The Fallen One

The Fallen One

A MYSTERY

RICK BLECHTA

DUNDURN
TORONTO

Editor: Matt Baker
Design: Courtney Horner
Printer: Webcom

Library and Archives Canada Cataloguing in Publication

Blechta, Rick
        The fallen one : a mystery / Rick Blechta.

Also issued in electronic format.
ISBN 978-1-4597-0196-0

        I. Title.

PS8553.L3969F34 2012   C813'.54   C2011-908010-9

1   2   3   4   5   16   15   14   13   12

We acknowledge the support of the **Canada Council for the Arts** and the **Ontario Arts Council** for our publishing program. We also acknowledge the financial support of the **Government of Canada** through the **Canada Book Fund** and **Livres Canada Books**, and the **Government of Ontario** through the **Ontario Book Publishing Tax Credit** and the **Ontario Media Development Corporation**.

While many of the locations in this work are real, the situations and characters described are fictitious. Any resemblance of the latter to real persons, living or dead, is purely coincidental.

Printed and bound in Canada.

Visit us at
Dundurn.com | Definingcanada.ca | @dundurnpress | Facebook.com/dundurnpress

Dundurn	Gazelle Book Services Limited	Dundurn
3 Church Street, Suite 500	White Cross Mills	2250 Military Road
Toronto, Ontario, Canada	High Town, Lancaster, England	Tonawanda, NY
M5E 1M2	LA1 4XS	U.S.A. 14150

For her love of opera and exceptional skill with languages, not to mention her unconditional support of all my endeavours, this book can only be dedicated to my wife and favourite travelling companion, Vicki.

Overture

Across the small pond, the trees had turned spectacular shades of yellow, orange, and red. The contrast with the scattered green of the pines could truly take your breath away. Autumn didn't get any better than this in eastern Ontario.

The man turned away, walking the few feet back to a house under construction. Somewhere in the forest a crow cawed loudly, breaking the late afternoon silence. Contemplating nature, unfortunately, had to drop to the bottom of the list — at least for the next little while.

He stood at the end of a very long road. Searching, waiting so long to catch sight of his quarry, had strained nerves to the breaking point. So much rode on what would happen over the next ... what? Ten minutes? A few hours? Even a day or two?

What did it matter? He'd waited patiently for this opportunity, and he could wait a bit longer.

Of course, it had always been possible to move on, give up, do something else, but what he needed to accomplish was too important for that. If he could pull this off, then he'd be a made man. He shook his head at the irony of his thoughts. What did they always say? "The world will be your oyster." Yes. That was it. He could hardly wait to taste that oyster.

During his long search, every variable had been calculated to the finest degree possible. He knew what he needed to do, and he knew how to do it. Now all that remained was the final bit of waiting.

Carefully, he risked a quick glance through one of the empty holes where windows would soon have been placed, listening to the swish, swish of the long grass in the lower field as his target approached from the driveway beyond the old log house. As an incredibly subtle alarm, it worked perfectly.

He faded back into a darkened corner to wait. The half-built house around him made the man feel as if he stood in a forest of naked saplings. In a few minutes, that forest would be a mass of flames, consuming itself long before help could arrive, covering his tracks. It would appear as if the whole sad episode had been a horrible accident.

Nothing could go wrong now, even though the man knew his target was smart and resourceful.

It had all been planned out too well.

Dying isn't hard. I've done it over a hundred times — more than one opera critic has deadpanned that Marta Hendriks can die with the best of them.

The performance of *La Traviata* that evening at the Metropolitan Opera was going quite well. It had been a huge break for me to get my first leading role with this storied opera company. My manager had pushed the Met hard to give me this chance, since they'd always looked on me as no more than a competent second-stringer. "Get Marta Hendriks. She's reliable and does a good job in supporting roles."

Three nights earlier, my first performance had not been everything I'd wanted it to be. It wasn't until late in the second act that I'd gotten my nerves under control. Even though I knew how much my career counted on giving my very best, I just didn't accomplish what I'd set out to do. Next day, I'd been too chicken to read the reviews, but I found out plenty quick. Bad news travels fast in the backstage world.

Tonight, though, was a different story.

Giordano Friuli, my Alfredo, had been on his best vocal behavior ever since the conductor had raked him over the coals for holding his dramatic moments far too long. My voice felt supple and strong, leaving me to concentrate more on my acting, something the New York critics seemed to find woefully lacking in the first performance.

Consuela, my dresser at the Met, had been fussing over my wig before the third act (and my big death scene), when someone knocked on my dressing-room door. She cocked an eyebrow questioningly.

"Better see who it is," I told her.

"Is she decent?" asked a basso profundo voice I recognized at once.

"Always decent for you," I called out.

Bernard Laliberté, the Met's general manager, swept into the room as he was wont to do, always seemingly in a hurry.

I thought he'd stopped by to wish me good luck or something, or maybe to ask if I'd like to go out for a spot of supper after we'd finished. Singers are always ravenous after a performance — one cause of the weight problems that dog most of us.

"Bernard!" I began, swivelling my seat. "How nice of you to come and see me."

Something seemed to be wrong with his face, but he quickly papered it over. Perhaps Friuli was acting up again. The course of a general manager's life in America's biggest and best opera house is seldom a smooth one. Singers are volatile creatures.

"I came up to escort you to the stage."

"Whatever for? I know perfectly well how to find my way down." I grinned at him. "Is this a new service at the Met for sopranos? I'm so touched."

Laliberté seemed on the verge of saying something, but merely held out his arm. "Is she ready?" he asked Consuela.

She shrugged and stuck another hairpin in my wig for good measure.

I should have twigged that something was up when we exited the elevator at stage level. Everyone turned to look. I remember thinking that maybe my performance so far that night had been even better than I believed.

Jeremy Cross, the Met's long-time stage manager, came over to tell me that they were ready to begin the act, and I could hear the orchestra out front making their usual getting-ready tootling noises. He glared at Laliberté as he led me to my mark, another thing out of the ordinary. I lay down on my side on the bed at the rear of the stage, waiting for the curtain to go up. The mattress smelled of dust even though the linens were spotlessly clean, so I turned my head up to avoid breathing in any crud. The evening's Annina (Violetta's maid) scurried out dangerously late and plopped down into the overstuffed chair where she was supposed to be asleep. She turned her head away from the audience and stared at me unnervingly, too.

In the wings, Laliberté and Cross seemed to be having words. Behind them, three or four stagehands stared out at me intently. The audience applauded from the other side of the curtain, the conductor struck up the band, and we were off.

As operatic death scenes go, Violetta's death in *Traviata* does take quite a bit of time, but being one who gets to sing this glorious music, I'm not complaining. The poor girl's expiry could go on all night for all we sopranos care.

There's a long aria at the beginning of the act for Violetta as she wakes up and is visited by her doctor.

Since she's in the final stage of tuberculosis, I didn't have much acting to do but stagger from the bed over to a sofa and portray, through voice and action, how very weak the poor girl is supposed to be — while still being heard at the back of the theatre — which is a good trick, when you think about it. The big wind-up for Violetta is when Alfredo arrives, not knowing he's seeing her for the last time, and they get to sing their damn fool heads off.

Friuli was in the wings early for once, and instead of his usual nervous pacing as he waited for the cue for his entrance, he glared at me with such ferocity that I felt I should check my body for burn marks.

At this point, I finally began feeling uneasy. It couldn't be my performance that was attracting everyone's attention. It had to be something else, but what? My focus began to slip as I sang the lovely and poignant aria about how Violetta feels her life coming to a close. The libretto, which I knew as well as any, was drifting out of my head. I struggled to bear down, relying on the prompter more than usual.

I regained my equilibrium when Friuli made his entrance. We'd been singing rapturously together all evening, drawing energy from each other's performance, but all of a sudden the tenor was holding me stiffly, almost at arm's length instead of pulling me in as he usually did.

This threw me completely, and when he let me go, I was shaking so much that I no longer had to act like I needed to sit down.

Once again, Friuli had to sweep me up at a touching moment in the opera when Alfredo realizes just how sick Violetta is, which quite often makes me dewy-eyed.

There is a little bit of musical interlude here, which gave me the time to seemingly stumble, allowing me to turn away from the audience.

"What the hell is going on?" I growled at Friuli.

His answer came out low and angry. "How can you be doing this? Are your veins running with ice?"

I had to sing again, so there was no time to ask him what he meant, but a cold fist seemed to be closing around my heart. My breathing was uncontrollable and my heart raced.

When Alfredo's father, Germont, made his entrance, I had a brief moment to hurriedly whisper to Friuli, "What are you talking about?"

"Did you not love your husband, that you can go on singing when he has just died?"

I staggered back as the weight of his words slammed into me. Now the meaning of those puzzling stares had a razor focus, and I was certain beyond doubt that what Friuli had told me was the truth. I spun to look into the wings and there was Laliberté. The expression on his face confirmed everything. Of course he knew and had deliberately kept this horrendous news from me so that I would go on and finish his damned performance.

Turning away, I gripped the chair, almost pulling it over. As the final moments of *Traviata* fell to ruins around me, I somehow managed to croak out my next few phrases through a rapidly tightening throat. Stuck where I was, what could I do? I just tried to keep a grip on things.

But when Barry Wheeler, playing Germont that evening, hugged me into his arms, I finally crumbled completely, forcing him to try to sing with the full weight of my body dragging him down. He is a big man, but I am not a small person, and I'd taken him by surprise.

By this time, everyone in the audience knew something was wrong. My next cue was to hand Alfredo a locket, and I almost managed it, but when I turned to look at Friuli, it wasn't his face that I saw.

My husband Marc stared at me across the stage at the Met, looking as he always did: head cocked to one side, a sardonic grin on his face, body slouching, broadcasting to the world that he just didn't give a damn about anything.

I took one step, then another, holding my hands out in front of me as I strove to reach him. If I could just touch him, I felt sure he wouldn't really be dead.

The orchestra kept playing as I missed one cue and then another. My fellow singers tried to keep going.

That night was an operatic train wreck of monumental proportions. Marc began to fade — or was it my consciousness slipping away? I called out. Some say I almost sang it; others say it came out as a choked scream. All I know is that I hit the stage hard. The side of my face was still bruised two weeks later. Everyone agreed that it was a collapse worthy of any opera, but no one had the courage to tell me that until nearly a year later.

Brief vignettes of the remainder of that terrible evening still float around in my head like bubbles of oil in a sea of water: lying on the stage with some stagehand's smelly coat under my head, a hastily-summoned doctor taking my pulse and shining the beam of a small light into my eyes, the wailing scream of an ambulance on the trip to the hospital, whispering voices all around me, and finally an injection, its brief sting bringing sweet oblivion.

Chapter One

Tonight was my night — for the first time in nearly two years.

Though I was usually calm before a performance, the thought of what I had to accomplish before the curtain came down at the end made my hands clammy and my legs wobbly. My heartbeat had been through the roof all day. These are not good things for a dramatic soprano who desperately needs to give a good performance.

No. Correct that. Not a good performance. A great performance. My job this evening was to make it crystal clear to everyone in the Palais Garnier in Paris that I'd come back from the abyss.

Once upon a time, I'd been a happy-go-lucky musical nomad, bemused at the extreme left turn my life had taken back in university when I'd discovered, much to everyone's surprise (including my own), that I possessed a very fine singing voice and the volume to fill an opera house. Until that point, I'd been studying percussion at McGill University's Music Faculty. The ironic thing? I'd been one of those many musicians who take great delight making fun of singers. We referred to those in the opera department as "mouth majors" and generally looked down on them as being "not quite musicians." Then, almost too fast for even me to catch, I became one of them. Some of my former instrumental comrades still haven't quite forgiven me.

After university I travelled the world for several years, learning my new craft, first with my mentor, Gerhard Fosch, then in the school of operatic hard knocks as I became a voice for hire. Gradually, the roles I was offered got bigger, until one day a journalist referred to me as a "diva," an overwrought term to be sure, but one that showed I'd finally scrabbled within sight of the summit of the operatic mountain.

Two years ago my little world had been dragged off that mountain to the edge of life's Grand Canyon and kicked hard in the derrière, leaving me to cling desperately to the edge by any means I could. Many times I came within one breath of giving up, letting go of the meagre hold I had, but something always held me back.

You see, two years ago, my dear husband Marc, the light of my life, had tragically been burned to death when a fire tore through the house he was building for us near Lanark in eastern Ontario.

It had been a long, painful road back, but with the help and support of my closest musical colleague, I'd made it.

Feeling like I was ready to resume my life, I'd been hired out of the blue by the Opéra National de Paris as a very last-minute replacement for a soprano who'd precipitously decided to retire from the stage because of vocal problems everyone else knew she'd had for years. My manager and I were aware that the ONP was grabbing for anyone they could get at the last minute with even a modicum of star power. Their season opened in less than two weeks with a new production of Verdi's most popular opera, *Traviata*, and the one thing I had going for me is that I am a very quick study. My percussionist's mind for detail gave me that small edge.

It was a delicate and poignant situation for me. The last time I'd trodden the boards had been that terrible night at the Met.

⌒

I completely fell to pieces after Marc's death, something that surprised me. Up until then, I'd always been dependable and capable Marta, the calm in the eye of any storm. But by the time my sister had dragged me off the plane at the Ottawa airport, I was medicated up to the eyeballs and barely functioning. Thank God for my much older siblings, who had immediately flown to my aid, my sister Narissa to New York to accompany me, and my brother Clark to Ottawa to smooth the way. I cannot say how grateful I was for their company on the long drive back to Perth, an hour west of the nation's capital. In the following two days, they organized it all. I'd turned into a complete zombie, unable to do a thing. There was no funeral, because there was barely anything left of Marc's body — the fire had been that hot. The only thing identifying him had been his partially-melted wedding band, the twin of the one I had on my finger. I refused to go out to the farm, so my brother handled all of that.

A policeman eventually came and told me what had happened. It appeared Marc had knocked over a nearly full tank of propane, somehow breaking off the valve and safety fence on top. He'd been caught when the resulting jet of gas ignited. The constable had apologized for my loss and quickly left. Case closed.

As the weeks dragged on, my depression had deepened, and I just could not pull myself out of it. By then I was back in my condo in Toronto. I didn't go out. I stopped answering the phone. I barely ate, even though my favourite place to spend a morning shopping for food, the St. Lawrence Market, lay right across the street. I simply ceased to care about anything.

Rightly or wrongly, I blamed myself for what had happened. You see, Marc had convinced me to let him build our dream house on my family's old farm near Hopetown, a forty-minute drive north of Perth. When our parents had passed on, I'd bought out my siblings' shares and had used it as my vacation home — until Marc came along.

My friend and vocal coach, Lili Doubek, had come to my rescue a month after Marc's passing, and not a moment too soon.

It was late afternoon and I was still in my housecoat, staring listlessly down at Front Street, six storeys below, contemplating how much it might hurt to land headfirst on the sidewalk. My phone rang.

It was Samatar, the building's Somali concierge. "I am very sorry to bother you, Madame Hendriks, but there is someone down here who wishes to see you. I told her that you told me, 'no visitors,' but she refuses to leave. It is most inconvenient."

"Who is it?" I asked wearily.

"It is that little woman from Czech land with the loud voice," he answered in his inimitable way.

Sighing heavily, I told him, "Put her on."

"Hello, Marta," Lili said as I held the phone a good distance from my ear. I knew that bulldog tone very well. "Tell this man to let me through."

"But Lili, I'm not prepared for visitors. The apartment is —"

"Nonsense! I have come all the way down here. I wish to see you."

Knowing she was stubborn enough to wait in the lobby until I gave in, I told Sam to let her get in the elevator. During the three minutes it took her to arrive at my door, I raced around the apartment, trying to pick up several weeks' worth of garbage and dirty clothes, left wherever I'd dropped them.

Lili's knuckles pounding on the door felt like a physical assault on my aching head.

When I opened it, the small, grey-haired woman stood there, inspecting me from top to bottom, wrinkling her nose at what she no doubt smelled.

"Aren't you going to ask me in, Marta?"

I stood aside for her to pass.

She stopped in the middle of the room. "Your apartment is a sty not fit for pigs! You should be ashamed."

Even though I was expecting a harsh comment, her words stung.

Lili came back to the door where I was still standing dumbly, took my hand off the knob and led me to the sofa. She had to move several unread magazines, junk mail, and a pizza box to clear enough space for both of us.

"You are not doing well, dear Marta. We are all concerned about you."

Averting my eyes, I lied. "I'll come around eventually."

Lili reached out and gently took my chin, forcing me to look at her. "You need to deal with this. You have had a very big shock."

"That's an understatement."

"Maybe so, but in life we must take the bad with the good."

"Oh, spare me the facile platitudes."

"Platitude or not, that is the only way. You still have your friends, the people who love you. You cannot push them away. Let us help."

"What are you going to do? Tell me that life must go on? Oh, that's a really big help. I feel like someone stuck a knife in my chest and cut out a huge chunk of who I am ... was. Maybe I don't want to go on."

"Are you serious?"

I sighed as she released my chin. "I don't know. I just don't know."

"You need help, Marta. You are suffering from severe depression and you need professional counselling."

"No! I'm not going to lay on some couch and pour my guts out to someone I don't know."

"Marta, be reasonable. There is nothing dishonorable in that."

"That's hardly the word I'd use. I just can't deal with strangers right now. Maybe later." I got to my feet. "Now, Lili, it was very nice of you to drop by. I'm just feeling a little low at the moment, but I'll snap out of it. Don't worry."

She looked around the room again. "You should see this apartment with my eyes. Don't forget I know you well. You have never been the neatest of people, but this place is like a garbage dump." Lili motioned with her head toward a sideboard that must have had fifteen or twenty empty wine bottles on it. "How many days does that represent? You have already been drinking today."

"Oh, come on! I'm not turning into an alcoholic."

"But you have never been much of a drinker. This is not good. You cannot medicate away your pain. When did you last sing?"

"I don't know. Maybe a week ago."

"You are lying to me. I can tell from the way you are speaking. This is not good. You must seek help."

"I'll pull myself together. Now, I think you should leave before I start getting angry."

Lili stayed put, her overcoat buttoned, her hat and scarf still on, her purse and gloves clutched in her lap. "You will not listen to your friend who cares about you very much?"

"No."

She went on as if I hadn't answered. "Marta, you are going through hell, I know, but you cannot continue like this. You need professional help."

"I don't need professional help. I'll be okay. Just give me time. I'm not going to pour out my guts to a stranger, and that's final!"

Lili looked pensive. "What if you could speak to a friend, a good friend?"

"I'm not friends with any shrinks."

"But you are."

"Who?" I demanded, feeling the leading edge of a slippery slope under my feet.

"Me. That was my training, as a psychiatrist, and that is what I did for many years in Czecho before I came to this country."

I wouldn't have been any more surprised if she said she'd been a fighter pilot or an Olympic wrestler.

"The reason I came to Canada was so I could return to my original love, and that is music." Lili got to her feet and began putting her gloves back on. "Now, it is all settled. I will come back tonight at 9:00 p.m. and we will begin. Please have this apartment clean by then. It stinks of old wine, body odor, and rotting food."

She let herself out, slamming the door as punctuation, while I stood mutely in the middle of the room, watching. Lili and bulldogs did have a lot in common.

Several minutes later, I un-stalled myself, turned to the buried coffee table, and began picking up empty takeout boxes.

That evening, we did indeed begin. And it was a long, agonizing way back up to the surface.

~⌒~

Two years and countless painful therapy sessions later, I found myself in Paris, City of Light, ready to pick up the pieces of my shattered opera career.

Rehearsals for *Traviata* had gone well, considering I'd replaced someone halfway through the rehearsal stage. The cast they'd assembled for the season-opening performance was one of the best I'd ever had the pleasure of working with, the director had some marvellously refreshing ideas on staging this old chestnut, and I was sincerely looking forward to once again taking on the role of Violetta, the tragic courtesan in Verdi's most enduring opera. To finally be performing it in the city of the opera's setting was simply icing on a mile-high cake.

Lili hadn't been sure I was psychologically whole enough to take on doing *Traviata* so soon, certainly not as my first major role since Marc died. The only thing I'd sung was the Countess in *Le Nozze di Figaro* for an outdoor concert performance by the Canadian Opera in Toronto the previous summer, when someone had taken sick at the very last moment. I found out afterwards that they tried everyone else before reluctantly calling me in. My manager was as astonished as anyone when the Paris Opera offered me Violetta three weeks later. For two days after signing the contract, as Lili and I rehearsed the part around the clock, I kept wondering — out loud — how many people turned them down before they called for me. Lili, fed up at last, yelled at me for being so negative.

We both knew I was considered damaged goods. Singers who cannot be relied upon don't get a lot of work. I had just begun to be seriously noticed in the opera world when I'd had my meltdown on the Met stage. Even though people might have been sympathetic to my situation at the time, Laliberté never publicly spoke about what he did to me on that awful night. I'd like to think it was because he felt ashamed. Regardless, the result was no one knew how badly he'd screwed me.

Lili and I had been speaking every evening since I'd arrived in Paris. She'd grill me on how I was feeling inside and out, the state of my nerves, how I was eating, sleeping, even how my bowels were behaving. It got to the point where it began irritating me, but I couldn't bring myself to say anything to her. I knew quite well that the only reason I wasn't dead was her intervention.

Accompanist, vocal coach, and finally my therapist, this unassuming woman had indeed been my angel at the time when I most needed something approaching divine intervention.

I couldn't help but ruminate on the past as I stood backstage at one of the world's greatest opera houses.

The company still performs a couple of operas a season at the original nineteenth-century theatre, and luckily for me, *Traviata* was one of them. The historic auditorium was packed, and the orchestra, backstage crew, and cast were ready.

As the brief opening prelude — lovely in its delicacy and overwhelming in its sadness — segued into the opera proper, the curtain rose, and the chorus began. I forcefully purged everything from my head except for the glorious music I was about to sing. By sheer luck, I'd been handed a brilliant opportunity to restart my career. I could not expect another. Tonight, it was swim or sink into operatic oblivion, becoming, at best, a mere footnote for the rest of time.

Nobody in that audience cared a jot about what I'd been through the past two years. For them, it was whether I gave a good performance or not, nothing else.

Lili and I both worked hard to get me to this point, and now my future lay completely in my own hands, which was as it should be.

There was my cue. I squeezed my eyes shut for a moment, then strode onto the stage, already in full voice.

⁓

Even though it had been a late night with a small reception for the mucky-mucks backstage after the opera, I woke up rather early the next morning feeling refreshed and with my motor still cranked from what I believed was a damn good performance.

Lying on my back, hands behind my head, I savoured a moment I thought — as recently as a few months ago — I'd never experience again. Regardless of what the usually harsh Parisian press thought of it, the four curtain calls had told me the audience considered my Violetta a triumph.

On the edge of my thoughts, however, stood Marc's shade, always there, always smiling his easy smile, head back, looking at the world as a big joke. My bubbling happiness immediately went flat.

I threw back the covers with a muttered "Damn!"

Even opera singers enjoy singing in the shower, but that morning there was no song in my heart as I tried to scrub away more than just dirt and sweat.

With *Pelléas et Mélisande* scheduled for performance at the Opera Bastille that evening, I had the whole blessed day to myself — no rehearsals, no demands on my time. With a decisiveness Lili would have approved of, I decided I'd be damned if I'd spend it moping around my hotel room.

I love walking in Paris. Like Vienna, it's a city made for feet. Slipping on jeans, runners, and a shockingly plain blouse, I planned the day in my head: poking around in my favourite shops along the Rive Gauche, perhaps lunch in a small café or bistro along the Rue Mouffetard, and then I'd catch a movie or visit some art galleries in Le Marais.

After a quick ride on the Métro to Saint-Michel, I walked along the Seine for a bit with Notre Dame just ahead. I really felt the need to stretch my legs, as

I'd been spending far too much time indoors. On all three off-days I'd had since arriving in Paris, it had positively bucketed.

The sky that day was bright and clear with just a few puffy clouds. The temperature had edged up enough that I threw my jacket over my shoulders, knotting the sleeves underneath my chin. Autumn was the perfect season to wander this wonderful city.

Parisians have the reputation of being brusque and rude, and it's certainly justified in some cases. Maybe it was a reflection of the way I was feeling, but more often than not, folks would return my smiles.

I'd gone without breakfast (even the skimpy Parisian version), so my stomach was rumbling pretty early on. Dropping into a friendly-looking bistro on Rue St-Jacques, I was a good girl, ordering consommé and a salade Niçoise with a glass of Chablis. A demitasse of espresso finished off my meal, as I kept firmly to my resolution that, despite how good the pastries looked, I would keep away.

The person at the next table had left behind his copy of *Le Monde*, and it was open to the review of the previous night's performance at the opera. What caught my eye was the colour photo, obviously taken during our dress rehearsal. It was very flattering to me and François Gutterand, the young Alsatian tenor who was my Alfredo and currently enjoying a meteoric rise on the opera scene. We made a handsome couple, as the caption pointed out. I wondered if François would feel the same way, because the review below had not been as kind to him as it had been to me.

The afternoon was spent ducking in and out of small shops. I bought a new handbag I didn't need and a present for Lili. Then it was on to a small café where I ordered another espresso, which came with two small ginger cookies.

Deciding that I preferred the open air to some stuffy gallery or other, I gave my legs a good stretching out and soon found myself again walking along the banks of the Seine. Notre Dame was now behind me, on its magnificent haunches, and tour boats and barges plied their watery way just below. Cars careened by in the street, and people occasionally jostled for space on the sidewalks. Ah, Paris!

A chill wind had sprung up and clouds were rolling in from the northeast — I hadn't bothered to check the weather report before leaving the hotel. The warm sunlight had long ago faded, so I decided it was high time to head back to my hotel, thrusting my arms into my Ottawa Senators jacket and zipping it up tightly.

Not having paid any attention to where I'd wandered, I had to stop to get my bearings. Up ahead, I spotted the Pont de Sully crossing the river, and while it was a bit out of my way, it would get me to the opposite side, where my hotel was located.

People around me were hurrying with more purpose now, and a storm seemed to be blowing in fast. The wind pushed hard against me as I crossed the Seine. I was thinking now only of the danger of getting caught in a downpour. The very last thing I needed was to have to bow out of a performance because of ill health.

Dredging through my mind for a hazy memory of the Paris Métro, I realized that the Sully–Morland station was not far from the bridge's end.

Somewhere near the middle of the long bridge, the rising wind began lifting bits of paper, and dead leaves into rustling eddies. Startling me with its force, a heavy raindrop bounced off the end of my nose, followed by a couple on my head. Around me rain began hitting the pavement with audible splats. The tangy smell of street grime moistened by the rain brought me back to the dirt road on which my old farmhouse stood, reminding me how much I used to enjoy the smell and feel of the first drops of a storm at the end of a hot, dusty summer day. A cold Parisian rain was a different matter altogether.

Slinging my bags over my shoulder, I began to jog with a purpose.

The heavens opened up before I made it, and every single cab in Paris seemed to have magically vanished. With no way to keep from getting drenched, I searched for a store awning or phone booth, some kind of shelter until the downpour slackened. Leaping over a fast-filling gutter, I ran alongside a small park. Through the sheets of rain, diagonally across the next intersection, I could just make out the stairs leading down into the Métro. Keeping my eye on the traffic, I waited for a break in the flow so I could race across. Would the bloody light at the corner behind me never change?

Finally, the traffic parted and I saw my chance.

The next moment, I stopped dead in the middle of the street, frozen in my tracks, not even daring to breathe. The world around me seemed to shudder to a halt, and I could feel bile burning at the back of my throat as my stomach heaved.

My eyes were locked on a person hurrying from the opposite direction. With one hand, he held a drenched newspaper over the soggy black beret on his head. The other supported a large item wrapped in soaked brown paper, balancing it on his shoulder.

He arrived at the stairs leading down to the Métro just as a pretty young woman approached from the opposite direction. Dropping his newspaper, he rested the heavy package on the ground, then ushered her down the stairs with a comical bow.

Even though the man had a neatly trimmed beard and moustache instead of the smooth face I was used to, his smile, his nose and his laughing carefree eyes, everything about him, convinced me that, impossibly, I was staring at my late husband, Marc.

Laughing, he looked up into the rain, letting it wash over his face for a moment before he heaved the package onto his shoulder again and disappeared down the stairs.

Chapter Two

*In the middle of the southbound lane of a
busy Paris street, I collapsed to my knees,*
cold rain streaming down my body as I fought to hold
back the darkness.

It registered distantly that a taxi had screamed to a
halt mere inches from my right shoulder.

Car doors opening and slamming. Excited rapid-
fire French. Hands helping me to my feet, handing
me my purse and packages where they'd dropped from
my hands. Shock. Numbness. Impossibility. My brain
simply shut down, unable to process what had just
happened. I bent over and vomited the remains of
my lunch.

Someone moved in front of me, putting his hands on my shoulders. His mouth was moving, but my overwhelmed brain refused to process his words.

"What?" I managed to croak at last, then remembering I was in Paris, I tried to think of the word in French.

Probably assuming I was an imbecile, the man repeated slowly, in English, "Is madame all right? Do you require a physician?"

I was already soaked to the skin and getting wetter by the moment, and that realization made it through my muddled thoughts. I got as far as saying, "Please," before my brain failed me again. I'd made the mistake of glancing at the Métro entrance. Somehow, my saviours understood what I was asking for and helped me to the taxi, just about lifting me onto the back seat. I started shaking uncontrollably.

The small group of people were discussing taking me to the nearest hospital, thinking that I had suffered a seizure. Perhaps I had. As the lineup of cars behind us grew, horns began honking. Parisians love their horns.

I blinked a few times, trying to clear the way for even one cogent thought. Assembling the necessary words into intelligible form, I told them in French that I wished to return to my hotel. "It was only a moment of lightheadedness."

The man who'd helped me to my feet shook his head. "I assure madame that I believe you are not well."

"I am fine," I said firmly, but smiled. "I simply need to get out of my wet clothes and into a warm bath."

A further discussion followed. It was almost comical. With only a few umbrellas between them, the crowd, which had grown to about a dozen people, was getting soaked as they argued over my medical condition.

The tremors were getting worse. "Please. Just take me back to my hotel. Please."

After a few generous Gallic shrugs from the assembly, the cab driver jumped behind the wheel with a purpose. As he did, one person was tapping the side of his skull knowingly.

"*Votre hôtel, madame?*" the driver prompted.

"*Le Millenium, s'il vous plaît,*" I said, dropping my throbbing head back against the seat and shutting my eyes as he screeched off.

I just wanted the world to go away.

Back at the hotel, the doorman helped me out of the cab, *tut-tutting* solicitously at my condition. I squelched across the lobby, water dripping from my clothes, soggy parcels under my arm. I knew I looked like a drowned rat but really didn't care.

Once in my room, I went straight to the bathroom, where I turned on the taps for the tub full blast. After pouring in an enormous quantity of bubble bath, I stripped off my drenched clothes, dropping everything on the tile floor. My body and mind felt as if I'd just performed all four operas of the Ring Cycle back to back. Sitting on the edge of the tub, I watched steam slowly filling the room as I paddled one hand in the water.

Once the bath was ready, I climbed in and leaned back, stretching out. Tentatively, I mentally poked at what had just occurred, not daring to really admit to myself that I was doing it. When I began to shake, I quickly shut my brain down again. "Keep yourself in one piece, woman," I told myself. "You can't afford to lose it!"

I stayed in the safety of the floating cloud of bubbles until my fingertips puckered and any hint of cold was gone from my body. One thing about first-class hotels is small things like heat lamps in the ceiling, so the room was comfortably warm when I finally stepped out.

Roughly drying my body until my skin tingled, I considered what to do next. Thank the Lord I didn't have to sing tonight. I knew there'd be no way I could step on the stage and do any role, but especially Violetta. Not tonight.

But would it be any better tomorrow when I did have to sing?

I slipped into a hotel robe and slippers, exited the bathroom, then crossed over to the phone and picked it up.

"*Oui?*" came a tinny male voice at the other end.

"Could you send up a pot of tea?" I stopped and thought for a moment. "On second thought, I'd like some cognac. Make it a double."

"*Oui, madame. Toute de suite.*"

I slumped down onto the bed, then curled up on my side. *Make the world go away*, I thought, but knew that would do no good. Things had to be faced. First and foremost, I feared for my sanity. I'd finally begun putting Marc behind me, and now hit this setback. Rubbing my aching temples, I decided to go in search of a pill for my pressurized skull.

Answering a soft knock on the door, I found a young waiter in a crisp white shirt and bow tie with my cognac on a silver tray. He came into the room, setting the snifter down on the coffee table.

"Compliments of the manager," he said. "Madame was noticed on returning to the hotel."

"Thank him very much for me," I answered and fumbled in my purse for some coins, grabbing several and pressing them into his palm.

He bowed, giving every impression of wanting to also click his heels together, and quickly departed. A handsome lad with a friendly, competent manner — he'd go far.

Perched on the edge of the sofa, I picked up the snifter with a shaking hand and downed the spirit in one gulp, feeling its burn all the way to the pit of my stomach. The glass almost slipped from my grasp as I put it down.

Leaning back, I shuddered. *Get a grip, Marta. Get a grip!*

The more I assured myself that I was okay, that there was a logical explanation to the afternoon's bizarre happenings, the more the knot in my gut and the throbbing in my head told me I was wrong. A half-hour later, I had the phone in my hand and was dialling Lili in Toronto. Hopefully, she wouldn't be out or already asleep.

I struck out on my first two calls: one to her home phone and one to her cell, leaving messages on both. They sounded pretty hysterical, even to my own ears.

Another double shot of cognac from room service earned a discreetly raised eyebrow from the young waiter. "Would madame perhaps like to order a bottle?" he asked with the utmost tact.

That sort of snapped me out of it. Piling on the alcohol would not do me any good. If nothing else, my voice would sound like crap the next day. Even so, I finished the cognac far too quickly. It didn't do a bit of good.

By the time the phone rang an hour and a half later, I was a complete wreck. Unable to sit still, I was wearing a groove in the carpet as I paced between the door and the window overlooking Boulevard Haussmann, four storeys below. I made a very unladylike dive over the bed to save time getting to it. "Hello! Lili?"

"It is me," she confirmed, her Czech accent stronger than usual, so I knew she'd spent the evening with friends from the old country. "What has happened? Your message made little sense."

For all my agitation since I'd gotten back to the hotel, I had completely neglected to figure out what I would say to her — or to anyone.

"Marta! Are you still there?"

"Yes. Yes, I am."

"What has you in such a state?"

"I ... um ... Something happened this afternoon." The pounding in my head increased dramatically. "I ... I saw ..."

"You saw what?"

"I thought I saw Marc this afternoon." There! I'd gotten it out.

The line was very silent for several heartbeats. "Sit down, Marta and —"

"Actually, I'm lying across the bed at the moment." I felt a giggle rising up inside me. That was not a good sign, so I took a deep breath to centre myself as Lili had taught me and rolled over onto my back. "I'm quite comfortable, Lili."

"Have you had anything to eat recently?"

"Not since lunch, but what has that —"

"Your blood sugar is very certainly low. Order some food and then you will call me back. All right?" Lili hung up, cutting off any argument.

She was probably right. In less than ten minutes, some bread, cheese, and fruit had been delivered, along with a cup of tea. No more alcohol for this girl. The waiter seemed clearly amused by my bizarre behaviour.

Lili answered her phone on the first ring. "You have done what I said?"

"Yes. The food just arrived. I'll eat while we talk."

"Tell me exactly the order in which things happened. I want to know all that has happened since we last spoke."

I gathered my scattered wits and plunged in. It took nearly a half hour to satisfy her.

"And what was your state of mind before this happened?"

"Lili! I'm going mad and all you can do is talk all clinical at me!"

"Marta, you've clearly had an episode of some kind and we must find the reason for it. You are not going mad. There is an explanation."

"All I had to do was call out and he'd have turned to me."

"You have probably seen someone who looked very much like Marc and just projected the rest onto this person."

"But it seemed so real."

"These things can. You said the man had a beard and moustache. Did you ever see Marc with facial hair?"

"No."

"No old photographs? Young men often grow facial hair at one time or another."

"Marc didn't have any old photographs. He didn't have much of anything. He told me all his possessions had been lost in a house fire a year before we met."

"So it is possible that the man you saw this afternoon just looked like you think Marc might if he had grown a moustache and beard? Yes? You admit yourself that you could not see all that clearly through the rain."

"And I wasn't all that close," I added, beginning to believe what Lili was saying. I *had* been thinking of Marc earlier in the day.

"This event is just your mind playing tricks on you."

"Like moving on with my life is somehow being disloyal to Marc?"

"Exactly! In your subconscious you must be feeling still that you should always mourn your husband."

"You must think I've been acting pretty silly."

"Not at all. I expected that going back to work would be challenging for you, especially doing *Traviata*. I would have preferred something like *La Bohème*. You've always done Mimi very well."

"Not too over the top?"

"Marta, I will be the first to tell you when you are, as you say, 'over the top.' I would enjoy very much telling you that you have been over the top."

Feeling more at ease, I laughed. Her calm words were very reassuring. "Perhaps if I continue to impress as Violetta, they'll ask me back."

"I have read all the reviews online and they are excellent. I was about to ring you up to offer my congratulations." Lili's voice became businesslike once more. "Marta, you must maintain your focus. Do those relaxation exercises that I have taught you. Also, think of Marc in a good sense, but also think of your time with him as being in the past. You are moving on to other and better things."

"You really think that?"

"Yes. The past is over. Done. You have mourned your husband sufficiently. It is now time to move on with your life. Be open to change. Keep telling yourself this thing!"

I was flooded with gratitude to this person who'd stood by me so tirelessly. "I don't know how to thank you, Lili," I began.

As always, she deflected my comment. "Go out there and give an even better performance tomorrow evening. That will be thanks enough for all my very hard work."

Hanging up the phone, I wasn't sure if she'd had her tongue completely in her cheek.

Vocal coaches, especially the good ones, can be tyrants at times. They need to be. No matter how good a singer you are, you require that outside set of ears, someone who really knows your voice to tell you if you're doing it right. Is the *passaggio*, that treacherous space between chest and head voices, smooth and even in tone? Singers can't completely tell that themselves. We rely on vocal coaches.

Lili Doubek was one of the best, even though she could be a filthy little slave driver if she felt her clients were not putting forth everything they had. One time, I jokingly began singing "All or Nothing at All" when she was particularly in my face about not trying, but she failed to make the connection. The more I got to know her, the more I realized she didn't possess much of a sense of humour.

Because of my breakdown, our relationship had undergone a profound and somewhat schizophrenic shift. She still remained my vocal coach, and I relied on her more than ever to help me keep all those singing muscles supple and in prime shape. As soon as she'd get up from the piano, though, she became my therapist, and if I'd thought she was hard on me vocally, it was nothing compared with Lili crawling around inside my head.

Now at the end of the two-year process, I was feeling more like my old self: the footloose musical vagabond I'd been when Marc had walked into my life. Lili made me realize that this had been the real me. When I'd been with Gerhard Fosch, I was very much the student, the one constantly being taught: how to sing, how to perform (two very different things), how to dress, how to behave in public, even how to make love. He very much formed me into the person whom I presented to the world.

This man had given me a great gift, showed me how to fashion myself a new skin that I felt completely comfortable in. After his sudden death, when I finally realized just what he'd taught me, I put it into use. The more I refined this skin, the more self-sufficient and confident I became.

Then Marc dropped into my life and I changed. I became one half of a whole — the lesser half, Lili had pointed out to me on numerous occasions. My life and how I viewed myself had diminished and I never even realized it.

Yes, I kept singing, and my career slowly blossomed, but it was far short of the meteoric rise that Gerhard had once predicted. The drive that had pushed me to succeed slowly began to dissipate. Puzzlingly, though, Marc stayed completely away from that part of my life. He only heard me sing once — other than around the house — at a party at one of the embassies in Ottawa. We never travelled together; he only came to my condo in Toronto a handful of times. He never really understood what made me tick and seemed not to care. It was the only thing he'd ever done that had hurt me.

Maybe I just loved him too wildly. I was blind to how I'd begun pulling back from everything that was so important to me, wanting to spend every moment of every day with him, not off in some hotel halfway around the planet.

Lili had seen all that clearly and worked hard to help me back to my previous state of equilibrium. I was struggling to stay afloat, and when Marc died, I had no anchor, nothing to hold on to. Somebody who was no longer there was still the centre of my universe. And his loss had been just too devastating.

Lili's gift was helping me understand why.

⟡

Marc had arrived in my life driving an old pickup truck with one of those cover things over the back. Inside were all his tools, not neatly laid out and clean, but looking as if they'd just been chucked in as he hurried off to his next handyman gig. I found out later that this impression was indeed accurate, when I'd hired him to re-hang the doors on the old barn behind my 150-year-old log home.

I didn't realize he was French Canadian until I saw the roughly lettered MARC TREMBLAY on the side of the truck. From a brief phone call, I had him pegged as Mark and firmly Anglo.

"*Vous êtes québécois,*" I said. "*Je m'en étais pas rendu compte au téléphone.* Your English is very, very good."

"*Merci, madame. Et votre français de même.*"

"It's not as good as your English," I said, laughing. "Where are you from in Québec? Montreal?"

He looked at me for a moment, then nodded. "Sort of."

As we strolled through the long grass from the log house to the unpainted barn two hundred feet away, he said to me, "I have passed this place before and wondered who lived here. Had I known it was such a lovely lady, I certainly would have stopped to offer my services."

I held back a snort at his outrageous words. Just over six feet, brawny and ruggedly handsome, Marc reminded me of one of those stud muffins you see on the covers of romance novels: all muscles, dark hair, dark eyes and full lips.

Me? In those days I'd admittedly gotten a bit plump (like many opera singers), and my brown hair was cut short to more easily accommodate the wigs many roles demand. I had a good enough body and a nice enough face. My best feature was undoubtedly my whiskey-coloured eyes. I figured Marc only saw an easy chance to score with a lonely, slightly older woman.

It took two days to re-hang the old barn doors. Since their size (each twelve feet tall and six feet wide) made it impossible for one person to handle them, I had to work closely with Marc the entire time — and I can't say that I minded. It had been a long time since someone stirred my blood the way he did.

"You are quite strong," he remarked on the first day, wiping his arm across his sweaty brow. "When I arrived here, I didn't think you'd be able to help me much even though you are tall."

Resting my hands on my hips, I fixed him with a mock glare. "Why? Because I'm a woman or because I look delicate?"

He grinned, knowing that he'd at least partially gotten my goat. "You seemed too much of a lady."

That time I did snort.

"Well, are we going to chatter all day, or are we going to get this job done?" I asked, tossing his hammer to him, maybe a bit closer to his head than he was expecting. "I'm still the boss on this job site. Get to work!"

Reflecting back on it now, it was amazing how well we fitted together right from the beginning. My yin complimented his yang in almost every way. I was seldom comfortable with people as quickly or easily as I was with Marc.

The second day was very hot with almost no breeze. By the time we finished in mid-afternoon, Marc and I were both drenched in sweat. When I came back from the house with another tall pitcher of ice water, the last having been finished during the afternoon's work, Marc was nowhere to be seen.

"Marc! Marc, where are you?" I shouted.

"I am here," his voice came from the farm's three-acre pond, just down the hill from the barn.

Walking through the waist-high grass and out onto the old, rickety dock my dad had built many years before, I could see Marc out in the centre of the pond. His clothes had been dumped in the long grass near the shore.

"You have trout in this pond!" he shouted.

"Yes, I know. There are also enormous leeches. Better be careful — especially in your state."

"You should come in. The water is really quite wonderful on this hot day."

"My bathing suit is back at the house."

"You should swim as God intended."

"I think not," I replied, but Marc's suggestion did cause a flutter in my stomach.

When he unselfconsciously hoisted himself onto the small dock, the flutters turned into a full-scale butterfly migration.

We eventually finished off the last adjustments to the doors, and as we stood around chatting after I paid him, I threw caution to the wind and invited him to dinner — then later in the evening, to breakfast. The following week he moved in.

Six weeks later, in front of a justice of the peace in Perth, we became husband and wife.

Chapter Three

Yet another Paris driver leaning on his horn in front of the hotel woke me up the next morning. The grey clouds and rain of the previous afternoon had blown away during the night, and I hoped they'd taken the disquieting events of the previous day with them. Standing at the window, looking out on a perfect autumn day, I took a deep breath and began to feel that my behaviour the previous afternoon had been pretty ridiculous.. Thankfully, too, my throat felt fantastic after I'd had some hot tea and done a bit of vocalizing. A second bullet dodged.

My manager, Alexander Bennison, had called from New York late the previous evening to congratulate me on my triumph and to let me know that he arranged for an interview with a reporter from an Austrian paper.

"I knew you had it in you to come back in a big way, Marta," Alex had said. "Already other opera companies are nosing around. The Canadian Opera had been sitting on my queries about future bookings, and they've called twice today. I can't say what it will be yet, but you're going to get something good from them."

"Too bad bookings work two and three years ahead. I'll be sitting on my hands a lot for the next little while, regardless of how well I do here in Paris."

"Don't you believe it. I'm pulling out all the stops to let everyone know that you're available and willing to come in on short notice. There's always a certain amount of fill-in work. People get pregnant, have vocal problems, or just bow out for personal reasons, you know that. And I've just heard that the Salzburg Festival might be looking for a Pamina for next summer's festival."

At this, my eyebrows had raised. It was very flattering. "I haven't sung that role in several years. Don't you think thirty-six is too long in the tooth for Pamina?"

"With the weight you've lost recently? I just got the proofs for those new promo shots, and you could pass for twenty-five easily. You might want to start dusting Pamina off. My sources are pretty good. That's why I've arranged for the Viennese paper to interview you. What's a good time in the morning for you?

"I'm pretty well wide open. I've arranged for a coaching with someone from the opera early in the afternoon, then there's a quick cast meeting before the performance. But my morning is completely free."

"Good. I'll call him back. Eleven o'clock okay?"

"Sure."

"Talk about your time with Fosch. That'll go over well. He was very popular in Vienna."

"Relax. I'll give him a full dose of the old charm. I know how important this is."

"That's it, then. Call me afterwards to let me know how it went."

"Thanks for all the hard work, Alex," I'd said before I hung up. "I won't let you down."

"I know you won't."

I wondered what Alex would have thought if he saw the state I was in earlier in the day. Gerhard, too, would have been very unhappy at my lack of control, which to him was an abomination.

It was midway through my second year of university that I found myself in the chorus for an opera, not the place you'd expect to find a percussion student. We all scorned singers of any stripe, but especially opera singers. To us, they were merely a target for infantile jokes and jibes. Perhaps it was a means of defence since there are probably more drummer jokes in circulation than singer jokes.

How did this turn of events come about? The flu was racing its way through the usual ranks of singers, and with the performance only five days away, they were very short on good, strong voices. Since I'd once sung in the faculty's choir, and also had a reputation for quick memorization of music, they asked. I refused. They pleaded. I reluctantly agreed.

You know what? I found I really liked the gig. The opera bug had bitten. By the end of the year, I'd quietly begun studying voice. By the next fall, the word was out: Marta Hendriks had switched allegiances and was now a de facto member of the opera department, even though I continued on gamely with percussion, not convinced my musical career should take such an extreme left turn.

The reason I finally gave up thoughts of banging on things for a living was Gerhard Fosch. The famous German director, voice teacher, and world-renowned expert on all things operatic graced the old school with his presence for two days of master classes in mid-December that year.

You can imagine my shock when I found out the previous week that he'd chosen me to sing on the first day. I hadn't even applied. Unbeknownst to me, my teacher and the opera department's director had decided to send him a tape of me singing two arias, "Sì, mi chiamano Mimì" from *Bohème* and "Porgi, amor, qualche ristoro" from *Figaro*. Fosch must have liked what he heard. The singers who didn't get selected really took it out on me, someone they regarded as a barely talented interloper.

Fosch had the reputation of being incredibly harsh with anyone slow in wit or lacking in talent, and I sat with increasing nervousness as he tore strips a foot wide off the first two students in the master class. By the time I got up on the stage to sing, I was contemplating repairing the burned bridges with the percussion department, thinking that Herr Fosch would inevitably send me packing.

Gerhard, well over six feet, still slender as he approached sixty and very distinguished-looking, had something in his demeanor that could make mere mortals tremble before he even opened his mouth. The man carried himself with an almost regal bearing. Even though he was dressed casually that day, his slacks and open-necked shirt were obviously bespoke. His blue eyes and swept-back, longish black hair (certainly dyed) did nothing to take away from his natural presence. Several of the female members attending his class were already seriously gaga over him. He was quite handsome.

With nothing to lose, I just let it all go, and at the end of the first aria, turned to find Fosch sitting in his chair, head down, eyes closed. I thought he'd somehow managed to nod off. I started to leave the stage to make my sorry way out of the hall and the opera singing world.

"Where do you think you are going?"

I froze, holding my breath, certain that I'd made a great faux pas. Toward the back of the room, someone tittered. The voice was definitely soprano, and it had a nasty edge.

"I, ah, I, ah ..." was all I managed to get out before being cut off with a wave of his hand.

"You have a very big voice, but you do not know how to use it ... yet. Your pitch and rhythm are very good, and I believe that you may actually be musical. You have something more to sing for me, ja?"

Oddly, I was a bit more relaxed when I began the Mozart, but that led me to be, perhaps, a bit too enthusiastic in the volume department.

Again, the decisive wave of the hand, this time only part way through. "No, No! You cannot sing Mozart like a rock star (more titters). This is not a tasteless Broadway entertainment, my dear. Mozart must be approached with delicacy, subtlety, and the voice with great warmth must be filled at all times. Do you not know what the words you are singing mean?"

"Yes, I am quite aware of their meaning," I answered in what I prayed was fairly decent German.

Fosch actually smiled and answered back in the same language. "Oh ho! You are cheeky as well as showing a bit of talent. Begin again and Fosch will walk you through this work of genius. Stand tall. Taller! Look like a countess! That is good. Now begin again!"

The next half hour was a revelation of not only how to sing, but how to sing Mozart.

"No, no! My dear, you cannot bellow like that! Focus your tone. Find its core. You have good lungs, and you must use them properly to support the voice. To sing softly, you must fill them and use them as a pillow to gently let each note be produced naturally. Mozart, even when fortissimo, must not ever be harsh. Smooth. Natural. Cultured. Now sing that passage once more!"

At the end of my session, Fosch actually smiled, stood, and kissed my hand. "I would like to work with you again in the future."

There was no snickering in the hall as I took my seat in the audience.

One month after my final year of school ended, by invitation I was staying at Fosch's chateau in Burgundy. When August turned to September and autumn was in the air, he'd taken me on as his protege. By the time all the leaves had fallen, we were lovers.

My real education had begun.

                                                      ~

Knowing that a lot was riding on every chance I got to speak with the media, that morning I carefully arranged the sitting room with a chair pulled close to the sofa for the reporter. The curtains had been drawn back, allowing the brilliant morning sun to flood the room. The little MP3 player I travel with was softly playing Beethoven piano sonatas, and on the table in front of me was coffee in a tall silver pot, with fresh croissants, jam, and butter at the ready. I'd gotten up early, done my hair, carefully applied makeup, and put on one of my nicest dresses, casual but elegant. Today, I needed to look every bit the diva. The only touch missing was a discreet "personal assistant" hovering in the background. With only three more gigs booked over the next year, there wouldn't be much for a personal assistant to do.

Perhaps I could go a good way toward making that a greater number. *Die Presse* was a well-thought-of newspaper, not just in Vienna but in all of Austria. Good coverage there would be noticed in certain places — the Vienna State Opera, for one. And perhaps the Salzburg Festival really would come calling. Thus far in my career, they'd ignored me.

Twenty-three minutes after eleven found me drumming my fingers on arm of the sofa, the coffee getting cold. No call apologizing for lateness. If I hadn't needed him more than he seemingly needed me, his arrival would have found me not at home. Being late for an appointment is unforgivable in my book.

I sighed, but didn't stop drumming my fingers.

A full half hour late, there was a knock on my door. Looking through the peephole, I saw a youngish man with overly long brown hair, glasses, and a very big nose, although that was probably mostly due to the fisheye lens I was looking through.

I made him knock twice.

Opening the door, I said, "Herr Theissen?"

"I got a late start this morning," he said in faultless English.

I heard my voice saying, "Oh, that's quite all right. I lay pretty low on performance days," and hated myself for being such a damned phony. "Would you care for coffee? I'm afraid it's not quite as warm as it was. I can order more, though.

He pulled a water bottle out of the knapsack slung carelessly over one shoulder. "I am quite all right, *danke*." A notebook, pen, and small digital recorder came out next. He settled onto the chair without being asked and proceeded to get himself ready. "I do not interview musicians as a rule, but since I am the only reporter for *Die Presse* currently in Paris, I was told to do it." His tone of voice made it clear he was not happy about this.

In an effort to apply oil to the troubled waters, as I

took my seat on the sofa, I asked, "And what is it that you generally write about, Herr Thiessen?"

"I believe in English you would call me an investigative reporter."

"Ah, I see."

"Still," he said pleasantly as he picked up his pen and notebook after switching on the recorder, "I have not been in my job long enough to complain too loudly. Shall we begin?"

I swallowed back at least three tart remarks as I poured myself some lukewarm coffee.

"So, Fraulein Hendriks, are you happy to be on the stage once again?"

"Certainly, and then being given the chance to sing in such a storied opera house as the Palais Garnier, how could I not be thrilled? As you know, most operas are staged at the Bastille now. Working with such a fantastic cast is —"

"And in the two years since the death of your husband," he interrupted, "what thoughts were going through your head?"

I could only manage a "Huh?" in response.

"You were undergoing therapy for extreme depression, is that not true?"

Perhaps that's why he'd been late. The little so-and-so had been on the phone to Toronto, trying to get some dirt on me. Just great. What the heck was Thiessen after?

In order to give myself some time, I grabbed my coffee cup and took a sip, then another. "I would prefer to talk about the production I'm in, or about my career. I do not wish to make my private life a matter of public record."

"I am just attempting to give the story of your triumph a context for our readers, *ja?*"

I considered the reporter's words, wondering what Alex would want me to do. I wished he were present to tell me. "After Marc's death, I needed time to evaluate a number of things and come to grips with what had happened to me."

"But you did suffer from depression?"

"Wouldn't anyone when the love of their life is so horribly taken away?"

The little bastard just shrugged. "And you are better now?"

"Yes, I am," I answered firmly.

"One of the reviewers said he felt your performance two nights ago had depths of which he did not think you were capable. Do you feel this was a result of the tragedy that befell you?"

Stay calm, stay calm. I could hear Alex's voice as if he were in the room. Here I had been expecting a puff piece, something to build up my name in the Austrian press, not a goddamn interrogation.

"I cannot say, Herr Thiessen. It may just be the result of singing once more in front of an appreciative audience, rising to the occasion of an opening night in Paris. This production I'm in is quite inspiring enough to not need any reading into the whys and wherefores of MY performance. Are you aware of the changes of context the director has added to the opera's libretto?" I asked, trying to steer the conversation into safer waters.

He didn't take the hint. "I do not care for opera. Do you have a photo of your late husband? I would like to use it in the article I am writing."

"No. I do not!" I shot back.

"He was younger than you, I understand."

"What does that have to do with anything?"

"Don't you think it's curious that I could not find a single photo of the two of you together? Didn't he ever attend any appearances with you? None of the big parties? It is always you alone in these photos."

"My husband preferred staying in the background. To be honest, he wasn't much interested in opera, either. He was a man of simple tastes."

Thiessen was relentless. "No one I have spoken to could tell me that they even met this mysterious man."

"Who have you spoken to?"

"People who should have met him. They socialized with you. He was never there."

"Plenty of my friends met Marc! It's just that he preferred living in our farmhouse in eastern Ontario. That's where his work was. He needed to be there!" I put down the coffee cup hard enough to make the spoon rattle on the saucer. "I will not answer any more questions about my private life."

With an expression that clearly said he wanted to ask a question that he knew I wouldn't answer, the journalist looked down at his notebook. My little outburst kept him on the straight and narrow for several minutes with general inquiries about what I was booked to do, favourite roles, and the sorts of questions I thought I was going to be asked in the first place.

It caused me to let my guard down.

I was telling a story of a colleague, a now-famous Canadian baritone, who had been all set to spend his life making cabinets and fine furniture until he appeared as a last-minute fill-in for an amateur Gilbert and Sullivan society in Montreal. Someone from the Met just happened to be in town visiting and was dragged to the performance. I was trying to work the story around to my situation of almost winding up as a percussionist.

Thiessen took a sip from his water bottle, and when I stopped for a breath, he snuck in his question. "Was your breakdown caused by tragically losing a second lover in a row?"

The way he did it was really quite artful, and I came very close to falling into his trap. I suddenly saw how easily people could be manipulated by skillful interviewers into saying things they later greatly regretted.

I actually began to speak, saying, "What does Gerhard have to do with all of this?" before realizing what was happening.

The stress of the past few days boiled out of me as I leapt to my feet, completely out of control. "Get out!" I screamed so loudly I'm surprised the windows didn't rattle. "Get out of this room now!"

Surprisingly, Thiessen said nothing. He put all his things back into the knapsack, got to his feet and scurried from the room without a word. Maybe the volume of my objection had frightened the little weasel.

I slammed the hotel room door hard and leaned against it, shaking with anger.

Alex would just have to understand when I told him what happened.

Chapter Four

With my whole body shaking as emotions surged this way and that, I felt completely rudderless, unable to control myself. It wasn't until I swallowed that it sank into my pea brain what I'd done. The saliva going down my throat felt like a dozen razor blades.

The human voice is a surprisingly fragile thing, and it doesn't take a lot of trauma to screw it up. Every singer is always aware of that — and deathly afraid of what can happen with the slightest misstep.

It was easy to feel that I'd just screwed mine up quite dramatically. I slid down to the floor and sat there, tears welling in my eyes. After all I'd been through, now this — and all because I couldn't keep my temper with a stupid reporter.

Swallowing tentatively, I tried to feel just how bad things were. My throat muscles were very tight and it was sore past my voice box. "Hello. Testing, testing," I said, with huge relief that something sounding fairly normal came out.

I read somewhere that a soprano at the Met screamed unadvisedly loudly during a rehearsal and knocked herself out of commission for several weeks.

Could I sing Violetta that evening? I couldn't see how. It's a vocally trying role at the best of times.

Among my toiletries in the bathroom was some special "mouthwash." I hadn't asked what its ingredients were when Gerhard gave a me large bottle nearly a dozen years ago, but it had gotten me out of a few tight spots in the past when my voice was tired or my throat was mildly sore.

"Use this very judiciously, my dear, and only when really needed," he'd said. "You cannot rely on it for more than one or two performances. It only masks; it does not make the throat better. You are risking serious injury by using it."

I said a silent prayer and crossed myself before gargling gently for twenty seconds, letting more than the usual amount of the potion slide down my throat. The soreness began to ease up within a few minutes, but the muscles remained stubbornly tight. The only solution I could think of for that was some sleep. Often those tender muscles relaxed when one didn't think about them.

Surprisingly, I drifted off fairly quickly and awoke shortly after two. Reaching out, I took a couple of good swallows of water from my bedside glass, then rolled over onto my back, trying to judge the state of my throat.

It still felt as if an unseen hand had a tight grip on it, but that grip had loosened somewhat.

"How does it feel now?" I said softly, then repeated it a few more times at increasing volume.

So far, so good.

I had arranged to warm up with one of the opera's vocal accompanists to get ready for the evening's performance, and shortly before three I left the hotel. Even though it was a short walk to the opera house, I had the doorman flag down a cab. My heaviest scarf was wrapped carefully around my throat to keep it warm. In my pocket was the bottle of Gerhard's magic mixture, and in my hand a large bottle of water, to keep myself hydrated.

We met at the stage door and the répéteur led me to one of the claustrophobic rehearsal rooms in the depths of the old building. I was reminded of scenes from *Phantom of the Opera*, which actually is set in the bowels of this building, subterranean lake and all. Fortunately, the man leading me down didn't have a mask.

Jean-Pierre Godard was excellent at his craft, and we'd enjoyed working together quite a few times over the past few weeks. He noticed one measure into the first warm-up that things weren't right.

"Cher Marta, you are not yourself today."

That's an understatement, I thought. "I'm sorry, Jean-Pierre."

"Your voice, it feels okay?"

"No, it doesn't," I told him. "Perhaps if we warm up very slowly and lightly?"

I sang *mezza voce* for about five minutes, feeling things out at considerably less than full throttle. It was still tight, but might be doable.

"Can you give me a little more?" Jean-Pierre asked.

I took a few swallows of water and we tried some things that were higher and louder.

I have this mental imagery I use when stressed. It involves a pump attached to my head by a large suction cup. In my mind's eye, when the pump is turned on, all the bad "sludge" in my brain starts coming out — sticky brown crud that looks quite disgusting. Probably smells disgusting, too, but I've never carried the imagery that far. At that point, I tried switching the pump on, and the process actually started working. As my voice rose through a series of ascending minor arpeggios, I could visualize the crap starting to leave my consciousness. Maybe it was the professionalism Gerhard had drummed into me over and over again, or maybe it was desperation, but behind the keyboard, Jean-Pierre finally began smiling.

"Much better, my dear!"

I smiled triumphantly, mentally blocking the return of any of the thoughts I'd just managed to flush out. My throat also felt slightly more relaxed. "Could we do those *passaggio* exercises you showed me last week? I wasn't quite satisfied during the first act the other night. I was thinking they might help."

"I think you must be more aware of supporting the notes right at the bottom of the *passaggio*. Ease into them more and feel the air coming from your toes."

Jean-Pierre liked talking about toes in his mental imagery.

By the time our forty-five-minute session ended, I was feeling a lot more confident and centred, but still apprehensive about the evening's performance. My reserves felt perilously low.

"I cannot attend this evening," Jean-Pierre told me as he kissed my hand, "but I know you will sing like a goddess. I do not think you should push too hard, though. Your voice still sounds fragile, but you may have enough petrol."

I smiled. "The word you want is 'gas.' Thank you so much for your help, Jean-Pierre," I said as I kissed both his cheeks.

"And remember your toes at the bottom of the *passaggio*!"

I often wonder what someone who knows nothing about singing would think about the bizarre way we talk sometimes.

⌒

Back in the hotel room, Alex had left a sputteringly indignant message, outraged by the disastrous interview and promising to do something about it. Whether he could or not was another matter. I put the whole thing out of my mind. Another hour of napping was what I needed most to recharge my batteries.

At six o' clock, I had a light meal in the hotel's dining room, keeping to myself at a table in the corner. Even though I don't normally touch alcohol before

I sing, I thought it wise to have one glass of wine to further relax me.

When I arrived at the Palais Garnier, the cast briefly met with the director backstage before the performance. One of the more temperamental cast members, Gutterand (my Alfredo), gave me a chilly reception. He'd been one of those raked over the coals by the critics, and obviously resented the fact that I'd gotten most of the kind words. Tough. There was no way I should feel guilty about a good review. I just hoped his petulance wouldn't carry over onstage. The stories of one singer trying to scuttle another's performance because of a grudge, for a lot less reason than a bad review, are legion in this business. I'd be well-served to keep on my toes, and decided it was best not to tell him about the three huge bouquets (one from the general director, one from Alex back in New York, and another from Lili, bless her!) that had been waiting in my dressing room when I'd arrived.

I felt hesitantly confident that I might squeak through the performance. I'd have to watch my volume, hold a mental image of keeping my still-tight throat muscles relaxed — and only resort to the magic potion hidden in my coat pocket as a last resort. It would be better to bow out of one performance than to wreck my voice for heaven knew how long, perhaps permanently.

By the end of the first act, I wasn't so sure I'd made the best choice. Gutterand seemed determined to redeem himself by singing louder and with more intensity than anyone in creation, taking enormous risks in the process — primarily with my voice. I had a natural edge since the human ear detects higher pitches as also being louder, but in order to match him in our duets, I was forced to push harder than I had intended. My throat muscles were feeling more and more tight, the soreness nearly overwhelming. I began to fear causing something drastic like a throat hemorrhage, the worst thing that can befall a singer.

In a quick moment while the orchestra had several measures to themselves, I whispered to him, "Can you back off a bit? My voice isn't up to this tonight."

His eyes narrowed and he shook his head, making his intentions clear.

I scrambled for some way to avoid impending disaster. Singing from my toes be damned, I wasn't going to make it.

Then it came to me: Violetta was already supposed to be suffering from consumption, right? Maybe I could compensate for easing back on the vocal throttle by some fancy acting. But how?

I could make it seem as if Violetta was even more frail than is usually the case. It might be natural for her not to stand there and belt it out toe-to-toe with Alfredo. Make her bravely stoic, but already failing, fanning herself, stumbling a bit against furniture, perhaps rubbing her throat? Hmm.... Why hadn't I thought of that before? It would be tricky to do on the fly, but I might be able to pull it off.

In the end, I just made it through the act, singing the final aria, "*È strano*," in a somewhat choked *mezza voce* as much as I could get away with, and saving a last major blast of full voice for the section around the "*Sempre libera*" reprise.

That curtain could not come down fast enough. I'd survived the act but I was perilously close to the edge.

The roar of the crowd was deafening when Gutterand and I came out for our bows, increasing in volume as I curtseyed — which wasn't lost on the tenor. I crossed my fingers as he bowed and indicated my approval to his performance with a smile and wave of my hand, acknowledging him. Thankfully, the applause level stayed the same.

Bullet successfully dodged.

I beat a hasty retreat to my dressing room and took another swig of the magic potion. Things felt better almost immediately, but I knew it was only the irritation being anesthetized. The problem of muscle tension still remained and was only going to get worse. Maybe I was a fool to go on, but I felt I had to at least try.

The first scene of the second act was more of the same but with almost no chorus to hide behind for a bit of a break. Toward the end of the scene, the thin ice I'd been skating on finally shattered when I cracked on a high note. An expression of concern crossed the face of Simon DeLong, the American baritone who was singing Germont that evening, and he cuddled me in his arms more than usual, immediately cutting back on his volume, the old sweetie. Hopefully he'd talk some sense into Gutterand during the intermission — if I even lasted that long.

I had a longer break between acts thanks to the fact that the second act ends without Violetta onstage. During that time I stayed resolutely silent, drank tea with lots of honey, gargled with salt water, and about five minutes before hitting the stage, administered the magic potion once again.

In the third act, Violetta is in the final stage of consumption, so my *mezza voce* scam could work really easily, and I played it to the hilt. I'm sure everyone in the cast was rolling their eyes discreetly as I lurched around the stage, but I really had to sell the consumption aspect. It would be a simple matter for the Paris critics to take back their kind words about opening night if they thought my voice really wasn't up to snuff, and I knew for a fact that one of them was in the audience, ready to give a second opinion. DeLong and Gutterand (finally) came to my aid and played along with the overacting. My death scene was even more touching than usual.

The audience demanded five curtain calls that evening, something that had never before happened to me, and their volume as they cheered and shouted and clapped was simply deafening.

With restrained happiness, I went back to my dressing room.

DeLong stuck his head in the door shortly after. "Are you all right, my dear?"

I shook my head.

"You were very brave tonight — and also very clever. That was a dangerous game."

I shrugged.

"Get lots of rest tomorrow for the matinee on Saturday." He raised an eyebrow comically. "As the father in this production, I demand you listen to me!"

My dresser fussed over me as several more people stuck their heads in the door, voicing both concern and congratulations. Oddly, there was no appearance by the general director. Maybe he was trying to avoid bad news from his starring soprano.

Everyone invited me out for supper, and on a better night I would have gladly accepted, but why go out with friends when all I could do was pantomime? An early night was certainly called for. My throat felt simply awful. I also had a splitting headache. But I felt like an Olympic champ, having against all odds jumped over every hurdle cleanly.

I had my dresser call down to the artist's entrance, to arrange for a cab to take me back to the hotel. When I got down there, it was ready and waiting. So were autograph seekers, and I knew I couldn't stop. They'd expect me to speak to them.

DeLong gallantly saved the day as he followed me out with Gutterand and the conductor. "Madame Hendriks is very tired and not feeling completely well. I hope you will excuse her tonight. But Monsieur Gutterand, I'm certain, would be most happy to sign autographs for you!"

As DeLong helped me into the cab, I whispered to him, "You're very bad. But from the bottom of my heart, thank you."

"I'm surprised that ham hasn't hired people to pose as autograph seekers to impress the rest of us. I'm going to have to talk to him. He has a great career ahead of him if he can keep his head on straight. Now, you get out of here. And no unnecessary talking tomorrow!"

DeLong slapped the top of the car twice after closing the door and it pulled out of the courtyard.

As we circled around the opera house to pick up an eastbound street back to the hotel, I was idly looking out the window, bone weary and daydreaming about nothing in particular, when I sat up with a gasp.

Among the crowd milling around the front of the opera house, I could clearly see that horrible phantom again. This time he was looking directly through the window at me.

"Quickly, stop the cab!" I croaked, then realizing I'd said it in English, repeated my command in French.

The cabbie shrugged and stopped. Behind us, someone jammed on the brakes and honked angrily.

I opened the door and leaned out, looking back at the crowd.

Marc was nowhere to be seen.

⌒

I will never remember the rest of my stay in Paris fondly. Basically, I barricaded myself in the hotel between performances, the curtains tightly shut, not answering the phone unless I recognized the number, hardly even going downstairs to the dining room for meals. I can't imagine what the staff thought of me.

No matter how much Lili reassured me, I was more than halfway convinced I was losing my mind. All that hard work for nothing. How else could you explain the two instances where I'd seen someone whom I knew to be dead? The carpet in my room did actually begin to look worn where I paced for hours at a time — or was that my imagination, too?

On the other hand, I was determined to keep going with what I'd been hired to do, and the time that I spent on the stage of the Palais Garnier over the next ten days was the most satisfying of my professional career thus far. Each performance was a triumph, and once recovered vocally after that unfortunate incident with the reporter, my voice got stronger and more supple. I was sorry to see the string of performances come to an end, but they were already talking to Alex about getting me back in three years' time to sing *Tosca*.

As for the article in *Die Presse*, it was not quite as bad as I'd been fearing. That damned reporter obviously worked it as though I'd been teetering on the edge of insanity, but the overall tone of the piece made me out to be more of a heroically tragic figure than anything else, someone bravely determined to carry on in the face of insurmountable odds.

Alex, a manager who can lie with the best of them, truth be told, claimed it was all his doing. Maybe it was, maybe it wasn't, but the coverage only increased the buzz around the name Marta Hendriks. The Chicago Lyric Opera signed me for two roles, San Francisco one, but there had been no word out of Salzburg yet.

Regardless of the positive turns of events, I felt as if I were walking on eggshells during the remainder of my time in Paris.

Whenever I stepped out of the hotel, I deliberately kept my eyes down, or unfocused so that details around me were a blur. I wouldn't come down from my suite until I knew the limousine was there and waiting. It cost me a pile to be chauffeured the few blocks to and fro the opera on performance nights, but I didn't think I could survive one more time seeing Marc staring at me.

At the opera, I would barricade myself in my dressing room and always tried to have someone with me, either my dresser or another cast member. The excuses I made for this became a bit ridiculous.

What I would have done if Marc had appeared to me at those times I was forced to be alone I cannot imagine.

It was with a profound feeling of relief that I watched the French countryside drop away on my flight back to Canada. I doubted that all my troubles were over, but I instinctively knew things were going to be better once I was home and in familiar surroundings again.

Part of the deal Alex worked out with the Opéra National de Paris was first-class plane travel, and with a sigh I leaned back into the wide seat, feeling a little guilty about all those who had to suffer through economy class — but it was only a passing thought. I'd earned first class with what I'd been through.

I couldn't wait to be home and safe.

Chapter Five

Dusty, stale air assaulted my nasal passages as I walked into my Toronto condo, bringing on a sneezing fit within five minutes. If I had half a brain, I would have called ahead to my cleaning woman to have the place cleaned and aired out. A shocking coating of dust lay on every surface due to my five weeks away. There was no food. The heat was at a subarctic setting. Some homecoming.

Mañana. Right now I was too jet-lagged to worry about anything.

Flopping onto the sofa, I picked up the phone. The flashing light told me I had messages waiting. It felt like some sort of rebuke — there couldn't be many, since

I'd cleared them from Paris the evening before. Maybe there was notice of another booking.

"Hello, Marta. Your manager gave me your number in Paris, but I missed you. This is the dean's assistant at the Schulich School with a courtesy call to remind you that you're giving two days of master classes here this coming week. We've mailed train tickets to your home and booked you into the Courtyard Marriott just down the street from the school. Please let me know if there's anything further you need and when you'll be arriving. First session is at nine o'clock on Wednesday morning. The dean also wanted me to tell you that he read some of your Paris reviews, and extends a brava to you for making the old school look so good. He's also looking forward to greeting you personally when you arrive. Bye for now."

Geez, I'd forgotten all about that. The opera department at McGill had gotten in touch with me four months earlier to say that they were arranging a series of master classes with various high flyers in the opera world. I distinctly got the feeling they were having trouble getting people at such short notice. At that point, I wasn't sure I could handle it, so I turned them down. The next day the dean himself called and applied a little gentle pressure to get me to accept.

Digging my agenda out of my purse, I checked. Sure enough, I'd entered it for the wrong week. Lovely. It might be time to computerize all these sorts of things and carry a laptop, or buy myself a more advanced cellphone and shove everything on there to keep myself totally organized. I'd resisted most electronic gadgets so far. My father's Luddite tendencies ran strong in his youngest child's blood.

The second message was a hang up, but the third was most welcome.

"Hi, baby sister! It's Narissa. I'm going to be in Ottawa this week for a high school reunion. I looked it up on the Web and I know you're done in Paris. Any chance you have some free time between engagements? I'd love to see you. Call me at the very least so we can chat. Congrats on the great reviews. We're all so proud of you!"

Arriving on the planet twelve years after my sister and fifteen after my brother, I'd been a "happy accident" for my parents. In many ways, I grew up like an only child. My sister Narissa had to put up with me more than was fair, since she was instantly elevated to the post of chief nursemaid. The novelty of a baby wears off pretty quickly when you're on the cusp of teenagedom. It wasn't until I was around fourteen that Narissa and I actually became close. Up to that time, she had generally referred to me as "The Creature." In a lot of ways I deserved that, since I really took pleasure in annoying her. She had eventually settled in Victoria, British Columbia, where, true to our family background, she now taught at the university.

My brother Clark, being even older and male, didn't really have contact with me that I remembered in those early years. By the time I was really aware of my surroundings, he was off at university studying philosophy, appearing occasionally — like a semi-familiar ghost — at various family events and holidays.

He didn't begin to know how to relate to me, and I was completely tongue-tied in the presence of my mythical "big brother." It wasn't until I was appearing with the San Francisco Opera and spent an evening in his home that I found out he had every one of my recordings, and his wife admitted that he boasted about me shamelessly to his colleagues at Stanford.

Narissa's phone call was a bit of a godsend. A few days of something normal like hanging out with my big sister might just help restore my equilibrium.

I also wouldn't have to face Lili right away. Despite what she'd told me repeatedly over the phone, I felt as if I'd really let her down.

Narissa picked up after three rings.

"Hi! It's Marta."

"Marta! Where are you?"

"Back in Toronto. Just walked in the door and picked up your message."

"Good flight?"

"As good as a flight can be."

"Fancy a trip to Ottawa? I can't make it down to you."

"As a matter of fact ..."

It was all set up pretty quickly. Narissa was staying with an old high school buddy since her husband had remained at home. I'd book into a hotel nearby, and we could spend a day and a half together before I had to move on to Montreal.

I wanted to talk to her about my problem.

I poured each of us another glass of wine. Narissa and I were in my hotel room, one of those places for visiting business people, so it had a small living room as well as a bedroom. We'd just returned after enjoying a seafood dinner at our favourite restaurant in the ByWard Market. Dad used to take us there for a special treat whenever Narissa or Clark came home for a visit.

About the only good thing that had come out of Marc's death was the strengthening of the tenuous bond between us. Certainly, a great deal of the distance had come because I was so much younger. But the distance was also the physical kind. I seldom got nearer to Victoria than San Francisco, and Narissa almost never came east — especially after our parents died.

She's much better-looking than I am: nearly six feet, congenitally slender, and with a long face framed by always impeccably styled brown hair. Where I'd been your typical tomboy — something that Gerhard had a hard time beating out of me — Narissa had always been a girlie-girl. What made me really envious was the fact that age only seemed to increase her beauty. We shared a common love of athletics and were both good at anything physical, but I enjoyed team sports, doing things with other people. She preferred solitary pursuits like running and working out. Since we'd bonded more firmly, I'd talked her into learning to play golf (I could outshoot her off the tees and on the fairways, but she trounced me in the finesse aspects of the game), and she'd introduced me to weight lifting.

Having consumed more than a bottle of wine with dinner, we were both pretty tight, but in very good spirits. The further libation I'd just poured was my way of trying to work up the courage to tell her what had happened in Paris. For the entire train trip from Toronto to Ottawa, I'd worked out just how I wanted to put it, but all evening I'd lacked the courage to pull the trigger.

Narissa sat in a corner of the sofa, legs curled under her. "So tell me all about Paris. I'm so envious. I love that city!"

I was in an armchair at a right angle to her. "Well," I began, "I didn't see too much of it. I actually kept to my room most of the time."

"Why ever did you do that? You must have had a ton of spare time."

"There were reasons."

My sister knew all about the problems I'd had, and I believe to this day that she sicced Lili on me after she'd phoned one night to see how I was and caught me very drunk.

Her pursed lips told me she was sizing up all the possible meanings in my statement. "Want to tell me about it?"

I nearly said no, covering my indecision with another swallow of wine, but I'd come all this way with an agenda and it seemed stupid to abandon it. "I went to Paris feeling really strong and in control. During rehearsals, this continued, but the day after the opening, well ... something happened."

With that, I told Narissa everything. She took it all in without asking questions, a habit of hers I'd noticed before. Her face was devoid of expression so I had no idea what she was thinking. That made it a lot easier for me.

After I finished, she sat swirling the bit of wine left in her glass before putting it down on the coffee table. "Has something like this ever happened before?"

I sighed. "Yes. First on that horrible night at the Met. Then there were a number of times after I'd holed up in my Toronto apartment. That could have been due to the amount of wine I'd consumed, though."

Narissa nodded. "I knew you were in pretty bad shape, but I didn't think you were that far gone. How about after you started therapy?"

"Only once, but I was already nearly asleep so it might have actually been part of a dream."

"And since?"

"No. Until Paris, not once."

Narissa looked at me, forcing my eyes to meet hers before she spoke. "Have you told me everything?"

"You mean about what happened in Paris?"

"I mean have you left anything out, anything I should know."

"Like what?"

"Are you drinking to excess again?"

"Of course not!"

"Drugs?"

"Are you kidding me? Narissa, I've told you everything that happened. I've left nothing out!"

"Have you told Lili about this?"

"I told her about the first time when I saw him at the Métro."

"Why not the second time?"

I put down my wine glass. I'd had enough for the night. "I got really worried that, despite what she was telling me, there was something ... something really wrong with me. You don't know how hard I've struggled to get this second chance."

"Yes, I do, sister mine."

"If this ever got out, I'd never get a booking again. Nobody's going to take a chance hiring a nut bar. There's too much risk involved. Yeah, if someone like Renée Fleming went flaky, she might get some bookings anyway, but I don't have close to her kind of profile."

"So what's the harm in telling Lili? She's certainly not going to blab. How can you think of not telling her?"

"I really can't say." I looked down at the floor and mulled over how to frame the next bit. "If I'm seeing my dead husband wherever I go, I guess I'm afraid that she may suggest that I need more help than she can give me, that I should be ..."

Narissa put down her wine, too, unfinished, and said it for me. "That you should be locked up? Do you think that's what you need?"

"If I really am seeing a man we all know is dead, wouldn't you say that's the case?"

Narissa leaned across the corner of the coffee table and took my hands in hers. "It may not be as dire as that. Talk to your friend. Level with her. She's the expert."

"But it also might be something else," I said in a rush. There. It was out.

"What are you talking about?"

"What if I actually did see him? What if Marc isn't really dead?"

⌒

Early the next morning, I was in a rented car, driving west from Ottawa.

Narissa and I had ended our evening having a pretty serious argument. She could not believe that I thought Marc might still be alive. My story had convinced her that I needed more help, if not from Lili, then from someone else. She had been emphatic on that score and when I refused to acknowledge it, she became very angry, probably hoping to shock me into agreeing with her.

But when I'd barricaded myself in that hotel suite in Paris, I had a lot of time to think, perhaps too much.

Yes, I was horribly frightened that I might be seriously disturbed, that despite all Lili's hard work, I really was crazy. It all made perfect sense: Marc had been my soulmate, the only person I ever really loved, and he was snatched tragically away from me.

Of course, my whole being ached to have him back. Right after the accident, I dreamed of Marc night after night: it had all been a horrible misunderstanding; the fire had been a lie; someone had kidnapped him; and perhaps worst of all, that it had just been a bad dream. Every scenario of hope had played in my head nightly on the big screen of my unconscious.

Pretty quickly, it led to my complete collapse and I knew beyond a shadow of a doubt that I eventually would have been dead if it hadn't been for Lili. Under the wheels of a subway train, throwing myself off a roof, or simply taking too many sleeping pills, it would have happened. I was just in too much pain.

After days spent lying on that bed in a plush Paris hotel or pacing the floor, I'd forced myself to relive the whole thing and at the end of it, I came to the realization that there might be another explanation, one that meant I was okay, that nothing at all was wrong with me. Before I could throw in the towel, I had to answer one question: had Marc really perished in that fire?

I had been hoping that my sister would accompany me on this trip. I desperately needed moral support, but she just couldn't bring herself to be a part of it. It was my guess that she was probably on the phone to Lili, perhaps right at that moment, explaining my state of mind, and there would be hell to pay upon my return to Toronto that coming Saturday — maybe earlier if Lili could get hold of me.

It was a beautiful fall day as I drove west from Almonte along Route 16 through the rolling Lanark Highlands. Everything seemed so familiar, yet so distant. I'd made this trip with my family hundreds of times over the years, but it was a bittersweet journey for me that day.

I remembered driving this road like a madwoman to get to Marc when I'd arrived back from one absence or another, longing with frightening intensity to be in his arms once again. Occasionally, he'd pick me up at the Ottawa airport, always waiting in the car until I phoned to say I'd meet him out front. On those occasions, I'd wanted the one-hour trip back to the log home to take just a little longer so I could listen to his voice, look at his profile, and feel that I was complete once again.

Until today, I hadn't been able to face going back, to see that empty, burned husk where all my joy had been incinerated. My brother, Clark, had seen to everything for me at the time of the accident: closing up the old log home, locking the outbuildings, and as far as I knew, no one had been back since. Our neighbors, good people that they were, had kept an eye on it, of course, and would have reported to me if anything seemed amiss, but those calls had never come, thankfully. I don't think I would have been able to deal with it.

One man down the road had been tapping the sugar bush behind the fields and paid me a small yearly fee and another neighbor cut hay which I was happy to let him keep, but that had been it. For two years I'd had no contact with the place that once had been the centre of my universe.

Today, for good or ill, I was returning.

I stayed surprisingly calm until I turned onto the dirt road that wound through the nearly unbroken line of trees leading to the old farm. At that point, my hands began shaking and felt slimy on the steering wheel. I had to stop twice to wipe them off on the legs of my jeans.

Finally, I came to the top of a small hill and stopped, looking down into the gully where the driveway lay on the left, mostly hidden by underbrush. It took ten minutes for me to be able to move the car forward.

Stopping well back of the big farm gate that blocked the driveway, I got out and leaned on it, staring at the old homestead two hundred feet away. It seemed to float on a sea of gently waving dead grass like some magnificent ship. The two-storey log house, now over one hundred and forty years old, didn't seem much changed. Maybe it needed a touch of paint around the windows and one of the shutters was a bit crooked, but it looked the way I imagined it would. The woodshed, which had been slowly collapsing for as long as I remember, peeped out from behind the half-dead apple trees to the right of the house, and·beyond that, I could just make out the peak of the old barn's roof, the barn whose doors I'd hired Marc to re-hang.

It was only when I allowed my eyes to move right that I could see the abomination on the highest point of land, the dream that Marc and I had shared so breathlessly together, the place where we had planned to live out our lives together.

The three white pines that stood close to the site were black and withered where the fire had partially consumed them, but their farther sides appeared all the more green and healthy for it. I felt glad they'd survived, although they were greatly diminished. The foundation of the house was nearly invisible in the tall grass. Other than that, I could only see a few blackened pieces of wood. Nature had already almost erased what had happened.

I stood for several minutes, my mind scrolling back through all the time I'd spent here with Marc. Was this a fool's errand? Was I desperately clinging to an explanation that had no basis in reality? I hoped that today would put me out of my misery — one way or the other.

Two fence posts down from the gate, there was a large rock. I rolled it away, and underneath was a small plastic container containing a key ring. Tears welled in my eyes as I looked down at them. They spoke to me of the good times that, regardless of what I discovered today, were gone forever.

I could see Marc hiding them under there when I'd misplaced my keys yet again. Bent over with the rock held up, he looked at me with laughing eyes. "Marta, do you think I should be hiding several sets under here so you will never be without?"

The padlock on the gate was well oiled and opened easily, speaking of the watchful eyes of my good neighbors. People out here took care of each other.

Hopping back into the car, I drove slowly up the overgrown drive, stopping in my usual place near the house. The barn with Marc's big doors was clearly visible now. They had held up well, but the wood was darkening to a grey that would soon match the rest of the building.

Once out of the car, I looked over to the ruin, more visible now than it had been down by the road. More blackened wood and two cement foundation walls, but I could still see the shape of the structure in my mind's eye as it had looked the day I took leave of my love for the final time. Little did I know, as I'd kissed him and driven off to the Ottawa airport, that so much tragedy would soon befall us.

I hardened my heart to the task at hand.

Grass had grown up around the house since they couldn't hay there, and I waded through it toward the barn, about a hundred feet away. Around back, the lower level was basically just a big opening. Generations of farmers had kept their livestock down there, the generated body heat keeping them warm and the building intact due to the moisture they also gave off. My father had redone the foundation nearly forty years earlier, opening up the back wall when he'd decided at the death of his father that he'd rather be a university professor than a hard-scrabble farmer. Having no doors made it easier to get the tractor and its tools in and out.

I'd spoken to my brother two days earlier and found out the last thing he did before leaving two years ago was to drive Marc's pickup truck under the barn to protect it from the elements. It had seemed the sensible thing to do.

"Unless someone's swiped it, it should still be there."

"I assume you locked it. Where are the keys?"

"They're on that nail in the floor beam near the stairs. You know, where dad used to hang his fishing gear. I figured no one would spot them there."

"Thanks, Clark."

"Why do you want to know about all this?"

"I'm thinking of going back for a visit."

"Really? Why?"

"To look around, see what there is to see."

"You take my breath away sometimes, little sister. You swore you'd never go back again. I can't understand why you haven't sold the place yet."

"I think I was waiting for a sign."

"What sign?"

"If I find it, I'll let you know."

Chapter Six

The trip along the side of the barn had covered my jeans with the burrs that always grew there — something I'd forgotten about. When I got around back, it took several minutes to pull them all off, after which I spent a few moments gazing at the familiar scenery. The sugar bush, spreading out behind the barn, held only a forlorn remnant of its fall glory. The hardy winter birds that remained around the property flitted around from branch to branch, but without any real purpose. The scene, lovely though it was, felt desolate: birds, plants, and trees, all making the most of those last few days before winter marked the end of another growing season by closing its iron fist.

The barn's foundation had been cleverly dug into an incline so that animals could be brought in at ground level in the back, while the upper hay storage area would also be accessible from ground level at the front. Even though animals had not been kept in the lower level for many years, the hard-packed earth floor, imbued with nearly a century of dung, still made the space's former use clear within a moment of entering. Oddly, I'd always loved the mixed smell of manure and dirt, and on that day, it sent me right back to my childhood. Most weekends had found our family out at the farm, and since there was such a huge gap of years between my siblings and me, this old barn had quickly become my pirate ship, my fairy tale castle, my dragon's cave, my friend.

When my eyes got used to the gloom, due to there being only two small windows high up on the side walls, I stepped farther inside, looking around. Our ancient family tractor was there, still connected to the rusty grass mower. In front of that, against the far wall, I could see the chopping block, the ax embedded in it, as if Marc had just left to take a barrow full of wood to the shed or to grab a quick sandwich back at the house.

Clark had told me he'd parked Marc's black pickup on the far side. As I turned to finally look, it was difficult to see Marc's name crudely painted on the fibreglass shell over the truck's bed.

I found the car keys right where my brother said they'd be. I was surprised, however, to find the passenger-side door wasn't locked. Upon examination, the whole vehicle was unlocked. Clark had told me differently.

A cold chill shot up my spine, and I took a good

look around to make sure someone wasn't hiding in the shadows. All seemed normal, but it was clear the pickup had been tampered with. In all likelihood, someone had been looking for something to steal, and certainly Marc had carried a lot of expensive tools in his truck, but when I lifted the back window and pulled down the tailgate, most of the familiar ones seemed to be there. Some of the bigger power tools weren't, but I assumed they would have been in the house when it had caught fire. The last time we'd spoken, Marc had told me he still hadn't installed the windows or the staircase.

I began my search in the cab.

The glove box was stuffed with an assortment of local maps, a number of receipts, and other junk you'd expect, all jumbled together. I laid everything out on the seat, carefully flattening crumpled bits of paper to see if they offered any clues.

I'd already done this once before.

Marc had never been what you would call neat, but he'd been surprisingly upset the time he caught me going through receipts on the truck's seat to get them ready for tax season. Usually, he was very grateful when I helped organize his handyman business for him.

"Mar, I am a big boy. I know how to take care of myself. Please leave my things alone."

"I just figured I could take them back to Toronto next week when I see my accountant."

"I don't feel like doing it now."

"That's why I'm doing it. You know damn well you're not going to get around to this until the last moment and then you'll be all frantic."

Marc angrily began grabbing handfuls of paper and stuffing them back in while I stood there fuming. I'd only been trying to help. As the last handful disappeared inside, he slammed the glovebox shut and stomped off to the house.

It was one of the only arguments we ever had, and I suspected now that maybe he'd had something to hide.

Twenty minutes of sorting the mess in the glovebox yielded absolutely nothing of significance. I crawled around in the back of the truck and only came up with a few more crumpled receipts for my efforts. There had to be something, and this was the most logical place for it to be. Marc had always used his truck as his office.

Hands on hips, I sighed, realizing I was getting cold, but I didn't want to just give up. I again returned to the cab and stared in. Then it struck me that I hadn't looked under the seats.

Both of them pivoted forward by means of latches, perhaps so it would be easier to clean underneath. After skinning my knuckles releasing the one on the passenger side, I stomped around for a moment, shaking my hand and cursing, then leaned into the cab and slammed the seat forward. It hit the dash, bouncing back and locking again, so I was right back where I started. If I hadn't been so tense, I probably would have laughed at myself.

Reaching under the seat again, this time the latch moved easier. I tipped the seat forward carefully, balancing it to rest against the dash, and leaned in to look underneath. There were six more crumpled, dirty receipts, all of them from Quebec, Montreal's west end to be exact, and none of them for anything remotely connected to building supplies.

Taking them out into the sunlight for a better look, I decided to go back to my car and check them against some old agendas I'd brought along from Toronto. I opened the door and sat crosswise on the seat, reaching behind me for my purse. A few minutes later, I had the whole story: all the receipts were from times when I was out of town for extended periods.

What that Austrian reporter had sussed out came back to my mind. I knew very little about Marc's past, other than he'd grown up in Trois-Rivières in eastern Quebec, moved with his family to Montreal when he was nine, had no siblings and that, like me, both his parents were dead.

"I never got along well with my relatives, Mar. Too judgmental and I cut off any contact with them after my father passed away. We never speak. End of story."

Obviously, when I was safely out of the way, he was making the three-and-a-half-hour trip to Montreal and keeping it to himself. What was he doing there and who was he seeing? What else had he kept from me?

And what else was I going to find? I hadn't even searched the log house yet.

That evening, back in Ottawa again, I convinced my sister to come and talk with me. What waited for her upon walking into my hotel room was a coffee table covered in neat stacks of various documents, photos, and receipts — the complete results of my day's efforts.

First, though, she took both my hands in hers and said, "Marta, I am so sorry I was cross with you yesterday evening. It was out of line."

"I know you meant well."

"It's just ... It's just that I think you need to face up to a few harsh — What's all that on the coffee table?"

It was hard not to smirk. "I drove to the farm today to have a look around."

"You did? You've never been back since it happened, have you?"

"Not until today."

"Was it because of what I said to you last night?"

"Not really. I was planning to go there anyway. I was just hoping you'd come along. You know, moral support and all that. Today hasn't been a very comfortable one for me."

Narissa sighed heavily. "And I went and got angry with you."

I kissed her cheek. "Don't worry about it."

She picked up one of the receipts. "And these papers? You were looking for this stuff?" Narissa seemed completely baffled.

"In a nutshell, I went there in the hope I'd discover how much I didn't know about my late husband."

"And what did you find out?"

I picked up my coat from where I'd dumped it earlier over the back of a chair. "I'm starving. Let's talk about all this over dinner. We can look at this stuff later if you want."

We carefully avoided discussing anything of con-
sequence on the drive to a nearby restaurant, but as we
each enjoyed glasses of white wine while waiting for our
appetizers, I began talking. Verbalizing it all brought
the reality of Marc's deception home to me. I should
have felt angry, betrayed. But by the end, I was only
incredibly numb.

"There's someone back in Montreal," I finally told
Narissa. "I don't know who it was, but he was visiting
there three or four times a year — and she was female. I
found receipts for toiletries and such. Girlie stuff."

Narissa frowned. "An aunt, his mother, a sister? I
only hope that he lied to you about his relatives because
that would mean —"

"He had another woman," I said, finishing her thought.

"Oh, Marta. I am so sorry. After all you've been
through, this is just too much to bear." She reached
across the table and squeezed my hand. "Are you going
to be all right?"

"Surprisingly, I'm better than I would have
imagined. It never even crossed my mind that he might
be two-timing me. At first this afternoon, I was puzzled,
then I got angry, really angry, now I'm just feeling hurt
and, well, more than a little bit of a fool. If it hadn't
been for that damned reporter in Paris, I probably
would have gone scurrying back to Lili for more help
and let the whole thing drop. Now...."

Narissa looked more than a little uneasy. "Now what?"

The waitress interrupted my answer as she brought
our food. I'm sure she didn't recognize me in the
slightest, but Gerhard had always drummed into my

head that I must always be circumspect with personal conversations in public places.

Once she was out of earshot again, I leaned forward, not sure that I should even be saying out loud what I was thinking, based on my sister's reaction the previous evening.

"I have to find out the truth about Marc, Narissa. I won't be able to let this go until I do."

As I expected, my sister tried a holding action. "Do you really think that's wise? What good is it going to do? You'll probably wind up making yourself even more miserable. Let it go. Walk away from this chapter of your life."

I pursed my lips, a forkful of curry halfway to my mouth. "You've been talking to Lili."

Narissa did have the good grace to look embarrassed. "Yes. How did you know?"

"She's already used most of those phrases on me." I smiled. "If you really want to deceive people, you have to at least change the phraseology."

"You're not angry?"

"I know you mean well, but you have to trust that I know what I'm doing. If nothing else, I must have closure. If anything is going to drive me crazy, it will be not knowing what's really going on."

"I don't like your use of the present tense. Am I to take it you're still clinging to the possibility that Marc is alive?"

I pushed my meal aside. Why eat it if I wasn't paying any attention to what it tasted like? "I don't like your use of the word 'clinging.' I am not clinging. I just want some answers. Wouldn't you rather that I, through some outrageous fluke, actually saw Marc in

Paris? The alternative is that I'm still suffering from mental problems. Is that what you want?"

Narissa looked down. "Stated like that, no."

"Look, at the very least Marc played me for a fool. When I'm in Montreal, I'll have the perfect opportunity to find out he still had a mom, or a sister, an aunt, or even a lover he didn't want to tell me about. End of story. I walk away a little bit wiser. Maybe he is dead and what happened in Paris was a leftover from my depression. But what if I really did see him? What if he's still alive? I have to know."

I think the thunderbolt hit us both at the same instant. Narissa says that my eyes suddenly got big. I know hers did.

If Marc was still alive, whose meagre remains had been found in the ruin of the house?

Neither of us finished our meals, and we didn't talk much more. Only when we got back into the car did Narissa speak about it.

"You're going to Montreal for that master class tomorrow."

"Yes, and I'm keeping the rental car to drive there."

"You're going to look around, aren't you?"

"Yes. There was a 514 area code phone number scribbled on the back of one receipt. I'm going to see where that leads me. I also picked up some photos from the log house when I was searching there today. I may visit some of the stores where he bought things and I'll need to show people what Marc looked like."

"Look, Marta, if you're determined to go through with this, maybe you should hire a professional."

"And risk having word of what's going on leak out? No thanks! My reputation is tarnished enough as it is."

Narissa undid her seat belt and hugged me tightly. "Then promise me you'll be very, very careful — and that you will keep in touch. I couldn't bear it if something happened to you!"

"You make this sound like I'm going on a secret mission to Soviet Russia. Don't worry. Like I said earlier, I'll probably just wind up feeling like a fool."

⌒

Next morning, I'd barely gotten through the door of the familiar old stone building on Sherbrooke Street West that housed the music school of McGill University when two very old friends pounced on me.

"Marta!" they shrieked like undergrads, instead of the serious and notable musicians they both were.

"Chloe! Lainey!" I shrieked as loudly as they had. "Oh my God! How good to see you both!"

Chloe pulled back after kissing my cheeks. "Our famous friend makes it to town so seldom, you didn't think we'd let an opportunity like this slip by, did you?"

"Lainey I might expect to see since she's head of the performance department in this joint, but did you get kicked out of the symphony, Chloe? Don't you have a rehearsal or something?"

"Sure, but they're working on some dreadful new string work we're premiering tomorrow evening, and the other piece on the program is Beethoven's 8th. I'm going to get a call on my cell as soon as they take a break. It's only a few minutes over to Place des Arts by cab. I'll make it."

"You know, Chloe, one of these days you're going to cut it too close," Lainey warned.

"Relax, girlfriend, it hasn't happened yet."

"The day of reckoning approacheth," I intoned right on cue, and then we all laughed at the old catchphrase we'd used far too often in the old days.

Chloe had always reminded me of a pixie: everything slightly on the small side, dark hair, delicate features, huge eyes, and extraordinarily pretty. Being barely over five feet allowed her to sneak up unawares on lumbering male percussionists and then crucify them with her awesome technical ability. She has the fastest hands I've ever seen. Lainey, on the other hand, was nearly my height, blonde, had long wavy hair, and had always been very slender. One of her boyfriends used to call her "Lanky Lainey." It fit. I'd always been the odd one out in the looks department.

The three of us had entered the faculty in the same year. Three female percussionists with big personalities had been a bit overwhelming for the normally male instrumental bastion. Shunted off on our own by the older students, we'd quickly branded ourselves "Chicks with Sticks" and told everyone we weren't percussionists, but "percussionistas." My two friends had been deeply hurt when I'd jumped ship for the opera department. Years had passed, and Chloe Smith had nailed the timpani chair in the Montreal Symphony while Lainey Martin had formed a renowned all-female percussion group using our old name. A year earlier, tired of endless touring, she'd disbanded the group and taken the job at McGill.

They were lucky to have her. She was a Québécoise — something I hadn't known when we first met, because her English was so perfect and her name sounded Anglo. She was also incredibly competent and dedicated.

"Everyone in the school is so thrilled to have you here," Lainey said as we made our way to the new wing of the building, a gift of a very generous benefactor who'd been honoured by having the entire school named after him: the Seymour Schulich School of Music.

Having attended the McGill Faculty of Music, I was finding it a bit difficult to adjust to the new moniker, but everyone else seemed comfortable with it.

"They're already there and waiting for you," Lainey continued. "That's why we were in the lobby. You cut it pretty fine."

"But then she always did," Chloe added with a smile, "and never missed a cue."

I shrugged. "Traffic. I thought leaving two and a half hours for the trip from Ottawa would be enough."

The morning's classes were being held in the new recital hall, named after the benefactor's wife. The place looked about half full, and considering the hall seats two hundred, I was gratified there was such a turnout for little old me.

Since we were now five minutes late, a very quick round of introductions to the VIPs in the front row was carried out, and I felt sure I wouldn't remember a single name after another five minutes had passed — except for one person: Julie Bouthot, my old voice teacher. I hugged her quickly in order to hide my shock at how much she'd aged since I'd last seen her six years ago.

She pulled away and held me at arm's length. "You are looking better than ever, Marta," she said. "I am so happy you have gotten over your recent troubles. And I am hearing good things about your singing, very good things."

"You know how the press can be," I said, deflecting her compliment.

"In Paris, I certainly do. A good review there is worth a dozen in any other city."

"Marta," Lainey said in my ear, "we have to move along. The sessions are all quite full."

"I'll talk to you later," I said squeezing Julie's hands. They felt bony, and her whole body seemed shrunken. "Lunch today or tomorrow?"

"I may not be able to stay that long. I get tired quickly these days."

"I'll call you then. I'm not leaving town without having a good chat."

Julie smiled. "I'd enjoy that."

The head of the opera department, someone new since I'd been a student, introduced me to the audience and we got down to work.

It was strange in the extreme to be sitting on a high-backed chair on a stage in my old school, just as Gerhard had done so many years ago when a young upstart soprano in the audience stepped onstage.

I generally don't do master classes. I'd wondered at the time I was asked if the dean might be headhunting for a new teacher, since many had gotten the idea that I'd retired from the stage.

The three-hour morning session flew by, and I was struck over and over by how dramatically the level of accomplishment at the school had risen since I'd attended — and it had been pretty high then.

Lunch was hosted by the dean, a very likeable man filled with great enthusiasm for his job, charming and with a very ready wit. His assistant, an equally likable blonde woman and obviously very competent, sat next to me, talking about all the changes at the old school since I'd last been through.

I excused myself a bit early so I could warm up properly. I'd been hampered that morning by not being able to demonstrate. Warming up while driving through traffic in downtown Montreal is not a good substitute for a quiet room with a good piano.

By the end of the afternoon session, I was completely wiped, but feeling quite exhilarated. I'd been able to work with a talented group of students and I felt that I helped most of them.

Lainey showed up to pluck me from the crowd that stayed behind, peppering me with questions — mostly related to securing a manager. The competition for singing gigs is always fierce.

"I'm taking you to dinner, girlfriend," she said in my ear, "and you're not saying no."

"Do you mind if I check in to my hotel first and freshen up?"

"Not at all."

As we transferred my rental car from a parking garage on De Maisonneuve to the hotel garage, Lainey brought me up to date on the lives of other friends from school. Always enthusiastic and funny, I'd forgotten how enjoyable she was to be around.

The woman had aged well, and even though she was dressed in business clothes, it was obvious she carried her youthful figure intact. Lainey's blonde hair was maybe a little darker and there were a few tiny wrinkles around her eyes, but she looked terrific.

Once up in my room, I made a beeline for the bathroom. A shower was definitely called for and, it went a long way toward refreshing me.

When I exited the bathroom, rubbing my hair briskly with a towel, Lainey, having raided the room's mini-bar, immediately shoved a rum and coke into my hand. It was the drink we'd cut our teeth on as undergrads.

I took a big swig. "Oh, that's good, just what I needed. Thanks."

"I love what you've done to your hair. Lighter brown, shoulder length, and those blonde highlights, yes, very nice."

"I felt I needed to change a few things."

"So you're back on the road again," she said, slouching back in her chair while I pulled on more casual clothes.

"Yup, and I have to tell you it feels great."

"Well, I can't tell you how happy I am not to be living out of a suitcase all the time. The job at McGill has allowed me to afford a terrific apartment in Côte Saint-Luc, and I feel like I'm finally able to put down some roots."

"Got a guy?"

"Yeah," she said, blushing. "I sure hope I'm not jinxing it, but I think he may be the one." Diffusing the subject, Lainey's eyes followed the jeans I was pulling up my legs. "You're looking good. Been working out?"

"Part of getting my life back together was joining a gym. I've been pretty lax since I left for Paris, actually." I looked over my shoulder at the mirror behind me. "I've certainly put on a pound or two."

The conversation abruptly changed again. "We really haven't spoken about your troubles. It must have been horrible."

I sat down on the corner of the bed, picked up my drink and looked at my old friend. "Marc was everything to me and to just have it all yanked away like it was.... It was nearly unbearable."

"You could have relied on Chloe and me."

Shaking my head sadly, I answered, "I know that, but at the time I couldn't reach out to anyone. It was as if someone had taken sandpaper to my soul. Everything was raw and bleeding, and I couldn't bear the thought of anything or anybody touching it."

Lainey got out of her chair, sat down next to me, and gave me a bone-crushing hug. "But you're all better now — and that's a very good thing."

The way she said it, I knew she wanted me to affirm that everything was indeed better now. A month ago, I would have been able to tell her what she wanted to hear, but now? Sadly, it was not the case.

I had been thinking on and off all day about asking for my friend's help, or at least her company, for what I planned to do later in the evening. She knew Montreal like the back of her hand and her French was home grown.

"Funny you should bring that up...."

Chapter Seven

My friend looked thoroughly perplexed.

So I told her about going out to the farm the day before, and among other things, finding a Montreal phone number. The part about seeing Marc in Paris I left out — at least for the moment. The way my sister had reacted made me very leery about sharing that information. If Lainey suspected I might not be telling the whole story, she didn't let on.

I swallowed the last of my drink. "I'm thinking that the phone number I found might be someone in Marc's family. He told me there'd been some sort of falling out and he'd cut off contact with them. They probably don't even know he's dead."

Lainey knocked back the rest of her drink and put down the glass with a decisive thump. "Let me see that number." Lainey whipped a BlackBerry from a little holster thing on her hip, and her thumbs flew over the keys for a couple of seconds, after which she announced, "Just as I thought. The number is for a phone in Verdun."

"How did you figure that out so quickly?"

"Reverse search."

"Reverse what?"

"Marta, you really are such a dinosaur. How do you keep in touch with the world? I'll bet you don't even have a computer."

"Uh, no. I do have a cellphone."

Lainey rolled her eyes comically and waved her gadget in my face. "I guarantee that within a month of getting one of these little babies, you won't be able to imagine how you lived without it."

"Perhaps you're right."

She stuffed her little marvel away, got to her feet, and slung her purse over her shoulder. "Eat first, detect later?"

⌒

Shortly after eight, we were sitting in front of what I mentally call "a Montreal apartment building" in the extreme lower west end of the city. They're sort of like row houses, and each building contains three flats. The bottom one is right at ground level, never more than a step or two up to the door, the second and third flats are reached by very distinctive, curving metal staircases on the outside of the building. The general design hardly ever varies, just the decoration. Every Montreal neighborhood has streets full of them.

Having never spent any significant time in Verdun, I knew little about it beyond its blue-collar origins. Once, there had been a lot of factories down here, but starting in the sixties that had begun to change as one after another closed or moved out of province. Always low-rent, the area was now looking pretty rough in places, with whole streets of rundown buildings and many vacant storefronts.

Not having a good map, it took us a bit of time to find the correct location. Finally, we turned into a one-block street, poorly lit and lined with careworn buildings.

"You're sure this is the right place?" I asked Lainey after she told me to pull over.

"Yup. That building over there, bottom flat. Ready to do battle?"

With a heavy sigh, I nodded. Faced with actually moving forward with my little project, I suddenly felt the first twinges of cold feet. Had I been alone, I might have chickened out.

Opening the car door, I answered, "Let's get this show on the road," with a lot more bravado than I felt.

My heart was thumping to beat the band as we crossed the street, mounted the one cracked concrete step, and looked down at a worn mat. I crossed myself for luck and pressed my finger on the buzzer. Beneath it was one of those embossed plastic strips with the name Lachance. I thought the name was appropriate, considering the circumstances.

To our left, the brick facade bulged out to contain a bay window, and a quick flash of light as the curtain flicked let us know someone was home. A moment later, a bare bulb went on above our heads.

A short, absolutely ancient-looking woman opened the door, safety chain on. Her face was so wrinkled it reminded me of one of those dried apple dolls you see in folksy gift shops.

"*Oui?*" she said. "*Puis-je vous aider?*"

I didn't answer right away, so Lainey gave me a bit of a nudge with her shoulder.

It was only then that I realized I'd never considered how I might open what could turn out to be a very uncomfortable conversation.

"*Bonsoir, Madame,*" I said, deciding it was best to speak French. "This is going to seem a very odd question, but does the name Marc Tremblay mean anything to you?"

She looked harder at me, then shook her head slowly. "No."

Opening my purse, I took out one of the photos I'd brought from the farm.

"Do you know this person?" I asked, holding it out.

The old woman studied it for barely a second, then looked up sharply. "Who are you and why are you here?"

"Well, you see, the man in that photo was my husband."

Her eyes opened wide. "I do not believe you!"

"But you do know who this is?"

"Of course! He is my grandson, but his name, I assure you, Madame, is certainly not Marc Tremblay."

Scattered drops of rain began falling around us, and a rising wind blew them onto our backs.

"Do you think we might come in and speak with you?"

She peered at us for a long moment, then nodded and released the chain but didn't issue any words of welcome as she stood aside for us to pass.

The sitting room was old, filled with heavy but worn furniture and oppressively hot. The television was on but the sound had been muted. Over the TV hung a print of the Virgin, de rigueur in a proper French-Canadian household.

The old woman gestured toward a sofa — lumpy, but with a bright Indian throw neatly covering it. She took a seat on a recliner but stayed perched on the edge, wary. No offer of tea or coffee was made, and that was out of the ordinary, too.

I reckoned Madame Lachance to be at least in her mid-eighties. She was short, rotund, and wore the expected black dress. A small gold crucifix hung from a chain around her neck, and her white hair was pulled back into a neat bun. In short, Marc's *grand-mère* looked exactly like thousands of others in la belle province.

"You said at the door that my husband's name was not Marc. Could I ask you what it was?"

She frowned at me. "How do I know that you are what you say you are?"

I was ready for that question and removed from my purse another of the papers I'd picked up at the log house the previous day: our marriage licence. From my wallet, I also produced my driver's license and a photo of Marc and me that a waitress had taken on the night of our marriage as we were enjoying a quiet meal together Mexicali Rosa's in Perth.

Laying out the various things on her lap, the old woman studied each one carefully. Lainey was fidgeting next to me, eager to see what was going to happen next in this little drama. The minutes ticked by.

"My grandson's name is Jean-Claude Lachance," she said, removing her glasses to rub her eyes tiredly. "I thought you might be from the police."

I had decided ahead of time to stick with the official line, that Marc had been killed in the fire, until I knew for certain this wasn't the case. It would be unfair, and probably very counter-productive, to tell this poor woman absolutely nothing about Marc's fate.

I took a deep breath. "Madame, before we go any further with this, I have to tell you some very, very bad news."

"He is dead then?" She didn't sound surprised.

"Yes. Two years ago in a fire at the home he was building for us."

"Where?"

"In Ontario, near Perth. Do you know where that is?"

She nodded. "He never told me he'd gotten married."

"Your grandson told he was completely estranged from his family."

"That is because of the trouble which was following him. He told me he did not wish to put me in danger. The less I knew about what he was doing, the better."

Tears welled in my eyes. Marc's grandmother, his flesh and blood, didn't appear upset. Her expression only transmitted weary resignation. I only hoped she wouldn't be hurt further at a later date.

Lainey, misinterpreting the situation completely, put her arm around me and squeezed.

Madame Lachance asked, "And my Jean-Claude has been dead for two years?"

I could only nod.

"I feared it was so. I have not heard from him for that length of time. How did you come to visit me tonight, so long afterwards?"

"There was a phone number on a scrap of paper in his pickup truck. I only found it yesterday and followed the trail here."

"I moved three years ago from our old house after my dear husband passed on. It was a new phone number." She chuckled fondly. "Jean-Claude had such a poor memory sometimes."

"You said a moment ago that you thought I might have been from the police. Why did you say that?"

At this moment, the old woman finally offered tea — quite possibly there might be things she wasn't sure she wanted to tell me. Somehow I had to wheedle out what I could. In the back of my mind, I could hear Narissa's voice telling me I should have listened to her and hired a professional.

Madame Lachance re-entered the room with what must have been her best china. She poured the tea, and we silently took a few small sips. The way I was feeling, a good shot of whiskey would have been more in order.

In order to get the conversation rolling again, I

asked, "Can you tell me about Jean-Claude when he was younger?"

The old lady looked up at me, the same expression of resignation on her face. "His home life was not of the best. It was not a marriage I would have wanted my son, Jean, to make. The mother was wild, drank too much, took drugs. She conceived a child and the families forced the marriage. Even before Jean-Claude's first birthday, she left. No one knows where. It was probably for the best. She would never have been a proper mother."

"Did he come to live with you?" I asked.

"He had to. His father drove transport trucks just like his father before him, mostly western Canada, but sometimes down to the States. He could be gone for a week at a time. We did the best we could for the child, but he had a wild streak — like his mother. There was always trouble, first with the school, then with the police as he got older. He took up with a bad crowd."

"Where was his father in all this?"

"Driving transport takes many lives. The long hours, the always pushing for more miles, it extracts a price. There was a pileup in the fog one night in Ontario near Windsor. At least I can thank our gracious Father that my son Jean's death was a quick one. Little Jean-Claude was only twelve and he did not take the news very well. His behavior only got worse after that. My Gaston, Jean-Claude's *grand-père*, spoke with him, the priest spoke with him. Nothing seemed to get through. Finally, when he was seventeen, there was a very big fight and Jean-Claude left."

"Do you know where he went?"

"You know about the motorcycle gangs in Quebec? It is a *grand scandale*! The big fight was because of this. Jean-Claude had become friends with some of them."

This came as a real shock. I knew my Marc loved motorcycles, especially big, noisy Harleys, and he talked constantly about buying one for himself someday, but I thought it was so much talk. Boys with their toys, nothing more. To me, Marc was always gentle and kind and funny, completely unlike what I imagined a biker to be.

Lainey finally spoke up. "Madame Lachance, was your grandson a member of one of these gangs, or simply someone who hung out with them?"

Madame Lachance hesitated before answering. "I believe he was on the outside with them, not a full member. In his heart, Jean-Claude really was a good boy. He was like a moth attracted to the flame, you know what I mean?"

We both nodded, and I asked, "So you completely lost touch with him after he left?"

"He never spoke to his *grand-père* again, but he did call me on the telephone sometimes when he knew Gaston would not be home, usually for holidays and my birthday. He once told me he was in Vancouver, working on a construction site."

I'd found a dirty blank postcard from Butchart Gardens in among Marc's tools. I could see him buying it to send to his *grand-mère*, then with his usual cheerful carelessness, losing it in the mess in the back of his truck.

"Five years ago, I stopped hearing from Jean-Claude. In my heart I feared the worst, but I hoped for the best. The priest assured me that God was looking after him. I prayed every day that I might hear his voice again. After one year and a half, the Virgin answered my prayers."

I thought back to the first dates on the receipts I'd found. I'd been singing at Covent Garden. "Was this in October?"

"Yes, it was."

"He came to visit."

"Yes. With his *grand-père* now at home because of his illness, we could not meet at the house, even though I begged for Jean-Claude to make up before it was too late. He would not yield, so we met at Place Desjardins."

Bingo! The three receipts I had from that October trip were for purchases made at that shopping mall. "And the other times he met you?"

"It was always at places well away from where Gaston and I lived. Jean-Claude made me swear on the Blessed Virgin that I would not tell anyone about his visits, before or afterwards."

Lainey stirred but didn't inject herself into the conversation any further.

Madame Lachance offered more tea, which neither of us accepted. Excusing herself, she went out to the kitchen and came back with a plate of Fig Newtons, taking two for herself.

"Now, my dear," she began after pouring a second cup of tea for herself, "tell me your story."

I gave her a rough sketch of how Marc (I was going to have a rough time forcing my brain to accept Jean-Claude as his name) and I met, fell in love, and the basics of our life together. She seemed especially amused that I was an opera singer. I asked about that.

"My Gaston loved opera. Every Saturday, he would listen to those broadcasts from New York on Radio-Canada. That is what he and Jean-Claude had their big fight about. He called all opera singers fat old women who screamed for a living. It is very funny indeed that he married one."

It certainly was. But it also gave me some insight as to why I'd often see a quizzical smile on my husband's face whenever I would sing around the farm house.

"Do you have any idea why he was using another name when he met me?"

"No."

"Do you remember the date you last saw Jean-Claude or heard from him?"

Madame Lachance hesitated again. I knew the last date for which I had a receipt. It was three weeks before the accident, and I was in Dallas then. He'd bought her a big box of very expensive chocolates in Pointe Claire on Montreal's West Island. Probably, he'd pulled off the highway when he realized he didn't have anything for her (he completely forgot my birthday once).

Finally, she said, "I do not remember."

"And you didn't hear from him after that?"

She stuck her chin up indignantly. "How could I? You yourself told me that he was dead."

Bitten. An expert probably wouldn't have made that mistake.

I felt suddenly weary. This sort of mental exertion after a long day of teaching preceded by a long drive from Ottawa was taking its toll. I could think of only one more question. By morning, I'd probably have thought of fifty more.

"Was he any different on that last visit? Did he say anything you think I should know?"

Again her eyes shifted away, and she answered, "No."

The old woman would have to ask God's forgiveness for lying when she said her prayers that night.

⌒⌒

I'd barely gotten my bum onto the car seat when Lainey erupted. "Just what the hell is going on?"

My shoulders slumped. I probably should have leveled with Lainey from the start and told her about the two incidents in Paris. I just hadn't wanted her to think I was a complete flake.

So I decided to lay it all out and not pull any punches. It took a good fifteen minutes. From the corner of my eye, I saw the curtains of Madame Lachance's front window flick at least twice. She knew we were still out there.

Lainey's only response at the end of my soliloquy was a low whistle. "So you think you actually saw him in Paris?"

I sighed and rested my forehead on the steering wheel, although I felt like pounding it. "I honestly don't know, but the thought that I might have is driving me crazy!"

"I can imagine it would." She patted my shoulder "Do you think the old lady was lying right at the end of our conversation?"

I twisted my mouth to the side, unable to avoid sarcasm. "Is the Pope Catholic?"

Lainey thought for a moment. "My grandmother died two years ago. My dad had to file a final tax return for her. How did your husband's estate get resolved?

Preparing to turn the car key, I just stopped, amazed that I'd missed that angle. "It, um, never got done."

"You're kidding!"

"I was in no shape to do anything. My brother searched the old farmhouse and found no will, but that wasn't unexpected, knowing my husband. What did he have to leave me anyway? Basically, just a beat-up pickup truck, tools, and some clothes. Anyway, I just ignored it all at the time, figuring it could be dealt with when his income tax forms arrived. Of course, they never did, because he wouldn't have filed any returns. I guess I just forgot about it."

"If you hadn't, you would have known immediately that something was up."

I started the engine and pulled out. At the far end of the block, another car also pulled out.

"What do you think I should do?"

"Well," Lainey began, "there's this guy I've been seeing...."

"So you said. And?"

"Well, he's a journalist and an author. His area of expertise is Quebec biker gangs. His books are actually quite good, but pretty gruesome."

"So that's why you asked that odd question."

Lainey nodded. "From what Sébastien tells me, it isn't all that easy to become a full member of a biker gang. It suits them to have hangers on. They can be made to do a lot of the dirty work in order to 'prove themselves.'" By that time, we were stopped for a light on Rue Notre Dame and it was beginning to rain in earnest. Lainey put her hand on my right forearm. "Did you ever get the feeling that your husband was frightened or worried? From what that old woman said, it sure sounds like he might have been into some heavy shit."

I thought back again over our time together, seeing if anything more had been jogged loose by the visit with my, well, grandmother-in-law.

Marc had just seemed to want to keep to himself, be his own man. He said all the right things to deflect any questions I might ask. He said he had no friends, no family, liked his solitude, and that I was all he needed. But then, he'd always been a glib rogue. He could easily have been hiding something. What other reason would he have had to change his identity?

"Lainey, to be frank, I'm open to anything. Sure, he could have been laying low. He had nothing to do with my career. I couldn't have gotten him into an opera house or party or concert with a gun held to his head."

I smiled at a memory of once threatening to do just that, even going so far as to pull the old shotgun out of the living room closet in the log home. Smiling broadly, Marc stood there, hands up in surrender, big grin on his face, deadly handsome.

"Go on, *ma chère*, shoot me. I will not go to that awful party. What would I say? I know nothing about the world you live in."

"Isn't it enough that you would be there with me?"

"Quite frankly, no." He kept smiling. "So I guess you will just have to shoot me."

Lainey pulled at my arm. "Marta, you've zoned out. The light changed about five seconds ago."

Amazingly, the car behind me hadn't honked, a first for Montreal.

"Lain, do you think you could arrange for me to speak to Sébastien?"

"Sure. When do you want to do it?"

I glanced at my left wrist. "It's just past ten. Tonight?"

She grinned. "I thought you were completely done in."

"I believe in striking while the iron is hot."

"Well, you're in luck because he's a real night owl. Let me see if I can run him down," she added, pulling out her cellphone.

Chapter Eight

Sébastien Bouchard's apartment in Old Montreal *was huge, one of those downtown* lofts with hardwood floors, ten-foot ceilings, exposed pipes, and enough windows to warm any voyeur's heart. It also contained almost no furniture. Book writing must be very lucrative. His place gave me the impression he'd just moved out of a much smaller apartment.

The man himself was tall, slender, dark, and while he wasn't particularly handsome, there was a certain magnetism in his presence. You at once got the feeling of a strong personality and inquiring mind lurking behind his very pretty eyes. In short, he was the sort of man to whom Lainey had always been attracted.

He greeted her with a peck to each cheek, followed by a quick kiss to her mouth. Though it was brief, it clearly showed the fire between them burned strongly.

I hoped it would work out for my friend. She perennially picked the wrong men for long-term happiness.

After planting quick air kisses on each side of my face, he stepped back and looked into my eyes.

"*Bienvenue,*" he said. "*Elaine parle de vous souvent.*"

"It's very good of you to see me this late," I answered in English. I was too tired to carry on this conversation in French.

Without missing a beat, Sébastien switched to English. "I usually stay up very late," he answered with a sideways glance at Lainey. Her hand snaked into his, and I got the feeling someone would be getting lucky as soon as I'd concluded my business and split.

At the far end of the room, they sat down on a leather sofa, and I took a matching chair across from them. A glass-topped coffee table over a nondescript rug and an ugly chrome floor-lamp completed the decor surrounding us. Other than two enormous book cases farther down one wall and a small desk, that was it for the living area, even though there was enough floor space to rehearse a good-sized orchestra. *Style at Home* magazine would not be calling anytime soon.

"So tell me what it is that you want. Lainey was very mysterious over the phone."

Certainly, I wasn't about to tell a journalist, regardless of his relationship with my friend, any more of my business than I needed to, and as we'd parked the car on the street below, I'd still been madly considering how to accomplish that. My recent experience in Paris showed me just how wrong things could go when the fifth estate is involved. On the elevator ride up, I made Lainey promise not to tell Sébastien anything about my situation past what I told him myself. I hoped I could trust her.

Since I was on record as being married to someone named Marc Tremblay, I felt I was on pretty safe ground if I used his real name — unless Sébastien started digging. But that was a risk I would have to take. "Does the name Jean-Claude Lachance mean anything to you? Have you ever run across it during your research?"

Sébastien considered for a moment, then shook his head. "No. Is he a member of a biker gang?"

"That's what I'm trying to find out."

"Why?"

Oh dear, I was hoping he'd hold off with a question like that until I'd had more time to gather my wits.

"He's a person I met, and we may do some business together," I said, amazed at how quickly the lie had come into my brain and how smoothly it slipped off my tongue. "There's something about him I don't really trust. You know, one of those feelings you get sometimes."

"What sort of business?"

"I'd rather not say."

Sébastien shrugged again. If he suspected I wasn't telling the truth, he didn't show it. Reaching down next to him, he pulled up a black computer bag and put it on the table. "Let me see if the database I keep has any record of him. There are too many players in this game for me to keep track of them only in my brain."

He explained that his files were heavily encrypted, so it would take some time for them to open. Lainey slipped off and returned shortly carrying a bottle of red wine and three glasses. We sat in silence while she was gone.

"Okay," he said. "We're up. Now what was that name again?"

He typed it in and waited, frowning. Then typed again, then again, finally shaking his head. "There is no one here by that name, and I believe my list is pretty complete."

"Maybe he's not a member anymore?" Lainey suggested.

"Once you are a part of these organizations, it is not so easy to leave — but we will look in an older database. Maybe his name will turn up."

While we again waited, Sébastien opened and poured the wine. I couldn't see the label, but from the taste I could tell it was expensive. Gerhard had taught me enough about wine to know that you don't get those sorts of nuanced flavours from plonk.

Soon, this new file was ready for work and Sébastien again typed a few words.

"Ah, here it is. Your friend is listed as being an associate of the Rock Machine."

"What does 'associate' mean?"

"He was not an inducted member, but was hanging around with them. Do you know what this means?"

I nodded. "How old is your information?"

"I created my new database five years ago. If I did not carry this Jean-Claude into the new one, it means that he was no longer active in Quebec."

"What if he'd gone somewhere else, like ... British Columbia?"

"If I had information that he had moved on elsewhere, I would have kept him on my new database. Now you must understand that I do not know everything. I certainly do not claim to have a record on every known biker in Canada. Your friend might well have gone west. Perhaps you have information about him out there? Do you know precisely where he was?"

"In the Vancouver area, I believe. Would there be any way you could find out about that?"

Sébastien looked at me closely again. He had these amazingly blue eyes and his face had a shrewd little squint to it. I got the feeling that I'd aroused his interest more than might have been wise. Certainly, an opera singer asking questions about a person involved with bikers would make any journalist's antennae twitch. "I will tell you what, Marta Hendriks, I will call a colleague who works at the *Vancouver Sun* and see if he knows anything. It may take a day or two. Will you be in Montreal long?"

"No. I teach again tomorrow and I'll be heading back to Toronto the morning after that."

"I may have word by then."

"That would be great." We exchanged cellphone numbers, and I prepared to get moving. Lainey walked me to the door as Sébastien left the room with the empty wine glasses. I retrieved my coat from the hall closet.

"You're quite the little liar," she said as she handed me my scarf.

I could feel myself blushing. "He caught me completely off guard. It just sprang into my head."

"So what do you think?" she asked. "Did you get what you wanted?"

"Not really. Hopefully, Sébastien's contact in B.C. will know something."

"He's pretty modest. His books sell really well, especially in Quebec, and he has a lot of sources of information. If anyone can find out what you want, it will be him."

She had the door open and I walked through, then turned and stopped. "Just make sure you stop off at home tomorrow and change your clothes. It doesn't look good to show up at work wearing the same thing two days in a row."

Lainey stuck her tongue out at me as she shut the door.

~

The next day was more of the same and all the students they'd chosen for me to work with were really quite excellent. Consequently, I'd been enjoying myself more than I expected. The day finished off with me bringing everyone up on stage to go through some breathing exercises that Gerhard had taught me. Julie had again been in the audience, but once again slipped out as I was demonstrating how to traverse the *passaggio*, going up and getting softer at the same time, always a very tricky thing for singers.

As I was walking out of the recital hall with the head of the opera department, I asked about my teacher.

She sighed. "Julie is very ill. I'm sure you noticed how frail she is."

"Cancer?" I asked with a catch in my throat.

The answer was a nod. "She does not like anyone to talk about it."

"I must go see her!"

"No, I don't think she would like that. It was enough, I think, for her to see you doing so well these past two days. They were marvellous sessions. You're quite good, you know. Some people are natural teachers. Julie was very proud of you, and so touched by how much you praised her teaching."

"I meant every word."

"That was obvious. I would suggest that you keep in touch with your old teacher by phone."

"How long does she have?"

"She will not say, if she even bothered to ask. She has only two students at present, but she struggles in gamely one day a week to work with them. She is an inspiration to us all."

I could only nod in agreement.

On my way out, I stuck my head in Lainey's office. Her secretary said she was busy with some people in her office, but would not be long. While waiting, I was struck by how much I owed McGill. I'd had four very good years here. It also seemed odd to be once again sitting in this particular office, only this time, on the other side of the door was not some crusty old man who'd always managed to make me uncomfortable, but one of my two best friends from my years in this building. Life sure takes some funny twists.

The door opened and two people exited. I recognized one of them immediately.

Victoria Morgan has been described numerous times as the "musician's violinist." I'll bet every classical musician has at least one of her CDs. Her premiere of the lost Beethoven concerto was the best-selling classical music recording of all time.

Lainey was saying, "So I will send you the proposed dates, and if you can let me know immediately how they fit in with your schedule, I would really appreciate it." Then she saw me. "Oh Marta, you're here. Great. Tory, this is my good friend —"

"Marta and I have met, what is it, two other times?" the redheaded violinist interrupted. She stuck out her hand. "How you doing?"

"Very well, Tory, and you?"

"Oh, the usual. Seems as if I've finally succumbed to the requests to do more teaching. Ms. Martin here drives a hard bargain." She indicated the man standing just behind her. "Where are my manners? This is my husband Rocky Lukesh. He's on the faculty here."

A light bulb went on in my head. It would certainly be a feather in the school's cap to have someone of Tory's stature listed among its staff, even if it wasn't full time. Some really great students would be lining up around the block for a chance to study with her.

I shook hands with the man I'd heard was an excellent teacher and player, but he seemed older and more careworn than I would have expected, given his age. For that matter, the violin goddess's eyes seemed to reflect deep exhaustion. Even with all the fame and money, her personal life had been fraught with difficulty — not the least of which was being accused of murder in Austria seven years earlier.

As they exited, I considered where I was going with my problem. Maybe it would be better to just let the whole thing drop. It was clear now that I'd been lied to, regardless of whatever reason, good or bad, there might have been. And if Marc was still alive, what then? Could I take someone like that back? Did I *want* someone like that back?

Lainey snapped her fingers in front of my face. "Hello, earth calling Marta. Come in, please." As my eyes slipped back into focus, she laughed. "Zoned out again, girlfriend? Hope you don't make a habit of doing that during performances."

My friend had a concert she had to attend at the school that evening, followed by a reception for invited alumni, so she wasn't available. Chloe also had a Montreal Symphony performance, coupled with a sick child at home, so she was out. As I walked back to the hotel, I decided that not being able to have a Chicks with Sticks reunion at our favourite restaurant on Avenue Parc might not be such a bad thing. It had been a long two days of teaching. I could use a nice, relaxing evening.

Once back in my room, I took a quick shower, raided the mini-bar for a split of white wine, and sat in the room's one chair, feet up on the bed.

The previous evening, I'd been too exhausted to consider anything but sleep, but now I let my mind spin for a bit, trying to come to grips with everything I'd learned in the past three days. That look in Tory Morgan's eyes came to mind, too.

What did I want to do? Would Sébastien be able to shed any further light on the issue?

As I was deep in my reverie, the phone ringing didn't register right away. "Hello?"

"Am I speaking with Marta Hendriks?"

I didn't recognize the voice. "Yes. And you are?"

"My name is Inspector Parker, Ron Parker, and I am with the RCMP organized crime task force. Would it be possible to speak personally with you?"

Even though I've never been guilty of anything beyond jaywalking, I suddenly felt nervous and defensive with a cop wanting to talk to me.

"What does this pertain to?" I asked, even though I felt certain I knew what he'd answer.

"Your dead husband, Marc Tremblay, or would you prefer that I refer to him as Jean-Claude Lachance?"

⌒

I'd had enough sense to agree to meet this man in the lobby of the hotel. He showed me his credentials discreetly, suggesting a quiet corner of the hotel's lounge for our little chat.

Parker appeared to be somewhere around fifty, slightly taller than me and sporting close-cropped greying hair that just screamed "cop," at least to my inexperienced eyes. He had on a light-grey suit and was obviously still very fit.

"Thank you for finding the time to speak with me. Would you like something to drink?"

"Sure. A glass of white wine, please."

He immediately signalled a waitress and gave her the order: wine for me and sparkling water for him.

"What is this all about, Inspector?"

He grinned. "You don't waste any time."

I cocked an eyebrow, not buying into the friendly routine. Yes, I was nervous about this, but I'd decided in the elevator on the way down that I wouldn't be intimidated. The fact that I'd been messing around with my knotty problem for not even three full days and the Mounties were already knocking on my door made it clear that I'd been poking a stick into a hornet's nest. I couldn't remember the last time I'd spoken even two words to a cop, and now I was being interviewed by one.

Parker kept me hanging until the waitress returned with our order. My heart was hammering the entire time and my hand was slick with sweat as I picked up the wine glass, but I refrained from wiping it off.

"How much do you know of your husband's past?" Parker began.

Between sips of wine to help calm my nerves, I told him all I'd known about Marc, well, up until the past three days. For whatever reason: loyalty, fear, or just orneriness, I decided to reserve the new information.

I'd been seemingly talking about this endlessly the past few days, but it felt ultra weird to do it as part of a grilling by a police officer, even in the civilized setting of a hotel cocktail lounge.

After finishing my little soliloquy, I added, "Look, my husband was killed over two years ago. If you had questions about him, why wait until now?"

Why did the look Parker suddenly flashed remind me of a shark about to attack?

"If you don't want to beat around the bush, Ms. Hendriks, then I won't, either. When the accident happened, it was deemed that you weren't of interest to us since you seemed to know nothing of your husband's past, so we left you alone — mostly because of who you are. Now, all of a sudden, you're asking questions. Why? It seems we may have misjudged your involvement in this situation."

That sounded ominous. "What 'situation?'"

"Ms. Hendriks, if you please, I will ask the questions. This is an informal discussion at present, and I'm sure you would like to keep it that way."

He leaned back to give his threat time to sink in. "Even if Jean-Claude really kept you in the dark about his past, I'm assuming that the old woman told you his real name yesterday evening."

"How do you know I visited her? Have you been following me?"

Parker waggled his index finger warningly. "Ms. Hendriks ..."

"Right. Sorry."

"We have had certain acquaintances of Lachance's under surveillance for the past two years."

I held up my hand as if I was in school. "Inspector Parker, may I ask a question?"

A smile flickered across his face. "Certainly."

"Just what did, um, Jean-Claude do? Obviously, it's pretty serious if the RCMP is involved." When Parker appeared to be hesitating, I added, "Look, I think I have a right to know. I was married to him and anything he did could very well have an impact on me."

"Let me give you the background to this story first. To cut to the chase, Jean-Claude was an RCMP informant. We recruited him in Quebec and he supplied us with some very important information that allowed us to arrest several of the kingpins of the Rock Machine about six years ago. Quebec was too hot to hold him, so he was put in our witness protection program and shipped out to British Columbia."

"I'm finding this all a bit hard to swallow. He was a secret agent?"

"That's a little dramatic. His job was basically to just hang around and keep his ears open. When there was something to pass on, he contacted us and one of our people would reel him in for a debriefing. We often work numerous people like this in the course of an investigation. Jean-Claude was more useful than most because he was one of those sorts that people naturally trust. You should know about that better than most."

It all made sense, except for one thing. "So why did he change his name and come back east to Ontario, then go through all kinds of subterfuge to visit his grandmother?"

Parker had a ready answer. "We had him in our witness protection program, then something spooked him about a year in and he jumped ship. You seem to have met him about six months after that."

The waitress came over with another glass of wine, although I hadn't seen Parker order it. "But at the beginning of this discussion you told me you'd been watching and waiting. If you knew where Marc ... I mean Jean-Claude was, why didn't you just make contact with him again?"

"I can't talk about that."

"Is that the cop equivalent of saying 'because?'"

Parker shrugged. "Sorry, but that's just the way it is." He leaned forward. "Tell me, are you in contact with Jean-Claude?"

Luckily, I hadn't started to swallow, or I would have sprayed wine everywhere. I still sputtered a mouthful of wine into the glass. "What?"

"Ah, sorry. I should have waited to ask you that."

People were looking at me again. "You should apologize. What the hell are you talking about anyway? My husband is dead."

The Mountie appeared unfazed. "Is he?"

"That is ridiculous!" I started to get up.

All around us, people had turned their heads, curious as to what was going on.

Parker kept his voice low, but loaded with authority. "Please sit, Ms. Hendriks. There is more to say."

I did as he ordered. "You're not expecting me to believe that he didn't die in that fire, are you?"

"That fire was awfully convenient, don't you think? We'd finally discovered where Jean-Claude was hiding and were about to pick him up when he's killed and his body pretty-well cremated. Now you suddenly appear at the scene again, then start asking questions."

"You were watching my farm?"

I was horrified. How could they do something like that? It had probably been some sort of electronic surveillance. I couldn't see them having someone hiding in the trees 24/7.

"Why did you start asking questions about your dead husband after you'd done nothing for two years? What were you looking for at your farm? Did he leave something there and ask you to pick it up for him? Why did you go there?"

Parker's demeanor had changed. Now, despite the surroundings of a Montreal hotel cocktail lounge, I certainly felt as if I was in a backroom somewhere, being accused of a crime.

At that point, I had a choice. I could have told him all about Paris. I probably should have told him. He was a cop, after all.

But I chose to keep my mouth shut and spent the next ten minutes doing some more lying.

Chapter Nine

I unlocked the door to my condo and peeled off my coat, leaving it and my suitcase on the floor of the entryway. After a stop at the sideboard, where I kept some Scotch in my dad's old cut-glass decanter, I walked over to the sofa, dropped my sorry bum down, and removed my shoes. My feet ached but not nearly as much as my brain. It had been quite a trip east.

My voicemail had a dozen messages, most of them useless telemarketing. Alex had called wanting to talk to me about a couple more bookings. Both Lainey and Chloe left messages saying how great it had been to see me and how we should get together more often. We always said that and then never did anything about it.

The way things had been going, I wouldn't have been surprised to have found a voicemail from Marc asking if there had been any messages for him.

My meeting with the Mountie had ended shortly after I'd decided not to tell him that I might have seen Marc while I'd been in Paris. A good part of the train trip between Montreal and Toronto had been spent contemplating just that.

Now that I knew Marc —

No. I had to get this part straight in my mind before I did anything else. The man's name was Jean-Claude Lachance. Marc Tremblay never existed — except in my memory.

I'd been lied to left, right, and centre, played for a complete fool. Pretty well everything I knew about my husband had been a fabrication. Now it appeared that he might not even be dead. So basically, I'd fallen to pieces, then spent two years picking them up and restarting my stalled career, when what I should have been doing was finding him and kicking his ass.

Picking up the phone, I dialled Lili and fortunately found her unoccupied.

"Marta!" she said. "Are you back in Toronto?"

"Got in about a half hour ago. Do you have any time to get together today? I need to talk to you."

"Business or pleasure?" she asked, using the shorthand we'd developed since she'd added the mantle of therapist and confessor to being my vocal coach.

"Mostly business."

I could hear her flipping pages. "Not today. I've got several coachings and then I'm accompanying at the

Royal Conservatory this evening. Is tomorrow at one-thirty suitable?"

"Anytime tomorrow is good for me. Could we work a coaching session in, too? I feel like I need a good workout and Alex is still saying there's a chance I might get Pamina in Salzburg next summer. I'd like to get that out now and dust it off. There aren't going to be too many more years when I can do that role convincingly."

"You will talk first and sing after."

"Not a problem. I'm going to be out and about during the morning, but I promise to be there on time."

The next morning was damn cold. October hadn't even concluded and already winter's icy breath was sending pedestrians scurrying for cover. It looked like it might be a very long winter.

However, crisp autumn days always give me an extra charge of energy, so I bundled up tightly and crossed Front Street to the St. Lawrence Market, where I enjoyed a big breakfast at Paddington's Pump, my favourite place for such things. It may be a wee bit dark and on the run-down side, but they know what they're doing in the kitchen. Throwing concerns about my weight temporarily to the wind, I ordered the Full Monty and revelled in it. There's little in this world more comforting than a good, solid breakfast. Once stoked and feeling ready for the world, I hailed a cab by means of my loudest whistle and headed for the Eaton Centre.

Today, Marta Hendriks was entering the twenty-first century. I was ready to buy a computer.

A young, very enthusiastic woman met me at the door of one of those chi-chi computer boutiques.

"And what can we do for you today?" she chirped.

I'd barely gotten a word out of my mouth when a tall man walked over.

"I'll take it from here, Jessie," he said, holding out his hand. "I'm Tony Lusardi, the assistant manager, and I'd like to say what a pleasure it is to have you in our store, Ms. Hendriks."

"You know who I am?" I can walk around most cities for a month without anyone recognizing me.

"I've sung with you several times."

"Excuse me?"

He smiled — and I swallowed hard. I would have remembered that smile if I'd seen it before.

"I'm in the COC chorus. First time was that 'gangster' production of *Rigoletto* six years ago."

That had been fun to do. The setting had been transplanted from sixteenth-century Mantua to Chicago during Prohibition with really great success, and the entire cast enjoyed themselves mightily as we'd camped it up to the hilt, requiring the director and conductor to rein us in on more than one occasion.

I looked closely at him, noting his broad shoulders and athletic build. I still did not recognize him. I'm pretty focused during a production, so I seldom even notice the chorus, let alone look at them. That's not a nice thing to admit, but it's the truth. And that was probably for the best if there were guys among them who looked like this man.

Lusardi appeared to be around my age and handsome in the Italian sort of way: slender build, large dark eyes, and wavy black hair. There was something aristocratic about his bearing, too, that made me immediately think of Gerhard, but his easy manner was a good foil for that, putting me at ease immediately.

I lied. "Oh yes, now I place you. I didn't recognize you without your scar." A lot of the cast in that production had scars.

It worked and he laughed happily. "Perhaps I should wear one permanently?"

Leaning forward conspiratorially, I told him, "I think people might talk. There are very few scarred computer store assistant managers."

As he led me over to a counter with tall chairs at the back of the store, I hoisted myself up, glad that I had slipped on jeans that morning. We sat with our knees almost touching.

"Now what can we do for you today, Ms. Hendriks?" he asked.

"Please call me Marta. After all, we've worked closely together so many times."

He laughed again. "Then you must call me Tony."

I had no idea buying a computer could be so fraught with decisions. He asked me dozens of questions about how I wanted to use it before making any sort of recommendation, and surprisingly, it wasn't the most expensive machine in the store, but a modest little laptop that was quite elegant in its titanium case.

After deciding on the machine, he suggested some software, which he had installed. Then he ran me through setting it up and basic operations. By the time we had that completed, Tony had spent well over an hour and a half with me. But I had a computer I could turn on and off with confidence, even if I didn't understand most of the other things he'd told me.

Marvelling at a satellite photo of Toronto that he was showing me, I said, "I thought you needed to have an Internet-thingy provider to look at websites."

"We have Wi-Fi in this store."

"Huh?"

He was off on another explanation, and if he thought I was a complete Neanderthal for my lack of knowledge, he didn't let on.

"I am totally at sea on all of this, Tony, and will never remember what you've been telling me."

He looked at his watch. "I can take an early lunch. Why don't we pick out a good reference book that will help you and I can explain things more fully while we eat. Are you game?"

"Only if I pay. I've already taken up far too much of your time."

He began slipping all the computer's pieces back into their plastic sleeves and everything went into the box. Then he again flashed that killer smile. "All right, but I also want to talk about singing. It's what I love best, and to have lunch with my favourite soprano and not talk about singing would truly be a sin."

I looked down at his bare left ring finger. The man was definitely flirting with me.

When I popped out of the cab at Lili's address in Cabbagetown, she was standing on her doorstep saying goodbye to a colleague, a baritone whose career had stalled a few years ago. I thought her eyes would bug out of her head when she saw what I was carrying.

I shook hands with Brian, and as we chatted for a moment, Lili's eyes didn't leave the computer box.

"So I see you've bought a new computer?" he asked at the end of the conversation.

"You know how it is; they get old and slow and you eventually realize you need something with a bit more under the hood."

"How fast is it?"

"Three-point-five gigahertz, I believe."

At this point Lili's jaw dropped open and it was very difficult not to laugh.

The door had barely closed when Lili erupted, pointing at the box I was holding. "Explain this!"

"Explain what?" I asked innocently.

"You have been telling me on many occasions that you would never get one of those 'awful machines.' I believe that is what you called them."

"Infernal machines," I corrected, and then gave her a hug and kiss on both cheeks as I also produced the box containing the scarf I'd bought her in Paris. "Relax. I had no clue what I was saying on your doorstep. That was just bafflegab I remembered from the sales pitch this morning. Got your goat, though, didn't it?"

We settled in her 'parlour' with cups of coffee while I told her about my morning excursion first.

Lili put her cup down and looked at me. "But you have not said why you suddenly decided to buy a computer."

Outside her window, a few golden leaves drifted down from the maple by the curb.

"That's what I want to talk to you about."

To Lili's credit, she sat there listening without comment while I told the story of my trip east yet again, but began with the second time I saw Jean-Claude outside the opera house, something I hadn't passed on to her at the time since I thought I understood what was going on. She didn't look happy when I got to the part where I began asking myself, *What if my husband didn't die? What if I'm not seeing things?*

"So when I got back to Canada, I decided to go out to the farm and poke around a bit, see what I could see." I pulled out the pile of receipts which I'd stuffed into my portfolio, along with my music. "I found this in his truck."

Lili looked at them carefully. "I don't understand the importance of these."

"They're all for shops in Montreal; they're all for times I was out of the country; and he never said anything about having been in Montreal — ever."

"And you were just in that city."

"Yes. You'll notice this receipt has a phone number on the back."

"You've spoken to someone, haven't you?"

"I know Narissa has spoken to you."

Lili didn't deny it.

So I told her what had happened in Montreal. The only other time Lili responded (a raised eyebrow) was when I dropped my little bombshell that the RCMP had come calling.

"So basically, my maybe-not-so-dead husband lied to me from start to finish."

Lili sat for several moments in contemplation, staring steadily out the window.

Finally she looked over at me. "What are you feeling right now, Marta?"

Knowing that question would be coming, I had a ready answer. "It seems to change from moment to moment. Sometimes I feel great anger that I went through all that agony, and maybe there wasn't a good reason for it. I feel betrayed. I feel foolish. I feel very unsure of myself. I've wept a few times and I've cursed, too."

"And what are you thinking right now, right at this moment?"

"I'm wondering whether my husband really is dead."

"Would you be happy or sad if that were the case?"

Good question. Really good question. "I honestly don't know." I looked up at her. "What do you think?"

Having her question turned around seemed to fluster Lili. I had never before in our therapeutic relationship challenged her in this way. "I think that it is the time to stay focused on your career."

"You mean, just let the whole thing drop?"

She curtly nodded once.

I was shocked. "Would you do something like that?"

"It makes no difference what I would do. You gave me your answer a moment ago when you said you didn't know how you'd feel if he was alive. My best advice is to move on. That part of your life is closed now. Marta, you have to believe that no good will come of this. To go down this road will only lead you to more heartache."

I pounded the arms of the chair. "But if it were you, wouldn't you want to know?"

Lili only looked at me, her expression unreadable.

Not able to sit still, I got to my feet and walked to the window, thumbs in the front pockets of my jeans because I felt like smashing some of the carefully laid out bric-a-brac filling Lili's parlour. I wasn't really mad at her, just incredibly frustrated by the whole situation.

"If it was not your husband in that fire, whose remains did they find and how did they come to be there? Have you thought of that?"

I nodded. "Of course!"

"Then you should have told that policeman who spoke to you everything you know. It is your duty."

"Is it? Lili, with all due respect, it's not my duty. My husband may well have done nothing wrong, other than to run away from their protection. Maybe someone was sent to kill him. That's his business, not mine. That Mountie, Parker, never even intimated that Jean-Claude had done anything illegal. He wasn't even clear about why they wanted to find him!"

"You seem to have stepped into a rat's nest."

"Hornet's nest," I corrected absentmindedly.

Lili stood and gave me a large hug, the top of her head barely coming up to my chin. "You are still fragile, my dear friend. Please don't do anything rash or foolish. Step back and be thinking hard about it. I know that you will do what you will do," Lili said, holding me at arm's length. "You always have. But come, no more of this! It is time to go into the next room and see what sort of shape your voice is in."

⌒

By the time I got home, there were a half dozen more phone messages waiting. After putting the computer box down on the coffee table, I looked at it, frowning. One thing the charming Mr. Lusardi had failed to mention in his sales pitch was that computers were darn complicated. Sure, everything appeared easy in the store with a pro running it. But me? I still hadn't figured out how to do more than program a few phone numbers into my cellphone, and I'd had it for five years now.

One of the calls was from management, Alex's assistant to be exact, telling me that he'd finally nailed down that booking in Salzburg for the festival. Oh boy! I'd once again be able to sing Mozart's sublime music, and the tenor singing Tamino was "The Next Hot Thing" in the opera world. It wouldn't hurt my profile to share a stage with someone like that.

"We've also had a request from *Opera Canada* for an in-depth interview," Natalie's voice said. "When you give us the thumbs up, we'll arrange everything. They also want to send a photographer. Call ASAP. Bye-ee."

I liked that. When I gave them the thumbs up, not if. After the disastrous interview in Paris, I'd told Alex I wanted full approval on any interviews. I guess they assumed I was still desperate enough that I wouldn't turn any down. Happily, though, the folks at *Opera Canada* weren't inclined to play hardball.

The other phone call I'd been waiting for, but it was made from a different location than expected.

"*Bonjour, Marta! C'est Sébastien.* I am calling from Elaine's office at the university. I have heard from my colleague in Vancouver. It appears that there is more to your story than you knew. We need to speak. I will try you again tonight. Until then, do not talk to anyone about this. *A bientôt!*"

Hmm. What could he mean by that last comment? I hadn't told him about the Mountie, and my sneaking suspicion was that Sébastien wouldn't like that.

I spent the remainder of the afternoon trying to initiate myself into the computer world and navigate its mysteries. Thanks to the book Tony suggested, I had success, but it was limited. After calling the Internet service provider he'd suggested, I was unhappy to find out that it would take several days for me to get connected. I assumed these things were instantaneous. I was in no mood to wait around before embarking on my search for the whereabouts of my formerly dead husband.

Out of frustration, I called back the computer store. "Hello, I bought a laptop from you this morning. Is Mr. Lusardi still there by any chance?"

"Just a moment. I'll find out if he's available."

A minute later, I heard, "Tony Lusardi."

"Hi, um, Tony. It's Marta."

"Having trouble already?" he chuckled, then sort of swallowed it as the implication of what he was saying sank in. "I mean, what can I do for you?"

Fortunately, I chose to ignore his inference. "It appears I can't get connected to the Internet for at least a week."

"Actually, that's pretty quick. If you need to be online sooner, you can just take your laptop to any place that has Wi-Fi. Most coffee shops have it, for instance."

"Frankly, that's not what I would prefer."

"Oh, I get it. Right. Well, you could try poaching on your neighbors."

"What?"

"If any of the people in your building have a wireless connection, they're broadcasting if it's turned on. If they haven't set up their network to require a password — and many don't — you can log on to it."

"Is that legal?"

"Well, strictly speaking, it's a bit of a grey area. Is there a neighbor you could ask?"

"Like a lot of people in this fine city, I don't really know any of my neighbors other than to say hello in the elevator."

"Then you're stuck with going out to a coffee shop or something."

What the hell, I thought. They probably wouldn't send me to jail. "So tell me, how does one poach?"

Within five minutes, my co-conspirator had helped me find six people's networks and taught me how to connect to any of them.

"How can I thank you?" I asked.

"Have dinner with me tomorrow."

⌒

The phone's ring at my right elbow startled me out of a pretty heavy doze.

I had made no headway in my search for information on my husband, and the only break I'd taken was to order some sushi for dinner, after which I apparently nodded off on the sofa with the computer on my lap.

Gathering my sleep-startled wits, I waited for a moment before picking up the receiver. "Yes?"

"Marta? It's Lainey."

"Lainey?" It sank into my head that she sounded upset. "What's wrong?"

"It's Sébastien. He's been hauled in by the police for questioning."

That fully woke me up! "Does it have anything to do with what we were talking about?"

"They wouldn't say. We were relaxing before going out to dinner when they knocked on the door, asked him to accompany them downtown, and off they went as soon as he got dressed. Sébastien didn't seem too concerned, but it's certainly knocked me for a loop. I thought they only asked people to come downtown in movies."

"Geez."

Lainey's voice went up a notch. "That's all you can say? What have you gotten us into?"

"First off, you don't know it's my problem that he's been hauled in about. Second, I would imagine, considering his subject matter, that Sébastien has been in a lot tighter spots than being hauled in by the cops. You should be asking me what I've gotten myself into. A few days ago, I believed my husband was a dead handyman."

She was silent for a moment. "You're right. I'm just a little freaked, that's all. It's pretty awful when the police come bursting into your bedroom."

"They didn't!"

"Not exactly, but it was certainly pretty obvious what we'd been up to when Sébastien answered the door, tying up his bathrobe, at 8:15 in the evening."

"Oops. Well, I apologize in advance if any of this turns out to be my fault."

"You'd better watch your butt too, girlfriend. They could be coming after you next!"

⌒

The next morning, I got up early and took a taxi to the gym. I couldn't make it to the end of my usual routine. Those weeks off had certainly taken their toll. I trudged back to the condo, thoroughly bummed out.

The rest of the morning and early afternoon was spent organizing my professional life for the next few weeks using my new computer, an exercise that turned out to be surprisingly enjoyable as I got more comfortable with it.

Sadly, I wouldn't be singing in any more operas until January in Chicago (*Bohème*) — unless someone broke a leg or something, but there was also another, Norma, for later in the spring season in Helsinki. Next summer, I was doing Pamina in Austria, of course, but other than that, there were pretty slim pickings for the next year.

Interspersed were a number of concert performances: two Messiahs in Canada and one in the States, Beethoven's 9th in Hungary, and shortly, a *Carmina Burana* in London (the conductor had the hots for me and had hung on through my "withdrawal" from performing).

Yup, pretty slim pickings. Looked like for the next eighteen months, I'd have to rely on those nerve-wracking, last-minute calls for help, something that happens all too often in the opera world. I began feeling like a musical vulture, living off the misfortune of others.

I had mixed feelings about my date with Tony for that evening. First of all, I hadn't been on a date for ten years at the very least. Since Gerhard died, I'd had a brief fling during an extended stay in London nearly eight years ago now, then there had been my marriage, and after that, of course, nothing.

Going into the bedroom, I took my clothes off and assessed myself frankly in the mirror. The weight had pretty well stayed off, but I looked a bit "soft" — and not in a good way. My face was in good shape with only a few wrinkles around the eyes, and I had the best hairdressers, so that wasn't a concern. My rapidly approaching forties, though, were beginning to put out telltale signs. I needed to redouble my efforts at the gym!

After a good, long soak in the tub, careful application of makeup, and basically tossing my closet for something casual yet nice to wear, I was pacing in the living room. Finally, Sam buzzed from downstairs that I had a gentleman waiting for me.

Tony, true to his Italian roots, had a hot car, in this case a black Corvette on which he obviously lavished a lot of attention.

"I cannot believe that I'm taking you out to dinner," he said as he helped me into the low-slung car. "You look absolutely stunning, by the way."

Said by anyone else, I would have rolled my eyes, but Tony was just, I don't know, so damn sincere.

"Where are we going?" I asked.

"You told me at lunch yesterday that you adore Italian food. Well, outside of my nonna, who is the best cook ever, I'm taking you to what everyone agrees is the best Italian restaurant in the Toronto area."

"Even your nonna?" I teased.

"Yes, even her," he nodded seriously, but then smiled.

He had some opera on softly in the background, and I recognized *Nabucco* immediately. It didn't hit me for a full five minutes that it was a recording of the opera on which I'd sung the role of Anna, because we had been chattering away about the Canadian Opera Company's fall season.

When he realized why I'd fallen silent, Tony said, "I hope I haven't embarrassed you."

"Not at all. It's really very sweet of you. I haven't heard it before."

"You don't listen to your own recordings?"

"Not this one. It was recorded just before my husband ... was killed."

"I'm sorry. I didn't know," he said, reaching forward. "I'll turn it off."

I stopped him with my hand. "No, please. I'm enjoying it." After a few moments, I went on. "A lot of things fell into the cracks around then. I haven't even opened the carton of them that the record company sent."

"That's a shame. You're really very good in it."

I couldn't tell if he was pulling my leg or not. Mr. Lusardi was turning out to be a very interesting man.

"Why *Nabucco* tonight?" I asked. "It's got more than its share of blood and guts."

Tony sighed. "I'm in an odd mood this evening. I have a cousin in Italy who's a journalist. His beat is the Mafia, and we all know it's dangerous. Anyway, there were two Canadian journalists found murdered today, and it sort of brought it all home to the family."

I'm certain my heart stopped for several beats. Please let it not be what I think it is! I screamed inside my head.

Stopped at a light, Tony glanced over at me. "Are you all right?"

I squeezed my eyes shut. "Where did this happen?"

"That's the odd thing. One was in Vancouver and the other in Montreal. The only thing linking them is that both of them wrote about biker gangs."

Chapter Ten

Needless to say, dinner was no longer on the agenda for that evening.

Embarrassingly, I began to cry, knowing in my gut that it couldn't have been two other journalists who'd been killed.

Tony, who naturally didn't understand what the heck was going on, pulled over and asked the usual stupid question these situations demand: "Are you all right?"

"No, I'm not all right! Please, just take me home."

"May I ask what's going on? Do you know either of these people? Can I do something?"

"No!" I said, answering his first question only. "Please, no more questions."

"All right," he said, "I'll take you home."

I nodded, turned my head to face the car window and stayed that way until he got me back to my building.

"We're here," he said tentatively.

Finally turning back, I rallied enough to say, "I'm so sorry the evening turned out this way."

"And I'm sorry you're so upset. Will you be all right?"

"Yes. Good night, Tony. Thank you for being understanding."

With that, I bolted from the car and ran for the elevator. I just wanted to get upstairs, get away from people and try to pull myself together.

Don't ask about the rest of the night. It was dreadful.

What a difference a day makes, I thought ironically as I wiped steam off the bathroom mirror after my shower the next morning. Twenty-four hours ago, I'd stood here thinking I had the world by its tail.

I don't know when I've ever looked worse. After my husband had supposedly died might have been the bottom of the barrel, but it had never crossed my mind at the time to bother looking in the mirror. Why stare at a car crash?

It had been nearly impossible to sleep. The best I'd managed had been a fitful doze as dawn began to lighten the sky. Lainey didn't answer her home phone or her cell. Chloe had no idea where she was or what was going on.

During the night, I'd been through it all as I ceaselessly combed the news networks on TV for information, alternately blaming myself for not just walking away. But I'd had to know — mostly for my own self-esteem — what had been going on. When Sébastien had offered his help, I'd gladly jumped at it. I vacillated almost minute-to-minute over whether to shoulder the blame or lay it aside. Sébastien might have only agreed to help because he smelled a story. Who knows? Given enough information, he might have turned the story I'd told him into a series of articles or a book. How would I have felt then?

The one thing I remained constant on, though, was that I had to talk to Lainey. She was my good friend, she was hurting, and even if I wasn't to blame, I had started the ball rolling by asking her to take that drive with me to Verdun.

Finally, at 10:15 that morning, someone lifted the receiver when I again rang her apartment.

"Lainey?" I asked almost in a whisper. "Is that you?"

The silence stretched more than ten seconds before she answered. "Yes."

I couldn't read anything from the inflection in her voice. Was she angry or resigned? I couldn't tell.

All the things I'd carefully rehearsed during the darkness of the night scattered before that one word my friend had uttered.

"Would saying I'm sorry beyond imagining count for anything?"

"It would be a start," she answered dully.

I got off the sofa and walked to my window. Outside, the sky was leaden, low, and the light diffuse and depressing. A mixture of brown leaves and litter swirled along the sidewalks and street below. Monday pedestrian traffic hurried along. As if to explain, a few large flakes of snow appeared, alternately drifting down and being whisked away by the frequent gusts of wind.

"Is this a good time to talk?" I finally asked.

"I have nothing else to do."

"You've told the school?"

"I didn't have to. It's all over the news here. The dean sent me an email saying to take as much time as I needed. He'd met Sébastien a few weeks ago at a concert and Sébastien had given me one of his books for him. I never got around to passing it on." She sighed. "What do you want to talk about?"

It overflowed out of me in a rush. "Who came to get Sébastien two nights ago? Is there any word on who they were?"

Lainey began talking, her voice zombie-like. "There were two of them. One of them showed Sébastien his I.D. I'm certain of that. The Montreal police have taken me through this so many times, I can scroll it in my head like a frigging movie.

"Everything was so jolly. The two men joshed with Sébastien, saying that he'd been through this sort of thing before, they were only the errand boys, blah, blah, blah. I was certainly freaked, but he just gave me a kiss on the forehead and told me not to wait up. I was ... I was ... asleep when it happened. When the alarm went off at seven the next morning, that's when I found out on Radio-Canada what had happened." Lainey began to cry. "Now I know what you must have felt like."

"Christ! What can I say, Lainey? Even though I only met him briefly, I could tell that Sébastien was a truly nice, generous guy. I am so sorry."

"When the cops asked me in for questioning, they made me feel that I'd done something wrong. It was horrible. I did finally get them to tell me that they have no idea who the two men were."

"How about his friend in Vancouver?"

"They said they wouldn't talk to me about him at all."

"I'm sure they asked you if Sébastien said anything to you about, you know, what he was trying to find out for me."

"Over and over again. They also searched his apartment. I went over there yesterday to pick up some things and they wouldn't even let me in. When I said I needed my laptop for work, they told me, "'*Tant pis*.'"

I had my fingers crossed. "So what did you tell them when they questioned you?"

"I want them to find the bastards who did this. I had to tell them everything."

"Everything?"

"What else could I do? Are you worried about being dragged into this?"

There was an edge to her voice that I didn't like, but I could understand where it came from. "No. Of course not. Did you tell them about me seeing my husband in Paris?"

"I'm not sure. I may have. Why?"

"I spent most of the night thinking this over. What would have caused somebody to take the drastic step of murdering two journalists? And it happened pretty quickly. Surely they knew there would be a huge uproar."

"What are you getting at?"

"Sébastien left me a phone message that said there was a lot more to this than I knew. He was in your office when he made the call. Did he say anything to you?"

"He called you? When?"

"The day before yesterday.

"He was alone in my office waiting for me. I was in a meeting that ran really late. I had no idea he even called you until just now. Why didn't you mention it when I spoke to you?"

"I just thought you knew."

"Listen, Marta, my mom and dad are due over here any moment to sit with me. And if I know my mom, she'll be bringing dinner. I've got to run. This place is a pigsty."

"I'm sure your mother won't mind."

"You don't know my mother. Even in the middle of a family crisis, rest assured, you could eat off her floors."

"Can we talk again soon?" I asked.

"Not tonight. A friend down the hall gave me some sleeping pills. I'm going to kick my parents out early and try to get some sleep."

"That sounds like the right idea. I may try the same."

"The cops are going to come and talk to you, Marta. I'd suggest you level with them. Even tell them about Paris. You don't want to mess around with something like this, and I know how you can be when you get your back up. You owe your husband nothing. He lied to you and now two people have died."

"Maybe three," I corrected with a sinking feeling, as I thought of the small amount of someone who had been found at the farm after the fire.

⟍⟋

Even though it was Sunday, the cops were at my door before noon. It was a scene right out of *Dragnet*.

There were two of them, white, both over six feet, both with brush cuts, neither with moustaches like the Mountie in Montreal, one older than the other, and neither with a sense of humour.

"Marta Hendriks?" the one on the right asked when I opened the door.

"Yes. What can I do for you?"

"We're from the RCMP," the second one said, expertly flipping open his ID "May we come in?"

The other also took out his ID I took them both and studied them carefully.

"How do I know you are what you say you are?"

"That's why we've shown you our IDs, ma'am," the first one, identified as Patrick Glover on his ID card, answered.

"Obviously. Do you have a number I could phone to verify this visit?"

I suppose real bad guys at this point could have just forced their way in, overpowered me in two seconds flat, then rolled me up in one of my carpets for a quick one-way trip to who knows where.

They were quite patient as I took their IDs, shut (and bolted) the door, and phoned the number they'd given me.

"RCMP," a crisp female voice answered. "How may I direct your call?"

Well, that was nice. Even with all the government cutbacks they had live people working the phones on a Sunday.

"This may sound odd, but I have two constables at my door whose IDs say they're from the RCMP. How can I verify that?"

"If you give me their names, I can check it for you, ma'am."

I read off the names and she was gone for about a minute. "Yes, both those constables are assigned to Toronto and they're out of the office at the moment. Would you like their badge numbers?"

"Yes. Certainly."

Everything checked out, but I wasn't taking any chances. "I was just wondering. What's your address in Toronto?"

"Constables Glover and Griffin work out of our office near the airport, 255 Atwell Drive."

"Thank you so much," I said as I madly began thumbing through the phone book to check. I was learning that it never hurts to be too careful.

Glover and Griffin were waiting at my door just as I'd left them. I handed them back their IDs and invited them in.

Fortunately, the cleaning lady had been through two days earlier so the place looked presentable.

The GG twins sat down stiffly on the sofa, and I plunked myself onto the upholstered chair by the window, the light streaming in behind me. Both took out notebooks, but only Glover wrote anything down. Griffin, the older one, seemed to be in charge and referred to copious notes in his book from time to time. Both declined the offer of coffee or tea. Good thing. Everything I had was stale, and I hadn't gotten around to picking up anything fresh. It was too easy to just run across the street to Second Cup when I wanted a brew.

"I suppose you're wondering why I didn't let you in just now," I began and immediately regretted babbling. Who cared what they thought?

Griffin looked at me. "We did wonder, ma'am."

Too late now. I had to answer. "That journalist murdered in Montreal, he was escorted from his apartment by two men posing as cops."

"You know that for a fact?"

"Come on, constable. You two didn't just wander up here to pass the time of day. I've already been interviewed in Montreal by one of your comrades."

"His name?"

"You don't have it in your notes?"

"His name?" Griffin repeated a bit more firmly.

"Inspector Parker, I believe, Ron Parker. Do you know him?"

Both Mounties just stared. If they were trying to unnerve me, they were doing a damn fine job of it.

Glover finally smiled. Perhaps the good cop of the duo? "Ms. Hendriks, we're just trying to gather some information for this case. I understand you knew Sébastien Bouchard. Wouldn't you like to help catch his killer?"

Taking a deep breath, I said, "I have no experience with the police outside of parking tickets. But I do know one thing, why are you here, Mounties and all? Shouldn't the Montreal police have asked the Toronto police to help them? Am I missing something?"

They looked at each other, then Griffin said, "Will you excuse us for a moment?" and they retreated to my foyer where they spoke in low voices for a couple of minutes.

Coming back, Glover again took the lead. "Did Inspector Parker tell you why we are still interested in your dead husband?"

"Not really."

Griffin thumbed a few pages of his notebook. "And your husband never told you anything about his past?"

"Absolutely nothing. Everything I've found out has come as a profound shock to me."

"What did Parker tell you about your husband's work for us?"

"Not much. He didn't really go into specifics, but I know he was supplying information on bikers."

Griffin stared at me with those bug eyes that sent shivers down my spine. "It would have been dangerous, ma'am. You see, when your husband disappeared, he was in our witness protection program, but he was due to testify in court with two other men. Their testimony would have put away some of the most notorious bikers in Quebec."

"You said 'would have.' I take it they didn't testify."

"No, ma'am. Two of the witnesses were murdered and your husband disappeared."

"And you think he may have murdered the two witnesses? I find that hard to believe."

Glover shook his head. "No. He fled after the other two were killed. But because of that, the crown's case fell apart. The key accused all walked. We only sent away a few of the smaller players."

My mind was racing at that point. There were so many possibilities here. "So they eventually found my husband and killed him, too. Is that what you're saying?"

"That's the way most of us read it."

"I'm obviously not getting something here. If these bikers killed the three key witnesses, why go after two journalists two years after the fact? Or are you going to say you can't tell me anything about that?"

Griffin ignored my question. "We know you spoke to Sébastien Bouchard. What was that conversation about?"

"A very good friend of mine was seeing him. It was she who suggested I speak to him since Sébastien knows ... knew all about bikers. I asked him if he'd ever heard of my husband."

"And what did he say?"

"My husband was in one of his old databases but past that, he knew nothing. He told me that another reporter, a friend of his in Vancouver, might know more about it, and that he'd check with him and get back to me if he got any further information."

"Did he say why this friend in Vancouver might have information?"

"No, he didn't."

"And did you hear from Mr. Bouchard any further on this matter?"

"Yes. He called me on Friday, but I wasn't at home."

"Did he leave a message?"

"Yes. He said that his colleague in Vancouver had told him there was more to this story than we suspected. He said he'd call back and not to speak to anyone about this." A shiver went down my spine, knowing that poor Sébastien had been only a few hours from his death. "He never called back."

"Are you sure that's all the message said?"

"Absolutely."

It was smiling Glover's turn again. "Is there anything else you think we should know?"

"No. Are you going to tell me what's going on?"

Griffin snapped his notebook shut decisively. "Thank you for your time, Ms Hendriks."

Thoroughly incensed, I leapt to my feet. "You ignored my comment about the fact that it should have been Toronto cops here today, not Mounties. You've said information Inspector Parker might have given me could be dangerous. Now someone I spoke to about my husband has been murdered, and you're just going to leave after thanking me for my time? I want to know what the hell's going on!"

Glover got up. At least he had the grace to appear a bit embarrassed. He looked searchingly at his partner who eventually nodded, but not happily.

"This is an internal RCMP matter, but what's being investigated by us is how the bikers were able to get to our three witnesses. Our suspicion is that the reporter in Vancouver dug up some information on it, if he didn't have it already. He passed it on to his friend in Montreal. Someone thought it was dangerous enough to take them out."

I didn't see what he was getting at and it must have shown on my face. "May I ask you one more thing?"

Griffin looked at me noncommittally.

"You said the unit you're working with thinks my husband was also murdered to keep him from testifying. If that's the case, then why did Inspector Parker ask me if I'd heard from my husband recently?"

"The unit believes your husband is dead. Parker doesn't. He's a man who operates on hunches, and this is one of them. Please do not pass on to anyone what we have told you today, or you'll be sorry."

With that, Griffin went out the door and Glover hurried to follow.

Fortunately, he shut the door behind him. I had zoned out to never never land with that last bit of information and didn't even notice.

Chapter Eleven

I spent the rest of that Sunday deep in thought. By mid-afternoon, it began feeling as if the walls were closing in on me, so the weather being fair, if a little bit chilly, I took the subway up to Davisville. I wanted to walk along the Belt Line, my favourite place in Toronto for a contemplative stroll.

An old rail bypass whose days were numbered even as it was being built, the Belt Line trail feels to me like a walk in the country, even though it's pretty well never more than ten meters from someone's backyard. There's a section of "forest" at the eastern end by Yonge Street, followed by "meadows" along Chaplin Crescent, then you're into a bit of "savanna" until you reach the end, just past Caledonia Road, whereupon you turn around and do the whole thing in reverse. With the last of the fall leaves swirling around me, it was a splendid place to walk that brisk day, even if I had to pay more attention to dodging the weekend runners and bicyclists than I would have preferred.

I must admit that a large part of me was very resentful of the whole situation. When I'd gotten on the plane for Paris on the third of September, I had believed that my recent past was finally just that: in the past. I was looking forward to working again and felt full of confidence and energy. Then that past rose up out of the Paris streets and bit me firmly on the bum.

I've never been one of those people who can easily let things go. I don't like people taking advantage of me nor being made a fool of.

My feelings toward my husband seemed to switch from hour to hour. While I deeply resented him not telling me about his past, I could at least understand why he'd done it. He even appeared to be a bit of a hero in my eyes. Biker gangs are horrible organizations that spread ruin, whether by drugs, prostitution, or the protection racket. Jean-Claude had certainly done something admirable when he'd helped the police, and it had not been his fault that everything had fallen apart, forcing him to flee for his life. It was only logical that he'd left me in the dark. But had he really thought so little of my strength, my resolve, my love? I would gladly have shared any danger and done everything in my power to help him.

The thing I faced that I couldn't get around or over, no matter how hard I thought about it, was what had happened in Paris. Had I actually seen the man who'd been wrenched from my life so painfully? Was it a figment of my obviously still-damaged psyche? That was the question that burned in my mind.

But the real point was could I avoid searching for the answers? Could I turn and just walk away?

I didn't get back to the condo until late afternoon, and I was famished. Since getting back into town, I had survived on takeout and a couple of frozen meals. It's hard to make anything edible when your fridge only contains mayonnaise, ketchup, jam, hot sauce, and six eggs that likely would have killed me, so I hiked downstairs to the big supermarket at ground level for some major shopping with an eye mostly toward long-term storage. Filling the freezer was a priority for someone in my line of business.

The only fresh meat I bought was two lamb chops that had called to me as I'd walked past the meat counter. Broiled up with a decent tomato and some sautéed spinach, it made quite a nice meal to sit down to less than half an hour later. Opening a bottle of Pinot Noir someone had given me, and with some candles on the table, I felt quite festive if rather blue. It's never fun to dine alone, and the nicer the meal, the deeper the funk.

I dug out one of the copies of the *Nabucco* recording Tony had been playing the previous evening on the way to our aborted dinner date.

Listening as if I were an outsider judging the recording, I felt I'd given a good, solid performance but one that, admittedly, fell a bit short. The baritone singing the title role was just terrific, the whole cast was — except for me. The performance by Careful

Marta as Anna, every note placed perfectly, resonant, in tune, quite simply lacked the emotion the rest of the cast captured in their performances.

As I sat glumly on my sofa, listening to the last act with a third glass of wine in my hand, the phone rang. I hit pause on the remote and picked up the receiver, glad for the distraction.

"Marta? It's Tony. I was just calling up to see if everything was okay. You were quite upset when I dropped you off last night"

"That's very kind of you," I answered. "I'm afraid I behaved rather badly last night and I'd like to apologize."

"Not necessary at all. Could I ask, though, what upset you so much?"

I wasn't about to go into things with a veritable stranger, but I felt I owed him some sort of explanation.

"The journalist from Montreal who was murdered. I'd met him. He was dating one of my close friends. She's a complete mess, as you can imagine."

"I'm sure there are plenty of journalists in Montreal who cover biker gangs. How did you know it was him from what I told you? "

"I can't tell you that. I just knew."

"Listen, I'd still like to take you to dinner if you're willing."

I detected a hint of apprehension in this otherwise confident man's voice, and marvelled at the fact that not only had he phoned, but he'd asked me out a second time. After my behavior, I thought I'd never hear from him again.

"I'd like that, Tony."

"Would tomorrow be good? Or Wednesday? I'm free on Wednesday."

"You wouldn't be skipping an opera performance on Wednesday to take me out to dinner, would you?" I laughed. "I couldn't live with myself if that were the case."

"No. They're doing *Bluebeard's Castle* and *Pagliacci* on Tuesday and Wednesday is dark. Thursday is *Der Freishütz*. You sang Agatha the last time the COC mounted it."

I felt quite flattered that he remembered.

"So it's tomorrow or Wednesday," I said. "Hmm ... All right, I choose Wednesday. Could we go to the same restaurant? It sounded awfully good, especially since it has your nonna's blessing."

He finally laughed. "I'll make the reservation as soon as I hang up. Pick you up at six o'clock?"

"That would be fine."

"Great!"

"And Tony, thank you for being so understanding. I wouldn't have blamed you one bit for tearing my phone number to shreds after last night."

"Don't even think about it. You had a right to be upset. A death of a friend is a horrible thing."

There was another awkward silence as he probably realized that I also lost my husband not all that long ago.

"Until Wednesday, then." I said.

"Unless something goes wrong with your computer and you need to speak to me sooner."

I was laughing again as I hung up. What a delightfully unassuming man. Why hadn't some intelligent woman snatched him up?

Monday was another coaching with Lili, and even though she seemed to be waiting for me to say something about my current problems, I decided I wanted to spend more time thinking things over before talking to her again.

Pamina's arias were once more becoming comfortable to sing, and there were several points where Lili just let me go through whole passages without stopping to correct things. She was smiling a lot, too, while she played, always a good sign.

Today, I felt ready to work on the exquisite aria, "Ach, ich fühl's, es ist verschwunden," from the second act — in the minds of many, the most beautiful moment in the opera. Pamina believes that Tamino, who has taken a vow of silence, loves her no longer, since he will not speak to her. Mozart wrote this incredibly sad and melodically ravishing aria with an astonishing simplicity that makes it something treacherous to negotiate successfully. One false step and the music is either lacking in humanity or completely unbelievable. Pamina is girl on the cusp of womanhood. There is no subterfuge or complex emotions behind the way she behaves, and that's what makes it so very difficult to sing. Those four and a half minutes are some of the most sublime moments in music. An operatic career can be made if a soprano can truly make her audience believe what she's singing.

When I told Lili what I wanted to rehearse, she looked at me from the piano, one eyebrow raised, as if to indicate, "Oh really?" Once in the past, I'd tried to work on this aria with her, but Lili gave up in frustration after only a few minutes. She loves Mozart more than any other composer, and try as hard as she might, that day she couldn't hide her disappointment in the way I was interpreting the music.

"Let us put this away for now," she said and rose to busily shuffle through some of the piano parts that normally littered the top of her grand piano.

Her rejection stung me and I quickly left, staying away for several weeks. I even contemplated switching coaches during that time. Eventually, we met and patched it up, but she never apologized and never mentioned the incident again, nor did I.

Having studied and worked on the aria for over two hours the previous evening, I felt hopeful we might actually make it all the way through this time. Now that the role was mine in Salzburg, this moment had to be faced.

A calm seemed to envelope me as I shut my eyes and sang the first notes, trying to grow them in my chest before exhaling them into the air. In the past, I would have been conscious of every small movement of my body as I worked to produce each note perfectly, not too loud, not too soft, all of them threaded together into the patterns dictated by the music. This day, I just shut off all of that and sang. The treachery of my husband and all his lies seemed to well up in me and I transferred those emotions to the music, understanding in the very fibre of my being how Pamina's heart must be aching, to reach out to Lili and try to make her understand what those feelings really meant.

The aria ends with a slowly descending passage in the strings with three solo woodwinds, a series of notes of such aching sadness that it always brings tears to my eyes. On this day, Lili's hands on the piano made those notes live in such a way that I began weeping. Opening my eyes, I saw that she, too, was overcome by emotion as her tears rained down on the keyboard.

The sound of the piano died away, leaving us in silence until the spell was broken by the clicking of someone's heels on the sidewalk as they hurried by the house.

Lili got up from the piano, walked over and wrapped me in tight hug, and I hugged back just as fiercely. We stood that way for nearly a minute before she pulled away.

"Thank you," she said.

"No. Thank you."

"Again!" Lili barked, drying her eyes and the keyboard with her sleeve as she sat down at the piano. "I have not cried enough yet today."

I smiled through my tears and poured a glass of water from the jug that always stood ready on a nearby table, then dried my own eyes, blew my nose, and took a drink. "I'm ready now," I said.

Lili's hands hovered over the keyboard for a second, then slowly dropped, giving the first notes a special weight as she set up the *dum-daaaa-dum* of Mozart's accompaniment.

I shut my eyes and again sank into Pamina's world, where she believes utterly that love has abandoned her and life is no longer worth living. I became that person, because now I understood and could use Mozart's sublime music purely to sing what had become my own emotions.

Midway through, the phone started ringing in the hallway. Lili, with a deep scowl, ignored it as she always does. When the same thing happened two more times in rapid succession, she apologized and left the room.

Reappearing almost immediately, she told me, "The call is for you."

"Who is it?"

"Tallevi from the COC. He is absolutely desperate to speak to you."

I walked into the front hall and picked up the receiver. "Leonardo, how wonderful to hear from you!"

Two years ago, Leonardo Tallevi had taken over the reins at Canada's premiere opera company. An excitable man, he nonetheless seemed quite competent, and the COC hadn't slipped a bit under his leadership, as many had feared would be the case.

"Marta, thank heavens I've found you! Our *Bluebeard* ... We have a very grave problem. Our Judith has been taken ill, and her understudy is also suffering from a very bad cold. Please, please, can you sing it tomorrow night?"

"You're asking me to jump into *Bluebeard* on a day's notice? It's been over four years since I last did the role."

"Could you? Would you? We have a sold-out house," he wailed. "I am just beside myself. A cancellation now would be truly abominable!"

I took a deep breath. Tallevi was asking a hell of a lot — and he knew it.

"There's no one else available?" I asked.

"Do you think sopranos are just falling off the trees who know this role? Our performance is in your hands. It is you or no one!"

I could hear my manager, Alex, saying, "You should do it, Marta. It would put him greatly into your debt."

What he wouldn't say is that I would be up on the operatic equivalent of a high wire with no safety net. Bartok is not easy music, and while I have a very good memory, there is a lot of singing in that one-act opera with only two performers in the cast — and it was in Hungarian.

"I don't know, Leonardo."

"Please say you will do it. I have read the reviews you received in Paris and I know your voice is in excellent form. You are at Lili's right now. I will bring over the music personally if it will help!"

Lili was standing in the doorway to her studio, arms folded in front of her and a quizzical expression on her face. Tallevi has a very piercing phone voice, so I had no doubt she could hear every word.

I put my hand over the receiver. "Should I?"

Lili said, "I can clear my schedule for the rest of the day and tomorrow, as well."

Jeez! What a position to be in. I wanted to do it, but I also didn't want to commit musical hara-kiri.

"Please, Marta!" Tallevi's miniature voice pleaded from the phone. "Save us!"

I took a deep breath. "Okay, Leonardo. I will do it. Call me tonight at home and we'll discuss details. I'm assuming the blocking is the same. And you'll need to bring in the costume from last time. I weigh twenty-five pounds less."

"I will do it myself, if need be!" he declared grandly, and I tried hard not to laugh as I imagined this very proper Italian gentleman hunched over with a needle and thread.

"Oh, and call Alex to explain what's going on. He'll talk money with you." *And I'll call him next*, I thought as I hung up the phone.

"Don't worry, my dear," Lili said cheerily. "I will help get you through this. And you will be fantastic."

"If I don't kill myself doing it," I muttered as I dialled New York.

⌒⌒

Tuesday evening at seven o'clock found me sitting in a dressing room backstage at the Four Seasons Centre, feeling as if I'd gotten hit by a train as the makeup artist fussed over me.

I was always one of those students who would wait until the last minute to study for exams and then would spend two days cramming everything in until my brain felt as if it would explode. Either that, or I'd reach for those answers and they just weren't there. I was praying that tonight wasn't one of those nights. Opera singers have nightmares about being onstage and either not remembering anything about the opera they're supposed to be singing, or they don't even know what opera they're supposed to be singing. We wake up with cold sweats from those, believe me.

Tallevi had pulled out all the stops and even had the offstage brass play a fanfare when I took to the stage mid-afternoon for a quick blocking rehearsal. My dressing room was so crammed with flowers that I had to ask the stage hands to clear them out, because the mingled perfume from them was absolutely overwhelming.

At 7:20, there was a soft tap at the door, and the stagehand on the other side of it said in a low voice, "Time, Miss Hendriks."

It sounded to me like the sort of thing they say to the condemned person just before that long walk to the gallows.

I made my way to the darkened stage. Crossing myself, I found my mark and prayed that I wouldn't make a total mess of it over the course of the next fifty-four minutes.

On the other side of the curtain, the orchestra began to play those potently ominous chords that begin the darkest of dark operas, one whose plot line concerns a serial wife murderer. I felt the evening's *Bluebeard*, a thoroughly nice Serbian bass-baritone named Slavos, fidget next to me as he slipped into the persona of a person so unimaginably sick and demented. I hadn't heard the man sing more than a few notes at our blocking rehearsal, but everyone told me he was marvellous. I tried not to feel intimidated. This was his fifth performance, and by now he'd be thoroughly comfortable in the role.

Musicians can sometimes get to a place where a performance becomes so balanced it's almost as if you don't have to expend any effort. I've heard it referred to as The Zone. All those hours of practice, all the thought, technique, and knowledge fuse together at the critical moment in such a way that you feel you can do anything. No matter how high, how fast, how difficult a passage is, you can suddenly just do it.

Whatever you want to call it, that night on the stage of the Four Seasons Centre in Toronto I was on fire, I was there, I was in The Zone, and my God, I did not want that performance to ever end. I felt as if I had just stepped onstage and then the curtain began descending as the audience was leaping to their feet. I had done it!

I knew that Tallevi had come out to make a little speech before the opera began, but I hadn't been able to spare the concentration to listen to what he was saying as he explained the last-minute substitution for the expected soprano. Lili, for whom I'd basically demanded a ticket, told me later that the general director had put things in such a way that the audience would have been on my side no matter what.

For that performance, though, I hadn't needed anyone's help.

I was blessed with six raucous curtain calls with the audience yelling, "Brava!" at the tops of their lungs in a show of excitement thoroughly uncharacteristic for staid old Toronto. What really touched me, though, was Tallevi himself bringing out the hugest bouquet of red roses anyone had ever seen this side of the Kentucky Derby.

Back in the dressing room crowded with well-wishers, I pulled Lili to me, trying to find the words to express the gratitude I felt for all her hard work, not just over the past day and a half, but for the seven years we'd been working together professionally.

The second opera of the evening was a pretty dark one also, *Pagliacci*, but less dark than *Bluebeard*. It's very hard to be completely black when you're singing in Italian. I guess the idea had been to stage two short operas about men who kill their wives, but at least in the latter work, they do it more tunefully, otherwise some enterprising soul out on the street might make their fortune selling razor blades after the evening ended.

Tony, in his peasant's costume for *Pagliacci*, stuck his head in the door to tell me how great he'd thought my performance had been.

"Why didn't you stop by before the opera to wish me luck?" I teased. "Or were you waiting to see if I'd make a complete fool of myself?" I immediately regretted being so flip with him because he quite noticeably flinched.

"Ah, no, it was nothing like that. I figured you were under enough pressure without some member of the chorus bothering you."

I was sitting on the chair in front of the dressing room mirror at that point as my dresser was removing the wig I'd worn, so I was actually speaking to Tony's reflection in front of me. Turning to look directly at him, I smiled and said, "Relax. I was just joshing with you. If Bartok himself had stopped by to wish me luck before the performance, I wouldn't have opened the door." I shot a glance over to the clock. "Now don't you think you'd better get going? You've got about three minutes to get to the stage."

"Will you be around afterwards?"

"Probably not. I'm completely done in." Noticing a slight slump in Tony's shoulders, I added, "We're still on for tomorrow, though, aren't we?"

"Absolutely. See you at six."

"Break a leg, Tony," I laughed, and felt that I was finally all the way back — and then some.

I had been great tonight and even I could acknowledge that.

⁓

In high spirits, Lili and I made our way uptown to the Park Hyatt Hotel, taking the elevator straight up to the roof lounge. It's my favourite place for a drink in the entire city. Tonight, I wanted Toronto at my feet, visually as well as operatically.

The waiter came over and I ordered a rather expensive bottle of champagne. I also told him to surprise us with some nice little snack, because I couldn't be bothered making any more decisions.

Toronto on a clear autumn night from the roof of the Park Hyatt looks as good as any city anywhere. We had a perfect view of downtown with Lake Ontario as an infinite backdrop.

"Here's to our success once again," I said as I held out my glass for clinking.

Lili held her glass back, looking at me curiously. "So you finally believe, really believe?"

"What do you mean?"

"I will tell you after we clink." We did and both took an appreciative sip. "Before I even met you, I had heard of you. Gerhard Fosch and I knew each other, you know."

"How come you've never said anything?"

She shrugged. "Lots of little reasons. Anyway, about eighteen months before his heart attack, we met by chance at the airport in Zurich. All flights were delayed due to snow, so we stopped and chatted for a bit. He was on his way to hear you sing in Oslo."

"I remember that. It was my first engagement in Europe and I suspected he'd pulled a few strings to get it for me. I sang Ines in *Trovatore*. God, was I nervous!"

"One reason I never told you about this meeting is that Fosch was quite irritated with you. He knew I was in Canada and asked if I had heard of you. I told him only by name. I had not heard you sing. 'She is the most frustrating creature with whom I have ever worked!'"

"Gerhard said that? Why?"

"Because you did not believe completely in yourself. He said you had all this talent and seemed content to dole it out in tiny portions. 'If she ever just lets go, she might be one of those singers for the ages. She has all the ability, but refuses to trust it. She thinks too much!' I have always remembered what he said."

"Why didn't you ever tell me?"

"It was not my place. I remembered, though, and tried to show you the door. But you're the one who had to have the confidence to walk through it."

"That's not fair!"

She smiled wistfully. "Oh, but it is. How many people, how many critics have felt this way and told you? Did you listen?"

"Of course I did."

Lili shook her head slowly. "Not until Paris — then again yesterday with the Mozart, and even more so tonight. Tonight," she said with a theatrical flourish of her hand, "tonight, Gerhard Fosch would have been so very proud of his little songbird."

I burst into tears. Lili had used his personal endearment for me, something I had not heard since he lay dying in my arms. To have told Lili something so private while not ever letting me know he'd so much as met her seemed just like him. I wished dearly that I could have given him that final gift while he still lived.

But he'd been right, as always. I just hadn't been ready.

I dragged myself into my condo around midnight, totally and completely done in. After a little food and another glass of champagne, fatigue had flooded in as the adrenaline left my bloodstream. The past two days had finally caught up with me.

I was humming "Una voce poco fa" from *The Barber of Seville* as I pulled the pumps off my aching feet. Not bothering to turn on the lights, I stumbled over to the couch and flopped down, rubbing first one foot, then the other. Tomorrow I wasn't budging from my bed until at least eleven.

As I looked out the window, my phone's insistently flashing light caught my eye. I was of half a mind to ignore it, but picked it up, dialling in the code.

"Marta, it's Lainey. I've been trying you all day. Where the hell are you and why aren't you answering your phones? Anyway, I dragged myself into work to make sure I didn't fall even more hopelessly behind and I found something on my computer — an email Sébastien downloaded while he was waiting for me in my office that last evening. It was in my mail program's trash folder, but he hadn't emptied it. It's from that reporter who was also murdered. I'm coming to Toronto to show it to you."

Chapter Twelve

Talk about crashing down to earth with an almighty thud.

I sat for a good five minutes playing space cadet while I thought over what this might mean.

Why hadn't Lainey read the email to me over the phone? Hell, she could have faxed it to me. Sent it via courier. Why did she have to bring it to Toronto?

The clock in the bookcase opposite the piano told me in its ghostly blue that it was nearly 12:30.

"Oh, hell with it," I said. "I'm calling her."

She wasn't on my auto dial, so I had to look up her number. The phone rang until her voicemail picked up.

"Lainey, it's Marta. Please call me before you set out. I don't care what time it is, I want to talk to you. Okay?"

I tried her cell with similar results, then sat stewing. Before I was a bit peeved. Now I was worried. What if the same people who'd killed her boyfriend had come after her? Was the email itself the thing that caused them to kill Sébastien?

And what would stop them coming after me?

Taking the phone into the bathroom, I jumped in the shower, but it wasn't the nice, long soak I had been looking forward to, since my ears were focused on the phone possibly ringing. Twice I was fooled and turned off the water before I just gave up and got out.

Ten minutes later, I was in bed with the covers pulled up to my ears. Even in my keyed up state, it didn't take long for sleep to creep up on me. The phone stayed obstinately silent all night, but maybe that wasn't a bad thing.

⁓

I was in the middle of one of those frustration dreams. I had to be on in moments. I could already hear the overture to *Rigoletto* echoing backstage, but for the life of me, I could not find the way there. I usually try to wake myself from this sort of dream, but I was too deeply asleep to make that climb back to consciousness. The dream seemed to go on for hours as I frantically searched for the way onto the stage. Then a fire alarm went off and water started shooting down from the invisible ceiling, completely soaking me.

Somewhere in there I realized it was my phone ringing. Reaching out, I nearly knocked it off the night table, but before the voicemail clicked in, I managed to fumble it to my ear.

"Marta? Lainey. I'm nearly to your place but I don't remember the exact address and nothing looks familiar."

"You're driving?" I asked groggily.

"Yes. I left Montreal at eleven last night and slept a bit at the rest area somewhere past Kingston."

"Where are you now?" I asked, pulling myself into a sitting position. Christ, it was barely 6:00 a.m.

Thank the Lord I'd gone to the grocery store. By the time Sam rang from the lobby that Lainey was there, the coffee maker was making its end of cycle burbling noises. Having no coffee would have been unbearable.

Lainey, literally falling into my arms two steps inside the door, quite frankly looked like shit. This is a woman who's never known a bad hair day, someone who, even without makeup, looks fabulous.

Her filthy hair was roughly pulled back and held in place by a rubber band. Her eyes were sunken black hollows, and her face had the colour of day-old oatmeal. I patted her back as she trembled against me. "You're in a bad way, girlfriend," I said.

"You can't imagine what I've been through the past three days."

"There's coffee ready. Maybe you'd like to take a shower?"

She pulled away from me. "Did you lock the door?"

I reached out and threw the dead bolt. "You really are spooked."

"I'm just glad I'm here safe and sound." Lainey took a deep breath and smiled wanly. "First, a quick shower and then we'll talk."

Hearing the water snap off in the bathroom, I roused myself from the sofa, where I'd been looking on my laptop at the news websites from Montreal, and got busy in the kitchen making toast with lots of butter, remembering that Lainey always had preferred it that way.

She padded into the kitchen bundled in my white bath robe with a towel wrapping her hair.

"That's better," she said. "I used one of those little shampoos you had on the shelf. Nice stuff."

I offered her a mug, which she took gratefully. "I only steal from the best hotels."

"Is that also the source of this very fine bath robe?" she asked with a hint of mischief.

"If you must know, the manager of the Intercontinental Hotel in San Francisco gave it to me when I told him how much I liked it."

We stared at each other for several seconds before cracking up. On more than one occasion in the past, both of us had stolen towels to help furnish the apartment we'd shared while we were in university. This time I was telling the truth, however. My hotel pilfering days were long over — except for shampoo and conditioner.

Lainey's face collapsed and I thought she might cry, but instead she rallied bravely with a tiny smile. "Thanks so much for being here for me."

"It's not as if I had a lot of choice. You were on the road long before I could stop you," I answered, but it wasn't harshly.

The toaster finally popped and I busied myself with the butter.

Topping up my coffee, I grabbed the plate of toast. "Let's sit in the living room. It's the first sunny morning in three days and I want to enjoy it." We sat side by side on the sofa, munching as we squinted into the sunlight streaming in. After a few minutes, I gave up the struggle. "Maybe I'll draw the sheers."

"Great toast. I haven't eaten it like this in years. Thanks for remembering. It's just what I needed this morning: coffee and toast with my bestest bud." This time a tear trickled down her cheek.

I popped a last corner of toast into my mouth and wiped my fingers on the leg of my sweat pants. Picking up my coffee, I lounged back, trying to smile. "I guess it's time we had that talk."

Lainey sighed heavily, and put down her mug. "The email is in the back pocket of my jeans," she said as she got up.

While she was gone, I took our mugs to the kitchen and refilled them.

She came back dressed again with her drying hair hanging gorgeously to her shoulders. I hated her. After every shower, I always had to spend a long time combing out the tangles.

Unfolding a piece of paper, she handed it to me.

Cher Sébastien,

How good to hear from you, my friend! I hope you're well and thriving.

You ask a very interesting question. I poked around in my notes since I immediately recognized the name, but the last thing I remembered hearing about him was several years ago. That caused me to make a few phone calls to contacts I've been cultivating, hence the delay in answering your email. Sorry about that.

So, here's the drift. There was a contract out on your boy and, if someone found him, the rumour is that they were going to make him suffer for what he did — before they put the gun in his ear.

Now you tell me that he was killed in an accident over two years ago back your way. I looked up the news accounts at the time, but they were pretty sketchy. Are they sure it was an accident? With the amount of money your boy had on his head, there was certainly a good incentive to go to the trouble of finding him after he ducked out on his handlers.

On the crown's side, he was also *persona non grata* because their whole prosecution went down the toilet since he was the only one left of their "dream team" of informers, the other two already having already been sent off for dirt naps. The profile info I have on the trio is attached to this email. You'll have better resources to find out about them than I do.

So I knew most of this shit before, but earlier today one of my sources gave me a new twist on the whole episode. Apparently, the way the witnesses were gotten to and eliminated was because they had somebody from the RCMP Major Crimes Unit in their back pocket. That person gave up the witnesses.

The delay in my getting back to you was in following up on that. It seems to check out at this point. It's more than likely, then, that they did get to your boy in eastern Ontario. I doubt very much that his death was an accident. What I do find curious is that the Mounties never stuck their noses into the investigation, although maybe they did and we don't know about it.

Here's the upshot: I smell a really great story here, my friend. Would you like to collaborate on it? At my end, I'm going to see if I can smoke out who the informer is in the Mountie camp and you can investigate whether this house fire really was an accident or not. Whether you're game or not, I'm going to put my investigation on the front burner. Quite frankly, things have been far too quiet out here for too long. It's about time I got hold of a juicy story. This one obviously has national implications and could be good for both our careers.

Call me soon to give me your thoughts. We should jump all over this right away. You might want to get started by talking to the other two witnesses' families to find out what they know, if anything. The details of their particulars as of four years ago are on the document attached to this email. It shouldn't be too difficult to track them down.

A bientôt!
Peter

Curled up at her end of the sofa, Lainey clutched her coffee mug as if she was trying to warm not only her hands but her heart, too. "So now you see why I was a little more than freaked out. Less than fourteen hours after this guy Peter sent out that email, both men were dead. Now I have it and I'm petrified that if anybody finds out, they're going to come after me."

"Come after both of us now that I've seen it, too," I pointed out.

"What should we do?"

"Is the email still on your computer at McGill?"

"I filed it under a different name and moved it to the university's encrypted storage. Do you think someone would search my computer at school or am I being ridiculous? From what Sébastien told me once, if you have the right equipment, you can get files off a hard drive even after it's been erased."

I shrugged. "Not being trained as a spy, I wouldn't know. It seems to me now that part of our education was sorely neglected. What kind of university degrees are they handing out today?"

"You can joke about this all you want, Marta, but I'm really freaked."

I put the printout down on the coffee table. "There's nothing in this email that points a finger at anyone, but it looks as if this Peter in Vancouver uncovered something too damaging to let him live. You're certain Sébastien spoke to him on the phone?"

Lainey nodded. "But he didn't tell me what was said. There really wasn't time before those two fake cops showed up at the door.

"Boy, am I glad he didn't. I'd probably be in Montreal right now for a double funeral."

My friend shook her head. "I spent the entire drive here thinking the same thing and trying not to feel guilty. It's all so horrible."

"If anyone should feel guilty, it's me. And believe me, I do."

"Did the cops come to interview you?"

"Yes, Sunday morning, not too bright and far too early."

"So what did you say to them?"

I tried to keep it as succinct as possible, but telling her still took nearly fifteen minutes. "At the time, I was certain those Mounties held back a lot that was important. Now we have a good idea what it was. And no wonder they didn't want to tell me. They've had enough bad press over the past few years."

"What are you getting at?"

"Surely they must know there's a rat in their midst."

"Well, yeah."

"And it seems to me that the most likely person who would want Sébastien and Peter dead would be that rat." I read through the email again to be sure.

"What is so telling is 'they' got hold of the information that someone was poking around where they shouldn't be and then acted on it so quickly."

We spent the rest of the morning using my poached Internet connection to browse all of the news outlets in Montreal and Vancouver to see if we could garner any new information.

The two deaths were still top of the news, but most of what we found was rehashed or little more than speculation. The prognostications of one CBC Newsworld talking head, a supposed globally recognized expert on "media assassinations" (as he dubbed them), were downright laughable — from the viewpoint of what we knew.

Lainey had grown restive and got to her feet. "We're no closer to a decision than when I called to tell you I was coming. Maybe we should just go to the Toronto police, show them the email and tell them what we know and be done with it. Surely that would be safe."

"For whom?"

"Why, us, of course."

"What about my husband?"

Lainey turned and stared at me. "Am I missing something here? You didn't find him, did you?"

"Ah ... no, but he might still be out there."

"So assuming he is, why do you think he counts?"

"Didn't you hear what I told you about the Mounties?" I said, anger rising. "I'm sure he cut out from their witness protection program because he knew they were going to kill him."

"How can you defend him?" Lainey shot back. "He screwed you over. Don't you forget that for one instant!"

"Marc was doing the only thing he could. If I tell the cops that I may have seen him in Paris and it turns out I did, I could be signing his death warrant. I'm not willing to do that."

"You certainly are a Pollyanna, I'll hand that to you." Lainey shook her head. "What do we do now?"

"Take our minds off it. I find sometimes that letting something percolate in my subconscious leads to new answers. How about we go to my gym? I made a vow the other day that I wouldn't put on weight again. It gets harder to avoid that every year, doesn't it?"

Lainey snorted. "Don't I know it."

"And maybe it will help us come up with something."

~

The gym I go to is for women only and it's a short walk away. So by the time I get there, everything feels pretty loose and I'm ready to work out. That day, I primarily used the treadmill with some work on the other machines after. Lainey, in a borrowed outfit, went at it with a vengeance, all her rage and frustration coming out as she threw herself around from one machine to another, much the same way she used to throw herself around the percussion studio at McGill after a particularly bad lesson. She even broke a timpani head once — and that ain't easy! By the end, when we hit the showers, we were sweaty messes.

I treated her to a massage after, and we got back to my place (by taxi) shortly after 1:00 p.m., completely famished, feeling rather self-righteous and totally mellow.

While Lainey got busy making soup and sandwiches, I listened to a string of messages that had come in. Most were congratulatory from various friends who'd caught one of the two reviews that had apparently been in the Toronto papers. Two more were from Alex, complaining that I was almost never home and never had my cellphone switched on when I wasn't. Managers can be such a trial.

"Alex!" I said when I got him on the line. "What is it you want?"

"You are very lucky that I'm a patient man, Marta Hendriks."

"You are?" I teased.

"Most definitely. How come I'm the last to know you had a major triumph?"

Oops! I thought. I hadn't thought about calling Alex. Feeling a bit like a scolded child, I answered, "I guess I was a little bit distracted. I haven't even seen the reviews. Something else came up."

"I can't believe I'm hearing this: a singer who doesn't read every word written about her?"

Getting a bit peeved, I asked, "Is this all you're calling me about?"

"Actually, no. My phone has been ringing off the hook. Suddenly my girl is a hot property."

"Who called?"

"First, Tallevi from the Canadian Opera. He wants to build a season around you. How would you like to do *Tosca*, *Lucia di Lammermoor*, and *Carmen* three years from now and be able to walk to work?"

"That's a hell of a lot of singing."

"One would be early in the fall and one later and the last in the spring. This is a tremendous opportunity. They'll make sure they schedule in enough rest, and you'll be the marquee attraction. There'll be scads of publicity, too."

I took a deep breath. "Tell Tallevi he's got a deal. Who else called?"

"Several other companies, including La Scala and Vienna. I told them you're only taking starring roles."

"Really?"

"I'm not kidding. The word is getting around. I take it you're agreeable to working at those houses?"

"Pinch me. I must be dreaming."

"In the meantime, I think we should see about doing a recital tour for next fall. It may be a bit late, but I should be able to swing something pretty good, call in a few favours. You need to get more income over the short term and keep that public profile high."

"I don't know...."

"Look, Marta, we have to strike while the publicity iron is hot. Don't you want to cash in on that?"

"Put that way, yes I do."

"Then listen to your Uncle Alex and let me do what I know is best."

"Okay," I answered, but I hope he heard how tentative my approval was.

I rang off in a state of disassociation. Sure, I wanted to revive my career, and La Scala and the Vienna State

Opera were high on any singer's list, but this was all happening so fast.

Lainey came out of the kitchen carrying a tray of soup and sandwiches and asked where I'd like to eat.

"I guess at the dining room table," I answered.

She stopped and looked at me. "Hey, are you okay?"

"I was just talking to my manager. It sort of feels like my life is taking off on me and I'm not on the plane."

"Huh?"

"The word seems to be getting out and all of a sudden, offers of gigs are streaming in. They want me to sing at La Scala and Vienna."

"And that isn't a good thing?"

"Of course it is, but it feels like I'm losing control here."

"Take it from someone who spent twelve years on the road: that's what you pay managers for."

After our meal, we sat at the table talking, and the subject matter was again not pleasant. Lainey had called Montreal while she was in the kitchen and found out that Sébastien's funeral was tentatively planned for Saturday.

"So when will you drive back?" I asked.

Lainey suddenly looked quite uncertain. "Could I stay here with you another day?"

I gave her a big smile. "Absolutely!"

After lunch, we adjourned to the living room and Lainey, after going through my CD collection, chose a movie soundtrack she hadn't heard that was pretty well all percussion. I zoned out, thinking over what Alex had said to me. Lainey put on a movie and I didn't really watch that, either.

Shortly before five, I drew myself from my reverie of fortune and opera glory, stretched, and glanced lazily at the clock. A little bell tinkled in my head, but it was a full three seconds before I realized why it had sounded.

"Holy God!" I cried, leaping to my feet.

Lainey looked up sharply. "What?"

"Someone is picking me up at six o'clock," I answered, scurrying for the bedroom. "I'll never be ready in time!"

My clothes were off and I was making a bee-line for the bathroom by the time Lainey followed me.

"Are you telling me you have a date?"

"Yes. And I already stiffed this guy on Saturday when I found out what had happened to Sébastien," I said over the water as I waited for the shower to heat up.

Lainey was leaning against the door frame, arms folded across her chest. "Sounds fascinating. Tell me more." Her face had a distinct smirk.

"There isn't much to tell. He's the guy who sold me my laptop."

"You let a computer geek pick you up? You *are* desperate."

"He's not a computer geek! He's the assistant manager of one of the biggest computer stores in the city and he sings in the COC chorus."

"And I'll bet he's the one who taught you how to poach Internet connections. He could be dangerous."

"It's only until I get the equipment I need."

"At which point you'll have to get him over to help you set it up. How very convenient."

"Get off it, Lainey. It's not like that at all."

"I'll just bet it isn't. Do you want me to make myself scarce tonight?"

"No. We're just going out to dinner. That's it. I'm not about to jump in the sack with some guy on the first date!"

"Why not? I can think of at least one time during university when you did."

"Lainey!"

It suddenly hit me: how could we be carrying on like naive co-eds with Sébastien's funeral around the corner?

Lainey's face told me she obviously felt the same sting. "I'm sorry. I shouldn't have said that."

As I got into the shower, I felt torn. I really was excited about going out with Tony. He interested me, and it amazed me that something like this was happening in the midst of all the turmoil in my life — and after the way I'd felt about my husband. But here I was going out on a date, leaving my friend to spend the night alone with her dark thoughts. The afternoon had brought Lainey out of her funk a bit, to the point where she'd actually been smiling and joking a moment ago. If she was anything like me, she'd be starting to hate herself about now.

"I'll make this a really early evening," I told her over the noise of the water.

Chapter Thirteen

Once again, Tony arrived right on time and that very hot black Corvette was waiting at the curb when Sam jumped up from behind his desk to open the front door for me, grinning as he stared out at the gleaming car.

Lainey had helped me with my hair and I thought it looked pretty good cascading down to my shoulders rather than just hanging limply. The bad part was that I had to put up with a lot more of her teasing, both of us falling into routines we'd established when we'd shared an apartment in the student ghetto near McGill. In many ways, it all seemed a bit hollow. I knew she was trying to help me feel good about actually going out on a date. Or maybe levity was the only way for Lainey to cope with all that she was going through. I was just glad Chloe, the third of our triumvirate, wasn't around, since she teased with far more devastating effect than Lainey.

Tony was waiting at the curb and opened the door of his car with smooth aplomb, taking my hand and kissing it as I stepped close. "You look lovely again tonight. You can't imagine how nervous I am taking out the belle of the ball the night after her great triumph."

I grinned wryly. "You'll get over it, I'm sure."

"How is your friend, you know, the one in Montreal?" he asked as the car roared to life.

"Actually, she's here, staying with me. We thought it was a good idea for her to get away for a bit."

"Really? That's very kind of you considering what you had to accomplish over the past two days."

"She arrived early this morning. I've already been up for twelve hours."

He looked over at me as we drove east on Front Street, heading for the Don Valley Parkway. "We should make this an early evening then."

"You're right, but I'm pretty wide awake at the moment — and hungry," I said, lying through my teeth.

Why couldn't I have remembered dinner before I'd bitten into that second sandwich at lunch? All my hard work at the gym was about to go down the drain.

The whole way up to Woodbridge, the radio stayed off. Tony told me he didn't want to take any chances. Instead we talked shop, meaning opera. That discussion went right through a quite fabulous dinner at the small trattoria. The owner had greeted Tony like a long-lost cousin and fortunately didn't recognize me. I wanted a relaxing evening, not to be the centre of attention. For dessert, we shared the best tiramisu I'd ever tasted.

"Your nonna is right about this place," I said, giving my fork a last lick. "I don't know when I've ever had better Italian food. That ravioli in the first course was pure ambrosia."

"I think that's why Nonna approves of this place. They will not serve any pasta that isn't homemade."

Our waiter brought espressos with some little hazelnut wafers, again homemade.

"I could become addicted to these," I said, biting into one.

"That's Nonna's recipe. She gave it to Paulo the chef because she didn't think his previous cookies were up to snuff. Believe it or not, that's a very high compliment from her."

"I hope to God I never have to cook for her. That would be far too intimidating."

Tony smiled. "She's actually a very nice, little old lady. You'd like her."

I put down my cup and smiled across the table. "Why?"

"She loves opera. When she was much younger, her family owned one of the finest restaurants in Rome. That's where she learned to cook. Her dad was the chef, but more importantly, he was a pretty good baritone, by all accounts."

"Are you going to tell me next that everyone in your family sings?"

He looked up. "Have you been talking to people down at the opera house?"

"No, but I've met Italians before who claim that."

"Well, I have two cousins in the opera orchestra, another cousin was in the chorus with me until her third child was born. My Aunt Annetta is in the chorus. My mother and father met in the chorus at the Rome opera and —"

"Stop. Stop!" I said, laughing. "I believe you."

"But I'm not done yet. I haven't told you about my two uncles, and my other cousins. I also have a second cousin who's studying in Europe. He may be the best Lusardi yet."

"Now you've got me thoroughly intimidated. I'm the only one in my entire family, which admittedly isn't anything like the size of yours, who's made a career as a musician. They all think I'm an alien."

With a wry smile, Tony said, "Then I guess aliens must be incredible singers."

I didn't know whether to laugh or feel embarrassed.

We'd dawdled over coffee and more cookies, so when we left the parking lot, it was pushing nine and time to get back to Lainey. I felt a bit uncomfortably full, but told myself that I'd be extra good the rest of the week. Meals like the one I'd just enjoyed don't come along every day. Thankfully, the restaurant was awfully far from downtown Toronto if you don't have a car.

Traffic on the ride home was quite light and we chattered away happily about our favourite singers. Naturally, they were mostly Italian. I felt very content.

It wasn't until we were a few blocks from my apartment that I thought about Lainey's teasing earlier. I don't know what might have happened if she hadn't been there, but I could have been tempted to invite Tony in for a nightcap. Right now it was a real boost to my recently battered ego to have a male, a nice honest male, so obviously interested in me.

He glided to a smooth stop in front of my building and shut off the engine. We sat for a moment then both started to say what a good time we'd had, causing us both to laugh.

I leaned over and kissed his cheek. "I really did enjoy myself this evening, Tony."

He looked at me, his expression quite unreadable. "I did, too ... very much." Smoothly, he leaned over and kissed my lips. It wasn't aggressive, but it was direct and quite, quite lovely, lingering and sweet.

I sighed as he pulled away. "Wow! I've always heard Italians were the best kissers, but I didn't believe it until now."

"I'm glad you didn't mind. I've wanted to do that all evening."

To emphasize his point, he leaned over and did it again, this time *con fuoco*.

Someone walking by the car slowed down to take a look and it broke the spell.

"I really should be getting inside."

If Tony was disappointed, his smile didn't show it. "You're right. I've kept you out too long."

"Thanks again, Tony."

"It was my great pleasure."

I was walking across the sidewalk when his voice stopped me. Turning, I saw him half in, half out of his car, speaking to me across the roof.

"I nearly forgot. Sunday is Nonna's birthday and we're having a little family get-together. I was wondering —"

"I would love to come, Tony. Can I bring anything?"

I couldn't believe I'd actually just said that, but I could always find something good at a bakery if he accepted my offer.

"No, no. My nonna is doing all the cooking with a few others helping her."

"She's cooking for her own birthday?"

"The old girl wouldn't have it any other way. She considers it a treat to cook for that many people. There will be lots of food, all served family style. Wait until you taste her pasta!" Tony kissed his fingers in a loud smack as Italians do. "*È come se Dio stesso discese per terra!*"

He compares his grandmother's cooking with God coming down to earth? No, they wouldn't be requiring food from me.

"What time does it start?"

"We're having it at Uncle Giuseppe's workshop near Eglinton and Caledonia. I could pick you up around five."

"How should I dress?"

"Hmmm," he said. "Something nice, but not too fancy. All the males will be wearing suits and the women will wear dresses, unless one of my younger cousins decides to risk censure and be more daring than usual."

"I think I can manage that. Okay, see you at five right here on Sunday."

I blew him a kiss and entered the lobby feeling more lighthearted and carefree than I don't remember when.

The TV was on when I walked into the condo, but I found Lainey stretched out on the sofa, completely down for the count. It had been a long day for her. Hell, it had been a long day for me, I realized with a face-splitting yawn.

When I turned off the TV, she stirred and propped herself up on one elbow. "What time is it?"

"A bit before ten."

She sat up, rubbing her eyes. "I think I fell asleep about two minutes after I switched on the TV."

"You've had a long day, girlfriend."

"A long week." Looking at me searchingly, she added, "So how was it?"

"The food was absolutely fabulous, some of the best Italian I've ever had. Great service, too."

Lainey rolled her eyes. "That's not what I meant."

"I know, but I don't kiss and tell."

"He kissed you, then?"

"Just good night in front of the building."

"Sounds pretty tame."

"He's a very good kisser."

"So do you think you'll bonk him?"

"Lainey, my dear, I am not going to dignify that remark with an answer. I'm simply out on my feet, so I'll bid you good night. Your bed is made up in the guest room."

"Just before you go: I checked my voicemail this evening. Sébastien's funeral has been moved up by a day, so I should head back to Montreal sometime tomorrow."

"I'm coming with you."

"You don't have to."

I walked over and hugged her. "I want to."

"Thanks."

As I got ready for bed, I felt a twinge of guilt. Moral support was not the only thing fuelling my urge to travel east.

I wanted to talk to the relatives of the two biker witnesses who had been murdered.

⁓

Sébastien's funeral on Friday morning was awful. First off, given the notoriety of his death, it was a full media feeding frenzy and that always brings curious onlookers. I wore sunglasses the whole time with a scarf tied around my hair, trying to look inconspicuous. It wasn't because I expected to be hassled because of who I am (as if), I just didn't want anybody asking awkward questions. Both Lainey and I also felt it quite likely that someone might be watching us.

Sébastien had been the golden boy of his family, the eldest son and successful. His parents were taking his death badly. Since no one in his family had ever met Lainey, she was left on the outside looking in, and that was very tough for her. I began to realize just how much she'd been in love with him.

I'd gotten in touch with Chloe during the drive the previous day, and she'd managed to book off from another morning rehearsal with the symphony. So there we sat, bracketing our friend in Mary, Queen of the World Cathedral while the service dragged on and on. Afterwards, there was to be a reception, but Lainey was in such a state that Chloe and I talked her into going somewhere else with us for a little private remembrance over lunch.

Montreal has no lack of good restaurants and bars, but we ended up at one of our favourites from our days together at McGill: El Gitano on Avenue Parc, a resto we used to frequent when someone had made extra money gigging, or there was something special to celebrate. I made sure there was a lot of wine.

Lainey laughed (and cried) as she spoke about a man who had been pretty special. I could certainly see what had attracted her to him. I also wished more than ever that I'd resisted her suggestion to visit him that night.

It was close to five o'clock when we helped Lainey into a cab and took her back to her flat just off Chemin de la Côte-St-Luc. We wrestled her upstairs and put her to bed, even though it was barely six o'clock. I felt sort of guilty for encouraging her wine intake, but I'd had good reasons.

"Just like old times," Chloe said with a smile as soon as our friend began to snore gently. "She'd been under a lot of stress before this mess happened. A few hours of forgetfulness will be good for her, despite the headache she'll have in the morning."

"Or whenever she wakes up."

"I do believe she's down for the count for today."

Outside on the sidewalk again, we stopped, neither wanting to go our separate ways.

"Thanks for making the effort to be here, Chlo. I had the feeling Lainey was holding a lot in."

The petite dark-haired woman smiled. "There's always time for my friends."

"If that's a bit of a nudge, you're right. Too often I've used the excuse that I'm too busy to get to Montreal, but that's garbage. Even if I can't get here, there's always the phone or the Internet."

"On our end, it's the same. By the way, Lainey told me when you were visiting the ladies that you've finally bought yourself a laptop. Communicating is a snap with those. You can email whenever and from wherever you want."

She stopped and looked me up and down.

"Why the visual exam?" I asked.

"Lainey also told me you have a guy," she answered with a semi-lecherous grin.

"It's hardly that. We've had a cup of coffee and he took me to dinner. That's it. Truthfully, meeting Tony couldn't have come at a worse time. My life is just too complicated at the moment. Maybe six months ago, maybe six months from now, but at the moment?" I shook my head. "It's just one more distraction I don't need."

"Lainey told me you sort of floated into your condo after your date with him. If you keep waiting around for 'the right time,' you're going to still be waiting when you're eighty."

"Between you and Lainey —"

"Listen to your friends." Chloe smiled again. "And speaking of not waiting, I've given myself the perfect opportunity to ask you if you're interested in reviving Chicks with Sticks for one last kick at the can. It would be a hoot to do some of those old pieces and routines again."

"What the heck are you talking about?"

"Just an idea Lainey and I had. We could play a concert at the school, a fundraiser for the percussion department. With you playing, I'm sure we'd fill the recital hall."

"Yeah, they'd come to see me fall flat on my bum."

"You and I both know better than that. Come on! Even if you haven't played in a dozen years, you'll get it back plenty fast. Lainey told me you've still got your drum set, some congas, and your stick bag shoved in the back of the closet in your guest room."

"That little sneak!"

The best stick handler of the three of us stood with her head cocked to the side, looking at me. "So are you in — or out?"

"Assuming I agreed, when would we do this concert?"

"Early next year? You could come into town for a week and we could rehearse our bums off. I can give you your parts tonight if you'd like. C'mon, say yes!"

"I'll have to check with my manager. The bookings are starting to roll in again."

"You'd get a lot of press out of doing something like this, I'll bet."

"You're too much. I'll talk to Alex and then let you know. Okay?"

"When are you going back to Toronto?"

"Not until eleven tonight. I've got a few things to take care of before I head out to the airport."

"I'm not doing the concert tonight since I wasn't at the rehearsal today. Need any help, or just a companion?"

Hmm. The last time I'd done something like what I had planned, two people had ended up dead. Still, I couldn't deny that it would be nice to have moral support, not to mention an extra set of eyes.

"You don't know any journalists, do you?" I asked as we watched for a cab to flag down.

⟿

It had all been set up the night before, right after Lainey and I had arrived back in Montreal.

With her Internet knowledge and some cash to an online search company, it didn't take long to track down the families of the other two dead witnesses the Vancouver email had spoken about. I spent the ride back from Toronto thinking about how to approach them, and I thought I'd come up with a good — and safe — plan.

One of the families was in Rivière-du-Loup, too far from Montreal for a quick trip, so I took a pass on them for the moment. This was not the sort of thing to do over the phone. The second family was in Boucherville, across the river from Montreal, and that was the family I called.

Afraid I might be in for a *joual*-filled conversation, I was wondering if I was up to it. My French was learned in an immersion program in Ottawa, and many of my teachers had been from France. All but one looked down on the rough-and-ready aspects of Quebec French. My years in Montreal had made me more comfortable with the language spoken on the streets, but I'd never quite mastered the sort of drawl and very odd vocab. I needed to sound like one of them, certainly not like an Anglo opera singer.

"Relax," Lainey said. "You'll do fine."

"They're going to hang up if I sound like I'm fresh off the plane from Paris. That's pretty off-putting."

She laughed at me. "Using words like 'off-putting' is pretty off-putting, I'd say. Sometimes you sound just like a university professor."

"That's 'cause both my parents were."

"Just do your best. I'm sure it will be fine. I can be listening in, and if you don't understand something, I'll whisper it in your ear. Okay?"

So I got on the phone and tried my best.

It didn't turn out to be as scary as I'd imagined. The father answered, and it was obvious from the beginning that he didn't want to talk to me. I told him I was a journalist writing about biker gang murders and I'd gotten a tip that led me to him. He didn't bite, and was about to hang up after soundly cursing me out, when someone else picked up the line — someone who sounded younger.

"Why are you hassling my father?" he demanded. "He is not a well man!"

"I'm not hassling him! Can't someone help me out here? All I want is a little background."

"On what?"

"On someone named Daniel Dubois."

Silence. "He was my brother. What do you want?"

I explained everything again and at least this guy stayed on the phone. "I'd like to talk to you about him if I might."

"What about? He's dead."

"About why he died."

I set my hook and hoped this fish would bite.

His voice was low, but it didn't sound so angry. "Who are you?"

It was time to level with the guy. I had the feeling that if he caught me in a lie that would be it. Like Inspector Parker of the RCMP, I was beginning to trust in hunches.

"If you will agree to meet with me, I will tell you."

"When?"

"Tomorrow evening."

"Where?"

"Someplace safe, public. Would you be willing to come to downtown Montreal?"

"Depends on who you are." Monsieur Dubois sounded amused. "Tell me."

"One more question first. You do know why your brother died, yes?"

"His testimony was going to put away some very bad men. The Mounties promised he would be safe. They lied. Now tell me who you really are, or I will hang up."

"My husband was another of the witnesses. They got to him, too."

"So what's there to talk about? They're both dead."

"Monsieur Dubois, there is a lot to talk about, but it is not something I wish to do over the phone. I promise if you meet with me, I will tell you something you will find most interesting."

"How do I know you're telling me the truth, that you're not just a journalist looking for a story?"

"Two things: your brother died in British Columbia, right?"

"Yes, but what does that have to —"

"I'm sure you've heard the reports about the two journalists who've been murdered, one in B.C. and one in Montreal. Both specialized in biker gangs. Don't you find that curious?"

Dubois spoke as if to himself. "I thought something might be up."

"So you'll meet with me?"

"What are you hoping it will accomplish? Like I said, my brother is dead."

"Just meet with me and listen to what I have to say. We may be able to help each other."

"Okay. I'm in." Then his voice dropped down very low and it was filled with menace. "But do not play with me, I warn you. You will regret it."

My bravado shrank to the size of a pinhead as I began to think I might have made another big mistake.

⌐

Twenty-four hours later, standing on a Montreal street, I whistled and Chloe shouted, and this time a cabbie driving by deigned to notice us.

As we were piling in, he turned and asked, "Where to, ladies?"

"Place Alexis Nihon. Let us off at the corner of Sainte Catherine and Atwater."

Chapter Fourteen

"*So let me get this straight,*" Chloe said
as we sat in the back seat of a cab bound
for Place Alexis Nihon, the location I'd set up for my
meeting. "I'm supposed to be the lookout? What are
you planning on doing, robbing the coffee shop?"

I needed my friend's help, but I'd decided that I
would try to keep her directly out of what I had in
mind. As far as the guy I was meeting was concerned, I
would be there alone.

"Chlo, quite frankly, you're my insurance policy."

Her eyes got big. "This sounds like something out
of a cheap spy novel. Just what have you gotten yourself
involved in?"

It was not part of my plan to tell her one iota more than I needed to, considering what happened last time. Chloe had a husband and two young kids, and I couldn't bear it if I was the cause of anything happening to them. She would just remain in the background, unknown. I'd make certain of that.

But I had thought this through very carefully, ever since I read the email Lainey found on her computer. I really needed to speak to someone who was involved in this whole mess, even if peripherally, and who wasn't a cop. It was something I owed to Sébastien in Montreal and Peter in Vancouver — and their familes. Also to my husband, if I'd guessed wrongly that he was still alive.

As the cab pulled up at the southeast corner of Place Alexis Nihon, Chloe got out, but then stuck her head in the door. "Right. Now I'm supposed to go into the coffee shop, find a spot where I can see everyone going in and out, then watch for the next hour to see who arrives."

I nodded. "And if you spot anything that stinks, someone who shouldn't be there hanging around, anything that doesn't feel right, you give me a call. The guy I'm supposed to meet will be wearing a Montreal Expos baseball cap, has a beard, and there's a scar on his left cheek. If it doesn't look like he's alone, I want to know."

"And if I can't reach you on the phone, I stop you on the way in." She shook her head. "I hope you know what you're doing, Marta."

"So do I," I mumbled to myself as the taxi drove off again.

I made the cabbie stop again two blocks later, earning raised eyebrows as I paid the tab. Walking one block north, then two blocks back west, I found myself diagonally across the street from my objective.

The coffee shop was near the northeast corner of the big mall with access either from the mall or from the street. With all the evening traffic, it would be a busy place and that was comforting. Dubois had suggested a few bars where we might meet, but that was something I was not prepared to do.

That's why I'd gotten Lainey good and looped during our lunch after the funeral. The previous evening, she'd insisted on coming. Now she was at home, safely asleep. Chloe being available had been a bonus. I could have done the recon and waiting by myself, but this worked out much better. Having her on watch as I was talking to Dubois seemed to me to be a much safer option.

Problem was, I had about an hour to kill before Dubois was set to show. Crossing the street, I went into the mall to look around. When I'd been a poor music student, I'd actually worked here in the big pet store, mostly as a cashier, but also cleaning fish tanks and puppy cages. Delightful job.

Fifteen minutes before the eight o'clock meeting time, I couldn't stand wandering around anymore and dialled Chloe. "What's up?

"Being an undercover operative is pretty boring," she said, "except for this young man, quite handsome in fact, who just tried to pick me up. Damned flattering, actually."

"You are paying attention to things, aren't you?"

"I'm all business, believe me, girlfriend."

I rolled my eyes. "You're behaving just like Lainey."

"Well, I am sitting in for her."

"So who's in the place now?"

"Five student-types, two couples, three older people, hardly dangerous-looking, any of 'em. Oh, now wait a minute. I think your boy just arrived."

"Is he with anyone?"

"Not that I can see. He's standing at the front ordering coffee." There was a five-second pause. "I don't believe it!"

"What's wrong?"

"He just ordered the grande espresso macchiato. Damn fool's going to be up all night if he drinks that."

"Chloe!" I barked. "Don't play around! My poor heart just can't take it."

"Sorry," she answered, but didn't sound it in the slightest.

"Is it safe for me to come in?"

Silence for a moment. "I think so. He just took a seat. He's opening up his paper. Oh my goodness, he can read!"

"What do you mean?"

"You'll know when you see him."

"I'll be there in three minutes. Don't take your eyes off us, but try to look as if you're not staring."

"How do you expect me to accomplish that little feat?"

"You're a mother. You must have learned how to watch without appearing to watch. If you see something you don't like, give me a call if there's time — or scream your bloody head off if there isn't."

"Relax, Marta. I've got everything under control."

"Why do I start getting nervous when you say that?"

By that time I was nearing the mall entrance to the coffee shop, so I put my cellphone away, crossed myself, and went in.

You couldn't miss Dubois. He was easily the largest man in the place and mean-looking to boot. I swallowed my fear and walked forward. Going to the counter, I ordered an orange juice and walked over to his table.

"This seat taken?" I asked in French.

"Are you the woman I spoke with on the phone last night?"

I'd noticed the previous evening on the phone that his French had a real South Shore twang. In person it was even more noticeable.

"I am." Leaning across the table, I stuck out my hand and we shook. Then I sat. "Thanks for agreeing to meet me."

Dubois had a full beard, dark eyes, and long wiry hair pulled into a pony tail. He looked to be in his mid-thirties, but it was hard to be certain with all the facial hair. The leather jacket he wore made him look like a biker, except that his hair was clean and neat. Any biker I'd ever seen had filthy hair. Maybe that's a requirement or something.

"You could almost pass as a biker." I meant to say it only in my head, but it came out of my mouth.

Dubois shrugged. "I build choppers, custom-made. It helps a bit to look like your clients."

"They're bikers?"

He shrugged again. "Some. Most are weekend warriors, living out a fantasy."

"Can you tell me something about your brother, Daniel?"

"Sure, but everyone called him Danny or P.A."

"Huh?"

"Short for Petit André. My name is André. Some of my customers enjoyed teasing him. Used to drive him crazy." Dubois smiled, but it didn't make him look any happier. "What about your husband?"

"His name was Jean-Claude Lachance. Did you ever meet him?"

Dubois shrugged. "Once or twice. Talked a lot."

"You don't sound as if you liked him."

"I didn't like the company he kept."

"Such as?"

"Two of the meanest bastards in the Province du Québec. Animals! They were the ones who were behind the butchering of my little brother. I am sure of it!" With a scowl, he lifted his cup and drained it, making a face as it scalded its way down. "So what is it you will tell me that I will find so interesting, eh?"

"I mentioned the two murdered journalists last night. They were looking into the deaths of those three witnesses. One was your brother, another was my husband —"

"And the third was Jacques Filion. I knew him, too, pimply faced little weasel. I wouldn't have trusted him as far as I could throw him."

I ignored the interruption. "The journalists, I don't

know what they found out, but within a matter of hours, they were both dead."

"Bikers don't like people who get curious about their affairs."

"I don't believe it was bikers who killed them."

His expression darkened. "What do you mean?"

I leaned forward so I could speak softly. It felt quite unbelievable, suddenly, that I was doing something like this. "I think their deaths were arranged by a cop, quite possibly a Mountie."

"You are a crazy woman!" Dubois stiffened and abruptly sat back in his chair, as if trying to put more distance between us. "I should not have come," he added as he began to get up.

I leaned across the table and put my hand on his arm. "Please stay. I am not a nutcase. Believe me, I'm as shaken up about what I suspect as you seem to be. It is pretty unbelievable. Let me tell you why I believe it's possible."

The story I told wasn't untrue in any way; I just left a lot of material out. First of all, I didn't want Dubois to know what I did for a living. I felt safe on that score because I didn't believe people who built custom-made choppers would follow the goings on of the opera world.

I told him I'd hooked up with Jean-Claude in eastern Ontario but that he hadn't told me about his past. Then there had been the fire and his death. Eventually I returned to the farm and ran across some information that made me curious. Dubois never asked where I actually live nor what I did for work.

"I found some papers when I was cleaning our old farmhouse to get it ready to sell. That led me to

Montreal and an old woman who turned out to be Jean-Claude's *grand-mère*."

"You must have been very shocked," Dubois said.

"More like angry. I couldn't believe that he would shut off family like that. Now I know the reason."

"I would have done anything for my little brother. He was always hanging around at the shop, helping me. That is where he met bikers. I did work for them. They made me nervous, and I knew where the money they paid me had likely come from, but there it is. My business was small and I needed all the orders I could get. Now I am more picky about who I will do work for."

I continued telling my story, about going to see Sébastien, about the interview with Inspector Parker, the murders and how quickly after my visit they'd happened, and then what the two Mounties in Toronto had said. I kept Lainey and the email on her computer completely out of the story.

At the end, Dubois nodded his head. "It makes sense. So why did you want to see me?"

"First, I don't want to feel I'm alone in this. If something were to happen to me, I want to know there's someone else who cares about what has happened. Second, is there anything more you can tell me? I'm going to find this person who has ruined so many lives. I want to see him punished."

"So you think this rogue cop murdered your husband and my brother?"

I shook my head. "No. I believe he set them up. Why should he kill them? The people they were going to testify against would have been perfectly willing to do that. But the two journalists, I'm not so sure about. Those murders had to be done by two separate people or groups of people. I doubt they could murder someone in B.C., hop a plane and do another in Montreal, all in the space of seven hours."

I looked across the table at this unlikely man whom I was asking for help. He returned my gaze, each of us sizing up the other.

"Did your husband cut a deal with the Crown?"

"Did your brother?"

"Yes. I do know that. He was involved in some bad things but just at the edges. The little fish always get caught first, then the Crown starts applying the pressure, turning the screws. They know the ones to pick and my little brother was the right one. They had him scared shitless. All of a sudden, they whisked him away. The family only got a note that he was going into the witness protection program, not where he was going to be or why this was being done. It nearly destroyed my parents. Danny was always the little angel of the family."

"Sounds a lot like my Jean-Claude. Why do people go bad?"

"It is because they wish to be 'big shots,' be something that they are not."

I didn't think that was true about my husband. Sure he was impetuous, hot-headed and prone to not thinking things through, but not confident? No. But it was best to keep Dubois talking.

"Did you ever hear directly from your brother again?"

"There was a card at Christmas. It was mailed from RCMP headquarters in Ottawa. He said he was okay, hoped to be able to see us soon and that was about it. The day before his death, though, I received a call at my shop from B.C. I wasn't in and the caller didn't leave a message, but my phone keeps the numbers. I believe it was Danny. Maybe he knew he was in trouble."

That was enlightening. Possibly it was Danny Dubois and not Jean-Claude who'd gotten wind of danger first. When Danny was killed, Jean-Claude would have known he was next.

"Do you remember where the call was from?"

"I looked it up about a week later. New Hazelton, a little place in the middle of nowhere."

It was getting late and I had a plane to catch, so I had to cut off the conversation. The whole time we'd been talking, Chloe had been constantly scanning the store, her cellphone ready in her hand, so I felt confident I wasn't in any danger.

I promised to keep Dubois up to date with anything I found out, but if I got any names, I didn't think that I would tell him. He seemed like the sort who would do something stupid to avenge his brother, and his parents or anyone else near and dear to him didn't deserve more pain.

⌇

The cab to Pierre Trudeau Airport made it with bare seconds to spare. It had been an incredibly scary ride, but I'd been the one to promise an extra twenty-five dollars to the cabbie if he got me there on time. Chloe had come with me and her face was noticeably pale as I handed her forty bucks.

"This is for the ride back downtown," I told her.

"No thank you! I'm taking the airport bus back downtown."

Outside the cab, she stood on tiptoes as we hugged. "I can't thank you enough for your help tonight," I told her.

She grinned. "It was certainly a different way to spend an evening, pretty nerve-wracking, though — and I don't mean the cab ride."

"I'll keep in touch a lot better, I promise."

"Me too. Look for a package of music from me in the next week. I'll get you some possible dates and we'll set up rehearsals. Plan on being here a week. You're staying at my place. Okay?"

"The sooner you can get me dates, the better. At this point, if I get a gig, I'll have to take it. Money is tight and you know what it's like finding work after you've been on the shelf for awhile."

She nodded and we hugged again.

On the flight back to Toronto, I thought harder than I had in weeks and began to see what must be done.

But how could it be safely accomplished?

∽

I felt sixteen again, getting ready for my first real date. It had been so long ago now I couldn't remember any details other than the boy's name: Ronald. Attending Tony's grandmother's eightieth birthday party certainly counted as a major date.

Going through the depths of the walk-in closet in my bedroom felt like exploring a deep, dark cave.

Coming out repeatedly with armfuls of unfamiliar skirts, dresses, and blouses, I laid everything out on the bed, searching for the perfect outfit for an Italian birthday. It became abundantly clear that I'd once had a serious clothes-buying problem.

Eventually, I settled on a simple midnight-blue dress. A colourful silk scarf and simple gold jewelry added just the right balance of personality and elegance. A shower and work on my hair and makeup took another hour, but I still found myself ready well before five. Pacing around the condo, looking for something to take my mind off my out-of-control nerves, I felt ready to scream.

Even though the cleaning lady had been in at the beginning of the week, all I could see was dust and grime and mess. First came the bedroom, where all the clothes on the bed got chucked back into the closet. *Mañana.*

Next came the bathroom vanity. Where the heck had all these cosmetics and hair care products come from? Opening up a drawer, I swept everything inside.

I was on my way to the broom closet in the kitchen for the vacuum so I could give the living room and bedroom carpets a once over, when I stopped.

"What the hell are you thinking, woman?" I said out loud.

Was my subconscious trying to tell me something? Why had I also bought croissants and fruit salad earlier in the day?

I plopped down on the sofa to think. Sure, Tony was a nice guy and all, but asking him up after the party, with the possibility of staying the night, was that really a good idea?

I still wasn't sure when Sam rang from the lobby at two minutes past five. "That same man is here for you again. Would you be wanting me to send him up?"

"No. Tell him I'm on my way down," I said, grabbing my coat, gloves, purse, and a small birthday present.

Some things are better dealt with on the impulse of the moment.

Chapter Fifteen

Tony hadn't been kidding when he said the party was being held in a workshop. Uncle Giuseppe was in the business of making and refurbishing moulds for plaster work, and judging by the workshop's size, business must be very, very good.

A whole battalion of Lusardis (Tony included) had spent the entire day clearing the main part of the floor, sweeping and washing it, then decorating. It was now filled with a long string of tables covered by an assortment of linen tablecloths, and the nicest place settings of several families had been brought out along with the best silver. Garlands of fake grape leaves threaded with fairy lights hung overhead and there were flowers and plants everywhere. It was the most charming re-creation of an outdoor taverna that you could imagine.

As Tony led me in, the buzz of conversation died, as if each person had been suddenly doused with a bucket of cold water. Every head swivelled in our direction. This was an opera-loving family, so they certainly knew who I was. I heard the chirp of a young one, asking, "Why is everybody staring at that lady?"

First up was the birthday girl, still wearing an apron from supervising in the makeshift kitchen set up in what looked like the shipping room. She was very short (probably not even five feet) with pulled-back white hair and had on the traditional black dress. Her one nod to the occasion was the inclusion of lavish necklace in addition to a large gold crucifix on a fine chain. Her eyes blazed with intelligence. The matriarch of the Lusardi clan was formidable indeed, I suspected, and not just in the kitchen.

"Marta," Tony said, leading me up to her, "this is my nonna, Benedetta Lusardi. Nonna, this is my guest for the evening, Marta Hendriks."

People were crowding into the doorway to see the presentation of the prodigal soprano. I decided to give them what they wanted.

"I am so pleased to be able to join you in celebration of your birthday," I said to her in Italian.

Her eyes moved from me to Tony, then back again before she stepped forward to shake my hand. "Thank you very much for your good wishes. It is our great pleasure to have you with us this evening."

Back in the main room, I was introduced to everyone there. Though nobody said more to me than "Pleased to meet you" as Tony led me around the room, it was obvious I was the topic of conversation among the adults.

When we finally got to our seats (near the middle of the table, thank the Lord), I leaned over to Tony and said softly, "Maybe I shouldn't have come. This is supposed to be your nonna's night. Everyone is staring at me."

He just smiled. "That is because you are *una donna bella*."

I could only blush.

I estimated that nearly sixty people sat down to eat. The food just kept coming out of the kitchen. First were platters piled high with all kinds of homemade antipasti. Then bowls of pasta, each with a different sauce and all fresh. Then there were more platters with fish and meats accompanied by grilled vegetables.

I wanted to taste everything, and realized pretty early on that even eating just one bite of each thing, I wouldn't make it through without exploding. After making it unscathed through just a few nibbles of the antipasti, the first thing that tested my resolve was a ravioli stuffed with ground walnuts and Gorgonzola cheese, covered by a rosé sauce of great fragrance and delicacy. I could have happily eaten a whole plateful.

"This is absolutely incredible," I told Tony around forkfuls. "You were not exaggerating the tiniest amount."

His face glowed. "My nonna is the best cook ever."

"I agree completely."

During the fish course while I was enjoying a tiny piece of grilled sole with a delicate lemon, white wine, and caper sauce, Tony's cousin Frank, who was sitting on my left, turned to me. "I think the old lady likes you. She's looked your way several times during the meal."

"That's just because my face was in the paper the other day."

He shook his head. "It's not that. We've had many visiting opera singers at various meals. Actually, I'm surprised that Tallevi from the opera isn't here tonight. He seldom misses one of Nonna Lusardi's meals. And don't forget Papa Biagio was a noted amateur baritone back in the old country — or hasn't Tony bragged to you about that yet?"

Tony noticed the dig and the two of them went at it behind my head in a good natured way. Across the table, the aunt and the cousin from the opera chorus had been chatting with us about singing. It was all very friendly, more like colleagues talking together (which it was, I suppose), and I began to relax a bit and not feel as if I were a centrepiece on the table.

Wine flowed throughout the meal, all of it Italian, of course, but none of it commonplace. When I questioned cousin Lina about it, she laughed. "Didn't Tony tell you? If you're a Lusardi, you're either a singer or in the food or wine business. Let's see, any pasta that Nonna and her helpers didn't make themselves came from my mama's shop. Uncle Antonio owns a butcher shop. The wine got here courtesy of Frank, who's next to you. His father began importing wine in the —"

"Hush child!" the aunt (Annetta?) said. "You'll make the poor woman's eyes roll up in her head."

Tony and Frank had finished ragging on each other by this point, and the conversation turned to everyone's memories of the birthday girl. All around us, family members chipped in with stories, and it became obvious this extraordinary woman was the glue holding her huge family together.

As the tables were cleared by the kids, toasts began, some in Italian, some in English, a few in both. Even the little ones stood to salute the family favourite.

I seemed to be one of the only non-family members present, and I realized to my horror that everyone was expected to say something.

When my turn came, I stood, looked down the table at Signora Lusardi, took a deep breath and began to sing "Happy Birthday." What else could I do? I hardly knew the woman. I could have toasted her with some generally appropriate words, but I hoped this might be more appreciated.

Little did I count on the Lusardi family. Before I'd even gotten through the first phrase, people had begun to join me — in three-part harmony! More and more people stood until the room was ringing with sound. By the time we got to the end (with Tony conducting the climactic notes), everyone was on their feet, singing their hearts out. Benedetta Lusardi stood to acknowledge the applause with a raised glass. Everyone filled their glasses, and the entertainment portion of the evening was off and running.

A violin was produced along with an accordion, and over in the corner, someone took a sheet off an old upright piano.

Naturally, we segued into "Libiamo ne' lieti calici" from *Traviata*. Everyone was grinning and enjoying themselves, even the young ones, who were either trying to sing along or just jumping up and down, cheering. Nonna was sitting in her seat smiling broadly and keeping time with one finger of her right hand. In the other she held her wine glass, which swayed to the three-four beat. For me, it was my first time singing this famous chorus with a glass filled with actual wine.

When we got to Violetta's and Alfredo's solos, everyone around the table looked to Tony and me. He grabbed my hand and we both took the solos. I was in my element, but I could tell from Tony's grip that he was pretty nervous.

He had a pleasant voice, not huge enough to be a soloist in a big house, but it was nice, round, and he had very good pitch and musicality. We meshed well.

After that, there must have been a solid hour of singing. The three musicians seemed to know every chorus and many arias in the Italian opera repertoire. There were solos, duets, trios, and several ensemble numbers. I eventually did two more solos: "Un bel di" from *Madama Butterfly* and Gilda's "Caro nome" from *Rigoletto*. Tony responded with "La donna è mobile" and from the laughter and good-natured ribbing from cousin Frank, I got the feeling it was his "party piece." He sang it with real gusto to great applause and cheers at the end. Frank filled Tony's wine glass and mine and we clinked them, holding them up in salute as we looked to the end of the table.

Now, I have pretty good ears, and even though it was in rapid fire Italian, I could have sworn Signora Lusardi turned to the people at her end of the table and said, "Who would have thought our little Antonio could have caught such a bright, shiny fish?"

There was laughter all around us, and Tony looked at his grandmother with fond exasperation and scarlet ears.

The singing eventually petered out and dessert was served. I managed to let it all pass by until the Neapolitan cheesecake, redolent of lemon and fresh pineapple, stopped in front of me. I allowed Tony to cut me a very slender piece. Next came espresso accompanied by little deep-fried crispy things dusted with sugar. Grappa was passed around, and I wasn't going to take any, but then Tony poured me some.

"Are you trying to get me swizzled?" I laughed. "I've had at least four glasses of wine!"

He handed me less than an ounce. "When you've finished your espresso, knock it back in one shot. Your stomach will feel a lot better later."

"Yes, but what about my poor head in the morning?"

Around us, the singing started up again and I sat back smiling. This was what making music was really all about.

Toward midnight, we were still saying our goodnights to everyone. Signora Lusardi gave me a bone-crushing hug and told me, in English this time, "Thank you for helping to make my evening very special. I have seldom heard better singing."

I was somewhat taken aback until Tony jumped in. "Relax, Marta, that's Nonna's way of teasing you."

She turned away for a moment, then said something in really rapid Italian. I only managed to catch a quarter of the words. Tony nodded and we actually made it to the door.

"*Ciao*, baby!" Frank cried to me from the end of the room. "If you get tired of my cousin, give me a call."

His wife smacked him on the arm, but the delivery seemed to be good-natured.

Tony had his cellphone out as we stood in the doorway, looking up at a very clear sky.

"What did your nonna say to you at the end there?" I asked.

Tony looked at me for a moment, then answered. "She thought I shouldn't be driving so she told me I should call a cab."

I twisted my mouth to the side skeptically. "All those words just to say that?"

"Yeah, why?" he answered with a grin. "Nonna has a large and expressive vocabulary. You should hear her when she really gets going."

On the ride back downtown — Tony insisted on coming along — he regaled the cab driver and me with stories about his nonna from when he was a little guy. He had us in stitches with one about her slugging the neighborhood bully who'd sucker-punched Tony when he was twelve, then chasing him down the street with a broom.

It seemed really natural when he reached out and took my hand.

Upon arriving at my building, Tony walked me to the front door. "I won't ask if you had a good time, because I know you did."

I leaned in to kiss his lips lightly. "That's for giving me the best evening I've had in a long time. Your nonna is quite a special person, and you're right: she is the best cook ever."

He smiled. "Do you have any spare time over the next week for a struggling opera singer?"

"After that much wine, you expect me to remember my itinerary? Lordy!"

"Well, I'd like to see you if I may. We could catch a movie. I only have one performance at the opera, so I'm pretty wide open."

He turned and started back for the cab.

"Tony, wait!" I blurted out. "Why don't you come upstairs and we can check my agenda?"

As he turned, his face was a mixture of surprise and hope.

Men are so transparent sometimes.

⁓

When I woke up, it was just barely light. Tony lay cuddled against me, his arm draped heavily over my waist.

"You're awake, then?" he asked, kissing my neck.

"I'm not sure yet. How long have you been up?"

"Not long. I generally wake up at seven, alarm or no alarm."

"When do you have to be at work?"

"Not until eleven. I should probably go home for a change of clothes."

I wiggled deliciously against him. "Are you sure about that?"

"You're not being fair."

"Why should I be fair? It's not every day you get to wake up in the bed of an opera star."

I was teasing him about something he'd said as things were getting hot and heavy on my sofa the previous evening.

Perhaps I had been too impetuous. All the wonderful music had done more to seduce me than anything Tony did. But it had been one of those special nights that happen far too seldom. Tony's kisses had sealed the deal. I might have actually consulted my agenda if his lips hadn't been so inviting. What followed after had me actively considering a repeat performance.

The clock was on the opposite side of the bed. "What time is it?"

Tony moved a bit, and I felt something very nice against my behind. "Nearly eight."

Duty called, and there really was no time for dallying now. Tony still had to go back and retrieve his car.

I got out of bed. "Let me make some coffee before you go. There's also fruit salad and croissants I could heat up."

"That would be nice, thank you. May I use your shower?"

He looked a bit disappointed as I put on my robe. "Sure. It'll take about ten minutes to get everything ready."

I was waiting to pour the coffee when Tony appeared. "Do you at least have time to eat a bit?" He nodded, sitting down and I handed him a steaming mug. "Do you take cream or milk? Sugar?

"I like it black."

"Now, something to eat?"

We sat silently as I doled out the food. The morning after a first night together can often be an awkward dance, especially when not that much water has passed under the bridge yet between the two people. Inviting Tony up to my condo had been the impetuous decision of a moment. Yes, he'd come willingly and I'd given willingly, but neither of us knew where the other stood. Were we just two people who had passed some very pleasant moments together — or was it the start of something more?

We both started to say, "About last night."

"Ladies first," Tony said when we'd stopped giggling.

"I was just going to say how much I enjoyed myself," I said, reaching across the kitchen table for his hand.

"But ..." he led.

"But what?"

"You were going to say something else."

"What are you talking about?"

He took a big breath and then let it out. "You were going to say something like, 'It was fun, Tony, but don't expect this to go any further.'"

Removing my hand from his, I sat back in my chair. "Tony, is this some ass-backwards way to give me the big brush-off?"

He seemed genuinely surprised. "No. Of course not."

"Then what are you trying to say?"

"Nothing."

"Clearly it is something."

"I guess I got this conversation off completely on the wrong foot."

"Really? What was your first clue?"

"Seeing the expression on your pretty face and knowing that it was all my fault."

With those words, Tony simply melted my heart. How's a girl supposed to stay mad when someone says something like that to her?

"And I shouldn't have gotten testy," I told him. "I have a beastly temper sometimes."

"Well, even imperfectly stated, my question is still on the table," he answered. "I was lying there this morning with you snuggled against me, listening to you breathe, and just marvelling that it had happened at all."

"Tony, I have to be honest and ask you this: is it me the person who is special or the opera singer I am who is special?"

He speared a chunk of cantaloupe. "Maybe a little of both."

This was all moving too fast for me to wrap my feeble brain around. What did I feel? Better to cut this conversation short before saying something I'd regret later.

Pretending to notice the time, I said, "You need to get going if you want to pick up your car before work." His face fell and I knew clearly what he was thinking, so I added, "You're not getting the brush-off here, Tony."

"May I see you this evening?"

"Why don't you call me late this afternoon and we'll see?"

"Sure. Anything."

He had been distractedly pulling apart a croissant while we'd been talking. As he rose he popped a piece in his mouth and took a last swallow of coffee, then we walked to the door.

Putting his finger under my chin, he eased my head up so I would have to look right at him. "The more I'm around you, Marta, the more I realize how special you are." Then he leaned in and kissed me gently. "I'm off. *Ciao, bella.*"

The door swung shut and I was left standing there, suddenly feeling very alone. That didn't last long. The lobby phone buzzed.

It was Tony. "There's a package for you from your Internet provider. Must be your modem. Do you want me to bring it up?"

"No, I'll come down for it later. Get yourself to work. You don't want to be late."

"Hey! I do up the work schedule, remember? If you want I can come back tonight to get you set up."

"We'll talk later. Call my cell at four."

I was at Lili's for a coaching well before my noon appointment. Needing time to think and the day being warmer than the recent cold snap, I decided to walk there. I must have been pretty hyper, because I made it in ten minutes less than I was expecting.

All the way there, my mind kept flicking back and forth between Tony and the other big problem: my maybe-not-really-dead husband. It was so strange that the two things had come together at the same time.

As I waited for Lili to finish up her eleven o'clock coaching, I could not sit still and paced her living room from end to end.

Upon entering the room, she immediately stopped and asked, "What is wrong?"

"Everything and nothing," I said, shaking my head in frustration.

"Stop being enigmatic, my dear," Lili answered firmly. "Sit down and we will talk."

"But I came here to sing. I need to clear my brain!"

"You will be useless the way you are now, Marta. Talk first, sing after. Would you like some tea?"

"Hell with the tea!"

"My goodness, you are in a state." She indicated the chair opposite her own. "Sit!"

I stomped around for another ten seconds and then plopped down on the indicated chair. Lili sat very still, looking quite unconcerned as I glared at her. I didn't know who I was more upset with: her for knowing me so damn well, or myself for being so transparent.

Eventually, I dropped my diaphragm, sucking in as much air as I could hold, then let it out slowly. Regaining some composure, I told her simply, "I've met a guy."

Forty minutes later, Lili knew more than I'd known myself when I'd begun talking. She has that way about her, and I suppose that's why she was so good as a therapist. Sadly for all those troubled souls out there needing help, she loved music more.

Along the way, tea had been made with me following Lili to the kitchen like a clinging little puppy as I poured out my story. Once the dam had been breached, I was helpless to stop the flood. If Lili felt any satisfaction at having learned to press my buttons so easily, she hid it well.

"So what do I do?" I wailed. "After everything that's happened, I'm afraid to let this guy get any closer. My life is too much of a mess right now. Hell! I may still be married for all I know. This couldn't have come at a worse time."

"Haven't you also wondered why he is not married or involved with someone already?"

"Of course!"

"Have you asked him about that?"

"No."

"You do like him, though?"

"Yes."

"How much? You are a person who is so proud of making snap decisions."

"I don't know if I'm prepared to find out how much."

"It is perfectly clear to me that you have worked yourself into a state of immobility, Marta. You are not trying to control the situation. You are letting the situation control you."

"What are you talking about?"

"Go to Paris. Find out if your husband is indeed still alive. Then you will be able to make a rational decision about this new man."

That sound I heard was my jaw hitting the floor. "You're kidding."

"No, I am not. It is the only way you will settle the situation." Lili got to her feet and began to walk out of the room. "Now, I think we should work again on the

238

Mozart today, once you have warmed up sufficiently," she said over her shoulder.

I followed along meekly.

As I sat in the back seat of a cab driving south on Jarvis Street, my mind felt refreshed and clear.

It had been a great session with Lili. She had been perfectly right to treat me as she had. Everything in my mind that had seemed so muddled earlier on was now all lined up in orderly little rows.

There was a lot to plan before I could just go trotting off to Paris, but the paralysis in my decision-making ability was gone. Obstacles would be overcome, and I had an ace up me sleeve in the way I might find my husband. I now knew what I had to do.

Entering my building and walking to the elevator, it was everything I could do to keep from bursting into song. It would have been "Zippedeedoodah." I shared the ride up with an old lady who lived down the hall from me and helped her carry her groceries to her door.

My good mood lasted until I opened the door to my apartment.

The place looked as if a hurricane had blown through. Every book and CD on my shelves was on the floor; the furniture was turned over and had been slit open. And my nice little laptop, which I'd begun to really like, was not on the coffee table where I'd left it.

I slammed the door and ran for my life.

Chapter Sixteen

I hit the lobby nearly running. Sam wasn't in his usual spot behind the desk, nor out on the sidewalk getting a breath of air, but I wasn't about to stop and look for him. My only goal was to put as much distance as I could between me and my apartment. The St. Lawrence Market area is a normally good place to find a cruising cab, but wouldn't you know, they'd all disappeared. As I hurried east, I kept glancing back, sure someone would walk up and shoot me.

I was on Wellington getting close to Yonge when a cab finally appeared, but he was in the far lane. I stuck my fingers in my mouth, whistling loudly. This startled an old lady, who glared at me as she yanked on the chains of her two little yappie dogs.

The cabbie did one of those hair-raising, last-second dekes right in front of a delivery truck and stopped smoothly at the curb to much angry horn tooting by the surrounding drivers. Normally, I might have been amused.

"Take me to the Eaton Centre, Shuter Street entrance."

I spent the entire trip trying to control my shaking hands. I'm sure the cab driver thought I was high on something.

Tony's face broke out into a huge smile as soon as he spotted me, but it quickly turned to concern when he saw the state I was in. "What's wrong?"

"Someone has broken into my apartment," I said, hugging him and feeling as if I was about to shatter into a million pieces. "I didn't know where else to go."

Tony took my arm and moved me over to the "Genius Bar" at the back of his store, sitting me down on one of the stools.

"We will sort this out," he said. "I just have to organize a few things, and then we'll go someplace where we can talk privately. Okay?"

The perky young lady who'd greeted me the previous week brought over a Styrofoam cup of mediocre coffee, but it was warm and sweet and kindly meant. I drank it gratefully.

It took Tony about twenty minutes to free himself up. I could tell when he came over to me, he wanted to do a lot more than just take my hand and lead me from the store.

"We'll find a quiet corner over at the City Grill. They're not busy at this time of day. You can tell me exactly what happened." He put his arm around me as we walked. "Quite frankly, you look like you could use a stiff shot of something."

Tony obviously ate lunch there a lot, because everyone seemed to know him. When the waiter came over, he ordered a Manhattan straight up for me and a mineral water for himself. "Hope that's okay. You told me the other night that you like Manhattans."

Smiling weakly, I said, "You pay attention."

"I try," he answered, gently squeezing my hand where it rested on the table.

I'll admit, I guzzled the drink, and Tony, with that astonishing panache some men possess, ordered another without me noticing. Making sure I just sipped the second one, I had begun feeling a little steadier, so I began to talk.

"In my second year at McGill, I was held up one night on the way back to my apartment. It had just been some young punk looking for quick cash, but the event made a lasting impression on me. He told me he had a knife, but I never saw it. Being smart, I just handed over all I had: twenty-two dollars and a handful of coins."

"You were very lucky," Tony said.

"I thought the whole thing was no big deal at the time. I picked my purse up off the sidewalk and continued on to my apartment. It wasn't until I got in the door and took off my coat that the reality of what had just happened began to sink in. I hate to admit it, but I got rather hysterical, scaring the crap out of my roommates. Over the next several months, I was plagued by horrendous nightmares and I wouldn't walk home unless I had two or three people with me. My roommates, Lainey and Chloe, put up with it, uttering nary a grumble. They could tell how much I was suffering, and actually threatened to go out and look for the guy, armed with lengths of pipe."

"They sound like interesting people." Tony replied.

"You can't imagine."

"Okay, now I've got the background. Tell me what happened today."

It didn't take long. What was there to tell? I'd been at Lili's for about two hours, and since I'd walked there and taken a cab back, I estimated I'd been gone just short of three and a half hours.

"I didn't get past opening the door, but the place looks like a hurricane went through it."

"Very wise. For all you knew, they might still have been there."

I took another sip from my glass. "My thought exactly."

"It was pretty ballsy of someone to go in and rob you in the middle of the day when they had no idea when you'd be getting back."

Even though I knew it would come to this, I hesitated. "I don't think they were there to rob my apartment."

Tony's face was a wonder of puzzlement, and he was silent for a good fifteen seconds.

"Does this have anything to do with those murdered reporters that upset you so much?"

He took my breath away.

I nodded. "Yes."

Tony looked at his watch. "I can't be away from the store much longer, and I get the feeling this is going to take a lot of time to explain. First, though, I think you should call the police. Or would you like me to do that for you?"

"No," I said firmly. "I'm not sure I want to do that."

This obviously surprised him. "Why not?"

"It's very complicated."

"Obviously." He thought for a moment. "Okay, I'm done work at seven. Why don't you go to my apartment and wait for me there?"

"I don't want to be a nuisance."

"Nonsense." He reached into his pocket and came out with a set of keys. "My building is on Merton south of Davisville east of Yonge. You can catch the subway right from here, and it's a five-minute walk from the Davisville station."

I shook my head. "No, thank you. I'll take a cab."

He looked at me again, then nodded, reaching for his wallet.

I put my hand on his arm. "No."

It looked like he was going to protest, but then he just nodded. "Okay. Here are the keys and I'll write out the address. When I get there, you'll have to buzz me in. Expect me around 7:40."

Tony insisted on taking me out to the street and seeing me safely into a cab. By this time, the traffic was crawling on Yonge Street, but I told the driver to stay on it. I wanted to be around as many people as possible at all times. It may have been paranoid of me, but I remembered Lainey's description of Sébastien happily going off with the two cops. That wasn't going to happen to this girl if I could help it.

⟞⟝

Tony's apartment was a pleasant surprise: spartan but with thoughtfully chosen furniture. What looked like an original oil hung on one wall, and a baby grand was tucked into a corner near the window. It was also tidy and clean, something I couldn't claim for my own place most of the time.

I was greeted at the door by a rather plump grey-and-white cat, who tried repeatedly to lead me into the kitchen, where I'd presumably be shown where his food dish was.

The view from the living-room window was very nice — if a little depressing under the present circumstances: it overlooked Mount Pleasant Cemetery. In the spring, I'd probably think it quite cheery. I thought of the walk I'd taken just a few days before. If Tony had been standing where I was now, he could have seen me set out as I crossed the old railroad bridge over Yonge. Perhaps he had been.

On the way north in the cab, I'd tried Lainey's cellphone, but hadn't been able to reach her. Becoming more concerned, I called her office at McGill and got her secretary.

"Ms. Martin is conferencing with the dean at the moment. May I take a message?"

I gritted my teeth at the use of the word "conferencing," and said, "Could you tell her that Marta Hendriks urgently needs to speak to her? She should call my cell. Would you like me to spell my name for you?"

"Oh no, Ms. Hendriks. I know who you are and I will pass this on as soon as Ms. Martin is free. Thank you for calling and have a great day."

"Yeah, some 'great day' I'm having," I told the cat who was busily rubbing against my legs. "At least Lainey's safe."

Tony called at three to make sure I'd gotten there okay. "There's red wine in the cabinet to the left of the sink or white wine in the fridge as well as plenty of food. Feel free to help yourself."

"Tony," I began, then hesitated. "I'm sorry to be such a pain. I just didn't know where else to turn."

"Well, I don't mind in the least that you turned to me. We'll talk this all over tonight and figure out what to do next. Everything will be okay."

I hung up knowing full well that he was being overly optimistic.

I pushed back my plate, picking up my wine glass. "That was really spectacular," I told Tony looking through the candles separating us. "I'd never even heard of *spaghetti alla carbonara* before."

Tony had shown up at the apartment not even an hour earlier. In less than forty-five minutes, he'd whipped up a fantastic meal and had it on the table.

"I know you're probably getting tired of hearing this, but it's Nonna's recipe and my favourite. I called it bacon and egg spaghetti when I was a kid."

"But that wasn't bacon you used."

"No. It's called guanciale and it's made from hog jowls. It's very hard to find around here. I was just lucky Nonna gave me some a few weeks ago, otherwise you would have been stuck with plain old bacon and that's nowhere near as good."

On top of all the other stuff, the guy knows how to cook, I thought. "And the salad dressing?"

Nodding sheepishly, he picked up his glass and we clinked again. "Nonna's recipe, I'm afraid."

"Tony," I said, looking at my wobbily reflection in the wine glass, "your parents weren't at the birthday party on Sunday, and nobody made a single reference to them. Why is that?"

"They're both dead. My mother died in childbirth, and that's how Nonna wound up in Toronto. She was a widow by that time and came over to help bring me up. I was a very late baby. My parents had long since given up on having a family when I came along. My dad? Well, he died nearly six years ago now."

We picked up our plates and took them to the kitchen.

"Would you like a bit of fruit for dessert? I bought some very nice pears the other day."

"Sure. That would be nice."

We sat together on the sofa, windows to our backs and Tony's TV, stereo, and book shelves in front of us. I'd taken a look at them while waiting around and found he was well-read, both in English and Italian. As expected, the CDs were mostly opera, but there had been a few rock and roll surprises.

Tony brought out two Anjou pears, pulling out a pocket knife to cut them up and handing me pieces on its point. I was grateful for the respite, since I had no idea how much to tell him about my troubles.

All too soon, the fruit was gone.

Tony sat back. "Now, tell me what's going on. I can't deny I'm very curious."

"How much of my personal history do you know?"

"Beyond the little you've told me? Well, some people at the opera have talked about you, and I, of course, listened, especially after I met you."

"And?"

"You were the protege of Gerhard Fosch, and yes, I've heard the stories about him, so I can imagine that you were very close, shall we say. After his death, you seemed to concentrate only on your career, then out of the blue you married a French-Canadian handyman. I haven't been able to find anyone who ever met the guy. After he died in a fire, you withdrew from singing for two years."

"I should hire you to write bios for me. That was pretty succinct."

Tony and I looked at the wall in front of us, the blank glass of his big-screen TV seeming to hold our eyes as our thoughts drifted for several minutes.

"Marta?"

"Hmm?"

"I was just thinking that both our pasts are more than a little operatic, wouldn't you say?"

I smiled. That's not the way I would have thought of it, but Tony did have a point. "What else has been going on in that devious brain of yours?"

"Does this break-in have anything to do with your past, your husband perhaps?"

My stomach immediately knotted. "Is it that obvious?"

"No. I just pay attention to not only what people say, but also to their choice of words and what may lie behind those choices. Will you let me help you?"

I made one of my snap decisions. It was about time I got the views of a completely disinterested third party, well, partially disinterested.

Telling my long story yet again took nearly an hour. I seemed to be getting much better at it, or maybe it was just that I felt so comfortable with Tony. For the first time, though, I told the complete story.

"Okay," he said when I finished, "since you came to me for help, I assume you're willing to hear what I have to say. Correct?"

I nodded.

"Then, it seems clear to me you shouldn't go back to your apartment. Certainly, someone has been watching you. And your friend in Montreal?"

"I spoke to her at six. She's fine, nothing to report, although who knows if someone hasn't been looking through her things, too? I assume we're dealing with pros here. I suggested that she goes to stay with her parents or friends."

"Do you think it would do any good to go to the Mounties with your concerns?"

"Who do I trust there?" I shook my head. "No, the Mounties are out."

"The Toronto police, then."

"What, for my apartment?"

"For everything."

"No. Let me put it to you this way: this rogue Mountie is staying ahead of everyone. You don't think the Montreal police aren't seriously looking for him? They have to suspect something. According to what Lainey told me, there haven't been any arrests there yet, nor for the reporter out in Vancouver. Would that give you a lot of confidence if you were in my shoes?"

"Frankly, no."

"Okay, then what do I do? How do I get myself out of this mess?"

Tony got up, disappeared for a moment, and came back with a bottle of cognac and two snifters. "This was a special gift from one of my uncles."

"Smells marvellous," I said as I swirled the amber liquid in the snifter he handed me.

We clinked glasses and I took an appreciative sip. I'd never had better, except for one time when Gerhard opened a bottle worth three thousand dollars.

Tony stretched out his legs on the glass-topped coffee table and I did the same.

"Here's what I think, Marta. The first thing is you need to go to Paris and try to find out if your husband really is alive. You won't have any peace until you do. You also can't tell the police about him, because it would probably put him in grave danger."

"So you do believe I saw him, that I wasn't having hallucinations?"

"If you had told me you keep seeing him wherever you go, then I would have said you need help. But to see him twice and only in Paris, then I have to believe it was real."

"Lili Doubek told me the same thing today. Anything else?"

"Yes. I think you should talk to the Toronto police, if for no other reason than you have to report what happened so you can claim the damage on your insurance. I also think that you should not tell them anything more than 'someone broke into my apartment.' Let them come to their own conclusions if they will."

I wanted to think about his advice a bit, and Tony, perhaps sensing that, got up, went to the stereo, and put on some music. It was *Beethoven's Concert Romance in F# minor*, the piece Victoria Morgan had suffered so much for in bringing it to the world. It's a work that's profoundly sad at the beginning and it perfectly mirrored my mood.

He left the volume down low and came back to sit next to me, sipping his cognac as he waited.

Finally, I nodded. "I'll do what you say. I think it's good advice."

"So we'll go to Paris?"

"No, Tony, dear. I'll go to Paris. Your only part in this is giving me shelter from the storm tonight. It can't go any further."

"But it could be dangerous! What if the people who tossed your apartment are still after you?"

"They probably are, but leaving Canada is going to make it very hard for anyone to follow me. They keep track of who goes in and out of the country very closely now, even Mounties."

"How are you going to find your husband, then? Paris is a very big place, and what if he isn't even living in Paris? The search could take months."

"I think I have a good idea how I might find him," I said. "It may not work out, but I won't know until I try. And that's where you can help me."

"By doing what?"

"I'm pretty sure my nice little computer got stolen this morning. I noticed you have one in the spare bedroom. Could we use it?"

"Sure," he answered and got up to retrieve it.

It was an embarrassing moment when his desktop came up because it was a photo of me singing Mimi in *Bohème* at the Dortmund Opernhaus.

"Nice photo," I commented dryly.

"Well, um, yeah."

As soon as the computer was completely started, he opened a browser window. "I'm assuming you want to look for something."

"Yes. I want to find a place in Paris that sells Harley Davidson parts."

"Motorcycles? Why that?"

"Because of the package my husband was carrying the first time I saw him. It was wrapped in brown paper, but I'm pretty sure it was a motorcycle tail pipe assembly."

"So you're going to have to search all the places around Paris that sell motorcycle parts?"

"No, only Harleys. Trust me, Marc wouldn't ..." I sighed heavily. "Jean-Claude wouldn't be interested in any other brand."

The computer thought about it for a second, then a results screen flashed up. The list seemed longer than I would have expected, but there were three places reasonably near the Sully-Morland Métro station.

"Those are where I'll search first. If I'm right, somebody is going to have information on my husband."

"You can't very well go in there and demand they tell you. After all, you don't even know what name he's going under."

"I'm sure I'll think of something."

Tony went to each of the sites and printed out information on the companies, although his printer was located in another room, and there were no wires between the computer and it. The wonders of modern electronics.

Stretching and yawning widely, Tony said, "I have to be at the shop early tomorrow. We're doing inventory and I have some things to get ready."

His comment was so transparent, I just burst out laughing. He blushed charmingly.

"Why don't you just say what's on your mind, big boy?"

"I didn't want to be crude or pushy. I'm perfectly willing to let you have the sofa."

"Oh, that's generous of you." I was struggling to maintain a serious expression. "I'm the guest you invited here. I should be offered the bed."

"Well, you can't have it unless you want to share it with me, because that's where I'm sleeping."

Grabbing his head, I pulled him close, kissing him hard. "Now that's a good way to let this lady know where your interests lie."

Tony's face had a bemused expression. "Why should I beat around the bush?"

"Exactly. And why should I play hard to get?"

The next fifteen minutes were spent having quite a wild make-out session on the leather sofa. It was amazing how Tony's kisses just melted my insides.

Our clothes were already half off when he said, "Hell with this! We have a perfectly good bed that's not being used."

With that, he swept me up, then in the bedroom, he swept me away. Our lovemaking that night was far superior to the first time. No more "opening-night jitters" to mar what we did to each other.

By the time I was finally drifting off to sleep, I remember thinking that it hadn't been such a bad day after all.

The next morning, I woke up at five, and after an hour of trying to get back to sleep, I realized that it was no good. For better or worse, that was it for me as far as sleep went. Quietly slipping out of bed, I went into the living room.

I'd been pointlessly staring out the window for nearly half an hour when Tony appeared in the doorway.

"And how are you this morning?" he asked.

I didn't answer.

Mount Pleasant Cemetery lay spread out before me, a beautiful spot with trees, shrubs, and grass during the good weather. But even then, you knew it was the home of cold, grey stones that marked the passing of thousands of lives. Now with life shutting down in preparation for the hard fact of winter, its desolation was palpable. Given my present situation, it was infinitely depressing.

Tony came in and stood behind me, but fortunately didn't touch me. "Penny for your thoughts."

"I feel as if my life has turned into a bloody opera." I answered without turning around.

He wasn't having any of my glum mood. I could see his teasing grin dimly reflected in the glass of the window in front of me. "What opera?"

"Isn't it obvious?"

"Quite frankly, no."

I turned, and must have had quite a scowl on my face, because Tony stepped back. "Try *Traviata* on for size."

"*Traviata*? How do you fit yourself as Violetta into your situation?"

"That's what I've been standing at this bloody window thinking about since I got up." I turned around. "You've heard the poetic translation of the opera's title in English, haven't you?"

He nodded. "The Fallen One. How do you figure that relates to you?"

"Maybe it is me. I fell for this guy I knew nothing about. I've been wondering if I missed clues that were there, things that might have caused me to step back. Or maybe my husband is The Fallen One. Heaven knows, that fits him well enough." I looked into Tony's eyes. "Thing is, I just don't know."

"Know what?"

"Where this is all leading."

"Sounds like you could use a good hug, for starters."

Tony wrapped his arms around me and pulled me close, something I didn't know I needed until he did it.

"When I woke up and found you gone, I was worried that you regretted what happened last night," he told me after a quiet minute or two.

I squeezed him a little harder. "No, that was really wonderful, a bit unexpected, but really wonderful."

"I thought so, too."

We kissed, not one full of passion like we'd shared the previous evening, but one expressing our growing closeness.

"I could use a cup of coffee," I said a few moments after our lips parted. "I'm never much good in the morning until I've had my coffee."

"I'll make a note of that."

Again that teasing note to his voice. I began to relax.

"Espresso, cappuccino, or plain old drip coffee?"

"Whatever you're making is fine."

"I'm making whatever you want."

"Cappu, then."

"And after that? What would you like for breakfast? And don't say, 'Whatever I'm having.'"

I finally smiled. "All right. Some fruit and cereal."

"Muesli, granola, or Cap'n Crunch?"

"Cap'n Crunch? You're kidding."

"Actually, I am. I just wanted to see if you were paying attention. So, Muesli or granola?"

"Either one is fine."

Tony waggled his finger at me. "A decision, please."

"Muesli, then."

While Tony got busy in the kitchen, I took a much-needed shower. Coffee was brought in partway through, and he stood for a moment watching me through the transparent curtain as I rinsed off my hair. I suddenly felt self-conscious, but then remembered his soft words of endearment the night before. It also crossed my mind that he might have stood just like this watching a whole parade of previous women that he'd seduced. Violetta Valéry again sprang to mind, but again the gender of those involved was reversed.

Life was currently far too complicated for my confused brain.

Chapter Seventeen

It had been a wild and woolly few days.

First, there had been the fact that I'd never gotten around to booking the flight to London for my gig to sing *Carmina Burana* with the Royal Philharmonic Orchestra. Once again, I'd been brought up short, and it also showed me how completely distracted I'd been by the mess consuming my personal life. It had only been a question from Tony about driving me to the airport that made me realize I'd made another potentially disastrous slip-up. The outrageous cost of the last-minute ticket drove the hard lesson home. For once, my travel agent couldn't work any miracles.

"Let me show you how easy it is to do this sort of thing on your computer," he said, as we sat on the sofa after another fabulous dinner.

I made a face. "Except I don't have one anymore, remember?"

"You can use this until you settle with the insurance company, and I'll bring one from the store for my own needs." He turned on his laptop and I snuggled in so I could see the screen. "Now we key in your flight information. Now here's where you set the computer to send you an email, reminding you about it."

I watched and learned. "What was that you just put in?"

"A reminder to call me."

"How come the calendar's now got one of those for every day?"

Tony looked at me patiently. "Just a hint." After kissing my forehead gently, he added, "You don't want me to be worried about you the whole time you're in Paris, do you? As long as I hear from you regularly, I won't be as concerned."

Taking a deep breath, I asked him, "Tony, why weren't you snatched up long ago?"

He pursed his lips. "All right," he sighed. "Fair question. I was engaged once."

"What happened?"

"I was twenty-seven and working for my dad's food importing business. That involved a lot of travel to Italy. I met a girl in Turin and we fell madly in love. After a year of seeing each other, I asked her to marry me. Her family wasn't sure, and it took me a long time and a lot of hard work to win them over. Finally, her father gave his blessing. I was one happy guy.

"Then my trips to Italy were less frequent after my dad became ill, and I was forced to take over more of the day-to-day operations. When I finally made it over for a holiday right after Christmas, I knew immediately that something wasn't right. Our wedding was only six months away and Raffaella didn't even want to talk about it."

I squeezed his hand. "She'd met someone else."

Tony looked at me sadly. "It was worse than that. It was someone I'd introduced her to. They'd been secretly meeting for nearly a year." He took a deep breath. "It gets even worse. Raffaella was pregnant by him. The whole thing was just too awful for words."

"I cannot imagine what that must have felt like."

"Soon after, my dad died. I completely lost heart in everything and sold the business. With the proceeds, I bought this condo, the car I'd always dreamed of, and invested the rest. I thought it might make me feel better, but it didn't."

"How long ago was that?"

"Nearly six years."

"And in between then and now?"

He just shrugged. "I got bored with nothing to do, took a job selling high-end restaurant equipment. Got bored with that and took the job at the computer store."

"And, ah, relationships?"

"There didn't seem any reason." Then a smile lit his face. "Until now."

In talking my plans over with Tony, we realized that the performance in London provided the perfect way to get into France unnoticed. With European Union integration, immigration checks once you were inside the EU had pretty well become a thing of the past. All I had to do was pay cash for a ticket on the Eurostar and I would be in France without anyone being the wiser. Of course, this meant I'd have to give the slip to whoever might be following me. We had great fun figuring out outlandish ways for me to get from my hotel to St. Pancras station, where I'd catch the train.

I spent the days in long sessions with Lili working on several things but focusing on *Carmina Burana*. I'd performed the solo soprano part in this groundbreaking cantata by Orff five times over the years, but it had been four years since the last one, and I did not feel really ready until my final coaching, literally on my way out the door to the airport.

Tony had been a brick throughout, first going with me to the police, where we promoted the idea that it was just a common robbery that had taken place in my condo, at which point I'd gone back to it with two burly detectives in tow. Once they'd found out who I was, the police had been great and promised to do their best to keep my problems out of the news.

The mess in my condo was worse than I imagined, and there was a very nervous moment when one of the detectives observed that it looked as if someone had been looking for something. The detectives said it was obvious the person searching my apartment had been going as fast as he could. They also later reported that the guy who lived on the floor below told them he'd heard several bumps starting around 11:45 on the morning of the break-in but had assumed I was moving furniture or something. I'd left the building barely five minutes earlier. Even more disturbing, they obviously knew I was going to be out for awhile, which meant they'd probably put a bug on my phone or something. I couldn't ask the cops to look for that.

Not wanting to stay a moment longer than I needed to, I stuffed clothes and other things into two large suitcases and then indulged in a bit of subterfuge at the Royal York Hotel. Tony had suggested the old "in one door and out the other" routine, in this case using the underground corridor to get from the hotel to the subway station. Anyone following me would think that I'd gone to the hotel to check in. Nobody followed me down the corridor in the five minutes I kept watch.

To keep pursuers further off track, Lili and I worked at a colleague's house in North Toronto. It all felt like living in a spy novel, but I was really that spooked.

At my final session with her, I introduced Tony. To my surprise, she asked him to sing some vocal exercises and "*Prendi, l'anel ti dono*" from Bellini's *La Sonnambula*. He seemed caught off guard, but she pronounced his voice good, which pleased me very much.

"I can work with what God has given you," she told him. "There are several deficits in your vocal production that can be easily fixed. Have you considered concentrating on the bel canto repertoire? Your voice is well-suited to it."

I knew Tony would be mildly disappointed, because he loved Romantic Italian opera so much, but he seemed surprisingly buoyed by Lili's comments, and he quickly made an appointment for their first session. I got her aside on the way out the door to ask if she was only doing this for me.

Her remark was characteristically blunt. "Partly, but the boy does have a nice voice, though small and with no real carrying power. Let me see what I can do for him. He might well surprise us."

At the airport, I silently watched Tony haul my two suitcases out of his car's trunk. All day I'd been dreading having to say *au revoir*. After London I had only six days to find my husband. After that I would need to be in Dallas for a benefit concert, then off to the San Francisco Opera for another last-minute appearance as Donna Elvira in *Don Giovanni*, something Alex had managed to dig up the week before. It would be nearly a month before we'd see each other again.

"You will call me if you need to?" Tony asked. "Don't be stiff-necked about asking for help."

"I will call."

"And promise you won't do anything foolish."

"I never do." Boy was that a whopper!

Tony smiled. "This has been a wonderful week for me."

I hugged him close. "And, despite it all, for me, too. You've been terrific."

He kissed me, but it was rather chaste, considering what we'd gotten up to the past few days. I wanted more, but his instincts were right: getting close in public could be problematic. One never knew who would spot you and where the resulting photos from their cellphones would wind up, something Gerhard had drummed into my head years ago when spotting paparazzi was fairly easy. Tony seemed to understand that innately, and I was extremely grateful.

"Have a great flight, Marta. Call me when you get to London."

"Yes, Tony," I answered, chuckling as I grabbed the handles of the two bags and wheeled them into the terminal.

As I joined the other passengers at the check-in line, I heaved a big sigh. I'd been dreading that Tony might say he loved me.

Why was I so afraid of hearing that?

⟳

The first rehearsal for *Carmina Burana* went very well indeed. I'd been in good voice and singing the part came really easily. The other soloists were top-notch, too, and the multiple choruses this massive work uses had been wonderfully prepared. We had two performances scheduled, one of which was to be recorded for later broadcast on TV. The producers wanted an interview with me about the resurgence of my career, and that was a very pleasant surprise.

Just before I'd left Toronto, the music arrived for the percussion concert I'd been silly enough to agree to do. There were some pieces I vaguely remembered, but it had been so long since I picked up sticks that everything looked far more complicated than I remembered. Since a good part of road trips are always spent sitting around hotel rooms, at the last minute I went back to the apartment (with Tony in tow), grabbed my stick bag and a couple of practice pads — small discs that feel like a drumhead when you hit them, but don't make a lot of noise — and stuffed them in one of my already-too-full suitcases. My wrists and hands were way out of shape after so long and would need a lot of work.

Since *Burana* uses massive amounts of percussion, I made friends with the percussionists, but I was too shy to tell them why. They probably would have playfully told me to prove I really knew how to play. That could have proved rather embarrassing.

But after two night's practice in my hotel room, I realized that a lot of what I'd learned way back when was returning more easily than I'd expected. Yeah, my wrists turned to jelly after a half-hour of rudiments, but the feel of the sticks was still there.

The next morning, I got to rehearsal early. When I saw that all of the percussion instruments were already set up and nobody present, I couldn't resist. Plunking myself down on the stool behind one of the two sets of timpani, I opened the music that was waiting on the stand, whipped them into tune by ear (something I've always been good at), and began playing.

Happily at it, I didn't notice how much time had passed, and when I resurfaced, I was horrified to find the entire percussion section and a good part of the orchestra silently watching me. The timpanist whose part I was playing had heard me from the Green Room and come out to investigate. Finding me, he'd gone for the rest of his cronies and several others had tagged along, sneaking out to watch.

They all burst into applause, and I was absolutely mortified, feeling like someone with her fingers caught in the cookie jar. The timpanist came forward with a felt-tipped marker.

"What's that for?" I asked.

"I'd like you to sign my sticks. People won't believe me when I tell them the story otherwise."

Another one gave me the backhanded compliment of the century. "Now we know why you're about the only singer who seems to have any sense of rhythm!"

After that, I became the mascot of the percussion section. They even snuck me back to play snare for one section, and when the conductor, Sir Michael Dickson, discovered me back there, he burst out laughing and told the orchestra's manager that I should be getting doubler's rates.

While everything had gone amazingly well so far in London, as my trip to France approached, I was getting more and more nervous, and asked myself nearly every hour just what the hell I was getting myself into.

Tony tried hard through numerous emails and phone calls to keep me in a good frame of mind. Never once did he succumb to asking if I wanted him to fly over, which was very astute and thoughtful of him. The last thing I wanted, if I did manage to corner my husband, was to have the new boyfriend hovering in the background.

The morning after the second concert, I packed my suitcases, called the hotel's concierge, and asked if he would arrange to have them forwarded to the hotel I'd been booked into for the Dallas gig. If I was going to avoid being followed, I didn't want to be burdened with two huge suitcases. What I would need for Paris went into two shoulder bags I'd brought. These I had sent ahead to St. Pancras.

An hour before train time, I left the hotel in a cab bound for Harrods (certainly a place a hotshot opera star could be expected to go). I walked in the front entrance, made a bee-line for the side entrance where there was a cab stand, and ducked into the first one.

"Where to, miss?" the driver said in a Jamaican accent.

"St. Pancras, but wait a moment, okay?"

"Sure thing," he said as he turned on the meter.

We waited about three minutes, but I didn't believe anyone came out looking for missing opera singers. Even as we moved into the traffic, though, I made note of cars that pulled out. Some stayed with us a surprisingly long time, and the cab driver probably thought I was nuts the way I kept looking out the back window. Usually, they're very chatty, but this guy eyed me warily through the rear-view mirror. Once we got to St. Pancras, I pressed some bills into his hand and ducked into the station without waiting for change.

Perhaps, the whole exercise was a bit juvenile, but I just didn't want to take chances. If anyone inquired after me, the desk staff at the hotel had been instructed to say I'd left for Dallas.

As I boarded the train, I felt I'd covered all the bases as best I could.

Our arrival at Le Gare du Nord in Paris was precisely on time, something trains don't manage to do all that often in North America. We'd barely stopped when I snatched up my two bags and ran for a taxi.

Drivers in Paris are completely mad, and the cab drivers are the worst. In Montreal, they say green means go, red means look before you drive through the intersection, and yellow means go faster. Paris traffic is just crazy all the time, permanently stuck on yellow.

When I get into a Paris cab, I usually just shut my eyes and rely on good luck to get me to my destination in one piece. Today, though, I needed to keep my eyes open, so I saw all the near misses and close calls. The important thing was that I didn't see anyone who remotely looked like they could be following us.

The cabbie was Algerian and peppered me with questions in highly unintelligible French when he found out I was from Canada. I did my best to carry on the conversation while keeping my eyes peeled, both front and back: back to see who might be following, and front because Amad had the disconcerting habit of turning around whenever he said something to me. I saved us from certain death at least a half dozen times before he got me to the B&B I'd booked in the 13th arrondissement.

The place had been recommended by two brothers who played in the Royal Phil: Glenn was one of the percussionists and his brother Barry played bassoon. We'd gone out for "a pie and a pint" during a break during that last day of rehearsal. Both liked to duck over to Paris for the occasional weekend and spent their summer "hols" in Normandy.

"If you want to come and go as you like, this is the place," Glenn had told me about the B&B. Barry had nodded enthusiastically.

They'd informed me that the proprietor also had a studio apartment a few blocks away that I could get for a very nice price and still have breakfast at the main location. Not wanting anyone to know what I was up to, I jumped at their suggestion.

Michel, the proprietor, his cute little grandson in tow, helped me get settled in the apartment, which was three blocks away from the main house. On the second floor of what seemed to be a very old building, the single room had recently been renovated to the point where it even had wireless Internet. As soon as I was alone, I tapped out a quick email to Tony, telling him that I'd arrived safe and sound — and un-followed as far as I knew. He responded almost instantaneously with a short message: "Thank the Lord. Please keep me informed. — Tony." I smiled at the thought of him sitting at his computer waiting to hear from me.

Even though I felt as if a nap might go down well, I forced myself to gather up my sheets of computer printouts and maps and head out into the city for a little investigative work.

The day (unnoticed on that nerve-wracking cab ride) was quite magnificent and warm for early November. I'd packed a knitted cap and my favourite scarf (always a prerequisite for a singer's vulnerable throat) but decided I didn't need either.

The nearest shop selling Harley Davidson motorcycles and parts lay west of where I was staying. It was not the most likely location to get a lead on my husband, but I wanted to try out my story to see how it would fly before I hit the place I felt would be my best bet. A little rehearsal never hurts if you want to give your best performance.

I had a bit of a hike to get to where I could catch a bus, but on such a fine day, that was no hardship at all. Walking briskly along several back streets, I felt good that I was finally doing something about my problems instead of waiting around for them to do something to me.

Getting on an eastbound bus when I reached Rue de Tolbiac, I took a seat and went over things in my head.

I'd first visited Paris on a school band trip when I was seventeen. That had been an eye-opener to kids from a small city like Ottawa. We were a pretty unruly bunch. Our teacher and the chaperones spent the majority of their time trying to corral us. One night, six of us, more on a dare than anything, snuck out to the infamous Moulin Rouge, where we saw the very sexy stage show and drank champagne. Everyone piled out of the cab back at the hotel pretty smashed, only to find the band director waiting for us in the lobby, his expression positively Vesuvian. He confined us to our rooms thereafter and said if we stepped out of line even one inch, we'd be immediately put on a plane back home. When the word of what we'd done got around, we were elevated to hero status, not only in the band but in the whole school. It was one of those childhood memories that both delights and shocks you when you get old enough to realize just what might have happened.

Being in Paris as little more than a tourist for the first time in years, I naturally thought of those youthful high-spirits. The parallels to what I was doing now were not lost on me, either.

When the bus passed over a rail line, I knew we were getting close. I had what I wanted to say pretty-well worked out, but rehearsal is always a lot different than the performance. If I ever thought I was a competent actress, today was the day to prove it.

I know nothing about motorcycles except that they're dangerous and noisy. When Marc had gone on and on and on about how he wanted to one day build his own special motorcycle, and pulled out all his magazines and brochures, I had to struggle to keep my eyes from glazing over. Sure, I felt I should share my husband's interests, but I also wanted him to stay alive and healthy. The only cold water I actually threw on the project was when I told him he would never catch me riding on the back of it. He just laughed and said he had ways of persuading me.

The motorcycle shop was nicely laid out, clean and actually looked quite swish. The places Marc had dragged me into were dumps by comparison.

"How may I help Madame this afternoon?" inquired the tall grey-haired man behind the circular counter in the centre of the shop.

I walked toward him trying to appear indecisive and unsure of myself — not much of a stretch, considering how much of a long shot this whole exercise could prove to be.

"I ... I am not sure," I began in the broadest Quebec accent I could manage. "It is my husband's birthday in a few weeks and I want to give him something special."

"Madame wishes to buy a motorcycle?"

"No, no." I tried to appear genuinely horrified.

Some of his shopkeeper's patience seemed to ooze away. "Then what does Madame wish?"

I leaned forward as if to tell him a secret. "Well, you see, my husband does not know that I know about the motorcycle he is building in the garage of our neighbour. We moved here about two years ago and he —"

"What are you trying to tell me?" The expression on the shopkeeper's face seemed to add, "you stupid cow."

"My husband knows that I do not approve of his dream of having one of your fine machines, so that is why he is building it in secret, but I have decided that if he wants it that badly, then he should have it and not hide things from me."

"And?"

"I would like to buy a part for it and give it to him on his birthday. It will be a very big surprise for him."

"But how can you buy a part if you do not even know what he is building? This is a foolish thing you ask!"

Reaching into my purse, I pulled out two photos I'd brought with me. Both showed Marc and me in happier times. In one we were sitting on a sawhorse in the shell of the new house. It was a good shot of him, smiling and looking as if he didn't have a care in the world. The other was on the occasion of our first anniversary, when we'd gone out with some neighbours to a restaurant in Perth. In this, Marc was more solemn and I remembered that just before the camera had flashed, he'd kissed me and told me that I was the best thing that had ever happened to him. I hadn't been able to look at that photo until this trip.

"This is my husband, although he now has a small beard," I said sliding the photos across the counter. "Perhaps he has bought some of his parts here?"

"You do not even know if he shops here?" the shopkeeper asked incredulously.

I decided to appear a bit put out. The man certainly deserved it.

"I have already told you, my husband is building his damned motorcycle in secret."

My use of the Quebec term *maudit* for "damned" seemed to set the man back on his heels a bit, and he actually studied the photos carefully for a few moments.

"No. I have not seen this man. I am afraid Madame is wasting her time here." As I dejectedly slid the photos back into my purse, he added in a kinder voice, "Perhaps you would like to buy an accessory for him?"

"It has to be a part so that he knows I am in support of him. Thank you for your time."

Once I was out the door and around the corner, I drew myself up to my full height again, stretching the kinks out of my back. This acting gig was hard.

Back on the bus, I was surprised I didn't feel depressed or even downhearted. I had just successfully fooled that snot of a shopkeeper, and I felt ready for the real test, which would hopefully come the next morning.

Chapter Eighteen

*The sun had pretty well set by the time I
got back to my romantic little apartment.*
I'd stopped in at a couple of shops I passed on the way
home, picking up one of those small roasted chickens
the French call coquelets, salad fixings, a half a baguette,
and a bottle of red wine. It's probably against the law
in France to drink red wine with chicken, but I really
didn't give a fig. Wine is so good and so cheap in this
country, I was going to indulge myself.

After eating, I poured a third glass and watched
a little bit of television on the small set. Nothing
particularly caught my interest, so I tapped off a quick
email to Tony, telling him about striking out on my first

try, then sent another to Alex, asking what was up for some pending European bookings that had been offered since my triumph at the Paris Opera.

I'd been twiddling my thumbs, lost in thought as the computer shut down. For some reason I felt completely wired, totally unprepared to go to bed. From the corner of one of my bags I could see Chloe's percussion music peeking out.

"Why not?" I asked no one in particular.

With my stick bag unrolled on the table, a practice pad in front of me on top of some magazines to get it to the right height, I happily practised rudiments and some of the music for the next hour, at which point my hands gave out. Not bad. I might actually avoid making a fool of myself at the concert.

After a quick shower, I felt more ready for bed. Checking my email, Alex had added two more opera bookings for two years on and one for the following year. Covent Garden was eager to discuss appearing in the premiere of a new opera. I was sort of disappointed to find that Tony hadn't answered my earlier email.

I switched off the computer again, then the overhead light after I got into bed. Lying on my back in the darkened room, I reviewed what I wanted to do the next morning. For some reason, I could not fall asleep. The clock told me it was just after midnight.

Since it was a fine night, I could still hear the frequent clicking of people's heels as they walked along the street below, either going to or coming from one of a number of restaurants and bars to be found at the top of the hill. When I'd passed by there on the way to catch the bus earlier in the day, I also spotted a bank of pay phones.

"Why not?" I said, throwing back the covers.

The area was alive with people, mostly young, taking advantage of what was an abnormally warm evening for so late in the year. One restaurant even had a couple of its glass doors slid back, and nobody seemed to mind. I went into a café, bought a phone card, and walked to the booths, which were located in a slightly quieter side street a block away from all the action.

I thought I'd check in with Lainey, see how she was doing, and find out if there was any news on the investigation of Sébastien's murder.

Her cellphone rang four times and then was answered by someone unexpected, Chloe, who sounded extremely odd.

"Having a girls night out, are we?" I asked playfully.

"Martha?" she practically shrieked. "Thank the Lord. Where the hell are you?"

"In Paris. I couldn't sleep so I thought I'd —"

"Paris? How the hell did you find out what's happened?"

It began to sink that something was very wrong. "Where's Lainey?"

"Oh Christ, Marta, they just took her to the hospital!"

I felt as if someone had hit me hard in the stomach. "You'd better tell me what's happened," I said a lot more calmly than I felt.

"Some guys broke into her apartment and beat her up."

"What do you mean? When? How?"

"Just before I arrived here, apparently. She'd asked me to drop over to discuss our Chicks with Sticks gig. I was a bit late and there were three police cars out front. I didn't think much of it, went into the lobby and on up to her apartment. About a second after stepping out of the elevator, I realized the cops were at Lainey's. I ran down the hall right into the arms of a cop, who asked me, not very politely, where the hell I thought I was going. 'That's my friend's apartment,' I shrieked at him. 'What's going on?'"

Chloe was normally a person who kept her emotions in check quite well. To hear her so beside herself was just shocking. "What did the cop tell you?"

"The brute just glared at me. 'You know the woman who lives here?' he asked. 'Yes! Is she all right? Let me see her!' He motioned another cop over and told him, 'The boss will want to talk to this one. Take over for me.'"

I felt physically ill by then. "Did you see Lainey?" I asked.

"Only as she was being wheeled out on a stretcher."

"What did they do to her?"

"Pounded her around pretty good. I could only see her face and it looked awfully banged up."

"Any other injuries?"

"I don't know!" Chloe wailed.

"Can you find out?"

"I'm going to the hospital as soon as I get off the phone with you."

"Do you know anything about what happened?"

"The cop in charge told me that two students who live in the next apartment heard noises like someone breaking things. They went to investigate and found the door not quite shut, so they entered. Two big guys had Lainey backed up into a corner. She was holding a lamp and taking swings at them with it. When the intruders realized they weren't alone, they decided they'd better split. Those brave boys didn't back off, though. One was knocked down pretty hard."

"And Lainey? Did you speak to her?"

"Only for a moment as they waited for the elevator. She told me I had to get in touch with you."

"Did she say why?"

"To tell you to be very careful."

That had been viscerally driven home by this phone conversation.

Chloe, who seemed to be thinking more clearly now, asked, "What are you doing in Paris? I thought you were going from London to Dallas."

I dropped my voice, even though there was no one within earshot. I couldn't help it. "Look, Chloe, you don't know where I am. You haven't spoken to me. Is that clear? I don't care who asks you. Don't say anything about where I am."

"Marta, what the hell is going on? Are you in some kind of trouble? Is that why Lainey got beat up?"

"Chloe," I said patiently, "these are probably the guys who killed Sébastien Bouchard. Tell the cops that, but don't say where you got the information."

"I don't understand."

"Just do it!"

"Okay, but can you tell me what's going on?"

"Not now, but I will. I promise. When you speak to Lainey, tell her I said to tell the cops everything she knows."

I stopped at one of the bars for a double of cognac to steady my nerves. After that, I scurried back to my apartment refuge and made sure the door was securely locked.

Normally, I sleep very well. When I finally took off my clothes and got back into bed around two, I tossed and turned and generally was completely miserable, as anyone might well imagine. I kept reminding myself that I needed to be well rested for the next day, but my brain just wouldn't listen. Sometime after 3:30 a.m., I finally got deeply enough asleep to begin dreaming. That wasn't any better.

In the first part of the dream, I found myself in the middle of a burning building. The heat was incredible and I thought my hair would catch fire. Wrapping a towel around my head, I stumbled through the flames and smoke, and I wasn't looking for my husband. He'd gotten out, and I couldn't believe he'd left me behind. I kept calling for help but heard no response.

I looked down at my hands and they'd started to char. With the usual disconnect you get in dreams, the burns didn't hurt, but I knew that I was probably close to death. Eventually, I spotted a door in a far corner. Whether it might be a closet or the way to salvation, I was going through it. As I began to run,

I noticed that the shoes had burned right off my feet. I didn't stop.

The door was smoking as I crashed through it. On the other side it was night and heavy rain was falling. As it hit my body, steam sprang up, making everything hazy and indistinct. I heard voices around me. "My God, do you see what's happened to her?" "That is absolutely disgusting!" A child began whimpering. "Make her go away mommy. She scares me!"

Stumbling on, I saw a puddle and looked down. As if in daylight, I could see my reflection perfectly and my stomach heaved. Except for a few shreds, my clothes had all burned away. Underneath my body was completely charred, my skin cracking and showing red underneath.

I soon found myself in a winding deserted street, like many you find in old Paris neighborhoods. Still night, there was now no one around to see me in my misery. I walked by a restaurant and was surprised to see my husband inside at the small bar near the back, laughing and talking with a man who was obviously the proprietor. I knew he was waiting for me.

Desperate for help because I knew the pain from my burns would soon hit me with crippling force, I lifted my hand to tap on the window when there was a bright flash from inside the restaurant and glass, bricks, and mortar flew out toward me. I knew we were all dead.

My eyes flew open. I was lying on my side, the early morning sun hitting my face as it bounced off an apartment window across the street and snuck by the carelessly closed curtain. Touching my face with my hand, the skin felt cool, smooth, and whole, and I began breathing again.

I sat up and pushed back the tangled mess of my hair. It was soaked, as were the pillow and the sheets. Looking at the bedside clock, I saw it was just after seven, so I got up and filled the coffee maker. I'd told my host that I'd be over for breakfast at 8:30 a.m., which gave me plenty of time to clean the sweat from my body and steam the crud from my brain.

When I came out of the bath alcove, coffee was ready. Still wrapped in a bath towel, I sat at the small table, sipping gingerly and thinking about what had happened to my friend back in Montreal.

I couldn't stop now. They'd keep coming until they got what they wanted. First Sébastien, then my apartment, now Lainey. Had she surprised them or had they been waiting for her? Thank the Lord for those two brave students who came to her rescue, or quite likely she would now be dead.

If the bad guys knew what I was up to, they'd be over here in a flash, since it was obvious this all centred around Jean-Claude. It always had. There must be something more to this than his testifying at a trial, something I didn't know yet. But what?

I just prayed that I'd been right all along and he was indeed still alive. Now, I *had* to find him.

I chose a pair of jeans, runners, and a black turtleneck sweater for the day, threw on a bit of makeup and forced myself to make the short walk over to the main house for breakfast. All I wanted to do was crawl back into bed and pull the covers over my head.

Unfortunately, the only other guest that day recognized me right off the bat, and I could not shut him up.

He was an elderly Brit who often came to Paris to see opera. He went on and on about how horrible the new Bastille opera house is and actually told me I should enjoy the Palais Garnier so much more. I hated to respond that I'd never yet sung at the Bastille, and if he thought the Palais Garnier was so wonderful, he should see the backstage area. His eyebrows shot up when I told him it hadn't been that long ago that there weren't any toilets near the dressing rooms, and during evening performances, one had to leave the theatre to use the facilities in a nearby restaurant.

"I am on holiday and looking forward to having some time to myself for a few days," I told the old coot as I autographed a piece of paper for him. "Let's make my presence here our little secret. Okay?"

He tapped his index finger against the side of his nose. "Mum's the word," he chortled. "Our little secret!"

I hoped he'd remember. He didn't seem like the sort who could keep his mouth shut if he had anything even mildly interesting to share.

The car I boarded on the Métro at Place d'Italie was jammed, and like a good Canadian, I moved well away from the doors. People continued piling on, and by the time the train pulled out, I was squashed in on all sides. Just before we got to the Bastille, someone groped me. It was all very subtle but also very definite. Pressed in the way I was, I couldn't turn, but I shook myself and gave a little yip. Surrounded as I was by males, I had no idea which one I should punch out, even if I'd had the room to get in a good swing.

As the train slid into the station and the doors

opened, enough people left that I could turn around, but the bastard, if he was still there, knew how to dissemble well, because there was no indication on anyone's face — and believe me, I looked. I had to squeeze through the closing doors to avoid going past my station.

The experience had shaken me up, and once above ground I looked for a place to sit and gather my wits.

Overnight, it had clouded up and a cold wind was blowing from the east. After the previous day's weather, nobody looked particularly happy. Near the old canal that runs up from the Seine and right under the Place de la Bastille is a small park. I found a bench and plopped myself down, hands still shaking from what had happened on the Métro. For the next ten minutes, I distractedly watched the demolition derby that is Parisian driving as vehicles circled the huge July Column in the centre of the Place with seemingly complete abandon.

The cold wind finally forced me to my feet, and I made my way around the west side of the roundabout, keeping a wary eye on the traffic whizzing by as I crossed two streets.

Tree-lined Boulevard Beaumarchais is the heart of a very welcoming, picturesque Paris neighborhood, and it struck me once again how different the area was from the places in North America where one generally finds dealers selling motorcycles. I'm well aware that not all people who love motorcycles are hoodlums or even bad people, but that's what many think of when the machines are brought up in conversation. This neighborhood was delightful, even on a cold day in late fall. Not a biker in sight. I began to feel hopeful.

Walking up the east side of the street allowed me to scope out the bike shop from a distance. The business seemed to have spread over several storefronts, and while appearing neat and tidy, it didn't have the same swish factor as the first place I'd visited. Being a weekday morning, things looked rather quiet, so I crossed myself and crossed the street.

The greeting I got as I entered the shop was almost the same as the previous day. An older man, who stepped out of the back room as a bell on the door tinkled, stared at me balefully as I walked toward him, once more sliding into character.

"*Oui, Madame?*" he asked.

I went into my routine about wanting to surprise my husband with some part or other for his "secret" motorcycle project. Carefully scanning the man's face, especially his eyes, my pulse quickened as I began to suspect he might know who I was talking about. When I produced my two photos, he looked them over carefully but would not commit himself.

"Madame must understand that we serve many customers here, including several from your country. I may know this person, but it is hard to tell with so old a photograph."

With my brain racing to try to think of some way to break this impasse and get the information I had come all this way to find out, I was saved by a young man who came through the same rear doorway. Dressed in greasy blue coveralls and wiping his hands on an equally dirty rag, he, at least, looked like he belonged in a shop that sold motorcycles.

"Hey, what you looking at, Alain?" he asked, snatching one of the photos from the old man's hand. "It's Luc! But who is this woman with him?"

The old man hissed over his shoulder, drawing attention to me with a jerk of his head, "It is his wife."

In back of the counter, the tension was suddenly thick and I saw immediately how to play this: I began to cry.

I made a big production out of searching my pockets for a handkerchief. Two were immediately offered, one greasy, the other pressed and pristine white. It wasn't hard to make a choice. The young lad got dispatched for water, and the older man fussed over me. Finally, I wiped my eyes, which I'd actually managed to get wet, and blew my nose.

"I am so sorry," I said in a shaky voice. "I should not have lied to you."

"Lied to us, Madame?"

"My husband left me over two years ago and I have been looking for him ever since. That pig of a brother of his finally admitted to me that Marc was living near Paris, so I came over here to find him. Ever since he ran out on us, I have been forced to work two jobs so that I can keep our house. Even so, it has now become impossible, even if I had three jobs. I took the last of my money to come here and beg on my knees for him to help us!"

The young guy had returned and I could hear him grumbling. His superior remained skeptical.

"How did you know to look here for him?"

"His brother Guy. He told me that Marc was building a motorcycle." I pulled out my list of shops. "I have been to most of these. He would need parts. Many people have refused to speak to me, and I know you would not have, too, if it had not been for the slip of this young man here, thank our Virgin Mother!"

The old man sighed heavily. "As you have probably guessed, your husband has another woman. I hesitated to give him away. He is a good customer."

"He also constructed some wooden racks for parts in the back room," the young one said. "He is a handy man."

"You called him Marc just now," said the old one.

"So he has made up a name for you?" I shot back scornfully. "That is because he ran out on his obligations to his family. The court ordered him to pay child support and he did not want to! My husband's name is Marc Tremblay and he came to France to hide."

"He told us it was Luc Duchene."

"Please, Monsieur, would you tell me where he lives? I beg you!"

Before he could be shut up, the young man said, "Beauvais. It is north and west of the city. You can get there by train from Le Gare du Nord."

I pounced. "Do you have his address or phone number?"

"No," said the old one.

"But of course," said the young one at the same instant.

The old man shrugged and left the room.

"You must excuse him," my saviour said. "He is from the old school. To him, discretion about our customers is everything."

"Even when the customer does not deserve it?"

"You know that, and I know that, but if someone spends their money here, then he believes we must be discreet if questions are asked."

I pressed. "Do you have my husband's address or a phone number?"

An order book was produced from under the counter. "There is a small hotel and bistro in Beauvais. I believe your husband works there." He scribbled something on a piece of scrap paper and slid it across the counter. "Here is the name, address, and phone number. He has ordered several parts from us. In fact, one is on order now."

I grabbed the young man's hand and brought it to my lips. "You have helped my family and me very much and I thank you for it. *Au revoir!*"

"*Bonne chance, Madame,*" he called after me as I left the shop.

Walking back to the Bastille Métro station, I wiped my mouth on my coat sleeve. This role playing was hard to stop once you got started.

I looked at my watch and saw that it was still quite early. I'd need to do a bit of online research, but I saw no reason not to go to Beauvais right away and strike while the iron was hot. Hopefully, the old man at the shop wouldn't rat me out. It would be a real kick in the head to finally find where my husband was hiding, only to discover he'd flown the coop again.

Back at the apartment, I fired up the computer, went to one of those map sites Tony had showed me how to work, and looked up Beauvais. It didn't have much to recommend: a large cathedral and some old buildings was about it. Located about halfway to the coast, the train schedule said I could get there in an hour and the departures were frequent.

If the stars were aligned right, it wouldn't be long before I'd be standing in front of the man who'd almost ruined my life and had cost several people theirs.

Chapter Nineteen

"Beauvais, messieurs, dames. Nous arrivons au terminus de Beauvais."

The confidence I'd been feeling that morning had slowly oozed out of me with each passing mile as the train drew closer to the town where I expected to find my husband. My mood had been buoyant right until the train began easing away from Le Gare du Nord shortly before one. All the doubts, the uncertainties began creeping up on me as Paris slowly melted away into countryside. At each stop the train made, I'd known that I had one chance fewer to put a halt to everything. Then I'd thought about Lainey and Sébastien in Montreal, Peter in Vancouver, and the person who had actually died in the house fire at the farm. Those evil bastards were still out there. I couldn't stop now, no matter how much I might have wanted to.

The dark heart of my doubts, though, was this: was I doing this because I wanted to set something right, or because I wanted to hurt Jean-Claude as much as he'd hurt me?

Now we were in Beauvais. I'd been told Jean-Claude lived here. The final decision was staring into my face. I could either go on with this to the end, or just sit and wait for the next train back to Paris. Once I walked out of this station, that would be it. Did I want to or not? At the last moment, I slipped on my coat, wrapping my scarf tightly around my neck, and departed the train. The die had been cast.

Exiting the station, I found myself on the southwestern edge of this Picardie market town. At my back stood an ugly industrial area and in front, two restaurants, one closed, one open, neither looking welcoming. A cold rain from the nearby Atlantic coast forced me back inside the station while I consulted my hand-drawn map for about the tenth time.

It became clear I would be waiting in vain for a taxi to show up, so I took out a beret I'd brought, jammed it on my head, and hit the road.

A check on the Internet had told me that Beauvais is very old, having been around since Roman times. Obviously, it had never risen above being a backwater country town. Toward the centre, Saint-Pierre de Beauvais — the partially built gothic cathedral for which the town is most noted — glowered down, greyly dominating the skyline as it had for nearly eight hundred years. A cathedral unfinished for that long was a pretty good indication of how things stood locally.

The address I'd been given at the motorcycle shop was between where I stood and that cathedral, so I crossed the road and headed off to find out where fate was taking me.

Part of it was the greyness of the late fall day, part of it was the bleakness of my mood, but this provincial town seemed unbearably grim as I walked down a long street of fast food shops and stores selling junk and services on the cheap.

Turning right at the first busy intersection where a sign pointed to Centre-ville, the shops began inching up the economic scale toward some sort of respectability.

With two more glances at my map, I managed to find Place Jeanne Hachette, the ancient town square now half parking lot, half park. Shops lined three sides of it, and the old town hall filled the remaining one. Beauvais's historic heroine, Jeanne Hachette, whose twice life-size statue dominated the plaza, had obviously been a determined woman. Depicted wielding her intimidating weapon in a rather operatic manner, she looked like someone I certainly wouldn't want to run afoul of.

The hotel/brasserie where Jean-Claude worked was on the west side of the square, directly in front of me as I stepped around the statue.

Getting closer, I saw the place was nearly empty, since it was a good half hour past the end of the lengthy French lunch interval. Two waitresses cooled their heels near the bar at the front, clearly eager for the last of the dawdling matrons and businessmen to depart. My husband was nowhere to be seen.

What was I possibly going to say when I came face to face with the rat who'd put me through so much agony? "Hi! Remember me?"

There was no way I was walking into that brasserie without some sort of great line. I had nothing, not even a mediocre one. Knowing Jean-Claude, he would seize the moment, say something incredibly brilliant and totally decimate me.

The cathedral looming over the tops of the buildings beckoned, offering me an excuse to avoid walking into that restaurant. Despite feeling like the biggest coward in the world, I dodged to another street and made my way there. The closer I got, the more overwhelming that grey hulk appeared.

It was the oddest church I've ever been in, seeming to go up more than it went out. I felt like I was in a huge tower with stained glass windows. The space was awash with thundering sound — someone was practising Phantom of the Opera music on the large pipe organ. I stopped to wonder at organists who have to do their "dirty work" in public, mistakes and all. I certainly wouldn't want to. Perhaps that's why they're often such strange people.

Off to the side, I lit candles for my two parents and Sébastien, then sat down nearby to think.

My inability to make those final few steps was really quite ludicrous. I'd come all this way, gone to so much trouble, stirred up so much shit. People had died because of my poking my nose into the situation, and here I was dithering at the very end of my journey. It was not only cowardly, but disgusting.

I put my head into my hands.

I've never been all that religious. The last time I'd spoken to God, I was in the throes of despair over supposedly losing my husband, and I was not kind in my words. Quite frankly, even though my faith had been on the wane over many years, that dark evening I'd severed all emotional and spiritual ties with Mother Church and hadn't been back until now.

I waited for twenty minutes, but God again didn't speak to me, so I got up and left.

The restaurant was completely empty when I got back.

The door to the hotel portion of the establishment was to the right of the brasserie, and through the glass, I could see a narrow set of stairs going up.

Taking a deep breath to steady my nerves, I opened the door and went in.

At the top, I found the hotel's small front desk, behind which a thin elderly woman was typing furiously at a computer as she leaned forward, squinting at the screen. Clearly, she was too vain to wear the glasses hanging around her neck.

I watched her for a good twenty seconds with no response, so I pointedly cleared my throat.

"*Oui?*" she asked, obviously put out that I'd interrupted her.

I answered, imitating Jean-Claude's accent as best I could. "I am looking for a friend from back home —"

"From Quebec, are you? You'll want Luc, then. He should be downstairs cleaning up." She dismissively waved her hand at the stairs behind me and turned back to the computer.

I went back down to street level again and moved to the corner of one of the big glass windows of the restaurant, waiting for my husband to appear.

Even though I'd imagined over and over during the past two weeks what the moment would be like, my heart still leaped into my throat as he appeared in a doorway at the back of the long room, a large plastic flat of clean glasses tucked under one arm.

Now that I had a chance to study him, Jean-Claude certainly looked quite different. Most startling was his shaved head, something I hadn't noticed that fateful day at the Métro, because he'd been wearing a beret. The goatee and moustache changed the whole lower portion of his face, and he appeared fit and athletic, having lost a fair bit of weight. It made him seem taller.

Would anyone else have recognized him? I didn't know, but I certainly would have, even in a crowd. Every single movement he made as he arranged glasses on the shelves behind the bar had been imprinted on my memory during our brief time together.

What did I feel? I had believed my husband irrevocably lost to me, and yet here I was spying on him like a guilty child, watching him as he did small things, unaware of anything but his task.

I waited until he'd brought out a second flat of glasses and his back was turned, intent on his work again. With sweaty hands and heart beating *molto vivace*, I pushed open the door.

"I am sorry but we are closed until five-thirty," he said without turning around.

His accent was softer, less twangy and angular than I remembered. In short, Jean-Claude definitely sounded more French than Québécois.

"Well, fancy finding you here," I responded in English.

The effect of my words couldn't have been greater if I'd dumped a full bucket of ice water over his head. His hands froze halfway to the shelves, a glass clutched in each, and stayed that way for several seconds. Then he slowly put them down as he gathered himself, not turning around but looking at me warily through the mirror at the back of the shelves.

"Nothing to say?" I prodded when his silence had stretched a good ten seconds more. "I've never known you to be at a loss for words, Marc. Or would you prefer me to call you Jean-Claude, although I understand it's now Luc."

His shoulders sagged as he turned and his expression held only apprehension. "How did you find me?"

"You ran out of luck back in September. It was at the Sully-Morland Métro station. You were running for the entrance just as I was coming from the opposite direction."

"I had heard that you were in Paris."

"I thought I was losing my goddamned mind," I snarled, unable to restrain my anger. "Do you have any idea what you've done to me, not to mention other people?"

"Have you told anyone about seeing me?"

"Didn't you hear what I just said? Are you just going to ignore it? Don't you think you owe me at least a frigging explanation?"

"Marta, please. Lower your voice."

"Why? Afraid someone might hear what a rat bastard you are, might find out about your sordid past?"

He stepped around the bar and moved toward me, attempting to take my hands, but I drew back.

"I do not blame you for being so angry with me, Marta. I did what I did because I had to. It was actually to protect you."

"What a complete load of shit!" I enunciated each word separately, practically spitting them at him. My body shook with the sudden uncontrollable rage boiling out of me.

Jean-Claude took a step back. He clearly thought I might slug him. *I* thought I might slug him.

"I've seen your grandmother and I've spoken to the Mounties."

Now he looked worried. "What did you tell them? Did you tell them about seeing me?"

I could have easily said yes and then watched him swing in the wind, but I wouldn't lie. I would not go down the same road he'd taken.

"They actually approached me after I began poking around. I had to be sure that I had actually seen you that day in Paris. They were watching, Jean-Claude. They got on to me within a day."

"But you didn't tell them that you'd seen me? I must know that!"

I took a deep breath to steady myself. "No. I did not."

The door behind me opened.

It was a young woman, holding the hand of a toddler just learning to walk. "And there is your papa," she said to the boy, then to Jean-Claude, "Gaston has walked all the way from the car. Isn't that great?"

She was maybe twenty-five, my height and my colouring. Her hair was longer, well below her shoulders, and she was quite slender. It struck me with the force of a blow that she looked very much like I had at the same age.

My husband, clearly distracted by this entrance, took a moment to gather his wits. "Ah, Marie, that is indeed wonderful. I am a bit busy for a visit, however."

Marie then noticed me, and with that sixth sense women possess, her eyes narrowed. "And you are?"

I was about to answer when Jean-Claude butted in. "She is an old friend from Montreal. She has dropped in unexpectedly and we were just catching up."

Marie's expression clearly said, *Oh really?*

It was my turn to say something, but I was spared by the child, who having successfully disengaged his mother's hand, had tried to wobble to the bar, fallen, and bumped his head on the leg of a chair. It was nothing serious, but he set up a lusty howl, more from surprise than anything, I expected.

"Isn't it time for the boy's nap?" Jean-Claude asked sharply.

"I suppose so, but I'll be right down once he's asleep." She turned to me. "And I look forward to speaking with you, an old friend from back home. Luc has told me nothing about his past."

As soon as Marie was out the door with the child, Jean-Claude looked at me with desperation in his expression. "You cannot be here, Marta. You must go."

I sat down at a nearby table, enjoying his discomfort. "Why?"

"Marie suspects something."

"Oh, and she counts more than I do, I suppose." A thought occurred to me and I glanced down at his left hand. "So you've married her, have you?"

His expression was a wonder of apprehension and fear.

"I believe bigamy is illegal in France, Jean-Claude."

"Marta, please, I beg you! There is the child."

"Yes, I had noticed. Adorable little tyke. He has your eyes."

"Why did you come here?"

"To talk. To ask you some questions."

"I will not speak to you if you stay."

"You'll talk to me or you'll talk to the police," I stated coldly.

Jean-Claude stared at me for a long moment, then said, "Do your worst! If you will not leave, then you will have no answers to your precious questions. You will ruin two innocent lives and you will go away unsatisfied. Do your worst."

I couldn't believe it when he turned and went back to his straightening of the bar.

Now what? A moment ago, I'd thought I had him over a barrel and with one deft move he turned the tables on me. I damn well knew if I stayed there would be a scene with his new wife. I would have to tell her what was what. Any papers that proved Jean-Claude was my legal husband were back in the mess in Toronto that was my apartment. I could ask Tony to send them, but it would take two days at least to get them here. Would it even do any good? By that time, Jean-Claude would no doubt be long gone.

"If you are thinking I'm going to run again, you are wrong," he said without turning around. "If you know my story, you know I had good reason for running. They came for me that day, and it is only through luck that I survived."

I squeezed my eyes shut. "You could have shared your troubles with me. I could have helped. That's what two people in love do when there's trouble."

He turned. "You would have gotten killed. If you had been with me that day, the man they sent to do their dirty work would have killed you. I can see by your eyes that you know I speak the truth." Wiping his hands on a towel, Jean-Claude walked around the end of the bar again and sat down across the table from me. "I am not proud of what I did to you. Not a day goes by that I do not regret it. I should never have let things between us ..." He sighed heavily. "But I couldn't help myself. You bewitched me from the first."

I shook my head at his twisting of the situation. "You regretted it so much you ran here and married someone else and now you have a son. Wow. Some regret. Excuse me if I don't get up to pat you on the back."

"It was not planned. It just happened. I did the right thing by taking Marie as my wife. Her family would have thrown her out otherwise. My old life with you was over. I could not go back." He glanced at his watch. "It is getting late. I will talk to you any time, any place you name, just not here and not now. I swear on the graves of my parents that I am not lying to you."

"Oh spare me. Your *grand-mère* told me all about your parents. You don't even know if your mother's still alive."

He had started to sweat, something hard to believe in someone who was always so cool, calm and collected. "I will come to you tomorrow. I swear! What can I say that will make you believe me?"

Jean-Claude's hands were gripping the edge of the table and I looked more closely at his wedding band. Not plain like the ones we'd bought in Ottawa, this was an intricately carved gold Celtic knot, obviously handmade. I suspected Marie had one like it.

I held out my hand, fluttering my fingers. "Give me your wedding band."

He looked truly shocked for a moment, then shrugged, knowing he had no argument. It took a bit of twisting, but it came off. When he dropped it onto my palm, its weight surprised me.

I consulted the train schedule I'd picked up. "Tonight you will take the train into —"

"I have to work tonight."

"Tough. Book off."

"That is not possible! Not tonight," he answered in a low voice. "Marie's mother —"

"Old broad with the nice manners upstairs at the front desk?"

"Yes. I must be here tonight. Tomorrow? Can we meet tomorrow?"

It was against my better judgment, but I agreed. I'd always had trouble saying no to Jean-Claude.

"Tomorrow morning then. There's a train from here at 10:31. Be on it. I'll meet you at the other end." I walked to the door leading out to the street, stopped and tossed the ring up. It glittered magically in the light before I snatched it out of the air. "Don't screw with me, Jean-Claude. I will not hesitate to come back here with this ring and tell your darling Marie what a lying rat you are. And I will show her papers that prove she's not the first Mrs. Lachance. Or should I say Luc Whatever-your-name-is-at-the-moment? Believe me, I will not hesitate one instant to ruin your life here."

The trip back to Paris was much different than the one out to Beauvais. I had faced down the enemy and sent him packing with his tail between his legs.

True, I didn't know for certain that he wouldn't pull a bunk again. If it hadn't been for little Gaston and the love that had sprung into Jean-Claude's eyes the moment he looked down at that child, I would have held my ground. I was betting this whole enterprise on the fact that he loved his son completely and utterly — that he loved his son more than he had loved me.

I arrived back at Le Gare du Nord in the middle of the evening rush, and it was not pleasant. With seemingly everyone in the city streaming toward the trains but me, I felt like a lone salmon buffeted and battered as it tried to swim up the fastest-flowing stream ever.

Backing up against a wall in the lee of a pillar, I pulled out my tourist book to look for a restaurant we could go to the next day. I was determined it was going to be good, and that also meant expensive. That was the least Jean-Claude owed me.

Of course, he would also be rather unhappy when I told him what I expected him to do.

I arrived back at my room tired and very hungry. I figured I'd go to one of the restaurants I'd seen the previous evening at the top of the street. But first I wanted a shower. The afternoon's work had left me feeling gritty. In more ways than one.

After stripping off my clothes, I glanced at the computer and realized I hadn't bothered to check my inbox before I left for Beauvais. This incessant checking of email thing everyone always told me about hadn't taken hold with me yet. Drumming my fingers while the computer turned itself on, I wondered if Tony had gotten back to me.

He had and I felt my blood pressure go through the roof as I read what he'd done.

Dearest Marta,

I was so worried about you that I have decided to come because I haven't heard from you today and I just have the feeling you will need someone on hand. I am en route to Paris. If I do

not hear from you in the meantime, I will head
for downtown. I am texting this on my cell, so
all you need to do is send me a normal email
and I'll be able to read it on this.

Tony

He didn't say when the plane was due in, but his email
had been written at nearly eleven o'clock the previous
evening. I did a quick sum in my head. Unless the flight
had a ridiculous stopover, Tony would have arrived by
mid-afternoon at the latest. Where the heck was he?

As if in answer, the computer pinged at me.

Marta,

I am finally in Paris, and I've had an awful trip.
My plane from London to Paris was socked in
by fog and I have only just arrived.

Please let me know that you're safe!

Call me. I'd like to take you out to dinner.

Tony

I felt like banging my head on the table. After the
day I'd had, a quick meal or even just some bread and
soup and an early evening was more my speed. The
last thing I wanted to do was get dressed up and go
out to dinner.

Since my cellphone only worked in North America, that meant getting dressed and trooping up the hill to the phone booth I'd used the previous evening. My thoughts were unprintable as I made the trek.

Tony must have had his phone in his hand, because it barely rang once. "Marta?"

"Yes, Tony, it's me."

"You sound angry. I'm sorry. I just couldn't stay away."

"I'm tired. It's been a very trying day."

"Would a nice dinner fix you up?"

I shook my head and sighed. Why was the man always so damn cheerful? It made it so much harder to yell at him.

"Where are you right now?" I asked resignedly.

"I had no idea where you're staying, so I just headed for the Opera Garnier. Are you around here?"

"Unfortunately, no."

"Do you want me to come to you?"

You shouldn't be here! I yelled at him in my head.

"Marta? Are you still on the line?"

I sighed again. "Do you speak French?"

"About as well as any Ontario high school student."

"That settles it. It's probably best for me to come to you. Do you already have someplace in mind to eat?"

"The Café de la Paix is across the street. Do you know it?"

"Yes, and it's very pricey."

"I've come all this way to take you to dinner. Why do it on the cheap?"

"It's going to take me some time to get ready. I can probably be there by eight. You do need reservations for this place, you know."

He laughed. "Made them an hour ago."

I shook my head. "Pretty sure of yourself, weren't you?"

"I always live in hope."

Getting into a cab an hour later, I felt that control of this volatile situation seemed to be slipping away from me again.

Much as I was growing to really like Tony, I did not need the distraction of having him around right now. To accomplish my task, I needed a tight grip on the reins and complete focus.

Husbands and lovers are never a good mix at the best of times.

Chapter Twenty

Cracking open an eye, I stared out at the murky light of the dull morning filtering through the partially closed curtains. Once again, I'd forgotten to check whether they were properly pulled together. Today, though, it didn't make much difference. Judging by the lack of light, the sky must have been piled with dark clouds.

I couldn't believe I'd done it again. When I'd left to meet Tony the previous evening, it had been with every intention of asking him to get a room in a hotel for at least that one night. Today, it was essential that my head be clear and my brain functioning at its very best.

At that moment, it was neither of those things.

Dinner the previous evening had been perfect in a way only the French can manage. The Café de la Paix, being right across the street from the opera house, plus the fact that I'd dined there several times with Gerhard in the distant past, meant that I'd been recognized immediately by its maître d'.

"Mademoiselle Hendriks! It is such a pleasure to see you again and after so long a time."

I knew a little polite French chiding when I heard it. "Actually, I am meeting a friend. His name is Antonio Lusardi."

"Ah! Monsieur Tony. *Oui*, he has been waiting rather impatiently for you," the little man had replied.

Tony had secured one of the best tables in the room. How, I had no idea. It overlooked the Place de l'Opéra with a perfect view of the Palais Garnier as it glittered in the night, alive with people attending the ballet on this particular evening.

He'd risen as I'd approached the table, producing a bouquet of roses and a huge smile. I presented my cheeks for rather chaste kissing. Charming as he might be, he was still in the doghouse as far as I was concerned.

The maître d' hovered for a moment to get me seated. The sommelier arrived shortly after with a bottle of rather expensive champagne, which he opened with a great flourish.

"Roses and champagne, too?" I said with a shake of my head as we clinked glasses.

"I had no idea how you would react to my being here," Tony answered. "This is a special night for me. Can you believe that despite my many trips to Europe,

I somehow never made it to Paris?" We looked across at the opera house for a moment. "I've dreamed of seeing it all my life," he told me.

"You've certainly picked an excellent vantage point."

"It is more beautiful than I imagined." Then he looked at me and lifted his glass again. "And so are you, Marta."

I smiled despite myself. "Look around you. Garnier also designed the interior of this café."

"Really? I didn't know that."

I picked up my menu. In line with the sumptuous decor, the location and the restaurant's standing, the expense of a meal was suitably horrendous. When I'd eaten here with Gerhard so many years ago now, I never thought about it. One never thought about anything as mundane as the cost of a meal when in Fosch's company. I'd probably ordered from one of the "lady's menus" — the ones with no prices.

The food was indeed as good as ever, and I found myself enjoying it. Tony was also just so damned enthusiastic about being in Paris. It made me think of my first visit and how smitten I'd been with the French capital. New York overwhelms you, crushing you down with its size. The City of Light overwhelms you but lifts you up. I'd forgotten that.

Over coffee and mille-feuille, a favourite dessert, I noticed Tony studying me intently.

"What?" I laughed. "Do I have a bit of pastry cream on the tip of my nose?"

He seemed to snap out of it. "No. No. I was just wondering if you've had any luck with your search, that's all."

The nice place where the meal, the location, and the company had sent me was suddenly blown into a million pieces. I had known it would only be a matter of time, but I still didn't welcome the intrusion. "Um, it's been going well, I guess."

He took both of my hands across the table and looked at me steadily. "Did you find him?"

"Look," I said, "can we talk about this later?"

He didn't answer for a moment, then tried smiling but it wasn't his best. "Yeah, sure."

Pointing at the long colonnade running the length of the front of the opera, where I could see people out getting a breath of fresh air, I said, "Must be intermission."

Tony turned and the bad moment drifted off to the side but not away.

After our meal (with complimentary cognac), Tony paid the bill without even wincing and we walked out onto the Place de l'Opéra. The night was chilly, but clearer than it had been all day, and the opera house twinkled magically under the spotlights focused on it from nearby buildings.

"What's it like to step out on that stage?" Tony asked.

"Amazing ... just amazing. You can't help but be aware of where you are. Vienna's like that, too. Imagine performing in an opera on the same stage where it was premiered. I've done that once or twice. These old houses have such history to them. We mostly lack that in North America. We're too young."

A cab drifted by and Tony had hailed it. "I want to see a bit of Paris. Will you show it to me?"

Tony's arm was draped over my waist, and I could tell from his breathing that he was still very much asleep. He'd been fine through dinner and the cab ride, which eventually led us back to my apartment.

Men have the reputation of falling asleep quickly after making love, but last night had to have set a record. Tony was out like a light within one minute. My pride wanted me to think that it had not been purely due to jet lag.

Over the course of the next five minutes, I slowly eased my way out of the bed so Tony would not wake. It wasn't quite 7:30, and we hadn't stayed up that late. So why did I feel as if I hadn't slept?

After throwing on the jeans and sweater I'd worn to Beauvais the day before, I slipped out the door and made my way downstairs to the street.

The previous day, the other person staying at the main house of the B&B had waxed poetic over breakfast about a small boulangerie he'd discovered at the top of the hill where this street led. "The best croissants in Paris," he'd told me enthusiastically. "And the coffee! Oh my ... Simply superb."

A good double shot of espresso was exactly what this girl needed.

Even though the damp chill really bit, the three-minute walk up the cobblestoned street did me a lot of good.

There is something about walking into the steamy warmth of a bakery early on a cold morning. From the back wafted the smell of some sort of sweet pastry, and the young woman behind the counter was just laying out an armful of crisp baguettes.

A few small tables ran along the wall opposite the counters, half of them occupied by elderly men looking as if they were missing their morning smoke as they drank coffee and read the newspaper or argued about politics with their neighbors. It still made me shake my head in wonder that France had successfully outlawed smoking indoors in public places. I remember being driven out of bistros and cafés by the thick pall of acrid smoke that bit at the back of my throat and made my eyes water.

I would have liked to sit for a minute and enjoy a coffee, but decided against it. So I bought two triple shots of espresso, four croissants, and a jar of apricot jam "bonne femme," then headed out into the cold again.

Even though it was nearly eight o'clock, the city still had not shaken off the gloom of night I sipped my coffee and thought about Jean-Claude as I walked downhill to the apartment.

The previous day, I'd been handed a gift in the shape of a baby boy. What I was going to ask the child's doting father to do was something I expected to be a really hard sell. Twenty-four hours ago, I would have given it a five-to-one chance I'd convince him. After my trip to Beauvais, the percentage was up to fifty-fifty — easy.

I could hear the shower running as I stuck my key in the door. I didn't think Tony would go for what I needed from him, but maybe a nice bit of breakfast would help my bitter pill go down with less difficulty.

"It's me," I said, putting the food down on the small table.

Tony heard me easily over the water. "Out for an early walk?"

"I went up the street for coffee and croissants. You going to be long?"

"I'm done," was his answer as he snapped off the shower and slid the glass doors back.

He began vigorously drying his hair, and I must say that my poor heart beat a little faster as my eyes ran over his lean, muscular body. Tony had a lot there for a gal to admire.

I was already sipping my coffee at the apartment's tiny table when he sat down across from me, pants on, no shirt, feet still bare.

"Mmm. Great coffee," he said. "I wouldn't have believed the French were as good at this as the Italians."

"Don't say that sort of thing in public," I answered, breaking off a piece of croissant. "The natives don't take those sorts of comments very well."

"So what's on the docket for today? Last night you were very close-lipped about what you've been doing since you got here."

I looked up. "I'm glad you brought that up, Tony. Actually, I'm meeting my husband for lunch today."

"I don't like the way you said that. Is there something you're not telling me?"

"No. We need to talk about some things, that's all."

Tony put down his coffee. "What sorts of things?"

"Things."

"Marta, you're stonewalling me. Back in Toronto, I felt we were in this together. Why am I being cut out now?"

"The situation is considerably more complicated than I expected. Not only that, I'm meeting with my husband for Christ's sake! I can hardly take you along."

"You are going to talk to him about what's been happening back in Canada, aren't you? Or have you already done that? Tell me, Marta."

"We really didn't get very far yesterday. Like I said, it's more complicated than I was expecting."

"Why?"

"Because he has a son ..." I paused. "And a new wife."

Tony took a moment to sort that out. I stared at his face in hopes of getting a clue about what was going on in his head.

"How can you possibly trust him to show up today?"

"Because I saw the way he looked at that little boy. He's caught between a rock and a hard place if I blow the whistle on him." I looked across the table. "And I threatened to do that if he doesn't play ball with me."

"But he's run out on people twice already — and one of them was you."

"I know, I know."

"You should have someone along today," Tony said and held up his hand as I immediately began to object. "No. Hear me out. I don't want to know what you talk to him about. That's private. I could just keep an eye on things from a distance. Make sure nothing goes wrong. I came all this way to help you. Please let me!"

I ate my second croissant silently and finished the last of the coffee, thinking things over.

"Tony," I began, reaching out for his hands, but he drew them back. He could read me too well by half. "I need to do this alone. Nothing will happen. How can it? We'll be in a public place, a restaurant. Why don't you just spend the day doing some sightseeing? Visit the Eiffel Tower or the Louvre? We can meet up again for dinner."

Our very first argument raged for a good ten minutes before my emotions got the better of me.

"I will not have you there! It will be too much of a distraction. If you won't listen, then I'll have to ask you to leave!"

Tony glared at me for a good five seconds before he got up, finished dressing, put on his overcoat, then left the apartment without a word, taking his suitcase with him.

I felt simply awful and suddenly unsure whether I'd made the right decision. I only hoped that after today's events were all over, I could patch things up with him. Why had everything conspired against me to have Tony come along at just the wrong time? The thought that I might never see him again caused my throat to constrict in panic. I considering sending him an email, trying to explain, but fought down that urge. The idea of giving in was too seductive.

I desperately needed to calm myself, get focused. Today's agenda required that. At the moment, it felt as if I was going to explode.

That's when I spotted my stick bag. Okay, I thought. If you want to hit something, Marta, make it a practice pad.

So for the next hour and a half, I worked out all my aggression on an inanimate object that was meant to be hit. I also broke two drum sticks in my fury. That was all to the good, since I ended my practice session limp and sweaty, but also more at peace and focused on what I needed to accomplish.

After taking a shower, I put on a warm wool dress, nicer clothes than what I'd been wearing the past three days, and left for Le Gare du Nord in good time to meet the train from Beauvais. With the early November wind beginning to pick up as I walked the tree-lined boulevard to Place d'Italie, I was glad I'd put on my beret, thick scarf, and gloves, all a matching shade of deep red. The Métro took me directly to the station with no transfers needed, and I parked myself impatiently at the track where Jean-Claude's train would arrive.

When it pulled in, my husband was not among the people getting off. The last few stragglers gave me a wide berth, probably due to the expression on my face as it became clear that I'd been had.

Well, I'd told him what would happen if he didn't do as I said, and I had every intention of carrying through on that threat as I looked up at the TV screen listing all departures from these tracks. The very next train to Beauvais was going to have me aboard.

Someone tapped my shoulder. I spun around and standing there was Jean-Claude, dressed all in leather, with a stupid grin plastered on his face. "I always loved the way you look when you are angry."

I continued to glare at him, knowing that if I opened my mouth, it would be to let loose a string of obscenities.

"I decided to drive my new motorcycle into town instead of taking the train," he told me when the silence got awkward.

I couldn't believe it. "And you honestly expect me to ride on a motorcycle in what I'm wearing?"

"Well, I cannot leave it outside the station. It will get stolen for sure."

I could have argued about it, but then decided it just wasn't worth the trouble. I'd planned on having Jean-Claude take me to the Café Marly, a chic resto on the north side of the Louvre — and expensive. He needed knocking down a few pegs. The thought of riding on the back of a motorcycle all the way into the heart of Paris was thoroughly without enticement for any number of reasons, so I searched my mind and realized that another very good (and rather expensive) restaurant was actually quite nearby.

Shaking my head, I sighed. "Lead on."

The motorcycle he'd built was pure Jean-Claude. It was big, it was loud, and it was colourful. I just hoped nobody from the press recognized me as I hoisted myself on the back, hiking my overcoat up in a rather unladylike way and slipping the helmet over my head. When we took off, I had to grip Jean-Claude hard to keep from falling off. I ground my teeth in frustration for even having to touch him.

The restaurant was one where I'd last dined more than a dozen years back while living in Paris for four months with Gerhard. He'd been preparing a production of *Tannhäuser* for the Paris Opera. Café Julien is a throwback to *La Belle Époque* with decor that hasn't changed in a hundred years. It would give me a touch more confidence for this meeting to be eating in a place with which I was so familiar.

With great aplomb, Jean-Claude pulled his motorcycle right onto the sidewalk out front. Back in Canada, he would have gotten a big fat ticket for doing that. Here it was the accepted practice.

I used my reflection in the front window of the restaurant to smooth out my hair. It was a good bet I'd be recognized as soon as we entered. Restaurants in Paris tend to keep the same wait staff for centuries.

The place was as I remembered: high ceilings, and murals of women and peacocks shared the walls with huge mirrors that made the large room seem limitless. But it was the stained glass skylights in greens and blues that I recalled most vividly. I'd once joked with Gerhard that it made me feel as if I were eating underwater. Odd coat trees, each with a large globe light on top, ran down the centre of the room, dividing the two groups of tables. I greeted them like old friends. Too bad frock coats and top hats have long since gone out of fashion. Ski jackets just don't cut it hanging from furniture like that.

Even after so many years, it felt like home. But I had returned to have lunch with my dead husband.

"Ah, Mademoiselle Hendriks, how good it is to see you once again!" the maître d' said smoothly as he swooped down on us near the entryway. "You honour us once again with your presence."

I couldn't for the life of me remember his name, but recognized him as having been a waiter way back when. I smiled and reached out to shake his hand, but it was snatched and enthusiastically kissed.

"Could I request a secluded table for myself and my friend?" I asked.

"But of course!" was the answer as he led us to one in the very back as far away from the other diners as you could get, seating me with my back to the rear wall of the restaurant. With a practised snap, he unfolded our napkins and placed them on our laps.

Our waiter arrived and took drink orders: Perrier for me, red wine for Jean-Claude.

"So I am here as you asked," Jean-Claude said, lounging back in his chair. "How did you track me to Beauvais?"

Looking over his head I could just barely see the brilliant red of his motorcycle out front and could not resist smirking as someone stopped to look over the attention-grabbing machine. "It was Harley Davidson that did you in."

His brow furrowed. "What?"

"When I saw you near the Sully-Morland Métro entrance, you were carrying the tailpipe for your motorcycle. The paper covering it had started to slip off. It just took me several weeks to realize what I'd seen. After that it was simple. There aren't many Harley dealers in Paris. I knew you'd buy nothing else."

Jean-Claude looked unhappy. "I brought Marie with me because she wanted to visit a friend. If I'd just had them ship the part to me, this wouldn't have happened. That was the only time I'd been in Paris all year."

I was suddenly confused. "But you also were outside the stage entrance at the Palais Garnier two nights later."

He looked across the table at me and sighed. "It was a very stupid thing to do."

"What was?"

"I had seen your picture in the paper and read a review. Since Marie was tied up with her friend, I had nothing to do that night."

"So you decided to hang around outside the opera?"

"No."

"Why were you there then?"

"I ... I went to hear you sing. It is a very long opera to stand through. Next time I will get a ticket for a seat."

I flopped back in my chair, completely stunned. Was Jean-Claude lying? Why would he? Was he trying to get to me?

The waiter setting down our drinks gave me time to marshal my thoughts. My husband mustn't know that he'd just delivered a brain-shattering blow, so I rubbed my brow and frowned, intimating that I had a headache, after which I rummaged in my purse as if looking for aspirin. He silently watched my every move.

I already knew what I wanted from the luncheon menu, but I made a pretense of studying it to gain additional time.

After all those opportunities to see me perform, he'd chosen that night? He'd certainly been there in the Place de l'Opéra. If he had used this story as a ploy to get to me, it had certainly worked.

When the waiter returned to take our order, I asked for a half-litre of the house Bordeaux. To hell with my good intentions to keep my head clear. I needed something to calm me down.

Jean-Claude's patience, or maybe his nerve, appeared to be at an end. "So why have you dragged me all the way into Paris? What is it you want, Marta? An apology? All right, you have that unconditionally. Maybe I just freaked out when that man appeared at our house. All I could think of was trying to survive. After that, I ran."

"What did happen?"

A pained expression flitted across his face. "I had been into Perth to pick up some supplies I needed. The guy they sent arrived while I was gone. You have to understand that bikers don't use things like high powered rifles, or I would have been dead getting out of the truck. They want their assassinations to have that personal touch.

"I had just started using my pneumatic nail gun and you know how noisy the compressor was, not to mention the gun, or I might have heard him. Next thing I knew, there was someone standing next to me. I looked up and could see right up the barrel of his pistol. He grinned down at me and said, 'Gotcha.'

"He was holding the gun in his right hand and I could see the fool still had the safety on. I quickly pressed the nail gun against the top of his boot and pulled the trigger a few times."

"Oh my God!" I said involuntarily, cringing at the thought of nails going through someone's foot.

Jean-Claude's smile was grim. "It was enough. He looked down for that split second I needed. I knocked the pistol from his hand by smashing it with the nail gun. After that, it didn't take too long. They hadn't sent one of their experienced men. I suppose it was someone trying to make his mark. You cannot be a full-patch member of a biker gang unless you've killed someone."

"And you used the fire to cover up your tracks."

"It was fortunate that he was nearly the same size as me. I knew that I had been given an unbelievable chance. I sat down to think and it didn't take too long to come up with a scenario that just might work. I switched my clothes with his and stuck my wedding band on his finger, although I didn't expect the fire would leave much trace if I did everything right. The propane tank I was using for the heater was nearly full and had seen a lot of years, so the safety fence around the top was loose and a bit bent. I just helped it along with a mallet. After that, I laid the tank down in the stone fireplace so it couldn't shoot off anywhere and placed the body about five feet in front of it. The rest you can figure out I'm sure. When I smashed off the guard and then the handle to make it look as if they'd hit something when the tank had been knocked over, you would not believe how the flames shot out. I almost didn't make it out alive." He chuckled. "I had to jump out a window."

"You did it all very well," I responded sourly.

The meal arrived but my confit de canard and potatoes simply stuck in my throat as I tried to eat. I've always had a vivid imagination and what I'd just been told would haunt my dreams for a long time to come.

Jean-Claude had been silent for several minutes, but as I swallowed a bit of my wine, he looked across at me. "You do know that I was working with the Crown and was going to testify?"

I nodded.

"It was either me or him, Marta. There was someone in the Mounties who was a rat. The other two witnesses had been brought down, and I only escaped twice by the skin of my teeth. They were at the front door of my house in B.C. only moments after I'd jumped out a back window. There were two of them that time. I was very lucky."

"You seem to jump out a lot of windows."

"The second time, I knew I had to leave without a trace and never come back, never contact anyone again. And that had to include you."

"Lucky me."

Chapter Twenty-One

We ate in silence for a few minutes and I relaxed a little as the wine began having an effect. The confit was everything I remembered, but I simply could not enjoy it, which I resented more than I probably should have. The sooner I could get this mess over with, the sooner I could get back to a normal life — if you could call the life of an opera singer normal. And in the background hovered Tony, if that was still a viable relationship after what had happened earlier.

I laid down my fork and knife. It could not be put off any longer.

"When I began to figure out what was going on,"

I told Jean-Claude earnestly, "the first thing I came up with was your *grand-mère*'s address."

He looked across the table at me. "How did you get that?"

"From the mess in your pickup truck. My brother stuck it underneath the barn after the fire and I searched it. There were papers and receipts behind the seat."

"Oh well," Jean-Claude grinned, "you were always after me to clean it out. And now I'm suffering for it."

"I got the feeling someone else had searched it."

He shrugged. "When I took the dead man's car to make my getaway, I had no idea where I was going, so it wouldn't have been easy to follow me. They wouldn't learn anything they didn't already know from what was in my truck."

"I learned what a bastard you are."

"Let's not get back on that again. You have your apology. What else do you want?"

"How did you get out of the country and into France without being detected?"

"False I.D. is not hard to get when you live on the fringe as I have. It just costs so bloody much now, though. When I arrived in France, I had only ten dollars in my pocket."

I pulled the conversation back from its detour. "Your *grand-mère* —"

"How is the old lady?" he asked, as if suddenly realizing he had a grandmother.

"Well, right now she thinks you're dead." When Jean-Claude frowned, I added, "She's the only relative you've got and she loves you. You really should let her know you're okay."

"You know why that's impossible. If anyone else finds out I'm alive, there will be no safety for me. I know too much for them to let me live. She will talk to her friends. She always does. And it could put her in danger."

"Jean-Claude, do you know who the rotten Mountie is? I need to know."

There was a flash of anger in his eyes, but also something else. Fear?

He leaned across the table, and asked with an intensity I'd never heard in his voice before, "Exactly who in the Mounties did you talk to?"

"When I was in Montreal, someone named Parker interviewed me."

"*Merde!* When was this?"

"Soon after I got back from Paris." I quickly sketched how I'd gone to the farm, then to Montreal, and finally about the Mountie turning up at my hotel shortly after I'd seen Jean-Claude's *grand-mère*. "I got the feeling they'd somehow been watching the farm. Parker also knew I'd spoken to Madame Lachance."

"And you told Parker nothing about seeing me?"

Again there was that intensity. I began to wonder if Parker, the cop who couldn't let go, was the bad apple in the Mountie barrel.

"Relax," I said grimly. "I can't afford to have it get out that I'm seeing dead people. Since my meltdown when you supposedly died, my reputation is bad enough as it is. I had to be sure about what I'd seen in Paris."

I paused until he looked up at me. "There's something else you need to know."

"What?"

"After talking to your *grande-mère*, I decided to talk to a reporter who knows all about biker gangs and —"

"*Tabernac!*" Jean-Claude said too loudly, causing several people in the restaurant to curiously look in our direction. "You told a reporter? You stupid, stupid woman!"

I sighed and shook my head. "I didn't tell him anything. I just asked if he'd ever heard of you, and if so, what had he heard. He only had your name in an old database, but said he would ask a reporter friend in B.C. who might know a bit more."

"You swear that was all?"

"No. That isn't all." I took a deep breath. "Two days later, both men were murdered."

It was as if the statement fell out of my mouth, rolled to the middle of the table and sat there while we both stared down at it. The silence lasted a good minute.

Finally, Jean-Claude's shoulders slumped.

I leaned forward. "The reporter in Montreal who died was Sébastien Bouchard. Did you ever meet him?"

"I had heard of him. Always eager for the inside scoop. Looks like he scooped a little too deep."

If Jean-Claude thought I'd even crack a grin at his little pun, he was sorely mistaken.

"He was the *chum* of one of my best friends," I said, using the Quebec slang for boyfriend. "And I want to get the people responsible for this."

"How do you plan on accomplishing that?"

"You."

There. It had been said. Jean-Claude's eyes bugged out of his head, and his hand, near his glass of wine, jerked, knocking it over, after which it rolled off the table and loudly shattered on the tile floor.

As a waiter rushed to our assistance, my husband's eyes narrowed. "You are mad!"

We kept our mouths tightly shut while the waiter cleaned up and the maitre d' came over with a fresh glass of wine.

Jean-Claude picked up the glass and swallowed almost all the liquid in one go.

"I barely escaped with my life last time," he finally said. "You can be certain the next time I won't be so lucky."

"Do you want to live the rest of your life looking over your shoulder? I asked you before and you sidestepped answering. I'll ask you again: who is the Mountie who ratted you out?"

"I have a few guesses. But surely after what you have just told me about the death of those two journalists, the police are investigating."

"Yes, but they don't seem to be making any progress." Using my fork to punctuate my words, I added, "What concerns me is that Parker's still on your trail. It was pretty clear from our conversation he believes you're still alive."

"He is the one who busted me. Of course he won't give up! You've met him. Can't you see that?"

"Busted you? He told me you had agreed to help them."

Jean-Claude rolled his eyes disgustedly. "That is not how these things work, Marta. People in the position I was in don't help the cops because they want to. They help them because they have to. You are so naive."

"Parker told me you were helping voluntarily, that you wanted to put those men behind bars."

He smiled sadly. "You would really like to believe that, wouldn't you? I was set up, *ma chère*, pure and simple. Your Jean-Claude got caught with his hand in the cookie jar. Isn't that the way you always used to put it, as if I was some naughty child you needed to straighten out?"

That stung. I hadn't been aware that he'd thought I was so condescending toward him. I also had to acknowledge that it might even have some basis in fact. We came from such wildly different backgrounds. That was what had initially attracted me to him. He was my bad boy, exciting, intoxicating, so different from anyone I'd ever met. Little did I know.

I shook my head in an outward effort to stay on track. "So what did you get caught at?"

"The leader of the biker gang wanted me to kill someone. That's how guys like this get their dirty work done. It would have allowed me to finally become a full-patch member. I was young and stupid and full of myself. I thought I wanted to be a tough guy. But when it came down to it, I just couldn't cross that line. Some tough guy, eh?

"Turns out it was a lucky thing I had trouble with my morals. The guy I'd been sent to whack was an undercover cop. Perhaps those who sent me knew that. I can't be sure. They were probably laughing among themselves about poor, stupid Jean-Claude. Anyway, it was a set-up and I walked right into it.

"What option did I have? Testify or get sent up for attempted murder of a cop. I was caught between a rock and a very hard place. If I kept my mouth shut and went to prison, I would probably get knocked off there for not carrying through the bikers' orders. It would be a matter of honour for them, and they would have made an example of me for the others, show what happens when someone crosses them. My only choice was to work for the Mounties, help them gather information, testify, and then try to disappear into the night. Do you know what happened in B.C.?"

I nodded.

"That's when I fled back east. I needed money so I started doing handyman work. Then I came to your farm."

"Was I just a stopping point for you along the way?"

For a moment, Jean-Claude looked at me in the way that used to melt my heart, but now it was like watching a magic trick when you knew how it was done.

"You were so ... different, Marta. Perhaps I was rash. I did a stupid thing, but I wanted to stay. In my arrogance, I thought I could keep a low profile in Ontario and make a life with you."

"And now?"

"*Ma chère*, I cannot go back to that life. It is over."

His arrogance stunned me. As if I ever would take him back! "Your son ..."

"Yes, my son. I am every day so surprised how fatherhood has changed me. You and I never would have had children. It was just not in the cards with your career always being first."

Dessert arrived and I looked down at the plate of tiny, exquisite one-bite pastries and pushed it away.

"Jean-Claude, you must come back to Canada, if not for yourself than for your son. Unless you end it, someday they will find you and it might not be just you who gets killed. Surely you can see that?"

He actually seemed to think that over. We were now out on the tip of the knife. One way or the other, he was going to finish this, but he didn't know that yet. I had that lever that had already forced him to Paris to meet with me. I would use it again — not that I wanted to. It would be better for everyone if he did this on his own.

Finally he came to his decision.

"No," he said with complete commitment. "I will not do it. I tried to do the right thing, and it twice nearly got me killed. They did not protect me. In fact, they did the opposite. Two of my friends died. No. I am through."

"Then you leave me no alternative. Don't think I —"

"You will not turn me in."

"I'm warning you."

"No, Marta. I cannot believe you have become so completely hateful that you would do that to my family." He caught the waiter's eye and signalled for the bill, then looked across the table at me and in his eyes was only tenderness and love, no anger. Whether it was truly there or simply another deceit, I could not tell.

"I am leaving now. You are going to fly off to wherever it is you are performing next. You will forget all about finding me and we will never see each other again. I know you will do this because you are a good person."

The waiter brought over the bill and Jean-Claude barely glanced at it before pulling out a wad of cash. He peeled off a few bills, then got to his feet.

"Marta, you do the right thing. There is nothing to be gained in this affair by ruining even more lives. Let it go. Know that I will always hold you in a special place in my heart because of what you will be doing."

Jean-Claude's voice and manner were so soft and gentle that I found myself responding almost as if hypnotized. Yes, it would be easy to watch him walk the length of the restaurant, then get on his motorcycle and disappear to Beauvais again. He was almost certain to be safe in such a backwater. He looked and sounded so different. Too many lives had already been wrecked. It would be on my head if anything more were to happen. I squeezed my eyes shut as he turned to leave. This was for the best.

While my eyes were closed, I could see Lainey as she'd looked when she'd arrived in Toronto: pale, ragged, miserable, and somehow physically diminished by her loss. Now she'd been physically attacked. It couldn't end here. This was what had hardened my heart. Things had to be put back into balance by making sure that those who had done evil were made to face justice.

"No, Jean-Claude, I cannot do what you ask. At least five people have died because a man, an officer of the law, did not do what he had sworn to do. I don't really care about the bikers. I care about a cop who broke faith. I will see him stopped. I can help you with this. We will take this right to the top with the Mounties and I will move heaven and earth to make sure you and your family are protected."

"You? How can you do that?"

"By using who I am. We can leave now for the Canadian Embassy. I met the ambassador at a party when I was last here, and I can get us in to see him. Tell him what you know, and they will catch this rogue cop. Please don't force me to go there alone, because I will if I have to. Do it for little Gaston and Marie. You must do the right thing."

I'd put everything I had into what I'd just said, every bit of sincerity, and I suddenly felt I could do what I had promised. I had to.

Jean-Claude sighed and shook his head. "No. I am through trusting — even you. Every time I have trusted, it has got me in trouble. No!" He got up from the table again and looked down at me grimly. "Do your worst!"

I got up and followed.

At the front of the restaurant, as we got our coats on, I thanked the maître d' for the lovely meal I'd hardly touched. Passing through the small entryway, we found ourselves once again on the jostling sidewalk of the busy Paris side street.

I started to give it one more try with Jean-Claude, unwilling to let go, but also unwilling to hurt his little family.

A truck that was parked directly in front of the restaurant pulled away and I could see across the street where a car was partially up on the sidewalk, illegally parked. Behind that stood a small taverne, its front covered in those big sliding glass doors, indicating that tables would have been spread across the sidewalk in warmer weather.

I don't know what caused me to look farther into the building. Maybe it was a movement on the other side of the glass, maybe it was fate, but suddenly I could see Tony sitting there, a glass of wine on the table in front of him.

My anger erupted. How dare he after what I'd told him?

Without even looking right for traffic on the one-way street, I stepped off the sidewalk. Jean-Claude, noticing my danger, grabbed at my arm. His gesture did little to stop my forward motion.

"Marta! What are you doing?"

"I can't believe he followed me!" I spluttered.

Tony saw me coming and threw some money onto the table as he quickly got to his feet.

By that point, Jean-Claude had let go of my arm. A truck's horn blared as it barreled down the street. Typical impatient French drivers.

As Tony came through the door of the taverne, I dodged around the illegally parked car, then turned to look back at Jean-Claude.

He was standing in the middle of the street, glaring at me with unmistakable disgust. It was easy to see that he thought my meddling had set him up, that Tony was either a cop or an assassin.

The truck driver honked again impatiently, and Jean-Claude stepped farther onto the road instead of back to the sidewalk.

Swinging quickly into the vacant parking spot in front of the restaurant, that truck saved his life, probably mine and Tony's, as well.

It hadn't even stopped moving when the bomb went off.

Chapter Twenty-Two

The whole universe came unglued.

The earth under my feet, the buildings around me, the very air itself seemed to become liquid, and I possessed no ability to stand against it.

Tony, barely five feet in front of me, had a look of horror on his face as I flew forward and landed hard on my side. He was knocked to his knees but had the presence of mind to huddle over, protecting his head, because it was suddenly raining glass. My right hand was under my body, but I'd used my left to try to break my fall and it was unprotected. I felt a sharp stab as something bit into it.

As suddenly as it had come, the wave passed, and everything solidified once again — painfully.

As I began to understand what had happened and realized the explosion had been behind me, I rolled onto my side and lifted my head.

Jean-Claude lay face down in the street. The truck that had protected us from the worst of the blast had been flipped on its side. Smoke rose from behind it. It fluttered into my rattled brain that it might explode, too.

Something touched my face and I moved my eyes again to see Tony bending over me. His mouth moved but all I could hear was a buzzing sound.

"I'm all right, I think," I told him. "Go see about Jean-Claude."

I had to repeat it twice, but finally Tony nodded and moved out of my line of sight.

Probably twenty seconds had passed since the bomb had ripped the world apart, but it felt like a day.

Can't lie here on the sidewalk, I told myself. *There must be people who need help.*

I sat up and took stock of how I felt. It didn't think I'd broken anything, but my whole body ached. Alerted by sharp pain in my left hand, I turned my head and saw a shard of glass several inches long sticking out of it. Quite calmly, considering how squeamish I am about blood, I pulled it out. Examining the one-inch wound further, it appeared as if it hadn't hit anything crucial. My hand still moved just fine, although flexing it caused blood to come out far more rapidly and hurt like hell.

I know now that I was suffering from deep shock, but I seemed so calm at the time, almost detached, as I took my wool and silk scarf, a Christmas present from my sister and something I dearly loved, and wrapped it tightly around my dripping hand. My badly-skinned knees would have to wait until later.

Suddenly remembering Jean-Claude again, I got unsteadily to my feet and went to where Tony was kneeling next to him.

"He's knocked out, but I think that's because he bounced off the car." The sound of Tony's words barely made it past the swarm of bees inside my head, but I understood enough by also reading his lips.

"He's not dead?" I asked, kneeling down, too, and putting my mouth near Tony's ear so he might hear me better.

"He's still breathing," he said into my ear.

"Do you think he has any internal injuries?"

Tony gave me a half-smile. "I'm not a doctor, Marta."

Jean-Claude let out a groan I could hear even through my diminished hearing. The fog in my head began clearing at the same time. I looked up. From everywhere, people were running toward us.

"We have to get him out of here!" I said into Tony's ear.

He said into mine, "No! We should wait here for medical help. You're both bleeding."

In the middle of all this destruction, it suddenly struck me how stupid we both must look having to talk into each others' ears. A giggle slipped out, then another. I firmly took hold of myself, knowing that hysteria was lurking just below the surface.

Jean-Claude moved with a groan and I sat down cradling his head in my lap, afraid that he might be dying and wanting him to not be without comfort on the cold street.

Blood was seeping from a cut on his forehead, along his left eyebrow, then down onto my skirt. I dabbed it as best I could with my scarf-wrapped hand, but what he really needed was a bandage — if not stitches. It was the only outward sign of damage we could find.

Tony and I looked at each other, knowing that there could well be serious internal injuries. I felt sick.

Jean-Claude's eyelids fluttered, then opened. Moving his bent left leg a bit, he looked up at me, his expression questioning.

I leaned down in case his head was also full of angrily buzzing bees. "It was a bomb. You've been unconscious."

At the word "bomb," Jean-Claude's brain finally caught and held. "Help me up. I must get away."

I looked up at Tony. "Help me get him to his feet."

Tony shook his head and shouted at me, "That's not a good idea."

I struggled with Jean-Claude's shoulders, trying to wrestle him to a sitting position. "Please!" I pleaded. "I need your help."

It looked as if he was still going to balk, but Tony finally took the injured man's hands, and easily got him to a sitting position. I rose to my knees and together we got Jean-Claude very shakily to his feet.

"Now, let's get going," I said, standing up, too. "It's not safe here."

"But there will be ambulances on the way!" Tony protested. "You both need to get to a hospital."

I shook my head. "No. That bomb was meant for us."

People continued to stream into the street from both ends, stupidly clogging the access emergency vehicles would need. Some probably wanted to help, but many were no doubt there to gawk at the dead and dying. Regardless, the crush would provide cover and protection.

Jean-Claude began moving, and needing our help to keep standing, forced us to go along, his arms around our necks. He seemed a little more aware, but his complexion was grey and he was limping badly. Between his cut forehead and my hand and knees, we must have been a sorry sight indeed. The passing crowd, looking shocked, opened up to let us through as we made our way toward a huge and very incongruous triumphal arch seemingly dropped into the middle of the intersection at the end of the block.

All three of us kept our eyes wide open for any sort of trouble, but if there was someone following us, I couldn't see them.

By the time we got to the circular bit of road that curved around the arch, the area was awash in cops, firemen, and emergency workers, all trying to get to the scene of the blast. In front of us, Boulevard Saint-Michel looked more like a parking lot than a busy Paris street.

"Even if we find an empty cab around here," Tony said, "it's not going to get us anywhere fast."

"There's the Métro," I said, pointing down the block.

"No. We need a cab."

At the next corner, we miraculously found one, and fortunately it was Tony who flagged it down. Jean-Claude was looking pretty bashed up, but I was horrified when my reflection in the cab's window showed I had a huge scrape on my cheek where it had slammed into the sidewalk. Tony, on the other hand, had escaped relatively untouched.

"Where are you staying?" Jean-Claude asked me in English as the poor driver, a man with skin as dark as night, turned in his seat and stared at the motley crew he'd allowed to stumble into his cab.

"Near Place d'Italie."

The driver understood enough of the conversation to pull out and deke down a side street. Even though he kept his eye on us throughout the trip, he kept his questions to himself. I suspected he was aware that the less he knew, the better.

No doubt it was due to shock and adrenaline, but I felt surprisingly fine. In a few hours, I knew I wouldn't be so sanguine. It was smart to go to ground before that hit.

"How are you feeling?" Tony finally asked as he dabbed at my cheek with a handkerchief.

The buzzing in my ears was slightly less. "Just a little stiff in my knees. I went down pretty hard."

Jean-Claude was slumped against the door on his side, still looking grey, his breathing rapid and shallow.

"You should both be going to hospital," Tony whispered as he looked down at the blood-soaked scarf wrapping my injured hand. "He could have serious internal injuries and you need stitches."

Jean-Claude answered in a surprisingly steady voice. "I am not going to the hospital, nor to the police. Now do you see how dangerous this little game you have been playing really is, Marta?"

"I can't believe that they found out where I was. I was so careful coming here."

My husband turned his head, his expression hard. "I could have stayed hidden indefinitely if you had not stirred up trouble."

I didn't have a good answer for that, and knew I never would.

The driver seemed a little confused about where to find Rue Alphand, the street where my rented apartment was located, so it was up to me to thread us through the maze of streets beyond the Place d'Italie. I made a few wrong choices but eventually got us there.

Jean-Claude and I struggled out of the car with Tony's help. The driver got horrendously overpaid, so he was happy as he raced off down the hill, tires bouncing noisily on the cobblestones.

Tony put one of Jean-Claude's arms over his shoulder, and helped him up the one flight on the curving staircase. I stumbled on ahead of them. We were quite the jolly crew returning home after a day's outing.

The apartment door had a really odd lock that had previously given me trouble, and in my state I just couldn't get it open. Tony stepped forward and took the key from me.

I told him, "You have to turn it twice and it sticks going around the second time."

It opened smoothly for him on the first try. Jean-Claude and I stumbled into the apartment after him.

"Don't lock the door," I said. "We may never get it open again."

Tony shrugged and just shut it, sticking the key in the lock on our side of the door.

Jean-Claude flopped down on the bed as I went into the bath alcove to see what I could do about cleaning myself up a bit.

The mirror told a rough story: that concert in Dallas next Tuesday would have one banged-up soprano on the stage. There was no way makeup was going to completely hide the two-inch scrape on my right cheek and the rising bruise and lump on my forehead. Inspecting the rest of my person, I discovered that both knees were equally scraped, so I set about gingerly cleaning the dirt out of them with a damp face cloth.

My scarf was a complete wreck, but at least the blood was now only oozing slowly from the cut on the back of my hand. It would definitely need stitches, but that would have to wait. I wrapped it up again in a hand towel.

My dress had two rips, and somewhere along the way I'd lost my beret and gloves. At least my heavy coat had padded my fall a bit. Still, all the damage was far better than having one's mortal remains being scooped up with a teaspoon. If that truck hadn't darted into the empty parking space when it did —

Out in the room, Tony and Jean-Claude were speaking in English. I cut short my self-nursing and walked back into the main room.

My husband was still on the bed, one arm over his eyes, and Tony was leaning against the bookcase on the far wall. I sat down heavily on one of the chairs at the small table, pushing my open drum stick bag out of the way so I could lean on my elbows.

"What were you discussing?" I asked.

"I was saying that they must have followed you to Paris," Jean-Claude answered. "How else could they have been at that restaurant today?"

I tightened my lips and shook my head. "Not with what I went through getting out of London."

"You've used credit cards since you've been here, though, haven't you?"

That was something I hadn't considered. I'd had to use my card to get some cash when I'd arrived two days earlier.

"They can access that?"

Jean-Claude lifted his head for a moment and looked at me. "They're cops, Marta, Mounties, for Christ's sake!" he snapped. "They can do whatever they bloody well want."

"But whoever is accessing bank records would be doing it illegally. He'd have to be worried about getting caught."

"He could be seen as legitimately searching for me."

The sun broke through my mental clouds. "Parker? He's the one who ratted on his own witnesses? That's a bit much."

"Do you have a better suggestion? There was always something about him that made my skin crawl."

Something bothered me, too, and I turned to Tony. "Did you see where the bomb was put?"

Jean-Claude finally sat up. "It had to be one of my cycle's saddlebags and I bet after it had done its job, they would have made out that I was going to kill you with it, Marta. That's just the sort of thing they'd do."

Tony looked at both of us for a moment. "To be honest, I wasn't watching the motorcycle. I was only there to make sure you were all right. My eyes were on the restaurant."

"It would have helped a lot if you'd seen something," I sighed. "It's like we're battling ghosts here."

As the effects of the adrenaline wore off, I was feeling worse and worse. My hands had begun shaking and the enormity of the situation was hammering at my aching head.

"Look," I continued, "we have to do something. We can't just sit here, calmly discussing this. People died on that street today. They died because we were there. The cops already know, or shortly will, that the motorcycle belonged to you, Jean-Claude."

Jean-Claude groaned, "Why did you have to come after me?"

I gave it right back, "That's a stupid thing to say! All along I've been trying to help you."

Tony stepped between us physically and verbally, talking in a surprisingly quiet and calm voice. "No. She's right. I shouldn't have let you leave the scene. I should have done what I was supposed to do in the first place. In all the confusion —"

I could feel the hair rising on the back of my neck. "Tony, dear God, surely you can't be —"

Neither of us ever finished our sentences because I heard the door swing open behind me.

"Can't be what, Ms. Hendriks?" said a voice I'd heard before but couldn't immediately place.

Whirling around, I found myself staring at Inspector

Parker of the RCMP, the suspected turncoat.

"You two look surprised to see me," he said, shifting his gaze to the left. "Hello, JC. It's been awhile."

The object of the cop's attention made no response but glared intently.

I was momentarily confused by Parker's comment. You two? Whom had he meant? There were three of us in the room.

The situation became crystal clear when Parker said to Tony, "You should have kept them at the scene of the explosion. Things are really going to be complicated now."

Tony shook his head. "You hadn't gotten there. I decided it was best to get Marta away."

Parker shrugged. "Like I said, it makes things more complicated, but it's not something that can't be dealt with."

I found my voice. "Tony, what the hell is going on?"

It was Parker who spoke. "Your friend, Mr. Lusardi, contacted me a few days ago and —"

Tony held my eyes defiantly as I shrieked, *"You did what?"*

"I'm sorry, Marta, but I thought you'd taken on something you really couldn't handle. I felt responsible for you. How could I have lived with myself if something had happened to you and I hadn't lifted a hand?"

I got out, "How dare you?" before words failed me.

"Coming to me was the right thing to do, Ms. Hendriks," Parker said.

I rounded on Tony again. "That's why you were so insistent on coming here last night. You were spying on me." I pointed in the direction of the cop. "For him!"

"It wasn't like that at all!" Tony protested.

"Sure it was! And fat lot of good your help proved, anyway. How many people got killed today?"

Parker spoke. "I was held up with the French police and didn't get to the restaurant until it was too late. You have to understand that as a Canadian I can't just —"

Jean-Claude finally spoke up. "So what happens now, Parker?"

"I take all of you to the Police Nationale."

"*Bien sûr*. You say you'll do that and then something will happen, and I, at least, will be dead, if not these two people, as well. You will be sorry that it all went so wrong. 'We underestimated the determination of those who were after him,' you'll say. Is that how it will work, eh, Parker?"

The cop's eyes flared and he walked further into the room. Jean-Claude rolled to the far side of the bed, getting to his feet with some difficulty. He had his hand on the window frame. From his body language, I thought he might try to get away by jumping.

Parker was going to have to go through Tony to get at him, and I was wondering what was happening as the cop seemed to be in the grip of some strong emotion.

I slammed my good hand on the table. "Everybody just hold it!"

They all looked at me.

"Correct me if I'm wrong, but Jean-Claude isn't guilty of any crime. You're here, Parker, because he ran away from your protection program that protected him from nothing. He fled to France to save his life. He's not guilty of anything."

"He entered France illegally," Parker pointed out.

"Big deal," I shot back disgustedly. "Jean-Claude, if you will only look at this logically, you'll see that you've got to speak to the French police. They can protect you and I'll be willing to bet that with your cooperation, they'll let any immigration faux pas slide."

"I am not going with this man!" he said, pointing at Parker.

"Do you have a cellphone?"

"What? What does that have to do with it?"

"It's simple. Call the police. Tell them who you are and where you are, and they'll come and get you. Get all of us, no doubt," I added with a grim smile.

That's as far as my little try at negotiation got, as the apartment door was kicked open with a splintering crash.

Coming through was one of the other Mounties I'd recently had contact with, Griffin was his name. His right hand held a gun.

"All right!" Griffin barked. "Everyone get your hands where I can see them."

I said, "Thank heavens you're here. Inspector Parker is the one responsible for the death of ..."

My sentence trailed off because Griffin wasn't paying the slightest attention to me. Seeing a movement to my right, I turned. Both Tony and Jean-Claude were putting their hands up.

Not at all grasping the gravity of the situation, I said, "You can put your gun away. We're not going to —"

For the second time, I was interrupted, this time by Tony. "Marta, foreign police aren't allowed to carry guns outside their home countries."

"Especially not with silencers on them," Parker added.

Chapter Twenty-Three

Griffin savagely kicked the door shut with his foot. "We don't need any more people involved in this mess."

Motioning with the gun, he said, "I want all four of you in a line with your hands behind your heads. Don't even so much as breathe wrong. Good. Now turn your pockets inside out one at a time, and slowly. Drop anything in them on the floor in front of you."

The men did as they were told. The only semi-lethal thing discovered turned out to be an old pocket knife Jean-Claude was carrying. At Griffin's command, he kicked it across the room where it smacked a baseboard with a loud crack. Despite myself, I jumped at the sound.

"You carrying, Parker?" Griffin asked. "No. Of course not. You always follow the bloody rules."

Parker spoke, fixing the other cop with an intense expression. "This is really stupid of you, Eli. You know that. The percentages are against you."

"I don't give a rat's ass about your bloody percentages."

"Whatever you have in mind, it won't work."

"Shut up! You think you're so smart, Parker. You see, right now I'm holding your gun."

"That isn't my gun."

"Sure it is. It's going to be the one you used to kill all these people. Unfortunately, I got here too late to save them, but I did manage to bring you down. But in the struggle it discharged and you were fatally shot. You know, I might even get a commendation for taking you on barehanded."

"That's the stupidest thing I ever heard."

Griffin's grin held no warmth. "You know it will work."

"The French police know where I am."

"Don't try to bullshit me, Parker. They have no idea where you are."

Parker seemed stunned. "You've spoken to them?"

"Of course. I was with their Internal Investigation Division this morning. You see, I'm here on official RCMP business." Griffin stopped and smiled broadly. "They sent me to France to keep an eye on you. And that's why you're wrong about me being able to get away with this."

"I don't understand."

"Seems that with a lot of pushing from me and a bit of false evidence, enough people in Ottawa now believe you may be the rat in our midst."

"Eli, you used to be a damn fine cop," Parker said with what sounded like real remorse. "How could you have lost your way so badly?"

I, for one, really wanted to hear the answer to that question. Everyone in the room was hanging onto each word spoken. Glancing quickly down the line, Jean-Claude's face showed only resignation. Tony's looked tense but watchful. Parker's face was dark with anger, but also showed no fear and that gave me a bit of heart. I hoped that he was just playing for time, that the cavalry might really be on the way.

Griffin paused for a moment, and it was easy to see what he was thinking by the way he moved his gun from one end of our line to the other. So far his eyes seemed to be focused only on Parker, but I became afraid that once he decided to start shooting, he'd just go on until we were all on the floor.

Griffin's face was like stone when he finally spoke. "It's not hard to lose your way, Parker, when the trap springs shut on someone you love, when, no matter what you do, you can't protect them."

Griffin was sweating, obviously in the grip of some strong emotional wash. I wondered if he was on drugs.

Parker obviously thought so, too. "It's not the first time one of us has gotten caught up in something we shouldn't have. We have drug rehab programs for our people. All you had to do —"

"I'm not talking about me!" Griffin snarled. "It was Laura ... my wife. The stress of not knowing when I went off to work whether I'd be coming home at the end of my shift. It took a toll on her. It only got worse when I joined the drug unit. The months when I was undercover, not knowing where I was or if I was safe, every time the phone rang or someone knocked on the door, it all took a toll on her.

"The worst part was, I didn't notice. I was too caught up in trying to do the job right, trying to be a good cop, trying to get ahead. First it was pills, then harder stuff. I can't believe I was too stupid to see it. If she'd only confided in me. You just don't think it will be someone in your family, not your own wife."

The longer Parker kept his fellow cop talking, the better our chances of staying alive. I think everyone knew that, because we were all barely breathing as we tried not to break the spell.

"So what happened, Eli? Help me understand."

"I was handed a golden opportunity one night when I was undercover, a chance to bust one of the big boys and I could do it all by myself."

"Mad Dog Clement? You were assigned to that surveillance."

"Got it in one," Griffin said, chuckling, but there wasn't a shred of humanity in it. "Another one of those 'moments of clarity' you're always prattling on about?"

"No. I just always wondered why that operation went south. We all believed we'd be able to bring that one home."

"I had him dead to rights and he had to know it. I mean, he had all the drugs in his house. You know the big guys never do something stupid like that. I felt like I'd won the lottery, but all he did was laugh at me. I found out why when he reached under the sofa he was sitting on.

"He handed me a box and in it was all the evidence they'd ever need to get Laura busted and sent up for a long time. In order to feed her habit, she'd been dealing. Clement sat there grinning at me like a frigging hyena the whole time I looked at that stuff. Names, dates, photos, audio, video, they had it all.

"'Now sit down, Elijah, and let's have a little chat about what you're going to do for me,' was all he said. You have no idea what that was like, Parker. Having to listen to that scumbag tell me what I was going to do. He not only would have brought Laura down, but me as well. I'd worked too hard and done crap assignments for too long to let that happen."

"So you went rogue on us. Went against everything you stood for."

"You don't understand!"

"No, I don't, Eli. There had to be some other way out. You should have talked with us."

"I couldn't take that chance! Laura's a stock broker. People trust her with their life savings! If even the slightest whisper of this had ever got out, she'd go down, all because of me, and I couldn't face that. If I'd told Clement to take his evidence and stick it where the sun don't shine, he would have dropped his bomb before I could have done anything to stop him."

Parker's next comment caught all of us off guard. "You ended up killing people for Clement, why not just kill him at the beginning and be done with your problem? Same thing, isn't it?"

Griffin shook his head. "Clement may be rotten to the core, a murderer and a psychopath, but he's not without

353

some brains. He had himself completely covered. Besides, I never killed anyone. I only provided information."

"Oh, don't give me that crap. You know the law. So you didn't actually pull the trigger, you're still just as guilty."

I could not hold my tongue a moment longer. "What about today? Or did you bring some of your biker buddies along to do your dirty work at the restaurant?"

Griffin licked his lips nervously. "That wasn't supposed to happen there. Something went wrong. I don't know what yet."

"But you didn't care who got killed? I suppose my death was just a bit of collateral damage you could live with? Is that it?"

"No, that wasn't it at all."

He said the words, but his eyes told me it was a total crock of shit. If I hadn't spotted Tony sitting in that taverne, Jean-Claude and I would have gotten on his motorcycle and immediately been blown to kingdom come. It was just luck that truck pulled into the parking space when it did.

Lucky for us, but not for the guy in the truck and the people in the restaurant. I was feeling sick about that.

"So you did have help," Parker stated flatly. "That's how you got the bomb, as well as the Beretta you're holding."

"Henri Clement, as you well know, has reciprocal arrangements with other biker chapters in Europe. Everything was waiting for me when I got here."

"Let me get this straight, you had help with the bomb?"

"Yes. I had to stay with the Internal Investigation boys so I'd have an alibi. I knew the guy the bikers sent was a screw-up the moment I spoke to him on the phone." Griffin laughed. "Well, he's going to take the fall for the bomb. That was all set up from the beginning. He has no idea who I am. He thinks I'm a biker, too."

The chatter had been going on for several minutes, and I didn't know about everyone else, but I was getting increasingly nervous. Zero hour was looming and I didn't see any way out. We couldn't keep Griffin talking forever.

The rogue cop's watch beeped and he stole a quick glance at it. The rest of us tensed to spring, but Griffin was back a good eight feet in the cramped room.

Looking around for something that might help us, my eyes dropped to the table in front of me. Right at the edge lay my stick bag, and as usual, I had removed every single drumstick and mallet from the pockets when I'd been practising that morning. The events of the morning seemed so long ago now.

All of the sticks were made either from very hard wood or plastic. Some had large heads. I remembered how much it hurt if someone in the percussion section lost one out of sweaty hands and you happened to be in the way as it flew by.

It just might work, I thought, glancing up because Griffin was looking in my direction.

When his eyes passed on, I stole a couple of quick glances downwards, estimating how long it might take me to grab a handful or two and fling them at Griffin's head. Two dozen pieces of wood flying at him would certainly be a big distraction. It might give someone else a chance to dive at him. I was out on that score because the table lay between the two of us. Parker was closest, followed by Tony. Jean-Claude was partially blocked by the corner of the bed.

I decided that the best course of action would be to fling everything — sticks, mallets, and case — at the same time, then make a dive for the floor. It would be up to someone else to take the bastard out.

Sooner or later, Griffin would work up the nerve to begin shooting. It was obvious that having your victims lined up like they do for firing squads was spooking him, since all of us were staring him down. We'd only been silent for maybe ten seconds, but already it was feeling like weeks. I decided I had to move then or not at all.

As Griffin's eyes swung once again to Jean-Claude, I made my move. Parker also chose that moment to act.

The next three or four seconds stretched for longer than seemed possible. Parker, about three steps away from the gun, started to make a vertical dive for Griffin's knees. Unfortunately for the brave man, his counterpart was lightning quick and rapidly swung his gun down. All I heard was two loud clicks as he pulled the trigger. Parker seemed to deflate, landing hard and sliding harmlessly along the wood floor.

I only saw this out of the corner of my eye, since I was focused on grabbing the near corners of the stick bag to fling everything in Griffin's direction with all the force I could muster. I was already well aware that if Parker hadn't done what he did, it would have been me on the floor with the two bullets. Griffin was too fast.

The spinning pile of sticks and leather bag seemed to take forever to reach their target, and I was already diving for the floor when they hit.

Griffin, responding by instinct, raised his arms to protect his face, and it was Tony who used his foot on the corner of the bed in order to launch himself toward the startled cop.

I was partially under the table when the two bodies collided with a sickening crunch. Whose bones had broken, I didn't know, but somebody was severely hurt. Both men slammed back into the wall between the bathroom and the apartment door and fell to the ground. They lay there stunned or knocked out, and Griffin's gun skittered across the floor.

Before I could react, Jean-Claude was around the bed, clamping my arm in his strong grip, half dragging me toward the door and simultaneously reaching down for the gun.

"Let go!" I shouted as I squirmed against his grip. "We have to help Tony!"

Jean-Claude answered, his voice tense and low. "He won't be in danger if we are not here!"

It couldn't have been more than seven or eight seconds since Parker had made his desperate lunge, and I was allowing myself to be pulled out the door. Jean-Claude was right. If someone was desperate to kill him, I wanted them as far away from Tony and Parker as possible.

I started to speak but Jean-Claude slapped his hand over my mouth and brought his face close to mine. "Do not make a sound. Could you not tell he was waiting for someone?"

A moment later, the downstairs door was opening and I could hear loud, anxious talking from the entryway.

"*Merde!*" Jean-Claude spat out as he once again grabbed my upper arm and pulled me toward the stairway, which we bolted up.

The old stairwell had rickety metal railings, and the steps were worn and badly lit, but we ran up as fast as we could, listening to the other footsteps that we hoped would be going to the apartment we'd just left. They did.

By that time, we were up two flights and had run out of stairway. Jean-Claude tried two apartment doors, then spotted a third door, looking like it might be a closet. I hadn't even managed to move my mouth to point this out when he smashed it open with his shoulder. In the dim light, we could see it was indeed a closet, and mounted on its right wall was a metal ladder.

Sticking the gun in his belt, Jean-Claude grabbed the rungs and looked up. Stepping into the doorway, I could see what had attracted his attention: a trapdoor in the ceiling.

"Follow me. The roof is our only hope."

Down below, I could again hear voices and footsteps. Were more people arriving, or was the first group coming up the stairs after us? I didn't hesitate. Jean-Claude was already at the ceiling, pushing furiously.

"Use the goddamned gun," I whispered as loudly as I dared.

Grinning down at me, he pulled it from his belt and pounded at what I assumed was a rusty latch. Nothing happened.

Dropping down to the floor again, he raised the gun, firing off three rounds. The expelled casings hitting the stone floor made more noise than the silenced firearm. The smell from firing the gun was overwhelming in the confined space.

He again shoved the gun in his belt and launched himself up the ladder; it clanked where one of the bolts holding it was partially out of the wall.

This time the wooden trapdoor gave way with a single smash from Jean-Claude's shoulder. Daylight flooded in as he pushed the door all the way open. His head and shoulders disappeared, then reappeared as he looked down.

"C'mon, girl! The roof is flat. We may be able to get over to the next building."

I stuck my head out of the closet. It wasn't loud, but several people were slowly making their way up the stairs toward us. I didn't have to be told twice to get the hell out of there.

I pulled the closet door shut and was up that ladder in a flash. As my shoulders came through the trapdoor, Jean-Claude grabbed them and hauled me the rest of the way.

The clouds above seemed very close and rain spattered our faces. Though it was only mid-afternoon, the daylight was already sliding toward darkness. Below us in the street I could hear shouting and in the distance the sirens of emergency vehicles.

"I think help is on the way," I said and started to walk toward the roof's edge so I could look down.

Jean-Claude dragged me back.

Sticking his face into mine, he shook me and said, "We have only a few moments to escape. Follow me."

He quietly swung the trapdoor shut and set out for the far side of the roof. I followed.

On the adjoining street, there was another flat-roofed building. Unfortunately, its roof was one storey lower and separated from our building by a good ten feet of alley.

"Oh well," I said, looking at the broken concrete of the alley a long way below.

"We will have to jump."

"Are you crazy?"

"It is our only hope."

"We don't even know who just came into that building. It was definitely more than one person and I don't think that Griffin brought a whole biker gang to back him up!"

"Do you really want to take that chance? Even if it is the cops, I do not want to see them. Stay if you will, but I am going."

I grabbed his arm. "Don't be a fool, Jean-Claude. You could die making that jump."

"We will both die if the wrong people come through that trap door."

As if in answer, we heard voices down below.

"They are coming, Marta! Take my hand!"

Jean-Claude pulled the gun from under his belt and grabbed my arm with his left hand. Down in that small closet, the ladder clanked against the loose bolt. Someone was climbing.

He moved us back three steps toward the centre of the roof. "When I say three, we will run and jump as far as we can. When you hit the other roof, just roll. If you try to do anything else, you will break a bone."

"I will break my fool neck, regardless of how much I roll!" I pried my arm from his grasp. "I'm staying here."

I think he was about to try to convince me when we ran out of time.

The trapdoor opened a crack, then was flung back and a torso appeared in the opening. The man was dressed like a commando and he had an assault rifle. He also couldn't fail to notice that Jean-Claude had a gun.

I moved toward the commando with my hands up and open, starting to say, "No! Wait! It's not what you think."

Behind me, Jean-Claude bounded toward the edge of the roof and an impossible bid for freedom.

The commando fired off three rapid shots before my husband disappeared over the edge.

Coda

As Jean-Claude disappeared over the edge of the roof, I stood frozen in horror. Then, as I started to move forward, knowing I'd see his still form lying on the ground three storeys below, someone grabbed me from behind, forcing me onto my stomach. At least three other men were now on the roof and they were all shouting.

Not listening to what I was trying to tell them, half in French, half in English because of my near hysteria, I was hustled back through the trapdoor without being able to see with my own eyes what had happened to Jean-Claude. On the way down, I asked if Tony and Parker were all right. I might as well have been talking to statues. The two tactical squad cops gripping me by the upper arm wouldn't so much as grunt.

Hustled out to the street, I was locked in the back seat of a police car while two men dressed in suits stood around, apparently discussing what should be done about me.

A crowd was gathering from every direction, for the moment being held back by stern-looking gendarmes. Down at the bottom of the street on Rue Barrault, one of those news trucks pulled up and started to unfurl their satellite uplink antenna.

A few minutes later, a man I recognized came out of the building and walked over to the two senior cops. It was Constable Glover, and the last time I'd seen him he'd been the partner of Griffin, who I sincerely hoped was lying in a pool of his own blood back in that apartment.

Was he on our side or part of Griffin's machinations?

Pounding on the window, I shouted at them to let me out. I had important information. The three men ignored me, but people in the crowd started gesturing in my direction, and not in a friendly way. I sat back, folding my arms while trying to control my anxiety. With all the law enforcement around, Glover of the RCMP wouldn't be trying anything. At least I hoped that was the case.

Behind me, two ambulances were slowly backing down the narrow cobblestoned street. They stopped near the door of the apartment building and several paramedics piled out, two of them carrying those simple stretchers with two poles and a canvas sling between, and disappeared inside.

A minute or two later, a tall man exited the building and walked over to Glover and the other two cops. The way the two French cops immediately stood a little straighter confirmed my guess that he was in charge. Going grey around the temples, he had a weary expression that spoke of a long career, during which he'd seen too much violence.

They were too far away for me to be able to hear anything through the closed windows of the car. As they talked for several minutes, punctuating their discussion with various gesticulations, one or another of them would occasionally look over at me as I stared out forlornly. Finally, the tall man came over and opened the door.

I was about to get out when he gracefully slid in, pulling the door shut behind him.

Speaking French, I pelted him with questions. "What happened to Jean-Claude? Where is Tony? Is Parker still alive? That bastard Griffin didn't get away, did he?"

The boss cop held up his hand and I stopped. "Calm down, Mademoiselle Hendriks. I cannot answer one dozen questions at the same time, *n'est-ce pas?*" He looked at me for a moment, then stuck out his hand. "I am Capitaine Andre Leduc."

"Marta Hendriks."

"Yes, I know. I saw a performance of your Violetta in September."

"Why have I been locked in this car?"

"It is as much for your own safety as for our investigation. This is a very complicated affair. Here, two men shot, one man with severe leg injuries, another with a suspected skull fracture —"

"Not Tony!" I squeezed my eyes shut and thought, Please God, let him be all right.

Leduc smiled and shook his head, but didn't elaborate. "And on the other side of Paris, a bomb detonated on a crowded street with an unknown number dead and injured. You expect us to instantly sort this out? That crowd out there believes that you may be one of those responsible, that you may be a terrorist."

After a deep breath, I asked, "Can you tell me how my friends are?"

"Which ones are your friends?"

"The man who was shot and fell off the roof; I suppose you could call him my husband —"

"And why were you up on the roof?"

That stopped me cold. "I really couldn't tell you. It seemed like a good idea at the time."

"Really?"

"We didn't know who was around. Jean-Claude wanted to get away, and then all those people started pouring in downstairs. What would you have expected us to do?"

"That is a good point."

"Is Jean-Claude dead?"

The old cop answered my question obliquely. "You know, it is a funny thing what fear can do to someone. I have known a mother to lift the front of a car to save her child trapped underneath. Even with a bullet in his leg and another in his back, your Jean-Claude managed to jump onto that next roof. Of course, he did not land well, and I have been told he also suffered a very bad break to his right leg. It is therefore astonishing that he was actually trying to climb off the second roof when we apprehended him. Amazing."

"But he's going to be all right?"

Chief Inspector Leduc took my hand. His face had lost the weariness I'd seen earlier, and I felt now I was looking into the face of someone's kindly French *grand-père*.

"I spoke to him briefly before they took him to hospital. Who is Gaston? He seemed quite concerned about him."

I sighed. "His son." When the detective looked puzzled, I added, "By another woman."

He had the grace not to inquire any further.

Using the silence, I asked, "And in the apartment? You didn't really tell me precisely how my ... how Tony is. Is he hurt? Do you know what's going on?"

My answer came as Leduc swiveled around and we both watched the paramedics, bearing loaded stretchers, begin emerging from the building. On the first one was Parker, and the plastic bag of saline solution being held above him by a third man, obviously a doctor called in to help, was an ominous sign. The Mountie's complexion was ashen, and I could clearly see a sheen of sweat on his face in the failing daylight. But at least he was still clinging to life.

The speed at which he was hustled into the farthest ambulance, which left immediately, made it clear that his injuries were grave. I said a silent prayer for the brave man who had probably saved my life, if not the lives of all of us.

Moments later, the second stretcher appeared in the doorway with that rat Griffin on it. It passed through my mind that it wouldn't be such a bad thing if the two men bearing him were to stumble and dump him onto the cobblestones. He certainly deserved it.

I could see into the ambulance as they transferred him to a more conventional bed-type stretcher and watched his former partner, Glover, lean in to say something. I would have given a week's salary to be a fly on that wall.

Last to appear was Tony, and he was at least able to walk, supported by one of the special forces cops. It was obvious he'd injured his left leg. He was also cradling his right hand in his left. I could see the pain in his set expression.

I waved wildly, trying to get his attention. "May I go to him?" I asked Leduc.

The old cop looked at me, then looked at the crowd now at least five people deep, and sighed. "As you wish."

Leduc tapped on the window and one of his people hopped to it, opening the door. I got out and hurried toward Tony, dimly aware that flashes were going off. As I got closer, Tony waved away the cop supporting him.

"Thank God, you're okay," Tony said as I hugged him. "They couldn't tell me anything about what happened after you and Jean-Claude ran out."

"There's too much for me to tell you out here on the street," I answered, looking up at him. "What's wrong with your leg?"

"My ankle, actually, but it's nothing more than a sprain. I had to stop playing soccer because of my bad ankle. It's not like I haven't done this before."

"And your hand?"

He smiled grimly. "I may have broken a finger. Seems like Griffin had a little bit more fight in him after my tackle."

I smiled at him. "It could have been worse."

Tony nodded. "Yes. A lot worse."

It felt extremely awkward standing in front of so many people, trying to tell Tony how grateful I was, how much I cared for him. I knew photos and video footage of our moment would be broadcast around the world, judging by the amount of light shining off the wet pavement, but I found that I didn't really care.

"We'd all be dead by now if it hadn't been for you," I said.

Tony shrugged. "I did what was needed. And if you really want to know, it was one of your damned drumsticks that caused me to twist my ankle."

I grinned up at him. "Sorry. That was all I could come up with."

"It was effective. I wouldn't have been able to spring at Griffin if it hadn't been for that bit of distraction. Actually, that was pretty quick thinking. We make a good team."

Yes, a good team, I thought. "We should get that ankle and hand looked at. I think the ambulance is waiting for you."

"There's your hand and all those scrapes, too."

I realized I'd completely forgotten about the slice that must still have been oozing blood, judging by the sodden state of the towel tied around my hand.

I put Tony's arm over my shoulder and we started moving. "When they've got you squared away at the hospital, we need to talk."

Tony stopped and looked at me piercingly.

I laughed, and it felt good. "Relax. I'm not giving you the big brush-off!"

I was aware that around us more flashes were popping and the camera light had increased. The gossip magazines and websites were going to have a field day with this.

So be it.

I put my arm around Tony's waist and let the paparazzi shoot away to their hearts' content as we walked to the ambulance.

Leaning my head back against the waiting-room wall, I rubbed my tired eyes. My watch told me it was not yet even midnight, but this day already felt at least a week long. Since the meal at the restaurant twelve hours earlier, I'd had two cups of coffee and no food. My head throbbed and I was finding clear thinking increasingly difficult. At least that annoying buzzing in my ears was a lot less.

It had been more than six hours since they'd wheeled Jean-Claude into surgery, and I felt that could be either ominous or good, depending on which minute you asked me. Next to me, Tony, his ankle heavily bandaged and his hand with a large splint on his middle finger, was slouched in his chair, asleep. Even dead to the world, I appreciated his company, because across the waiting room from us sat Jean-Claude's other wife, Marie, and her occasional glances were filled with quite enough venom, thank you. Even though it had been me who'd gotten Leduc to order her brought to Paris so she could be near her husband in his need, she obviously blamed me for everything that had happened.

The expression on little Gaston as he slept peacefully against her chest was quite angelic by comparison. He was a beautiful child.

Finally, a doctor appeared in the doorway. "Madame Lachance?"

We both started to answer, but I quickly suppressed my response. Whatever happened from here on in, I was definitely not Madame Lachance anymore.

"Might I speak with you out in the corridor?" the doctor continued, after looking at us in confusion.

Marie sighed, clearly at odds over what to do with her child.

"Would you let me hold him while you speak with the doctor?" I asked.

At first I thought she'd refuse, but in the end she accepted my offer. Standing, she transferred Gaston into my arms. The child barely stirred.

I walked to the far end of the room and sat, looking down at the child who might have been mine. Despite his age, it was clear he had the nose and chin of his father. He was also a solid little guy and would probably grow up to be thick and muscular like his dad. But around his eyes and mouth there was a softness that was his mother's gift. If he continued growing as his face and body hinted, he'd break more than his share of hearts when he got older.

Knowing the discussion in the hall could go either way, I said a silent prayer for Jean-Claude, Gaston, and even Marie. They deserved to be a family, and Gaston should have the chance to grow up happy.

Barely daring to breathe, I waited for an outburst from the hall, signalling that the worst had transpired, but with each tick of the second hand on the clock on the wall opposite, I dared to feel more hope.

About five minutes after she'd left, Marie appeared in the doorway, but I could not read from her expression what the doctor had told her.

"Is he ..." I began.

She answered simply. "He will live."

Looking at me piercingly, I could detect multiple emotions sliding across her face. The overwhelming one was uncertainty, and I thought I could guess why.

I patted the seat next to me. "Come and take your child."

She sat down heavily but made no effort to take Gaston back.

"I knew that he was coming to meet you today. Luc ... Jean-Claude made up some stupid excuse, but I can easily tell when he is lying. That is how I know that you two were ... are married. I made him tell me last night."

I snorted. "That's a lot better than I could do. That man could talk the hind leg off a mule and make me believe anything."

Marie didn't respond for a moment, then unexpectedly grinned. "I did not know what you meant at first. We don't have a phrase like that in this country, but yes. I agree. He is too easy with his tongue for his own good."

I handed back her son and she waited, looking at me nervously.

"My, um, our husband," I said, "has made a right mess

out of all of our lives, and I guess it's up to us women to sort it all out. Jean-Claude ... Marc ... Oh hell! *Luc's* life has moved on from me. He has you and he has a son and you should be a family. My time with him is over. I know that."

She seemed startled. "You do not mind?"

"I'm too tired to know what I think." I paused, rubbing the bridge of my nose. "Yes, on some level, I do mind. That man profoundly transformed my life when we met. I was so desperately in love with him ... but now? Too much water has gone over the dam for me to go back. Jean-Claude has you two now," I finished, lightly ruffling the sleeping child's hair.

He smiled in his sleep.

"But what about you?" his mother asked.

I looked at Marie. "It is not difficult in Canada to end a marriage. From now until then, no one has to know he's also married to you."

"My mother is going to be so angry with him!"

"If I know Jean-Claude, he'll have her eating out of his hand again in five minutes flat."

I remembered something and went over to my purse, thoughtfully returned to me by Capitaine Leduc.

Handing Marie JC's wedding ring, I said, "Your husband will probably want this back."

She looked quite puzzled. "Why do you have it?"

"Long story."

We shared a sisterly smile.

Marie got down to business. "The doctor said that Luc ..."

"I know the confusion you're feeling. I've been there, too. His name is Jean-Claude, regardless of who we know him as, that's probably easiest."

"Jean-Claude," she said thoughtfully. "He sounds much more Québécois like that."

She playfully imitated the French-Canadian accent in the word "Québécois" and we shared a little additional bond. Too bad. I could have liked this woman a lot if we'd met under different circumstances.

The doctor had told her that Jean-Claude would be a long time recovering. The wound to his leg had been very clean, the bullet luckily just missing an artery on its way through. The bullet to his lower back had been much worse, having broken a rib and damaging his spleen. The broken leg required surgery to try to put it right. He was very lucky to be alive.

He'd always had more than his share of luck.

Eventually, a nurse came back for Marie and I was left alone with my thoughts — and a snoring Tony at the other end of the room.

Walking over, I gently shook him.

He had been deeply asleep. Even though I'd been up just as long and had as little sleep the previous night as he had, I was beyond tired but unable to sleep, in that twilight land where you keep moving simply so you don't fall over.

"What's happening?" Tony asked groggily.

"Time to go."

"Where?"

Clearly, his brain hadn't slipped into gear yet.

"To find a nice warm bed," I said, looking down at my watch, "at twenty past midnight. I don't suppose you bothered getting a room after I threw you out yesterday morning."

He had the grace to look sheepish. "No, I asked at a café up the street if I could leave my bag there."

"We're going to look so respectable, showing up at a hotel in the middle of the night with no bags."

Tony's eyes showed a bit more life. "Does that mean you'll stay with me?"

I touched his cheek and smiled. "Tonight, I think I need someone to hold me."

"I'll do the best job holding you that anyone's ever done." He stood up quickly and winced, then looked into my eyes. "I don't want to lose you, Marta."

Leaning forward, I kissed him tenderly. "I know."

Nine months after that awful day, on a sweltering August afternoon in Toronto, Tony and I married. Even though neither of us wanted it, the Lusardi family would hear of nothing less than a big Italian wedding. Nonna Lusardi's insistence on doing all the cooking was what clinched it for me.

As we ran out of the church, the entire Lusardi clan playfully blew soap bubbles at us. My brother and sister and their families were there, as were Lainey and Chloe, my manager Alex and his wife, all with broad smiles. Over to the side, I spotted Lili with a thoughtful expression on her face.

The reception was held at the restaurant in Woodbridge where Tony and I had first gone out to dinner. Part of the choice was due to the fact that the owner was more than happy to give Signora Lusardi the run of his kitchen. Personally, I think he wanted the opportunity to observe her.

We'd invited Inspector Parker to the wedding, but he was spending the summer fishing at his cottage in the Eastern Townships of Quebec while he finished his extended leave to convalesce. It had been a close thing for him, but he pulled through, more by sheer cussedness than anything else. He wanted to be healthy for the trial of Griffin and his biker bosses when they got Jean-Claude back to Canada to testify.

I'd only seen my former husband once since that horrible day. It had been in early April. I was performing in Stockholm, and on my way to Montreal for the Chicks with Sticks concert (a roaring success), I had planned a very quick stopover in Paris — for a costume fitting at the opera. That fall, most of my honeymoon would be spent singing the title role in yet another fill-in gig in their production of *Norma*. This time, though, I expected to see my husband every day and as often as possible.

Paris in April is absolutely lovely, gently warm with the whole city decked out in spring colours. I had wished that Tony could have been with me to see it. He'd been back in Toronto with Lili, being run through her vocal ringer to get him ready for a minor role in *Fidelio* that he was given at the last minute. I had the distinct feeling that the COC was hoping some smaller roles for my soon-to-be husband would keep me closer to home and on their stage. I was thrilled for Tony regardless, and under Lili's tutelage, his voice was improving tremendously. We all harboured no illusions that he'd ever be a major soloist, but his voice was clearly too good to be relegated to the chorus forever.

But I'd also come to Paris for another reason. The previous month, I had arranged with Marie to bring some documents to her.

I again took the train out to Beauvais and grabbed a taxi to take me to the small cottage that Jean-Claude and Marie had rented a few miles out in the countryside. I felt a wrench in my heart as Marie and I stood in the kitchen, looking out on the backyard where our husband sat in a garden chair, throwing a ball to be chased and picked up by a laughing Gaston. Next to the chair lay two canes.

"He is getting stronger every day," she told me hopefully.

The man had undergone three operations since I departed Paris the previous November: one for his internal injuries, and two for his badly broken leg. But now he seemed to be firmly on the long road back.

"Has the Canadian government told you when the trial will be?" I asked.

"There have been delays, but they think it will begin before the summer is over." She looked at me for a moment, searching my face. "We have had many talks while he has been recovering. He told me all about what happened between you two." Again, she stopped. "You have been very generous and forgiving."

"Our lives have moved on. Even if you and Gaston hadn't come along, things would have been over between us." Reaching into my purse, I held out a fat envelope. "These are the divorce papers and everything my lawyer thought Jean-Claude —"

"He has decided to use Luc," Marie said almost apologetically. "We are all used to it here."

I nodded. "Tell Luc that if he wants his old pickup or anything in it, it's out at the farm. I also have a few cartons of his personal effects. I will be putting the property on the market soon, so he doesn't have much time to make a decision."

"Won't you go out to see him?"

"When I arrived, I thought I might, but no. I think I'll just take my leave." I gave Marie kisses on each cheek. "And I wish you all the very best."

The train trip back into Paris was a melancholy affair for me. The tender greens of spring in the market gardens of the Picardie countryside giving way to the clutter and graffiti of northern Paris did nothing to brighten my mood. Staring out the window, I forced myself to focus on the future where brighter things would happen.

Did I wish I'd never started down the path that had led to a bomb on a Paris street and near-death on a rooftop? Certainly. Almost every day.

But Lili, in one of our continuing sessions, had recently told me, "If we could see the consequences of our actions, no matter how small or large, before we did them, we would bring ourselves to a state of complete immobility. Marta, you did what you felt you needed to do. The outcome was not all that you wanted, but you started with the best of intentions. Could you have lived the rest of your life not knowing, thinking that you were maybe not right in your head? No."

Most days, I believe what she told me.

Acknowledgements

The author would like to acknowledge the help of several individuals in bringing this novel to its final form. First to Vicki Blechta for her help with research, French translation, and her great eye in spotting my "excesses" and errors. Thanks must also be given to Robert Kuenzli, a great singer and traveller in the opera world who was very generous sharing his expertise and experiences. Cheryl Freedman again took a first look at the manuscript and brought her editor's skill to bear on my unruly prose. My expert in all things French was the redoubtable Louise Pambrun. Ellen Gurwitz looked it all over with fresh eyes and discovered several things no one had considered. Allister Thompson and Sylvia McConnell believed in this novel from the very beginning and have my heartfelt thanks for that. And finally to my editor, Matt Baker, who oversaw the final work and asked the hard questions: this novel is better because of you.

Rick Blechta brings his musician's viewpoint to the thriller genre in such novels as *Shooting Straight in the Dark*, *When Hell Freezes Over*, and *A Case of You*. *Cemetery of the Nameless* was shortlisted for an Arthur Ellis Award for Best Novel. Rick is an active musician in Toronto.

Visit *www.rickblechta.com*.

Also by Rick Blechta

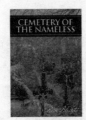

Cemetery of the Nameless
978-1894917179
$16.95

Victoria Morgan, violin virtuoso extraordinaire, and her devoted piano accompanist are on yet another European tour currently stopping in Vienna. While playing to a full house, Tory leaves the stage and disappears in the middle of this important concert, leaving behind a puzzled (and angry) audience. Why would a seasoned professional so intent on maintaining her well-established career do something so damaging? Especially after some very negative reviews from local press? Tory's decision to leave proves to be especially fatal to her career, since the rumours of her disappearance involve the accusation that Tory has committed the brutal murder of a high profile Viennese figure. While the press continues to hound everyone who knew Tory for answers, it appears she is running from them, the police and her long-suffering husband Oscar Lukesh, affectionately known as Rocky. Or is she? The action is set around the appearance of a mysterious score for a recently discovered violin concerto of incredible worth. Is it truly by Beethoven as the owner claims, and will Tory be the first to debut this dream violin piece, or are all of these things just hollow promises and a way to bait a trap? Now it looks like it's up to Rocky to help save Tory from herself and figure out who is committing the growing number of murders — if it really isn't his wife.

When Hell Freezes Over
978-1894917414
$16.95

Michael Quinn, former rock star, turned his back on a band on the verge of superstardom twenty-four years ago. He's spent his life since hiding from everything he'd been. When a woman chased by thugs jumps into his car, he tries to help. But this sets in motion a chain of events which turns his life upside down, even more so when his best friend is murdered and the girl disappears. Meanwhile, the thugs are looking for Michael. Only by finding the mystery girl can he hope to get out of a hole that's getting bigger. To do this, he must confront what he was, what he is now, and what he might have been.

A Case of You
978-1894917681
$15.95

Meet Andy Curran, drummer in a struggling jazz trio. When a distinctly odd street person sings at an open mic night at the club where they work, it's clear they've found their salvation: a vocalist of incredible talent. After she departs as abruptly as she'd arrived, Andy sets out to discover where Olivia Saint has gone and who she really is. That knowledge soon proves to be deadly indeed. In *A Case of You*, a crime novel that sweeps from the jazz clubs of Toronto, to New York City and Northern California, Rick Blechta has created a compelling story, rich in detail and compassion, and populated with characters not easily forgotten.

Of Related Interest

The Devil's Dust | A *Charlie McKelvey Mystery*
C.B. Forrest
978-1459701922
$17.99

Retired Toronto detective Charlie McKelvey runs from a cancer diagnosis and the violent memories of the big city and retreats to his hometown. A small declining mining centre, Ste. Bernadette offers McKelvey a chance to resolve old family issues, including his father's involvement in a deadly wildcat strike in the late 1950s.

When the local police force enlists his help in tracing an upswing in youth violence and vandalism, McKelvey stumbles into the hornet's nest of a crystal meth industry. The timing couldn't be worse for the town to expose its drug problem to the world: the mayor is hoping a new transmission line will be built through the town, bringing power line jobs and construction dollars; the police chief is trying to close a deal to truck Detroit's garbage to a local site as well as vie for the mayor's job; and a sleazy businessman is attempting to buy up the town's land to open a casino and resort.

Despite searches and seizures, the flow of drugs continues, leading McKelvey to suspect a local is manufacturing the drug. *The Devil's Dust* holds a magnifying glass to the current decline of rural life, the scourge of meth, and what happens when an entire town loses faith.

Lake on the Mountain
Jeffrey Round
978-1459700017
$11.99

Dan Sharp, a gay father and missing persons investigator, accepts an invitation to a wedding on a yacht in Ontario's Prince Edward County. It seems just the thing to bring Dan closer to his noncommittal partner, Bill, a respected medical professional with a penchant for sleazy after-hours clubs, cheap drugs, and rough sex. But the event doesn't go exactly as planned.

When a member of the wedding party is swept overboard, a case of mistaken identity leads to confusion as the wrong person is reported missing. The hunt for a possible killer leads Dan deeper into the troubled waters and private lives of a family of rich WASPs and their secret world of privilege.

No sooner is that case resolved when a second one ends up on Dan's desk. Dan is hired by an anonymous source to investigate the disappearance 20 years earlier of the groom's father. The only clues are a missing bicycle and six horses mysteriously poisoned.

 **DUNDURN**
www.dundurn.com

Visit us at
Dundurn.com
Definingcanada.ca
@dundurnpress
Facebook.com/dundurnpress